TRUMAN'S
SPY

Also by NOEL HYND

Novels
REVENGE
THE SANDLER INQUIRY
FALSE FLAGS
FLOWERS FROM BERLIN
THE KHRUSHCHEV OBJECTIVE
(with Christopher Creighton)

Nonfiction
THE COP AND THE KID
(with William Fox)
THE GIANTS OF THE POLO GROUNDS

Screenplay
AGENCY

TRUMAN'S SPY

SPY

.

NOEL HYND

ZEBRA BOOKS
KENSINGTON PUBLISHING CORP.

ZEBRA BOOKS

are published by

Kensington Publishing Corp.
475 Park Avenue South
New York, NY 10016

First printing: February, 1990

Printed in the United States of America

for
e.d.h.
with love

If you feel sick, you go to a doctor. If you're in trouble you go to a lawyer. If anything else is wrong, you go to a banker.

—American business axiom

PROLOGUE

■

They were a small group, only three of them—Milenkin, Sejna, and Filiatov—an unlikely troika of comrades who had never worked together before. They were in the United States to handle a pair of jobs considered too dirty and too risky for the Soviet residents.

Good espionage work, particularly a major Soviet operation within the United States, often rested upon a gentle cultivation of resources, a gradual easing along of the personnel involved, and a meticulously patient brand of timing. Milenkin and Sejna may have been an example of this rule, but Filiatov was the exception to it. There was nothing gentle about him and nothing gradual about his association with the two others. And timing? The timing of the operation—the murder of two American citizens—had been forced upon them.

Viktor Milenkin had been in the United States the longest and knew the country best. He'd been born in the Ukraine in 1925, the illegitimate son of a prominent Soviet chemist. His mother died in childbirth. At the age of four he'd come to the United States with an aunt named Liliya who became his legally adoptive mother. He was educated in the public school system of Palo Alto, California.

In 1939 Milenkin and his aunt were obliged either to apply for American citizenship or return to the Soviet Union. They chose the latter, repatriating to Moscow. From 1940 to 1942 Liliya worked as a stenographer at the Soviet Defense Ministry. At this time, she became the mistress of a handsome colonel named Andrei Klisinski. Klisinski was no ordinary officer of the Red Army. Rather, he was very "Western style"—perfectly fluent in English as well as Russian. He had extensive experience in the United States as well. He moved across international borders with spectacular ease, and it was even rumored that for a time at least he had had a family in England or America.

Klisinski, who was widely believed to have been born in what was now occupied Poland, was also assigned to the Glavnoye Razvedyvatelnoye Upravleniye. The G.R.U., as it was more commonly known, was the chief intelligence directorate of the general staff of the Soviet Defense Ministry. Most enlightened observers saw the G.R.U. as the military cousin of the N.K.V.D., the Soviet secret police agency that would become the K.G.B.

Colonel Klisinski saw possibilities for his mistress's boy. Like Klisinski himself, the teenager had a perfect command of English, a native's knowledge of the United States, and a flawless American accent. So the colonel and those whom he worked with began planning ahead.

From the time the tide of World War II turned on the German-Russian front in 1944, through the hours of the Soviet victory in Europe, Klisinski trained Viktor for an assignment in the West. Weeks turned into months, months to years. By the time Milenkin had perfected his cover, had memorized his contacts, and had demonstrated his devotion to his specialized line of work, he was no longer a boy. It was 1948 and he was a young man of twenty-three.

In June of that year, the G.R.U. equipped Milenkin with a freshly printed Swiss passport. He entered the United States in New York, destroyed the passport the next day in his room at the Hotel Astor and assumed the identity of one George Mulligan. Mulligan had been a young soldier who'd died in a Soviet hospital in 1942. Soviet operatives in America had retrieved his birth certificate from Davenport, Iowa, and had been further delighted to discover that the young soldier had no surviving family. He was perfect. And for that matter, so was Milenkin.

Thus with little fanfare, on a balmy summer afternoon in 1948, Viktor Milenkin checked out of the Astor and walked through Grand Central Station as George Mulligan. He had five hundred dollars in cash. With it, he rented a small apartment on Perry Street in Greenwich Village. Intelligent and well-spoken, he had within another week found employment as an installation man for New York Telephone. Here was a perfect cover profession: Milenkin had flexible hours, access to people's homes and private buildings, and no one looking over his shoulder. Every Saturday morning, in accordance with a routine established by the G.R.U. back in Moscow, he would look for "mail" in a piece of discarded piping nestled shoulder-high in the brickwork under the Williamsburg Bridge.

About a month after his return to America, in July 1948, Milenkin found the first message in the base of the bridge. A note summoned him to a meeting in Battery Park the following Monday evening. Milenkin went and was surprised to find Klisinski waiting for him, sitting calmly on a bench reading—of all things—a *Wall Street Journal.*

The two men spoke to each other in English. To speak Russian even in subdued tones would be to invite suspicion, even on a park bench.

Klisinski explained that a critical operation was about to begin against the Americans. It would be a long, important campaign with global implications, Klisinski said, even though he was only a small part of it. It would firmly test the will and resolve of capitalism in the postwar years.

"Even though you will probably never see me again," Klisinski explained to him, "I will personally serve as your control officer within the United States. You will continue to look for messages in the usual place and you will learn a method to communicate back with me. But you will contact me only in extreme emergencies. Your role will be that of a conduit. It is an important role, an essential one to the operations planned for the worldwide Communist revolution. Thus you must do your job, never question an order, never think about a message you may be relaying, and never try to exceed the role that our exalted leader Joseph Stalin has assigned to you. Is that clear?"

"Yes, comrade," Milenkin answered.

The younger man was in awe of Klisinski's flawless English. Milenkin thought back to their previous meetings in the Soviet Union and recalled that Klisinski had a strange hitch to his Russian. The conventional wisdom had it that he was a Polish Communist whose wartime valor had been rewarded with his current high appointment in the G.R.U. Young Milenkin, however, knew better than to pursue such points of curiosity.

"I'm sure that you're familiar," Klisinski added softly, "with the repercussions suffered by those who have *not* fulfilled their assigned roles within the Marxist master plan."

Uncomfortably, Milenkin said he had. Even Trotsky in 1940 had paid a pretty heavy penalty for revisionism.

Klisinski nodded. Then he patted the younger man on the

shoulder and said a few words of reassurance. "I know I can have considerable confidence in you," Klisinski concluded. "Just do what you're ordered. Don't try to think things out too much. For a young man in your position, that's where trouble always begins."

Time went by. Few messages came Milenkin's way other than the initial one to confirm the methods of contact in the United States. What bothered Milenkin was that he had heard only once from his mother, Liliya, back in the U.S.S.R. Adoptive or not, he loved her as much as any son could. She was the one person he was allowed to communicate with, and the one person allowed to communicate with him. Letters from her, like the other messages, were to come only through Klisinski, her former paramour, at the usual drop point in the base of the bridge.

The silence from back home bothered the young man. But he sought to put it out of his mind. And so Milenkin—or Mulligan, as he now wanted to be known—settled into his job, made a few friends, went to movies with a female acquaintance here and there, attended baseball games and boxing events, and lived a very ordinary life. He was, to all appearances, just like millions of other American men of his generation.

Alexandr Filiatov and Marina Sejna arrived more than a year later.

Filiatov had cut his teeth during the final days of the war. As a sergeant in the Russian infantry, he had been in one of the first divisions to reach Berlin from the east. In the final days of the Third Reich, teams of Soviet, British, and American hit squads fanned out across Berlin looking for specific S.S. officers and various Nazi officials deemed unworthy of postwar trials. The Russians went about this task with considerable enthusiasm and needed as many extra guns as possible. Filiatov's division commander, knowing an efficient killer when he saw one, recommended him. A tractor mechanic before the war, Alexandr Filiatov finally had work he enjoyed.

In the days after the peace of April 1945, Filiatov remained in the army. The military life provided free food, heat, a uniform, and a few extra rubles each month upon which to get drunk. His division stayed in Poland for many months. A Polish government-in-exile in London had been recognized by the United States. But Joseph Stalin—the Exalted One—had other ideas. The January

1947 "elections" in Poland were dominated by Stalinists, who not only ran for government office but also counted the votes. The Soviet Army remained present to see that the new government of Poland was protected from the democratic aspirations of the Polish people.

Around this time the N.K.V.D. was on a talent search of the satellite countries. They found Filiatov in Gdansk, kicking around the docks, getting into fights with Polish longshoremen, and looking for a bosomy ex-barmaid named Teresia who was scared to death of him. Over her, or at least over the physical rights to her, Filiatov had already redesigned one steamfitter's face with a broken bottle. The Soviet Army transferred him back to Warsaw before he could cause a civil insurrection on his own. There his war record was checked. When he passed muster for the type of three-fisted operations the state security people had in mind for the next few years, he was sent back to Moscow for a more thorough look. Again it was Colonel Klisinski who did the evaluation. Klisinski was a rising star in Soviet intelligence: his operations against the West had paid dividends for several years already.

In Moscow, in the oppressive gray office building at 10 Dzerzhinski Square where the Soviet secret police made their home, Filiatov was cashiered out of the infantry and into the military intelligence section, under the control of the G.R.U. Thereafter, he would prove as effective an instrument of Soviet foreign policy as any battalion left behind in the satellite countries.

In Hungary that same October, for example, he strangled a non-Communist labor organizer in the back room of a Budapest union hall. And in a doorway outside a Sofia nightclub early the following year, Filiatov shot an obstinate member of the Bulgarian Socialist Party who'd had the bad manners to criticize Moscow's agricultural policy in the Balkans. The criticism had been made during confession, but these things did have a way of getting back.

All of this brought Filiatov certain rewards. He was promoted to captain in the Soviet Army. He was returned to Dzerzhinski Square and immersed in an intensive English course for further work abroad. He was given a small apartment in Moscow. And to keep the apartment cozy and interesting for the star pupil, he was given a Russian wife. Again, this was Colonel Klisinski's idea. A woman, he theorized, might have a civilizing effect on Filiatov, as well as give him something to do. It would also give the G.R.U. a bit of leverage against Filiatov working out any ideas of his own.

"If Filiatov steps out of line," Klisinski explained to his own superiors, "we can always take her away from him. Females are useful like that."

She was a girl more than she was a woman. Her name was Marina Sejna. She was pretty, blond, nineteen years old, and the niece of an admiral in the Atlantic fleet. She also spoke some English, which would later be improved with an extensive course in Moscow. She was also, as Filiatov would later boast to friends, "factory fresh" when he received her. A civil ceremony was performed on August 15, 1948. The official consummation was performed less than a half hour later when Filiatov dragged his tearful, frightened new bride into his apartment and, never a man of subtleties, rammed himself into her on a divan in the sitting room. Here was the one step along the way that gave pause to the colonel: a pregnancy would greatly complicate things, particularly if Marina wanted to keep her child. The next day the doctors implanted her with a device that she didn't understand.

"There will be time for babies sometime in the future," Comrade Klisinski told her, "as long as you faithfully do your duty to the Soviet state."

For Marina Sejna, this was a portion of the grand scheme which the party had in store for her. At first she contemplated hanging herself. But she soon discovered that as long as she gave in immediately to her husband's sexual whims and desires, she would be spared his other brutalities. So she dared not complain. Worse things had happened to other young women, she knew, both during and after the war. She even came to think of Filiatov as her protector and, in a strange sort of way, with her uncle ranking high in the navy, she became his.

So Alexandr Filiatov and Marina Sejna settled into Moscow. They learned English. She was better than he, but helped him along. This, in turn, even prompted some tenderness on his part. Time went by. At a moment in history when many Russians suffered, they were not unhappy.

After they had reached a certain level of accomplishment in the English language, they began to study American culture. They listened to tapes of American radio and were shown selected American movies, particularly those which showed—as their instructors explained it—bourgeois excesses or the genocidal warfare waged against the once-peaceable tribes of native Americans. Secretly, however, Filiatov enjoyed watching outnumbered brigades of white men mowing down wave after wave of feather-clad tomahawk-waving Indians. In spirit, the "B" westerns reminded him of the Eastern front against the Germans.

Midway through 1949, Klisinski met with them again. He told them that they would soon be leaving their Moscow apartment to commence an important assignment abroad. They would be rewarded with an even better living location if they were able to complete their mission successfully. So in October, a few days before the thirty-first anniversary of the Great Revolution, Marina was given pistol training. "You may someday need to save your husband's life," she was told. And shortly after that the couple was equipped with Finnish passports.

Pistols. Passports. Marina was under no illusions what her husband was. Nor did she have any real doubts as to the purpose of her own training. So it came as no surprise when a military aircraft took them to Leningrad. There they met a bus that transported them through several brick, concrete, and barbed-wire checkpoints and across the border to Helsinki.

From there they flew to London, and from London to Toronto. In a Greek restaurant on Queen Street two days after arrival, Colonel Klisinski met with them a final time. The rendezvous had been prearranged in Moscow.

Klisinski told the couple that he had extensive networks of Soviet patriots in the United States, all working for the worldwide revolution of laboring people. Then Klisinski handed Filiatov an envelope containing two passports and the couple's new identity. They were now Mr. and Mrs. Gregory Abelow. Their cover story was that they'd been displaced persons after the war, but had been legally able to emigrate to the United States. Mrs. Abelow already had a sister who was an American citizen, the tale went. The passports were excellent forgeries, even bearing exit stamps from the United States five days earlier.

Filiatov and Sejna returned to their hotel and memorized their new identity. The next morning snow fell heavily in Toronto, but the couple traveled by rail to Windsor, Ontario. The day after that was a normal business date in Canada, but it was the American holiday of Thanksgiving. Comrades Filiatov and Sejna took advantage of the slow day at the American immigration control to walk across the Ambassador Bridge and enter the United States.

That easily, the assassination team was completely assembled within the borders of the United States. With Milenkin in place in New York and Klisinski left behind in Ontario, Alexandr Filiatov and Marina Sejna boarded an eastbound train in Detroit. Thereafter, they promptly disappeared.

PART ONE
■

ONE

Someone set a man on fire a few hours after midnight on the first day of January 1950. The victim's body was found near Barrier Point, a lonely section of warehouses and oil refineries, nestled against the grounds of the United States Navy Yard in Philadelphia. The man had been murdered with a single bullet fired into the crown of the head, a shot that had taken a course straight downward inside his body and came to a stop in his stomach. Then he had been saturated with gasoline and turned into a human torch.

A young chief petty officer named Dennis O'Brien was on New Year's guard duty at the navy yard. It was an inhumanly frigid morning, less than ten degrees Fahrenheit. The wind gusting up the dark Delaware River from the Atlantic Ocean made the air feel even colder. So O'Brien had permission to remain in his sentry booth for much of his shift and walk his four-hundred-yard section of the navy yard's perimeter only twice an hour. This he did for the final time at 3:43. That's when O'Brien first saw the flames.

"Something big, sir. All crumpled up and lying there, sir. Better call the city fire department, sir," he said when he phoned the night command post. A few minutes later an alarm interrupted the New Year's party of the fire company at 6th Street and Oregon Avenue. The smoke eaters responded with a single engine and sloppily hosed down what they had thought to be a trash fire in a vacant lot. Only when the blaze subsided did the firemen realize that this particular call would have to be passed along to the Philadelphia police department as well.

Yet, by this time the victim already resembled a passenger in a small airplane that had made a one-point landing. Whoever he had been, wherever he had come from, how ever he had gotten there, for whatever reason he had died, he was now completely unrecognizable. Only parts of his shoes, a tiny piece of clothing here and there, his bridgework, his eyeglasses, some jewelry, and a small piece of skin under his left arm had escaped the flames. If this—in the first hours of 1950—was an indication of things to come, the second half of the twentieth century promised to be just as unforgiving as the first.

The body was lying on a strip of land that belonged to the Atlantic Oil refinery. So it was the homicide division of the Philadelphia police department, Fourth District, that was notified at twenty-two minutes after four A.M. Two officers of that unit, Sergeant Fred Castelli and Detective Mike Proley, arrived at ten minutes before five. Neither could say that he was happy to be there.

They came in the same car, parked near the fire engine, and walked toward the wet, steaming remains. The dead man's charred limbs were contorted at impossible angles, from which rose a mixture of steam and smoke. There was a repulsive odor of death in the air—somewhere in between that of burning rubber and seared pork. Neither cop was particularly moved by the scene. What hurt was the icy wind off the Delaware River.

"Jesus," Castelli grumbled. "What a night for a barbecue." Behind him he heard two of the firemen laugh.

Castelli was a good homicide cop when he cared to be, which was less and less as the years marched by. He was forty-one years old, single, five feet nine, 205 pounds before a good Italian meal, and 210 afterward. He drove a '46 DeSoto and had what they referred to in his police district as a duckass hairdo. An aura of small-time violence seemed to cling to him: he always *looked* like he was on his way to a murder scene.

Some men made the Philadelphia detective bureau the hard way—through diligent work. Others made it the easy way—through political favors. Castelli had made it the unusual way—by shooting dogs.

Feral canines had been a problem in certain South Philly neighborhoods in the postwar years. They'd been kicked out of homes by their female owners when the men had come back from the war. Major league dogs: Dobermans. Rottweilers. German shepherds. They'd run wild in packs, and when they were hungry enough, they bit chunks out of people. Eventually they maimed a couple of white children. "Enough of this bullshit with the dogs," then-Patrolman Castelli announced in April 1946. Along the back streets came a red and white Ford police cruiser for the next few nights. Arf, arf, arf. Bang, bang, bang. Each morning for the next few months residents would find a couple of dead animals on the sidewalks, waiting to be picked up by the health department. Hey, who's shooting those mutts? Silence from the cops. No one knew. But Castelli's district captain recommended him for promotion out of gratitude. A complex social problem had been solved—frontier style.

In comparison, Mike Proley, Castelli's partner, was a quiet, thin, spare family man of thirty-six. He had been a cop for eight years and a homicide detective for five. He had light, thinning hair and impassive blue eyes behind thick, silver-framed glasses. He looked a little like a high school math teacher. With Castelli, Proley completed an unlikely couple.

There was nothing unlikely about the abilities of Castelli and Proley as murder detectives, however. At the end of each fiscal year they usually had several dozen arrests between them, at least half of them "quality." They were authorities on big-city underlife and, amid a politicized and frequently corrupt police department, represented law and order west of the Delaware River. All of that was how they came to be standing on the other side of a chain-link fence from the navy yard as dawn broke on the first day of January 1950.

Castelli stared down at what remained of the corpse, his breath making small cones in front of him. He touched the dead man's left arm with the toe of his shoe. "Know the worst thing about this?" he asked. "The gentleman's wallet may have burned up with him. Perfectly good money up in smoke." He shook his head. "Some days you can't catch a break at all."

Proley broke out a pack of Pall Malls and they both smoked. Castelli turned toward the sound of an arriving car. "Here's the M.E.," he said to his partner. "Finally."

The doctor from the medical examiner's office was named Harry Wolf. Castelli and Proley liked Wolf a little less each time they saw him. He was a man in his thirties who was on the staff of one of the city hospitals that specialized in D.O.A.s. Wolf's father-in-law was a ward boss in Kensington, which was how Harry picked up an extra check each week pronouncing crime and accident victims dead at the scene. Wolf specialized in tough calls such as this one, where he could take one glance and proceed straight to the paperwork.

"Don't forget to check his pulse, doc," said Castelli.

"What do you think, Wolf?" Proley added. "Natural causes?"

"Fuck you guys, all right?" Wolf answered, fumbling with both his glasses and his medical notebooks.

"Where the hell were you, Wolf? Home playing with Sally Five-Fingers while we're here freezing? You're supposed to be on call, you lazy turd."

"How'd you guys like to wait for two hours next time?" Wolf asked, looking up from a pad of death certificates. "Or maybe I'll go get some coffee right now. Were you first officers on the scene? That means you stay until a doctor pronounces this guy dead and *signs* the form."

"So fucking sign it," said Castelli. A contingent of young sailors in pea coats looked on from the other side of the fence.

Wolf might not have signed it, but the wagon from the morgue arrived with a body bag and a set of shovels. So did Captain Robert Heintz from the Fourth District police command, along with the department photographer.

Heintz was a big, strapping man with gray hair and wide shoulders. He'd seen things go bump in the night in South Philadelphia since the days of Prohibition. Much of what he'd seen had been stranger than this.

"Just wrap him up and get him out of here," Heintz said. "Wolf, shut your trap and sign the friggin' form." So with little further discussion the charred remains of a human being were loaded onto the body wagon and removed.

There it was. A single, unidentifiable man murdered, his body mutilated beyond recognition. Off he went to the city morgue where, in the absence of his connection to any missing persons report, his case would diminish daily among the priorities of the homicide division. It was all too typically the sort of case that drifts into the oblivion of the unsolved and forgotten among the big-city police forces of North America.

But for anyone who cared to look deeply in the ashes, bones, and rubble, there were nonetheless certain physical clues and—just as important—certain deductions to be lifted. All of these, when added up, would be more than sufficient to change the lives of scores of men and women throughout the United States, Europe, and Asia. Equally, the conclusions from the crime, were it ever to be solved and made public, would shake the foundations of at least one respected American financial institution, undermine the reputations of intelligence services on both sides of the iron curtain, and even touch upon the highest levels of the United States government.

The fire at Barrier Point in the opening hours of 1950 would prove, in other words, to be hot in more ways than anyone present could reasonably imagine. All that was missing was one person who cared.

■
TWO
■

L ike Philadelphia to the north, Washington shivered through its coldest midwinter in a dozen years. Ice hung from the cherry trees along the Potomac with such tenacity that it was difficult to imagine that spring would ever come. A mantle of snow adorned both Jefferson and Lincoln Memorials. Even Pennsylvania Avenue itself, where traffic crawled in both directions, seemed more like a New Hampshire snowscape than the center of the American government.

In the White House things were warmer. Sixty-three-year-old President Harry S. Truman dug in for an increasingly acrimonious battle with the Eighty-first Congress. He fought with the nation's legislators over everything from increased social security benefits to public housing to his frequent use of the term *god damned* in public, a word frequently applied by the President to the leadership of the U.S. Congress itself.

But if Truman looked for solace in the tide of world events, he found none there either. In 1949 the President had succeeded in breaking the eighteen-month Soviet blockade of West Berlin with massive American airlifts of food and medical supplies. But Joseph Stalin was so freshly invigorated at home, and had so thoroughly terrified the heads of his puppet governments throughout Eastern Europe that he merrily launched a new and exhaustive generation of purge trials in Russia. In Asia the North Korean government made ominous noises about reuniting their country in a manner they saw fit, and using their huge army to do it. Nearby, General Chiang Kai-Shek and his pro-American Kuomintang Army had been driven from the mainland of China to Formosa late in 1949. It was evident that the U.S. consular staff would soon follow. In Europe the Fourth French Republic, founded after the war, teetered from week to week on the brink of ruin. Even in England, Truman's final and most loyal wartime ally, Winston Churchill, was out of office, suffering daily as the vocal but essentially powerless leader of the Parliamentary opposition. It was a time when, from the perspective of the American capital, enemies were ascendant and friends were either disloyal or halfway into their graves. It was a time when the support of public opinion deserted the President and galvanized around the conservative senator Robert Taft, grandson of the three-hundred-pound former president, as well as the increasingly vocal, hard-drinking, and—in the opinion of many—mean-spirited Joseph McCarthy. There was even talk that if the lid could be kept on the little guy from Missouri for two more years, a possible presidential candidacy by Dwight Eisenhower, the former supreme allied commander, might rescue the country. Ike was currently drawing a paycheck as president of Columbia University. If only he would announce whether he was a Democrat or a Republican, matters would be greatly clarified. But in the end, it was a time, as Charles Dickens might have written, much like our own. Just five years after a war that compromised all humanity, and already the world was again on its way to hell in a handbasket.

Perhaps in an attempt to prevent the world from going to hell, and perhaps as a final response to Pearl Harbor, the United States government four years earlier—in 1946—had sought to reorganize its intelligence community.

The sneak Japanese attack on Hawaii had not only carried with it a devastating shock to the American public, it had also taught a lesson to some of those in government. Inquiries during the world war had revealed that there had been significant indications before December 7, 1941, that Imperial Japan was up to something. Crates of documents, retrieved after the fact, had lain around unused and unnoted by American military and naval commanders in the years 1939 through 1941. Information that could have saved thousands of lives and perhaps have shortened the war had been ignored. Why? Simply because no single effective unit of the government had been equipped to assemble and analyze foreign intelligence. Thus, in the early months of World War II, President Franklin Roosevelt created the Office of Strategic Services, the nation's first official espionage and counterespionage agency. But after the war—and within months of Truman's ascension to the White House following Roosevelt's death in April 1945—the O.S.S. ran afoul of special-interest lobbyists. Specifically, the military intelligence services and the F.B.I. of J. Edgar Hoover insisted that in peacetime the O.S.S. would only duplicate the efforts of previously existing agencies. Eventually President Truman came to agree and abolished the O.S.S.

Within a few months, however, the President acknowledged his mistake. Whatever the faults of the O.S.S.—and there were many—it had at least been a single agency collecting and evaluating foreign intelligence and sending the information into the Oval Office. Without a central agency Truman received an avalanche of contradictory, superficial reports. One day, confused, irritated, and ill informed, he exploded to his Secretary of State, James F. Byrnes.

"As soon as possible," raged the President, "we've got to get somebody or some outfit that can make sense out of all this stuff!"

Truman expressed much the same wish in identical letters sent on January 22, 1946, to his military adviser, Admiral William Leahy, Secretary of War Robert Patterson, Secretary of the Navy John Forrestal, and Secretary of State Byrnes. These four men were asked to consider themselves as the National Intelligence Authority. They were to plan, develop, and coordinate all foreign espionage and counterespionage activities. Within a few weeks the four had assigned funds and personnel from their own departments to the authority, and they had formed what they called the Central Intelligence Group to carry out the mission of the authority. To head the new C.I.G., Truman appointed Rear Admiral Sidney W. Souers. Souers bore the title of Director of Central Intelligence. The appointment caused some grumbling in official Washington. Souers was an admiral in the naval reserve and his civilian employment was currently as an executive in the Piggly Wiggly grocery chain in Truman's native Missouri. He had the President's ear and trust, in other words, but no experience in intelligence matters. Or, as some Capitol wags put it: "He wouldn't recognize a spy, but he sure knows fruits and vegetables."

Yet President Truman wanted nothing more than a reliable method of being kept informed. So this, for a while, satisfied him. But the setup was distinctly *un*satisfying to many others, including the directors of military intelligence and J. Edgar Hoover—all of whom continued to fear the erosion of their own powers—as well as Admiral Souers himself, who constantly found the four members of the National Intelligence Authority looking over his shoulder. Then there was another man who found the arrangement unsatisfactory: Allen Dulles. Dulles had been one of America's most successful spies during the two world wars. He also had the President's ear.

Dulles began to agitate the President for a change in the intelligence system. Simultaneously, General Hoyt S. Vandenberg of the army air corps succeeded Admiral Souers in June 1946. Vandenberg was named chiefly because he was the nephew of the powerful Senator Arthur Vandenberg, and managed to last only about as long as his predecessor, slightly less than a year. He in turn was succeeded by Rear Admiral Roscoe Hillenkoetter, whom Truman personally didn't like and whom many in the White House referred to openly as "a third-rate navy guy." America's new spy establishment, in other words, was off to a staggering start.

Yet, during Hillenkoetter's tenure, Congress passed the National Security Act, unifying much of the American defense establishment. The act also replaced the National Intelligence Authority with a new structure called the National Security Council. Similarly, the Central Intelligence Group was abolished and replaced by a stronger and more independent unit: It was called the Central Intelligence Agency. Its purpose was to gather and coordinate information from outside the forty-eight states. The agency would have no official police or law enforcement powers. And, in turn, the new C.I.A. was to be responsible—in theory, at least—to the National Security Council. Not by coincidence, President Truman then appointed a professional spy, Allen Dulles, as the agency's first director.

Thus the embryonic C.I.A. moved into the battered old complex that formerly housed the United States Public Health Service at 2430 E Street in the gashouse section of Washington known as Foggy Bottom. The complex bordered on an abandoned brewery and sat squalidly—almost disgracefully—amid a jungle of underbrush enclosed by a wire fence and topped with barbed wire. From this location, and for many years thereafter, little green government buses ferried passengers—frequently mysterious men bearing secret messages or documents—to and from the Pentagon and the White House. And at this humble inception, the one-hundred-forty-acre spread that would eventually house the C.I.A. in bucolic Langley, Virginia, was merely a gleam in Allen Dulles's eye. But it was a beginning, nonetheless.

In contrast, in 1950 the Federal Bureau of Investigation was housed in baronial splendor at Constitution Avenue and 10th Street, in a suite of fifth- and sixth-floor offices at the Justice Department. J. Edgar Hoover presided from a corner throne room, surrounded by his ablest assistants in adjoining chambers. This was a straight-arrow squeaky-clean place with light green walls, deep pile carpets, mahogany paneling, and countless American flags. A visitor to the Director's office, were he kept waiting in the anteroom, would be faced with an armada of plaques—given by various religious, fraternal, school, and state police organizations—that exhausted the space on the wall and heaped superlatives and praise upon the Bureau and its peerless Director. A revolving rack carried scores of editorial cartoons, mounted individually on hard cardboard backing, and was there for the perusal of the casual or serious viewer. If these displays left the observer ready for more, there were also some of the more macabre relics of earlier bureau adventures.

John Dillinger's death mask, for example, was in a glass case in the same anteroom, along with the straw boater Dillinger wore when gunned down by the combined forces of Hoover's G-men and the Indiana State Police. Completing the display, and looking to be in very good condition, all things considered, was the Corona-Belvedere cigar from the pocket of Dillinger's bloodstained, bullet-ridden shirt. This particular Corona-Belvedere was a quality smoke that the Depression-era outlaw never lived to enjoy.

But equally, this was a time when the Bureau was threatening to collapse of its own weight. Though the Director was an American folk hero in law enforcement, Hoover nonetheless had never led an investigation and had personally never made an arrest. Despite being photographed weekly with an array of weapons, he'd also never even learned to use a handgun. Yet the image of the bureau before the public had never been more immaculate. Hoover flitted about the country at his own whim, stayed in the finest hotels as the guest of the management, and had his picture snapped hobnobbing with celebrities such as Milton Berle, Shirley Temple, Toots Shor, Bing Crosby, and Jimmy Cagney. (Hoover would always love the latter for his galvanizing performance as an F.B.I. agent in the 1935 Warner Bros. production, *G-Men,* a film that did much to mold the public perception of the Bureau.) And the weekly radio serial, *This Is Your F.B.I.,* remained a hit in its sixth year on the air.

Yet behind the scenes, the Bureau increasingly reflected the disparity between the public image and the gritty, sweaty, day-to-

day operation of American law enforcement. Equally, the Bureau
also reflected Hoover's personal biases. Almost daily the F.B.I. was
formidably preoccupied with cases of a political slant or which emanated from a political favor. In October 1949, for example, eleven
members of the Communist Party of the United States had drawn
prison sentences of three to five years apiece for advocating the
violent overthrow of the United States government. They hadn't
done anything, they'd merely expressed their opinion. But in the
climate of the day, that was enough to land them in prison after
arrest by Hoover's men and a speedy trial in New York City.

The second perjury trial of Alger Hiss was concluding in Manhattan also. All indications were that Hiss would go to prison too.
The best was yet to come, however, as a section of Bureau spear
carriers in a newly renovated suite on the fifth floor continued a
long inquiry into the affairs of one suspected Soviet spy named
Martin Sobell. The investigation of Sobell had also led to some
alleged American accomplices named Julius and Ethel Rosenberg.
In the few remaining liberal and moderate circles in Washington,
the second half of the twentieth century looked to be an uncompro-
mising stretch of years, sort of a distant echo of the ninth century,
when all human enlightenment was systematically obliterated.

In a small, stuffy office in a far corner of the sixth floor, Special
Agent Thomas C. Buchanan sat at a black Royal typewriter. He
pecked out his final account of an investigation involving a securi-
ties swindle. Recently put out of business were a pair of Miami-
based land developers who'd raised money and sold homesites from
the Catskills to Sarasota. It was the kind of a case—hundreds of
small investors burned by a pair of slick carpetbaggers—that provoked Buchanan's righteous indignation. The case had ended with
indictments, convictions, tons of favorable publicity for the F.B.I.,
and—miraculously—the recovery of almost sixty percent of the ill-
gained loot. Within the next month, checks would go out to most of
the investors returning significant parts of their money. It was a
piece of work for which Buchanan could be proud.

He stopped typing for a moment. Buchanan reread his report
as it neared its conclusion. One could never be too careful in choos-
ing one's words within the F.B.I. Not only did Buchanan's immediate superior, Francis W. Lerrick, assistant director for the mid-
Atlantic region, attempt to read all completed files, but Hoover
himself also liked to pick up reports at random and breeze through
them. Here was where trouble could sometimes materialize from

nowhere. Hoover's attention might settle upon anything, no matter how large or small, negative or positive, real or imagined. One ten-year veteran of the New York office was abruptly transferred to Topeka when his report contained a quote from a Canadian ballistics expert who'd been used as a witness during a trial. "We keep *all foreigners* out of Bureau business!" Hoover had roared. On another occasion a special agent in the Atlanta office found himself placed on an immediate diet and ordered to lose fifteen pounds in three weeks. A final case report had included his medical records, revealing his six-foot one-hundred-ninety-five-pound stature. Hoover, as it happened, had been placed on a diet by his own physician the previous Monday.

Buchanan typed the final two paragraphs, then removed the last of fifteen pages from his Royal. He leaned back in his chair and carefully reviewed the report from start to finish.

Had anyone walked into the office at that time, he or she would have seen a sandy-haired man of thirty-two, a handsome man with a square jaw and dark blue eyes. He wore a white shirt and a red and blue striped tie. The jacket of his navy blue suit was draped over the back of his chair and his hat—mandatory for all special agents—rested on a coat rack in the corner.

Had it not been for a turn of fate and the course of history, Buchanan at this time might have been the architect he'd planned on being when young. He'd grown up in a comfortable town in the southeastern quarter of Pennsylvania. His mother had taught the third grade in the local school. His father had been a medical doctor in family practice, the now-vanished breed of man who used to drive over snowy winter roads to call on patients. As a teenager Thomas had shown an uncanny aptitude for numbers and sciences. He'd set his heart on going to Princeton University, his father's alma mater.

The turn of fate: A massive heart attack claimed Thomas's father at age forty-three in August 1932. His mother moved the family closer to Philadelphia, where they took up residence with his mother's unmarried sister. Thomas was enrolled at a private academy in Chestnut Hill, in accordance with his father's will. Here he demonstrated again his exceptional aptitude in sciences and math, and built an impressive academic record. Princeton accepted him as a full-tuition student. Lehigh University, however, offered him a full scholarship in engineering. This was 1936, and his father had not died wealthy. He went to Lehigh, graduated with high honors, and had every intention of continuing on for his graduate degree in architecture. Then, with the deplorable world events of 1939-40, the course of history interfered. A career, and, as it turned out, a potential marriage, would be misplaced in the tide of a global conflict.

Buchanan served as an infantry captain in the United States Army's North African and Italian campaigns in World War II. He won two silver stars and as many purple hearts. But when he left the military with an honorable discharge in the autumn of 1945, he was restless, too much so to hit the academic books again, even on a graduate level. So he looked for something else. A retired colonel who'd commanded his infantry unit told him that the Federal Bureau of Investigation was hiring. "The work can be interesting and the employer isn't likely to go out of business," the colonel had said. "If you decide not to make a career of it, it still won't look bad on your résumé. I'll write you a letter of recommendation."

So Buchanan entered the National Police Academy, the Bureau's training school, in early 1946. An eighteen-month tour in Chicago was his first assignment. He didn't have the commanding physical presence or bulk that typified many enforcers of American law, nor did he have the traditional gangbusting mentality for which the "G-men" had become the heroes of the somewhat gullible public and tabloid press. But he did have an outstanding analytical intellect. This he coupled with an easy, calm manner that inspired confidence in people and made them willing to talk to him.

Surprisingly enough, even suspected perpetrators—when investigated or confronted by Special Agent Buchanan—received much the same treatment. Frequently criminals took his civility, his sense of fairness, and his reluctance to resort to force as signs of weakness. Only later, usually from hours of leisure in a prison cell, were these malefactors able to understand that they'd underestimated the quiet, contemplative nature of their adversary. As a result, for his age, Buchanan was as fine a detective as the Bureau had to offer. And, despite the Bureau's growing pettifoggery and its inevitable lapses into cliques or office politics, Thomas Buchanan had rarely regretted becoming a law enforcement officer. The career did have its rewards from time to time. The rewards were frequently moral, but they were there.

Buchanan reached to a fountain pen to affix his signature to the report. It was ten minutes before six on Thursday afternoon, January 12, 1950. With good conscience Buchanan could call this a day. Not only had he completed a laudable piece of work, he could safely go home: The daily "he's gone" message had buzzed through the Bureau's corridors at four forty-five, signaling the departure of J. Edgar and his handsome, ever-present partner, Clyde Tolson.

Buchanan signed the report. A few seconds later the intercom rang on his desk. Buchanan hadn't even replaced the cap on the fountain pen. "Yes?" he answered.

"Tom!" cried a voice. Buchanan recognized it as Frank Lerrick's. "Tom, come down here this instant or there'll be gunfire!"

The "gunfire" was figurative. This was Lerrick's flowery style of demanding that an agent drop everything and get to his office. It struck terror into the uninitiated.

Moments later Buchanan walked into Lerrick's office, which was four doors from Hoover's. Buchanan found the graying, craggy-faced, sixty-two-year-old assistant director sitting at his desk. Standing nearby was a wiry, sharply featured, dark-haired man in a gray suit. He was forty-year-old William Roth, chief of the Philadelphia field office.

Roth nodded to Buchanan as Buchanan came in the door. "You know each other, I assume," Lerrick said.

"We do," Buchanan said. He and Roth shook hands. They'd worked on cases together in the past. Both had spent time assigned to a special operation in southern Illinois.

"How cozy," said Lerrick sourly. "That, I suppose, Mr. Bill Roth, is why you intend to ferret him away from my command."

Roth shrugged. Lerrick motioned to a folder on the corner of his desk. It was manila, thick, and closed. In bold red letters it bore the enticing instructions that if it were to be lost and found by a stranger, it was to be RETURNED IMMEDIATELY UNREAD to the nearest F.B.I. office.

"Sit in that chair over there, Tom, and take a look at this horse shit," said Lerrick, indicating the file. "It came here by hand today from Philadelphia. I won't identify exactly whose nonwhite hands" —Lerrick glared at Roth—"but God knows we should drop everything we're doing here in Washington whenever anything comes our way from our Brothers in Christ in Philadelphia. Right, Special Agent in Charge Roth?"

Roth again had the sense not to answer directly. Lerrick's eyes sparkled with fury. Lerrick looked at the file. "I'll be interested in your reaction, Tom," Roth said mildly.

"Reaction?" Lerrick snorted. *"Reaction? What are we here, a* radio audience for *The Great Gildersleeve?* Might as well be, the way we get blown about by every little puff of suspicious wind." He handed Buchanan the file. Thomas took it. "Don't speak again till you've digested this," the assistant director ordered. "If there's anything there *to* digest. Then we'll talk."

Buchanan seated himself in a corner chair. The only light was from a standing lamp. As Buchanan began to read, Roth took a position at the room's only window, a large eighteen-pane one that faced Washington Monument. Against the evening sky the monument was illuminated by yellowish-white beams from a series of floodlights.

While Buchanan read, Roth lit and smoked a cigarette. From time to time Lerrick's fingers drummed rhythmically and impatiently on the top of his mahogany desk from the General Services Administration.

Buchanan read for almost half an hour. The file focused upon a man named John Taylor Garrett and his most recent family business, the Second Commonwealth Bank of Pennsylvania. Buchanan was twice startled to see J. T. Garrett and Commonwealth Penn as the centerpieces of an F.B.I. file. Spending his final teen and high school years in Chestnut Hill, one of the better-heeled suburbs of Philadelphia, Buchanan had closely known Garrett, his bank, and his family. Garrett was as unlikely a subject for a federal investigation as could ever exist.

John Taylor Garrett was the epitome of old money. A distant Garrett ancestor had been on the *Mayflower* in the 1640s, and a later member of the Garrett clan had moved from the Massachusetts Bay Colony to Philadelphia with the young Benjamin Franklin in the early 1700s. The Garretts had been a family of genteel Protestant merchants in Pennsylvania since the days of Franklin. To this day they still owned a network of department stores bearing the Garrett name. The family had money in America before the newly independent colonies even had their own credible currency.

And yet . . . and yet . . .

According to the report before Special Agent Buchanan, the inner workings of Commonwealth Penn were a maze of question marks. Garrett had taken over Commonwealth Penn in 1934. The bank had been on the brink of ruin. Garrett had not only saved it, but had also built it into a respected financial institution. It was not a large bank, but it was prominent and significant—particularly as a privately owned independent. All of which made the bank's behavior—as well as its owner's—all the more bizarre.

Garrett was away to the world war for five full years, leaving his wife and two daughters behind. During this time Commonwealth Penn was managed by a board of trustees. *Mismanaged* by a board would be slightly more accurate, said the report, as the enterprise turned nose-down and plunged toward the ground again. The war ended just in time. Garrett came home and got his bank clicking again. Yet at the same time, after the world war, Garrett turned into something of a social recluse. He took an occasional meal in his favorite Philadelphia spot—the dining room of The Barclay—and was rarely seen anywhere else. At the same time, he seemed to deliberately cease communication with even the best of his prewar friends.

Then, while overseeing the renaissance of Commonwealth Penn, he presided over the disintegration of his own family. As Tom Buchanan well knew, Garrett had two beautiful daughters, Ann and Laura. He had a socially prominent wife. Between the last weeks of 1946 and the first days of 1950 his wife divorced him and both daughters inexplicably moved away.

The rumor mill in the Delaware Valley had all kinds of explanations for Garrett, his behavior, and the breakup of his family. Some said that he was a conduit for dirty money through the eastern United States. Others insisted that he'd been shellshocked in the war and had come home a different man. Others alluded to a career in a U.S. Army intelligence unit, complete with unsavory associations, a mistress, and even a second family somewhere else around the globe.

Yet none of this fit with John T. Garrett, the personification of the dour old-fashioned Quaker City Protestant. Improprieties of any sort, as Buchanan knew well, just didn't fit the man.

Buchanan finished the report, closed the folder, and looked up. "Who wrote this?" he asked.

"God," replied Lerrick. "God and his son, Jesus H. Christ. Didn't he, Roth?"

"I wrote it," Roth said. "It's a briefing file. It's a condensation of a much larger piece of work."

"It reads nicely," Buchanan said. "But with all due respect, it's almost entirely hearsay. I don't see anything indictable here at all."

"That," bellowed Lerrick triumphantly, "is exactly what I'm

telling people until I'm blue in the face. But no one listens to his uncle Frank these days!"

Roth was undeterred. "I'm sorry. But there are a multitude of serious questions here. They demand answers."

"If there's a problem with Commonwealth Penn," Buchanan reasoned, "that's the jurisdiction of the U.S. Attorney in Philadelphia. If his daughters and wife are missing, that's a matter for the local police."

"The Philadelphia police can't be trusted, particularly the detective bureau," Roth said flatly. "And we don't want to tip our investigation by asking any questions."

"The three Garrett women," Buchanan asked. "Any chance they were kidnapped?"

"There's no evidence to suggest that."

"Then what's the point?" Buchanan asked politely. "This still doesn't strike me as the basis of an F.B.I. investigation."

There was a finality to Roth's response. "I'm afraid it will have to prove as the basis this time."

Buchanan looked to Lerrick, then back to Roth. "Oh. That's why I'm here, is it? You're making an assignment."

For a moment a silence enveloped the room. Lerrick leaned forward at his desk and his mood seemed to change. "Tom, an inquiry upon John T. Garrett isn't my idea. You know who makes decisions like that."

It took Buchanan a moment. "Ah. Hoover," he said.

"The Director wants Garrett thoroughly investigated," Roth said. "He's read this report and he's read a more detailed one that's back in Philadelphia. You'll be seeing it soon."

"I will, will I?"

Lerrick nodded.

Buchanan felt something between anger and indignation rising within him. "I assume," he said, "that there's no coincidence here. About my being given the Garrett file?"

He looked Lerrick and Roth back and forth. For a moment both men were silent.

"Tom, once Hoover decided that he wanted Garrett investigated," Lerrick began, "he asked for a list of men who'd be qualified to do it. He wanted someone young and energetic as well as someone who'd have an insight into Garrett. Your name came up. I noted—and I said this to the Director myself—that you'd grown up in close proximity to the Garrett family. You went to the same private academy in Chestnut Hill as both of his daughters. In fact, it's right there on your background profile in personnel that you, uh—"

"That I was engaged to his younger daughter before the war?" Buchanan said. "To Ann Garrett. Is that it?"

"Yes," Lerrick answered. "Engaged to her. But you never actually—"

"Ann Garrett broke off the engagement in April 1943," Buchanan said. "She wrote to me in Italy. She said she'd met someone else. I never saw her or anyone in her family again. Nor did I try."

"Do you feel awkward about this?"

"What the hell do you think?"

"I wanted to get you eliminated from the investigation on those personal grounds," Frank Lerrick explained. "I said, 'Mr. Director, you don't want John Taylor Garrett investigated by an unsuccessful—for whatever reason—suitor of his younger daughter.' " Buchanan bristled slightly as Lerrick forged ahead. "But J. Edgar just laughed at me, Tom. He said, 'No, Frank, you have it all wrong. I want a *zealous* inquiry. I want a *relentless* inquiry. And that's exactly what I'll get from a former fiancé.' "

"You know the Director, Tom," said Roth. "Whenever he can pump a personal or even a sexual angle in a case, he damned well goes for it."

"Hoover asked if you were in the middle of anything important," Lerrick continued. "I had to answer truthfully. I said that you had testified in a real estate fraud case this past Monday, and a conviction had been obtained on Tuesday. The chief seemed to be aware of the case, thanks to the favorable publicity."

"Naturally," said Buchanan.

"So I told him you'd be wrapping up your present work this week. That did it, I'm afraid. Thereafter, the Director would hear of no name other than yours."

"There's nothing in that file that merits our involvement," Buchanan said. "Why a Garrett investigation at all?"

"Who knows?" snapped Lerrick. "Ask J. Edgar yourself. Garrett gets investigated because Hoover wants it done. It's as simple as that."

Another silence held the room. "I don't like losing men from this office," Lerrick concluded, "particularly quality men such as yourself. God knows, I never get them back." He sighed. "You're assigned to the Garrett case, Tom. And starting Monday you're transferred to Philadelphia. That's what Brother Roth is doing here in Washington, Tom. He's here to take you back."

THREE

"**D**amn! Damn them all!"

Buchanan cursed vehemently to himself as he pulled his overcoat tight against the cold of the midwinter Washington night. It was almost eight o'clock. He charged down the steps of the Justice Department in a controlled rage and hit the sidewalk, still struggling with the belt of his coat. "Of all the outrageous, impertinent, moronic ideas."

Him? Thomas Buchanan? Investigate the Garrett family? Sure, he told himself as he avoided a slick patch of ice on K Street, he could do a fine investigation. He could investigate *anyone* thoroughly. But why even *flirt* with the semblance of bias? If he found something significant against John Taylor Garrett, and later went to court with it, his actions would be seen as the vendetta of a young man who'd been unsuccessfully in love with Ann Garrett. And wouldn't that come out at a trial?

Yet if he found nothing, wasn't there the inherent suggestion of a whitewash? A young agent assigned to probe into the Garrett affairs but still wishing not to offend the family. The foundations of any investigation had to be clean and sound. Didn't Hoover know that? Didn't Hoover always *say* that? Wasn't that one of the first things they'd taught back at the National Police Academy in Quantico, Virginia, where Buchanan had reported after the war?

"Damn," he cursed to himself again. He stepped off a curb on Pennsylvania Avenue and a piece of packed snow gave way. There was slush underneath. His foot rode the cracked ice to the pavement and a small, unwelcome flood of freezing water rushed into his shoe.

Roth's fulsome words returned: *You know the Director, Tom. Whenever he can pump a personal or even a sexual angle in a case, he damned well goes for it.*

Hoover! Lerrick had even admitted that it had been J.E.H. himself who had made the decision. Hoover! That bombastic, unproductive, semi-effeminate fraud! A Republican appointment during the illustrious Warren Harding administration, Buchanan muttered, who was somehow still entrenched during the Truman administration. It was common currency around Capitol Hill that the man from Missouri wanted to get rid of him but either didn't know how or didn't dare. Hoover sure had an instinct for survival, Thomas concluded. In the Washington political jungle, J. Edgar knew how to swing with the top apes.

Buchanan walked a few more blocks against the bitter Washington wind. He gripped his hat. He'd lost more than one good Stetson fedora under the wheels of a Washington bus. Then, very gradually, Buchanan began to settle down.

He tried to be rational. Maybe, he sometimes wondered, the F.B.I. wasn't for him after all. For the past three months he'd worked on the land fraud case. Last week he'd been in court and this week he'd obtained convictions that would deliver a pair of swindlers to justice. At five o'clock that same day he'd concluded his report of the case. Surely this stellar effort should move him up the F.B.I. ladder to bigger, better, more important cases. Hadn't he earned that much? Then a mere hour later he was assigned to investigate a man who, were it not for the world war, might have been his father-in-law. Some step up!

He turned onto D Street at 9th. Even on these cold District nights he enjoyed walking home. He needed the exercise as well as the air. And tonight he needed to cool off in more ways than one.

There were proper channels for grievances, he told himself, and he would go through them. He would get an audience with J. Edgar Hoover and appeal to the man's reason. Give me a case with some big city hoodlums, he'd request. Or what about all the Red spies and saboteurs that Hoover constantly claimed were infiltrating the country? Put me on the trail of some of them, he'd ask, and I'll give them to you hogtied by Mother's Day. That's what he'd do! And if Hoover didn't respond, he'd slam down his resignation on the old man's desk.

Buchanan trudged another block through the Washington night. Why didn't the Sanitation Department get out here and get some rock salt on these icy sidewalks? He was a man who still thought of himself as young and fit, and he'd nearly fallen twice.

His wet foot, freezing as it was, was doing him no favors of comfort either.

He came to the corner of his own block. There was a small bar there. It was named The Haypenny and was fashioned after an English pub. It was a favorite of law and government students from Georgetown as well as secretaries from the Justice Department and the National Archives. There was a large plate glass window in front, and Buchanan glanced in. Lately he perceived the crowd as growing younger at The Haypenny. Tonight did nothing to dissuade him, so he kept walking.

The generational break, he'd long since concluded, would be defined by who served in the war and who'd been born too late. Unlike some men he knew who sought to recapture their lost youth after leaving the armed forces, Buchanan had no illusions as to which side of the generational gap he was on. When he saw groups of happy young drinkers, an uncontrollably morose feeling sometimes gripped him, and he thought of young men who'd been born the same year as he—1917—who would lie for all eternity in unmarked graves in Italy and North Africa. But that was past history, too, just like—he couldn't help but think—his romance with Ann Garrett. It was just that sometimes he would watch groups of men and women in their twenties and he would feel very old.

His apartment was on the third floor of a clean brick building on the 100 block of 7th Street, S.E. The flat was part of a house that belonged to a Mr. and Mrs. Elvin Rafferty. The Raffertys were a couple in their sixties who lived on the first two floors but who had created a separate, locking apartment at the top of the stairs. Rafferty himself didn't do much except sit around the living room or, in the summer, camp out on a big wicker chair on the front porch. There on summer afternoons he would turn on a big Philco console radio and follow Arch McDonald's broadcasts of baseball's Washington Senators—home games from nearby Griffith Stadium and road games from seven other disastrous points around the American League.

"Washington!" Rafferty habitually ranted. "First in war, first in peace, and last in the American League! Next thing you know," he once complained to Buchanan, "they'll be integrating with niggers like the Dodgers, the Indians, and the St. Louis Browns."

"Maybe when they do," Buchanan had answered gently, "they won't be in last place anymore."

Rafferty had thought about that all of August 1949.

Rafferty had been a grocer when he was younger. He was the grandson of a Confederate soldier—or so he liked to claim—but he'd had a knee shattered in the First World War. He'd hobbled around with a pair of canes for most of his adult life, but in the last few years arthritis had afflicted him. So he'd sold his store and now sat home on a veteran's pension, plus social security, plus rent from the third floor, which his wife collected.

"It ain't the money, Mr. Buchanan," Mrs. Rafferty had said the day she first showed the apartment to him. Mrs. Rafferty spoke with the lilting inflections of the Mississippi Delta, which she admitted that she hadn't seen in years. "It's these old legs of mine," she continued. "Ain't much better than my husband's these days. Don't have much use for a third floor, so we don't mind having company. 'Specially a nice young man."

"Yes, ma'am," he'd said.

She'd looked carefully at him. "If you bring ladies back here," she said knowingly, "make sure they're nice ladies. And don't make too much noise. I don't mind none, but Elvin don't sleep so good. The rent is fifty-five dollars." Buchanan, seeing the fray on the carpets in the entrance hall, was sure to pay it on the first day of every month.

Buchanan walked through the front door and up the two flights of stairs. He could smell the pot roast Mrs. Rafferty made every Thursday. He arrived at his own apartment, put his key in the door, and turned the lock. He felt the morning's mail brush against the floor as he opened the door. He threw on a light and soon found his way into the bathroom. There he hung his wet coat in the shower.

Philadelphia. Monday. He made himself a Scotch and settled into an overstuffed club chair in his living room. God, he was tired, he told himself. God, he could use a day off. He was hungry and there was no food in the apartment. Well, he could find his way to the little Italian place around the corner on 6th Street, where a plump but endearing little woman named Cora held court each night. Cora owned the place, along with her brother, Ray. Ray kept the beer cold. Cora made good spaghetti with meatballs and wasn't shy about serving man-size portions. This would not be the first time Thomas Buchanan had eaten dinner there alone.

God, he thought again as he sipped the scotch. How could he investigate a John Garrett? What would this lead to? After ten years, would he come face-to-face again with Ann Garrett, the infatuation of his prewar youth, the first woman with whom he'd ever fallen in love?

No, he couldn't take this case. This was ridiculous. Philadelphia on Monday was out of the question. He finished his scotch.

He'd made his decision. First thing in the morning, he'd tell Hoover exactly what he thought.

He went to Cora's, had a fine dinner, and read his mail and the evening Washington *Star*. He came home, slept soundly, and went in to work early the next morning. But by that time, of course, he'd recalled that the best path to advancement in the bureau was to successfully complete the work placed before him.

So on second thought . . . Well, most of the other agents said the Philadelphia office wasn't such a bad assignment. It was in the east, after all, and had the attractive reputation of never being personally visited by Hoover. So Special Agent Buchanan decided he'd keep his mouth shut, after all, and accepted the Garrett assignment without comment or protest.

In Philadelphia that following Monday morning, homicide detectives Fred Castelli and Mike Proley were, as usual, busy. Going into the year, they'd had a backlog of six cases, and had added to that the unidentified man found on fire at Barrier Point. That made seven. Fortunately since then, they'd been breaking even.

A woman named Hazel Blackmun who lived on Juniper Street in South Philly had been found at home with her head bashed in. No sign of a break-in, no sign of a struggle. Just a couple of quick, sudden blows. A little digging around the neighborhood pointed to a stepson named Ralph who was in the habit of cleaning out the woman's bank account. One afternoon while Ralph was at work, Castelli broke into the toolshed attached to Ralph's garage. There Hazel's stepson had stored not just a bloodstained hammer, but an undershirt with some matching bloodstains as well. Murder was, as this case demonstrated, the felony most frequently committed by amateurs.

Then there was the burglary of Quinzani's grocery store two blocks from the Italian market, again in South Philly. Some malefactor had taken it upon himself to visit Mr. and Mrs. Quinzani's cash register one night while they—a couple in their sixties—slept upstairs. The intruder was noisy. Mr. Quinzani—a well-known and much-loved grocer in the neighborhood since 1921—called the police, then came downstairs with a pistol. Mr. Quinzani was noisy too.

Shots were fired. Less than a minute later Quinzani was lying on the stairs, bleeding to death while a robber fled through the rear window, leaving a wake of cash in every direction. By the time that Quinzani expired at St. Agnes' Hospital, Proley and Castelli were already on the case.

The killer had parked his car two blocks away on the other side of Ninth Street. Above a cheese and meat retailer at the Italian market, Mrs. Mary Giancobini often sat in the window. Mrs. Giancobini hadn't slept well at nights since her husband died in 1937. So she saw a dark-haired, wiry man about five feet eight in height flee across Christian Street and jump into a car. She also saw the man push something dark—a pistol maybe—into his jacket. Mrs. Giancobini noticed that the car was from New Jersey and wrote down the license number. But she didn't call the police. Instead, she told her son Francesco. Frankie Giancobini worked at night in the previously owned automobile business. Frankie had been in and out of prison twice himself. He knew some other people who had unusual professions and he knew what went down on the streets.

A day later Castelli's home phone rang. "You the guy investigating the Quinzani killing?" a voice asked.

Castelli allowed that he was.

"The guy who done it. His name was Joey DeNovellis," said the caller. Castelli noted immediately that the concerned citizen referred to DeNovellis in the past tense.

DeNovellis was a two-bit hood from Trenton. And he could currently be located, the caller concluded, at Front Street and Snyder Avenue, right next to a furniture warehouse. Nor was DeNovellis liable to hurry off, as he was spending the evening in the trunk of his brown-and-white Nash Rambler, his throat cut, his testicles chopped off, his gun—the murder weapon—stuffed in his mouth, and the remainder of receipts from the Quinzani's cash register wrapped in brown paper for return to the victim's widow.

There were, as Castelli and Proley knew, certain families in South Philadelphia who exerted considerable influence in the area of the Italian market. These families appreciated a nice, safe God-fearing neighborhood as much as anyone else. Thus the Quinzani slaying was solved, at virtually no expense to the taxpayer.

Some cases, such as the slaying of Hazel Blackmun, have straightforward resolutions. Others, such as the Quinzani murder,

all but solve themselves. Still others, such as the grilled man at
Barrier Point, require a bit more inquiry and legwork.

Thus Castelli and Proley began the Barrier Point inquiry exactly where the Quinzani investigation had concluded. In bars, grocery stores, and barber shops south of Snyder Avenue or over morning coffee at the Melrose Diner on Passyunk, they put out the word.
They knew no one would tell them the killer, but would someone—
in exchange for a favor in the future—be kind enough to tell them
who the victim had been? This being South Philadelphia, someone
had to know something. This being South Philadelphia, someone
always knew something.

On the 1900 block of Mifflin Street, for example, around the
corner from where Fred Castelli lived, resided a woman named
Maude Romero. She was a widow from the war. On Saturday evenings she would draw every shade in her row house, assemble a
stack of Sinatra 78's on the Victrola, tart herself up a little with
some perfume from Bravo's Pharmacy on South 17th Street, and
cook dinner for two. Then her policeman, Sgt. Castelli, would visit
for the night. Maude was six years Castelli's senior. But she kept
herself in shape and easily passed for thirty-seven in four important
categories: age, hips, bust, and carnal enthusiasm. There were many
men in the neighborhood who would have liked to have been in—
among other things—Castelli's shoes.

Castelli and Maude tried to keep their affair a secret. Castelli
used the back door to her home and they went to Mass at Holy
Redeemer separately on Sunday morning. They kept things so quiet
that the whole damned neighborhood—including their priest, Father Manzi—knew they were sleeping together. Captain Heintz was
even in the habit of phoning Castelli at Maude's if anything urgent
came up on weekends.

All of which illustrated Castelli's current problem. "No one in
this city can keep his mouth shut. Everybody knows where I go for
a good piece of ass," he growled to Mike Proley three weeks into
the new year. "And yet not one person will tell me who got grilled
on New Year's morning."

No, no one was talking. It was even possible that no one knew.
There wasn't even a hot rumor. No citizen of the city's underclass
was reported missing, no one had vanished from a hotel room, no
low-rent hood was vacationing in Cuba with a sudden windfall, no
one had been scratched off any loan shark's debt books, and no

names were unaccounted for on anyone's hit list. Fred Castelli and
Mike Proley had never experienced any murder quite like this one.

Even the bullet that had killed the man returned from its ballistics inquest with peculiar biographical notes. The murder weapon
was unassociated with any previous crime in Philadelphia. And the
markings upon the death bullet suggested that it had been fired
from a low-caliber handgun of military origin, though not necessarily American.

Castelli moaned long and low when he learned this. There was
so much junk artillery floating around since the war. "It makes my
life murder," he liked to joke. But there wasn't anything that
amused him or his partner about the Barrier Point case. The victim
was a cipher and the killer, it seemed, was a spook.

In any event, the absence of any information helped him draw
one supposition. Whatever had happened, its genesis had been outside of the normal working activity of his district. And that meant
that the Barrier Point case could be a long haul, indeed, and that
1950 promised to be one bitch of a year.

■
FOUR
■

"Commonwealth Pennsylvania Bank," said Special Agent
in Charge William Roth, "was a tiny little operation in
Dublin Township out in Bucks County back in 1933.
Roosevelt closed the banks for fourteen days after he
came into office. Commonwealth Penn came within twenty-four
hours of not reopening." That, Roth announced portentously, was
when the bank's savior appeared. So it was also there that the F.B.I.
investigation had to begin.

Roth lit a cigarette. Thomas Buchanan sat across a desk from
him at the Philadelphia office of the F.B.I. It was three-thirty Monday afternoon. Several neat manila files were piled in front of Buchanan, but he'd spent most of the day listening.

Roth enshrouded himself in smoke, emptied an ashtray, and
continued with ancient history. "At the end of the Depression,"
Roth said, "Commonwealth Penn had five employees. A president,

a vice president, and three tellers. No guards, no secretaries, not even a cleaning lady. The president and vice president took turns with the key to the bank's only building. They'd unlock and lock the doors each day, serve as loan officers, and answer the phone if it happened to ring. The tellers would sweep the floor, dust the potted plants, and empty the wastebaskets. I doubt if they had more than eight hundred depositors. The place was a local joke."

And as jokes went, Roth continued, Commonwealth Penn was a pretty funny one. The Bureau had done its homework on this, and Roth had all the numbers.

"At the end of 1933, deposits were $316,000 and the purported capital was a very flat $100,000. But the bond depreciation was $298,000 and there were bad debt losses of $89,000, not yet taken. Add it all up quickly in your head, Tom? What's that mean to you?"

"The bank was broke," Buchanan said. "It should have gone belly up."

"Should have. Would have. But the banking law was different back then. A stockholder in the bank could be liable to the depositors for double the face value of the stock he owned. In Commonwealth Penn's case, that meant the bank was worth more dead than alive—except to the president and vice president—a pair of incompetent brothers named Paul and Joel Schusterman."

"How had they come to own the bank?" Buchanan asked.

"How else do morons come to own things?" Roth asked. "They'd inherited it. I call it the 'lucky-sperm syndrome.' "

"Any family money?"

"A little," Roth said. "An uncle had made a bundle in the oil business in western Pennsylvania in the 1870s. The money had filtered down through the family, but these clowns were running out of it."

Buchanan listened indulgently. "Go on," he requested.

"Paul and Joel Schusterman wanted to keep the bank's doors open until they could think of something brilliant. They weren't equipped to think of something brilliant, of course. But they got lucky. John Taylor Garrett came along." Here Roth paused long enough to snuff his cigarette and check a date in one of the folders in front of him. "May 3, 1934," he announced genially. "That was the day everything changed at Commonwealth Penn."

That was also the day, as Roth described it, that John Taylor Garrett began walking on water with other people's money.

Apparently Garrett had been bored to death running the family department store for the last decade. He'd been on the lookout for another venture. So he drew a bead on the Commonwealth Bank of Pennsylvania and its impending financial collapse. Here was a natural. The bank was right in Garrett's bailiwick and easy to be had. So Garrett first made a nonnegotiable offer to buy the bank. He had a pile of family trust money behind him as well as the cash flow from the department stores. But he wasn't planning to use much of his own resources.

Garrett offered the Schusterman brothers a simple deal. He'd assume their debts and Commonwealth Penn's liabilities if they signed everything over to him. The brothers couldn't see how Commonwealth Penn could go in any direction except down the tubes. So they accepted the offer and jumped what they perceived to be a financially sinking ship.

"The second thing Garrett did was hop a train to Washington," Roth continued. "He went to the Reconstruction Finance Corporation. Familiar with it?"

Buchanan shook his head.

"It was a government agency, founded during the Hoover years but beefed up by F.D.R. It floated loans to businesses to keep them from going under. But the loans had to be collateralized, which was why the Schusterman brothers couldn't get one. You wouldn't have loaned a number two Ticonderoga pencil to those two guys. But John Garrett left the R.F.C. with a loan for $150,000. Know what he talked the feds into taking as security? Eighty-five thousand dollars of preferred stock in Commonwealth Penn, plus a note for $65,000 from Garrett himself, secured by the title to his own home. The latter, I'm told, you are familiar with."

Buchanan nodded. "I've been there," he said. As understatement, the remark was almost a conceit. But Roth was wise enough to let it go.

Thomas Buchanan pictured the sixty-acre estate with its Pennsylvania stone manor house, its stables, tennis courts, guest and gardener's cottages. The Garrett enclave was a big, delicious chunk of the American dream, surrounded by woods, streams, and meadows. He could picture it well. He'd last seen Ann Garrett there in June 1942, one day before he'd gone into the army. She'd worn a red dress with bare shoulders that night. At age twenty she had never looked lovelier. Nor had she ever looked more grown-up. Ann Garrett and Thomas Buchanan had been engaged for a month and in love for more than a year. Looking back on it—from the perspective of a W.P.A.-era federal office building almost eight years later—those months before the war seemed to glisten with an unreal, magical perfection, a dreamlike quality that he should have known would disappear. Their plans were to marry as soon as the war was over, or as soon as he came home. Whichever came first.

He'd borrowed his father's big dark green Packard and had taken Ann dancing at a rambling summer ballroom at the Bucks County Cricket Club. Afterward—

Bill Roth jarred Thomas back to the present. "After the visit to Washington by Garrett, Commonwealth Penn's purported capital was reduced to a more realistic $40,000 and the losses were written off. On paper John Garrett was in hock to Uncle Sam. But he also had himself a small, clean bank."

Buchanan tried to concentrate: There wasn't much in the way of business in Bucks County back then, Roth explained, which meant Garrett had to create some fast. In the eyes of the public, Commonwealth Penn was still a shaky operation, not the type of place a family wanted to put their money, especially after the daily bank failures of the early thirties. But Garrett, thirty-six years old at this time, reasoned that his community was one of homes. He further saw that the county was expanding. So Commonwealth Penn went into real estate.

"Most banks at the time were scared to death of builders' loans," Roth said. "They were afraid the builder's house wouldn't sell. But Garrett outwitted the larger banks. He'd issue the loan to the builder, then kick a few bucks back to the builder when the builder brought the buyer in for the mortgage. Then he'd write the mortgage. Any mortgage. Well, he'd guessed right again, because the government began guaranteeing the mortgages under the new F.H.A. law. Soon, however, he'd written more mortgages than he could cover through deposits. So he went on the road again, up and down the East Coast, from Maine to Florida, selling the guaranteed mortgages to larger banks. When he ran out of larger banks he started peddling the investment to insurance companies. As soon as one bought, they all wanted to buy."

Soon, Roth continued, Garrett had built branches in five other towns, where he repeated the same procedures, always a few weeks ahead of the larger banks. By 1938 he'd bought out two irritating small competitors. By 1939 Commonwealth Penn had assets of

$7,000,000. And by 1941 the bank was in eight figures, worth about $12,000,000.

"And it bears remembering," Roth concluded, "that Garrett *was* Commonwealth Penn. It was a one-man show, and he was it. So he was worth approximately what the bank was worth. Plus what the family trust had been valued at to start with."

"Sounds simple," Buchanan said. "How to make a fortune in banking."

Roth crumpled his cigarette pack and prowled through the top drawer of his desk for a new one. "It *is* simple, Tom," he answered. "If you have twenty-twenty foresight and are five times as smart as all your competition." Roth rejoiced: his hand settled on a fresh pack of Chesterfields. Ah, the pure poisonous ecstasy of tar and nicotine.

"What happened next?" Buchanan asked.

"Unforeseen problem. Someone started a war. And at the end of 1941, the United States was drawn into it."

Buchanan remembered that too. "And if Garrett went away to war like everyone else," Thomas guessed, "that left a one-man bank without its one man. No leadership, in other words."

"Exactly," Roth said. "Ever been in a boat without a rudder? That was Commonwealth Penn in Garrett's absence."

The bank drifted, Roth said, continuing the metaphor, straight onto the rocks. Garrett left a three-man board of directors in charge of the institution's business, the smallest-sized board then permissible under Pennsylvania state law. One of the board members was Garrett's family attorney, a personable old geezer who would have been more at home writing wills or defending drivers accused of making illegal left turns. Another board member was the department store's accountant, who knew how to tally up sums of money but not how to make it. And the third was Garrett's nephew, who was twenty-two years old and straight out of Wharton at the University of Pennsylvania. The kid had a recently punctured eardrum that would keep him out of the war. But he needed a job.

"For all the board accomplished," Roth said, "Garrett might just as well have invited the Schusterman brothers back into the chicken coop." Deposits fell off and competitors sprang up like mushrooms following a spring rain. The Philadelphia banks established outposts in Bucks County and systematically picked off Commonwealth Penn's base of business. The main branch was even held up at gunpoint by a deranged sailor, a source of considerable amusement in local banking circles: Why rob a bank where one could just as easily obtain a large unsecured loan, then default?

A few beads of sweat ringed Roth's forehead near his hairline. He stood long enough to open a window a crack. Outside, overlooking Chestnut Street and the federal courthouse, it was almost dark. A tiny current of cold air sliced into the office.

Commonwealth Penn tried to play catch-up, Roth resumed. The bank hired some new loan officers. They were like arsonists summoned to a roaring blaze.

They wrote loans to anyone who came in the door. Soon bad-risk borrowers were traveling from as far away as Pittsburgh with untenable—and in some cases downright idiotic—business plans. No matter. They all came away with credit. When the bank examiners came in November 1944, they discovered that sixty-two percent of the new loans written in 1943 and 1944 were to applicants who had been turned down by at least one other bank somewhere in Pennsylvania. Another ten percent had been turned down in Delaware, Maryland, or New Jersey.

"And by June 1945," Roth said, working on a fresh Chesterfield and moving toward a conclusion, "the bad paper was thundering home to roost. A quarter of the commercial credit was in default and the bank was virtually insolvent. Take a guess what happened next."

"You tell me."

Roth answered his own question. Garrett reappeared, Roth said. Only this time Garrett didn't have the mortgage and building businesses to save him. The bank floundered for several months. But Garrett mesmerized the state examiners, kept the institution open, and eventually was able to generate a respectable loan demand in the postwar economy. But by then he didn't have the resources to cover the loans he wanted to write. So off he went on the road again, trying to sell loans the way he'd once sold mortgages: Massachusetts, New York, and Virginia. Then Maryland, Ohio, and Florida. This time the magic was gone.

"So what did he do?" Buchanan asked.

"No one knows exactly. This was sometime in 1947. But apparently he took his show even further on the road. Went to Europe, if our sources are straight. There was even a pair of rumors. One said he'd taken off for South America with what remained of the cash assets of the bank. The other tale had it that he'd killed himself. Neither were true. The fact was, he showed up again after an absence of a few weeks. He was all bright and chipper. And the next thing anyone knew, Commonwealth Penn was rolling—I mean *rolling!*—in money again. How did he do it?" Roth opened his hands and arms in a wide dramatic gesture of wonder. "I don't know. That's for you to find out."

The summation suddenly finished, Buchanan held Roth in his gaze for several seconds. "Any theories?" Buchanan finally asked.

Roth motioned to the stack of files. "It's all in there," he said. "The bank is awash in unidentifiable corporate accounts, holding companies that only have initials, transactions that may or may not be coming from Europe and Asia, and letters of credit from London and Zurich used to generate loans from Commonwealth Penn. All this for a remote, struggling suburban bank? You tell me something's not wrong."

"It sounds like a textbook example of money laundering," Buchanan said.

"It's more than that. You'll see when you go through those files. Whatever happened, wherever the money comes from, it caused Garrett's wife to leave him and his daughters to move far away. We assume they're alive, but we can't locate them. To give you a further example of what you're getting into," Roth said, "we can't even locate *Garrett* from day to day. He's a recluse. Works out of his home when he's in the area and disappears for the rest of the time. An invisible man running a bank with millions in assets from phantom sources." Roth blew out a long stream of smoke and fiddled with his cigarette. "Again, that's why the Bureau is investigating and that's why you in particular are on this case. You'd have a better insight than any man in the Bureau. You *knew* the family."

"Years ago," Buchanan said evenly.

"At least that's somewhere to start. Do you and Garrett still have any mutual acquaintances?"

"There might be a few," Buchanan answered, pondering.

"Use them," Roth advised. "Even if they're remote. Make your own good luck."

Buchanan said he would.

"Here's something else," Roth said. "You worked in the Chicago office for a time, didn't you, Tom?"

"In 1946. For about ten months. My first assignment."

"Did you know a special agent there named Mark O'Connell?"

Buchanan's attention perked. "Yes," he said with mild surprise. "Of course. I knew him quite well."

"He resigned from the F.B.I. about two months ago. He was working on something that may have touched upon the Garrett case. I don't know. He quit in anger over something petty one day. Took a job as a local police chief somewhere out west. The location is in one of those manila folders," Roth said, pointing with an index finger, "along with the reports he wrote of his final cases." Roth cleared his throat, a rasping, guttural sound. "No one knows for sure if O'Connell turned up anything that touched on Garrett," Roth said. "But you might consider . . ."

"Taking advantage of the friendship and looking O'Connell up?" His tone suggested his annoyance.

"Exactly. Even if you have to travel. I'll authorize the expense." Roth paused for a moment, then moved right to the point.

"Look, Tom. You know how things work here. J. Edgar himself decided that he wanted a report on Commonwealth Penn," Roth said again. "So you'll have no more than sixty days to get to the heart of things. I'll try to protect you, but the Director's going to be glaring right over our shoulders. And I think you know that failure—real or imagined—is not tolerated very long in this agency."

Buchanan nodded.

Roth managed a sympathetic smile. "I better let you get reading," he said. An inch and a half of gray ash tumbled from his cigarette onto his shirt. He made a show of brushing it off, but was finished talking anyway.

"I'm going to assign a full-time secretary to you," Roth said, standing up. "Her name is Mary Doyle. She's been with the Bureau for years. She's more than a secretary. She can be a top-drawer assistant as well. Don't let her gray hair fool you. She knows how to cut through Bureau bullshit."

"I'll remember that," Buchanan said. "Thank you."

"Any further questions for now?"

"Just one."

"Shoot."

"I can tell just from your presentation and my assignment that the Bureau has made this case a priority. Why?"

Roth looked him straight in the eye. "Because that's the way J. Edgar Hoover wants it."

"But *why*?" Buchanan pressed again. "Surely he doesn't set priorities completely by whim. We all know that. Wouldn't it be helpful for my own investigation to know what's really lurking here? What's the ultimate purpose of Hoover giving priority status to a case like this?"

"Oh, Tom," Roth said, sounding like a disappointed uncle. "Don't you know? That's the one question it doesn't pay to ask around here." Then, "Good luck," Roth concluded. It sounded like a benediction.

Outside, it was night. Thomas Buchanan walked slowly down a long corridor from the office of Special Agent in Charge William Roth. In his arms he carried the Bureau's complete files on the life and times—personal and professional—of John Taylor Garrett.

Buchanan entered his own office, the one to which he had been newly assigned. With a sigh he set the files on his desk. Near them was a small reading lamp with a green glass shade. Thomas turned it on and sat down.

A thousand questions besieged him. Where *had* Garrett's new solvency come from? To where had his daughters disappeared? What about Garrett's wife? A terrible emotion was upon Thomas when he reasoned that all three women could be dead.

Why was foreign money pouring into a remote bank headed by the heir to a department store fortune? And whose money was it? Was this the repayment of a wartime favor? Or was this just good, aggressive business by John T. Garrett at a time when Commonwealth Penn needed it most?

For a moment Buchanan brooded on it without touching any of the files. Garrett had been an intelligence officer during the war, he reminded himself. Frank Lerrick had told him that much. What kind of intelligence work? And for whom? Was this an angle, or a trail leading off into darkness? Could the F.B.I. get Garrett's wartime record from the United States Army or the State Department? Or would one of these files currently on his desk be able to guide him?

There was a night porter in the office, an illiterate old Negro named Charles who would run long errands for a fifty-cent tip. Buchanan sent him up to Broad Street to retrieve a sandwich and some coffee. Then, while still waiting for Charles to return, his interest gradually heightening, Buchanan drew toward him the stack of files on John Taylor Garrett.

He noted his watch. Nine-fifteen. He noted the date. January 16. In two months he would have to have answers. So be it. That was now the challenge. Thomas Buchanan opened the nearest of the files and diligently set to work, attempting to reconcile his own memory of Ann Garrett's father with the man whose life the Bureau now wanted turned inside out.

■

FIVE

■

Laura Garrett turned off the gentle spray of the shower in her London flat and stepped onto the deep carpeting on the bathroom floor. She reached for a towel from the heated rack. In the warmth of the steam that remained from the shower, she ran the towel over her skin until she was dry.

Her stomach churned with anticipation. She had two hours to get ready. At six that Saturday evening a man named Henry Walters would call on her. It would be their first date. He would take her to dinner, then to the theater. It remained to be seen how the evening would go. But Laura had already made a decision about Henry. He was the man whom she wanted to marry.

Laura Garrett was twenty-nine years old and worked as a buyer for an expensive jewelry store named Pace's in one of the fashionable arcades near Savile Row. She maintained a comfortable flat on Brook Street in Mayfair. Like her younger sister, Ann, Laura was of considerable beauty, though with dark brown hair and greenish-blue eyes, she looked little like Ann. Beauty—the type of all-American beauty that turns grown men weak at the knees—was a funny thing to Laura. She knew how to show it and how to hide it, and made conscious decisions when to do either. Tonight she had decided to show it.

Two months previously, in early November 1949, she had seen Henry Walters for the first time. It had been at a gallery opening for an ex-patriate American artist in residence in Knightsbridge. Henry was a thin, bookish-looking man of thirty-one with glasses and short brown hair. Henry, who was also an American, was in a party of people from the United States Embassy in London. He was not the type of man who habitually turned the heads of beautiful women. But Laura Garrett, in many ways like her father, saw things where others didn't. She found out his name and who he was. She also learned, much to her pleasure, he was unmarried. He was, in short, just what she was looking for.

Meeting him directly, and getting him to ask her out, was more difficult. She began taking her lunch at the Audley Pub in the street of the same name. The Audley was around the corner from the embassy and not far from Pace's either. By early December they had "met," by what he considered chance, when she had asked him to save her place on a banquette during a crowded noon hour.

Obviously he was aware immediately that she was American. But Laura could always tell when a man was intimidated by her beauty. Henry was too shy to talk to her. So next, while allowing him to think that he had initiated the conversation, she asked him where she might catch a bus that would take her to Kensington. He explained.

"I'll never find the bus stop," she said helplessly. "Maybe you could show me." This way, she knew, he would have to remember her the next time.

It was a four-block walk, during which their conversation continued. She said she had graduated from Smith College at the end of the war. She was from Pennsylvania, she told him, and had worked for her father's bank briefly, then had moved to New York and worked as an assistant buyer at Tiffany's. Now she planned to work in London for a year.

"Where are you from?" she asked next.

"Shaker Heights, Ohio," he'd answered, explaining that it was a suburb of Cleveland.

"I knew a girl at Smith who was from Shaker Heights," she said. They exchanged names but had no mutual friends. Henry had a degree in international politics from Amherst College, he said, further elaborating that he was assigned to London for two years on business. But when she gently inquired what sort, he evaded the question. Then they arrived at the bus stop.

More lunchtime meetings. Over sandwiches of Scottish beef, accompanied by Spanish sherries and English ale, much small talk followed. Henry revealed that there was no woman in his life, either in London or back home. Laura let it be known that she sat home in her flat most evenings. Shortly after Christmas, Henry—slow as many men are to pick up the danger signals—worked up the nerve to ask her out for the first time. Much to his amazement, she accepted.

Laura finished drying herself in front of the full-length mirror on the wardrobe of her bedroom. She studied her own body. She perfumed her neck and breasts. She was proud of herself. She had seen how childbearing, the drudgery of housework, and sedentary life-styles had taken their toll on many women of her age. But not Laura. She stood before the mirror for a few extra moments and looked at herself approvingly. She had the pink nipples, full breasts, and nearly flawless figure that could turn a strong man into a bumbling fool.

On some dates she might have added a dab of perfume upon the lower part of her tummy, but not tonight. Few lovers had ever touched her in those special places, she liked to recall, though her Henry would surely be the next. She guessed that he might never have had a woman as beautiful as she. Well, that would make her task of winning him all the easier.

She dressed carefully and was ready by the time her doorbell rang at 6:01.

Henry brought her flowers which she graciously accepted at the door. She invited him in. He sat patiently in the living room while she returned to the bedroom to put on a final piece of jewelry. Eventually he stood up and walked around, examining, as she knew he would, the appointments of the living room.

From where she was dressing, Laura could tell where in the room he was. She knew he had stopped at the mantel above the fire grate and was more than likely examining the photographs upon it. Then she was ready, and came out to the living room.

"I like your apartment," he said.

"Thank you. I share it," she answered. She nodded toward a color portrait in a silver frame on the mantel. She knew Henry couldn't have missed it. "The other girl in the picture is my sister," she said. "Her name is Ann. It's her apartment too." She pointed to another portrait on the other end of the mantel, this one black and white and very prewar. "Those are my parents," she said.

"You have a very attractive family," he said, ever the diplomat.

She gave him her most appreciative smile. "Thank you," she said.

Henry took her first to dinner at a small French restaurant in Whitfield Street, then to an English bedroom farce that played to a capacity house in the West End. As it turned out, it was an altogether pleasant evening.

He brought her back home by taxi. They arrived by eleven

o'clock. Laura made two cups of tea, as she always did when she brought someone home. She expressed surprise, however, that her sister was not home yet. Laura played shy, attentive, well-spoken, and chaste. She let Henry lead the conversation. They revealed a bit more about each other. Her father owned a bank back in America, she said, and she admitted that she had grown up with riding lessons, country clubs, and private schools. His own background was thoroughly middle class, he told her, and his father was an insurance executive back in Ohio. After Amherst, he said, he'd taken a civil service exam just to see where it might lead. He'd tested well and had gone into the state department.

"That's where I am now," he revealed to her for the first time. "My first tour of duty was Havana. I was in Washington for my second. London is my third."

"So you're a *diplomat*?" she said with some surprise. "For all the times we've had lunch, you never told me that."

"You never asked," he joked, loosening up.

"You said you were in business," she said.

"I am. Political business."

They shared another laugh. She was cautious about not asking him too much about his work. But he did venture the information that he was a political officer. Laura seemed to have a good impression of that.

"Well, I think that's very patriotic," she said at length, "working for the United States government. More people should serve their country instead of just finding ways to make money."

"It's not terribly exciting," he said modestly. "It's a job like anything else." Yet he was pleased that she seemed so impressed. Impressing the women of his choice was something that Henry had never quite been able to master. Eventually he did admit that his job as a diplomat did have more cachet than, say, figuring out automobile collision rates.

They laughed and talked for a while longer, enjoying each other's company. Forty-five minutes later she began to yawn and said that she really must be getting to bed soon. He picked up his cue and rose to go. Laura let him kiss her at the door. She did not wish to proceed too quickly with him. But as he kissed her, she leaned to him in such a way that he knew her superb body might be his to someday enjoy.

The tactic worked. He called her the next day and asked her to attend a party with him. She accepted. It was a private black-tie

affair thrown at the Savoy by the staff of the United States Embassy.
The evening was complete with Persian caviar and California champagne, courtesy of their wealthy Uncle Sam.

Another date followed after that.

Within another two weeks, toward the final days of January
1950, the relationship had blossomed nicely and had turned serious.
One Friday evening, after drinks at the Café Royale, Laura told
Henry that her sister was away for the entire weekend. She let him
think about this while they watched a drama at the Duke of York
Theatre. Then Laura invited him back to her flat.

This time she never made the two cups of tea. Instead, as she
knew he would, he moved toward her on the living room sofa.
Laura, in turn, fell into his arms. He clumsily began undressing her
and, after a few token gestures of resistance, she allowed him to
continue. When virtually all of her garments were at least partially
unhooked or unbuttoned, Laura reached to the light, turned it off,
took Henry's hand, and led him to her bedroom.

There she slipped out of the rest of her clothes. She pulled a
satin robe around her and sat down on the edge of her bed. Henry
sat down next to her. She took his hand.

"I'll sleep with you only if you love me," she said.

"I do," he answered.

"Then let me hear you say it."

"I love you," Henry said. He kissed her as if he really did.

She told him that she loved him also. That meant that the satin
robe could come off, also, and that he could spend the weekend
making love to her. As it turned out, she had him worn out by
Sunday morning.

So began their affair. Henry, on the threshold of a great romance as well as a glamorous diplomatic tour in the English capital,
felt himself very much the man of the world. Laura, for her part,
kept her innermost thoughts to herself, nurturing her new lover and
her career, knowing—as women frequently do in such circumstances—that she was completely in control. It was, it seemed to
both of them, a magnificent time to be young and American and
making limitless plans for the future.

SIX

There wasn't a mile of the county roads that he didn't know by heart already, Chief of Police Mark O'Connell thought to himself. It was a week before Christmas 1949, and the former special agent of the F.B.I. had been in this new job for less than two months. It was strange how things worked out, he further pondered as he listened to the squeak of the well-worn windshield wipers on his police cruiser. He'd always thought that he would retire from the F.B.I. at age sixty with high honors and accolades. Then he and his beloved Helen could enjoy their retirement. Maybe they'd go to Florida, he'd always thought. Maybe they'd buy a small motel and spend a busy, profitable retirement in God's bright sunlight.

Instead, he'd been hounded out of the bureau. His departure had been sudden, arbitrary, and—to his way of thinking—grossly unfair. Not that he'd had any recourse other than to leave. Then, shortly after his enforced retirement, he'd accepted an offer from the town of Peterton, Oregon, to become their chief of police.

Peterton was a friendly, rainy community of forty-six hundred people fifty-two miles southeast of Portland. It was populated primarily by the descendants of liberal New England Protestants who'd migrated from East Coast to West across the northern United States late in the nineteenth century. And it was a predictably amiable blue-collar sort of place, complete with two gas stations, a hardware store, a general store, three groceries, a lunch counter, a restaurant where children were always welcome, and a branch of one of the smaller state banks. The Dobbs Lumber Company, which operated a sawmill five miles away in Harrisville, was the main local employer. Peterton was a place of good hunting, great fishing, and little crime. It was not at all a bad place to live or to be a police officer, particularly if a man liked his relaxation.

The previous police chief, a gregarious, well-liked soul named Bill Lucy, had grown old gracefully in his job. Chief Lucy had retired after twenty-six years, having never seen a gun fired in anger. The town even paid two part-time deputies to assist its chief. What more could a peaceable former F.B.I. agent want?

He slowed down his car on state highway 45. There was a truck pulled to the side of the road, its lights flashing, its right rear tires on the highway's soft shoulders. The Pacific Northwest had been slightly warmer than the rest of the country of late, but near-freezing rain could put a truck in a ditch just as fast as ice or snow.

O'Connell pulled to a stop. He switched on the flashing red lights on the roof of his car, a signal of caution to any vehicle approaching from ahead or behind. He stared at the empty cab of the truck. There'd been no crash. The truck was intact. Its engine was running. So what was wrong? Why was he so suspicious about everything?

Recently O'Connell had entertained a lot of strange ideas. When he'd started this new job as chief of police of the town of Peterton, Oregon, for example, he'd had the unbanishable feeling that he was . . . well, being watched. Or followed. Or something. It was an instinct more than anything, a sixth sense developed during his fourteen years of field work for the Bureau and three years as a soldier in the jungles and on the beachheads of the South Pacific. It was something he could not shake.

His wife, Helen, told him he was creating worries for himself. "We're better off here," she said. "A good job. A respectable community. Better for the kids." They had two children, a boy, four, and a girl, eighteen months.

"No excitement and no challenge," he'd countered.

"The people here appreciate the work you do," she said. "The F.B.I. didn't."

"The salary leaves a bit to be desired."

"We have a nicer home here than we've ever had before," Helen said, putting things in perspective. "And you have better working hours. You have dinner with your family every night. If we need extra money, I'll get a job. The lumber company needs book-keepers."

"My wife work?" he'd asked. "No, ma'am. Not unless I'm dead and buried." There would turn out to be a certain sad irony to his remark.

The rain swept into his face that night as he stepped from the car, a heavy flashlight in his left hand. He recognized the truck as belonging to one of the logging camps. Why then . . . ? Who then . . . ?

He walked to the front of the truck and stood in its headlights for a moment. That creepy, eerie feeling returned. He knew he was being watched now! He knew he was under observation by a pair of unseen eyes that very moment. He put his right hand on the stock of his service revolver and—

A man's voice called unexpectedly out of the darkness. "Mark!"

O'Connell squinted toward the woods. He felt his heart kicking in his chest. He saw a movement and began to draw his weapon.

"Hey, Mark? Jesus! Take it easy, would you?"

O'Connell shined his flashlight toward the voice. A bearded trucker stepped from behind a clump of small trees. O'Connell recognized him. He was a big, hulking man named Walt Kowell. Kowell lived in Hibbing, the next town toward Portland, and worked for Dobbs Lumber.

Kowell's rain slicker was disheveled. His hand was at the fly of his trousers. "Jesus fucking Christ!" he said. "Can't a man take a leak around here without someone calling the cops?"

O'Connell felt an overwhelming surge of relief. His pistol had been a quarter of the way out of its holster. He pressed it back in.

"Kind of jumpy, aren't you?" Kowell asked. "I don't think Bill Lucy drew his iron in thirty years."

"I'm not Bill Lucy," O'Connell snapped. "And that's no place to leave a vehicle on a rainy night."

O'Connell saw Kowell recoil, and the man's bemused expression vanished. O'Connell was also aware of how belligerent his own words had sounded.

The rain poured down upon both of them. "I saw your truck," O'Connell said in a more conciliatory tone. "So I stopped. Couldn't you wait till you got home to take a piss?"

Kowell shrugged sheepishly. "Not today."

Another car went slowly by, framing them in its headlights as it passed. O'Connell waved the car on, indicating that there was no problem.

"Come on, Walt," O'Connell said. "Get your rig out of here before someone skids into you. That's all I'm worried about."

Kowell nodded and thanked O'Connell for stopping. In another three minutes Kowell's truck had disappeared down the road toward Hibbing and O'Connell had turned back toward town. It was six o'clock in the evening and O'Connell had completed his drive along the roads immediately surrounding Peterton, a trip he made at the end of every tour of duty. Now he could go home to dinner. If anyone had a problem, the police chief could be reached at home. Or one of his two deputies could put in the time to solve it.

The nearly fatal problem for Mark O'Connell, however, was having too much time to think. That and the fact that his current job didn't exactly maintain him at his old fighting edge.

At age forty-two, he'd recently fallen into the habit of examining his life in assiduous detail. He'd put in all those years in federal law enforcement and he'd fought with distinction in the marines. His résumé sparkled. Until recently all of his career decisions had looked good.

He'd served the F.B.I. in the Atlanta office as well as in San Francisco, Tucson, Washington, D.C., Chicago, and Seattle. Up until 1949 he'd never had a blemish on any professional record, either military or Bureau. But in 1949 funny things began to happen.

Those funny things, as he called them, were now the matters he struggled to put out of his mind. There had been the Great Wobblie Witch Hunt in Tacoma, a massive waste of time fully sanctioned by the F.B.I. Then there had been the Great Handsaw Caper —as it had disparagingly become known in the bureau—at the Krieger-McGhie army base in Spokane, Washington. And finally there'd been the Magnificent Morning Glory Investigation which had stretched from San Francisco all the way up to British Columbia. All of these, as the special agents liked to recall, were full-fledged wild goose chases.

The problem was that after all those years as a professional investigator, Mark O'Connell's instincts told him that somewhere among these three cases he'd been onto something—something so subtle or so complex that even he, with all his experience, couldn't recognize it. And whatever it had been, it had made him a marked man.

Helen told him repeatedly that he was imagining things. She even suggested that he should see a psychiatrist. "Professional counseling" is what she called it. After fourteen years of stress, who could blame a man for needing a little help sorting things out? A lot of soldiers needed just such treatment, and not even that much of it, when they'd come home from Japan and Germany. No one held anything against them.

"I'm sure the citizens of Peterton would be pleased to know that their chief of police is seeing a head doctor," O'Connell answered. That meant, no, he wouldn't go. But temporarily at least, he did discover another form of therapy.

At an army surplus store in Seattle, O'Connell found an old Dictaphone with a generous supply of recording reels. So instead of talking to a psychiatrist, he sat at home many nights and talked to himself. He stayed up well into the black hours of early morning on more occasions than he could count. When there was nothing else to do, and when the recent past seemed a more oppressive burden than he could bear, Mark O'Connell sat in the solitude of his cellar at an old workbench by the oil burner. He sipped local Oregonian beer from long-necked amber bottles and put his thoughts on the Dictaphone. He carefully marked each reel and stashed the full ones in a tool chest.

This went on for a month. Then the horrible feeling gripped him again, starting early in December. He was possessed by this unrelenting sense that the more he talked into the Dictaphone, the more scrutiny he was under. After that, every night had its own madness. He became obsessive about pouring his thoughts into the recorder, starting with the Handsaw case, moving through the Wobblies, then concluding with Morning Glory. As he spoke, more thoughts came back to him. Little details that he'd never put into his final reports at the Bureau, tiny observations that hadn't even merited being set in writing in his notebook.

During the days his nerves were taught, his expectations askew. He began to see the signposts of every ordinary working day —a truck traveling too slowly through town, a telephone that rang unanswered, a neighbor's light flashing on and off for five seconds— in apocalyptic terms, the handwriting of a dire conspiracy against him.

Once, sitting alone in his basement at two-forty in the morning, instinct told him to turn. He did. His gaze rose and quickly settled upon the dark two-paned cellar window at the summit of the cellar wall about ten feet from where he sat. For a moment a bolt of fear transversed him that felt like lightning, because he was sure—positive!—that through the darkness the face of a man had been staring back at him.

He yelled, whirled in his swivel chair, and pulled a forty-five-caliber pistol from his drawer. He charged up the stairs and bolted through the living room of his home. He threw on the outdoor floodlight and burst outside through the storm door. It may have been the middle of the night, but the hour of reckoning was obviously at hand.

He stood on his doorstep, a preposterous figure in bedclothes, slippers, robe, and handgun, perusing a quiet, misty night in the peaceful Northwest. He stood as motionless as a statue for several seconds, regarding the darkness. Again, nothing. Not a rustle of a footfall on the wet leaves, not a car engine, not a crunch of a branch under an unseen shoe.

Then he turned and reentered the house. In the dim kitchen he bellowed with fright a second time when he felt a human hand fall on his arm.

"Mark! Mark!" It was Helen.

"What in God's name—?" she began. She stared at the gun. "I heard you scream," she said.

"I thought I saw someone," he said.

"Where?"

"Looking through the cellar window."

She thought about it for several seconds. Quietly he closed the kitchen door and extinguished the outside light. "Did you see anyone out there?" she asked.

"No."

Helen exuded a long sigh. Then she reached to her husband and held him. O'Connell clicked on the safety catch of the pistol and pushed the weapon onto the kitchen table. He held his wife firmly. "I wish you'd talk to someone," she said softly.

Several seconds passed before he answered. "Okay," he said at length. "After Christmas. In January."

"You mean it? You promise?"

"Yes," he said. And he meant it. Never before in his adult life had he screamed out in fear. Now twice in the space of five minutes. Helen was right. It was time to get help.

But *was* he imagining things? The next morning he affixed new bolts to the doors of his home. As for the basement window, he placed a cardboard screen across it. No one—real or imagined— would be peering through. Then that same evening he was again down in his basement, talking into the recorder. Okay, so it was a little nutty, he told himself, but he felt better making a spoken record of everything. And as for the recorded reels themselves, the more than two dozen that he'd now completed, there was no use leaving them sitting around. He placed them all in an orange crate, removed a loose panel from the basement wall, and put the entire collection in hiding.

For the next few days Christmas took his thoughts in a more pleasant direction. On a day off he took Helen to Portland to see the holiday lights and do some shopping. Helen bought some toys for the children and an electric razor for him. He slipped away for a few minutes to buy his wife a wool sweater, plus some eau de toilette—the new fad from France—from one of the expensive perfume counters. Even after eleven years of marriage, he wasn't sure what Helen wore. But it smelled nice on the salesgirl, so he bought it.

The next day was December 24. The bank threw a noontime Christmas party for everyone who worked in the town center. Chief O'Connell attended. There was a light snow that day, and everyone made corny remarks about a white Christmas. Most of the shops in town closed toward three in the afternoon.

Chief O'Connell's nerves had been less on edge since the cellar window incident. While not convinced that he'd imagined what he saw, he had nonetheless confronted his nightmare, and the nightmare had vanished. So much the better. He'd also agreed to go to Seattle to talk to a police psychologist instead of an actual psychiatrist. Probably Helen had been right all along about this, too, he told himself. She often had answers before he did.

By four-thirty the day before Christmas, the sky was dark. The light snow continued to dust the area. Chief O'Connell went to his car to make his final run across the county roads surrounding Peterton. His deputies would be off this evening too. Nothing serious had ever happened on Christmas Eve in Peterton since Oregon became a state in 1859. So by all odds the town would be safe if he went home a half hour early.

It was on Route 31 just to the southeast of the town that Chief O'Connell saw the brown Plymouth that had apparently skidded. There was a woman looking at the front end of the car where it had left the road. He slowed to a halt and turned on his overhead lights. He stepped out, noticing the California license plates on the car. A single woman driving home for Christmas was O'Connell's first impression. Yet, his suspicious nature always aroused, he observed immediately that the car was pointed north toward Washington State, not south toward California.

"Trouble?" he asked.

"I'll say," she said. "I skidded. Take a look." She was blond and very young, he noticed. Well, if she'd skidded, he reasoned, maybe one big push could get the car back on the road. Or maybe he'd use a heavy rope and give it a pull with his own car.

Then, by happy coincidence, another car appeared behind O'Connell's police cruiser. Fine. With the help of another man, O'Connell thought, he'd have the girl on her way in no time.

O'Connell walked to the front of the car. It was off the road, all right, but frankly he couldn't see any damage. The other car pulled to a stop. O'Connell looked at the girl's tire tracks. No skid marks.

"What exactly is the problem?" he asked.

The damned fool in the other car parked but kept on his high beams, irritating O'Connell. The other driver stepped out and walked a step or two in their direction.

"I don't know," the girl said. "Won't go."

"What won't go?" he asked.

"Car."

She was talking strangely. She looked anxious. And for that matter, again, her car's motor was running. Then he looked at her more closely and—instinct again—saw something in her eyes, something he didn't like at all. Something that—*Oh, Jesus Christ!*—scared him just like he'd been scared the other night.

The other driver stopped walking. The girl quickly stepped back and away from him.

"You're not even off the road," O'Connell said to her. "Won't your car move?"

She said nothing.

"Answer me, will you?" The other headlights blinded him. Where had the other driver gone? The man had moved laterally. In fact, who in hell was—?

In the fraction of a second before anything happened, O'Connell knew he was as good as dead. The man behind him, the man he couldn't see because of the headlights, was raising a pistol.

Within that moment Mark O'Connell's mind was perfectly lucid. It was as if he were grasping a small victory in the knowledge that he had been imagining nothing, after all.

In a reflex to stay alive, O'Connell leapt to one side and groped for his sidearm. But the man whom he couldn't see opened fire. Two bullets hit O'Connell squarely in the chest. The force of the shots hurled the police officer backward and to the side. His own weapon flew from his hand.

As the hot pain in the middle of his body seared through him, he was aware of very little except his own agony. He steadied himself against his police cruiser, clutched his wounds, and stared. He had no idea where the woman had gone. He was only aware of yet another set of headlights coming from somewhere else, accompanied by the rumble of a truck.

The assassin fired twice again. Two more times on this Christmas Eve O'Connell felt the cylinders of death ripping through his insides. The final shot blew him away from his own vehicle and sent him sprawling violently backward onto the snow.

He heard voices talking. It was a man and a woman. They sounded increasingly distant and they didn't converse in anything he understood. Their words sounded garbled, and in all rationality, he thought that because he was lying in the snow dying, he could no longer understand the English language.

His final moments of consciousness had their own insanity. Everything seemed to be getting darker and brighter all at once. The pain wasn't in any one place anymore, it was all through him. And the wetness around him wasn't rain or melting snow. It was his own blood.

Something—a woman's body moving, or was it an angel's?—crossed quickly in front of those damnable headlights. For an immeasurably short moment in time O'Connell had a silhouetted vision of the man who'd shot him. The figure struck a chord of familiarity in his memory, and O'Connell battled with it as he heard the roar of a motor. Then, seconds later, he'd placed the man who'd shot him. The shoulders and the outline of the head matched with the nightmare that had fled from his cellar window.

All that made perfect sense to Mark O'Connell. His nightmare had come alive just long enough to kill him. As his strength faded, that seemed to be the logical order of things. A final vision of his wife and children spun wildly before him, and he was unhappy that he couldn't reach out and hold them. But a strange contentment swept him next, while simultaneously everything closed in on him and the entire world spiraled violently into blackness.

SEVEN

About seven thousand miles west of London, and slightly less than a thousand miles south of Peterton, Oregon, the actress known as Lisa Pennington lay in a nightgown on the bed of a garishly decorated Los Angeles apartment. A paperback book of mysteries titled *Prescription: Murder* lay across her lap. But about an hour earlier she had lost interest in reading.

It was three A.M., several evenings into the new year of 1950, and her only companion was the nearly empty glass of bourbon and water that sat at her bedside. Her eyes tried to close, but she resisted sleep. Lisa was one third drunk, one third depressed, and one third out of her mind with anger. She was, in other words, waiting for her errant husband to stagger home.

In her mind she spun wild fantasies about smashing him over the head with the Jack Daniel's bottle when he came in the door. And as he lay dying—which was what he deserved—she would calmly step over him carrying her bags. Then off to another country she would run with a younger, different man. One who would love, respect, and appreciate her. Not a man who stayed out nights whoring like her husband did.

Whoring. She held the term in her mind and wondered about its vagaries. Was it whoring if he didn't exactly pay cash in exchange for getting laid? Was it whoring if he was simply working his way through the meat rack of willing starlets, just like every other two-bit film director in Hollywood? From the opposite viewpoint, was it whoring for a woman to sleep her way into a film?

Her mind drifted. It was midnight back east. It was too late to call any old friends. It was too late to try to find a friendly voice on the telephone and admit that, yes, with her ambition, her abuse of drugs and alcohol, her misjudgment of the character—or lack of it —of certain men, she'd maneuvered herself into one hell of a mess. There really wasn't *any* possible retreat into the past. No longer, it seemed, did she have any hope of reclaiming who she'd been or what she wanted to be.

"Christ!" she said to herself. The sound of her own voice jarred her in the empty room. She reached for the glass of bourbon and water. She drained it with one long, loud, self-pitying gulp. She returned to the thought of running off with another man. She came back to it increasingly these days. There was, after all, no contract in Hollywood so ironclad that a sharp lawyer couldn't break it. Marriages were small stuff compared with some of the things she'd seen.

Again her thoughts drifted. Here she was staggering through her twenties wondering how she could have allowed things to get so far out of control.

Growing up, she'd always been the prettiest girl in her class. In college she'd moved easily into acting. She'd left college for two years during the war, but then as a junior and senior at Northwestern University she had done exceptionally well in the college's dramatic productions. In 1946 she'd gone to New York to test her aspirations on a professional level.

She took a single room at the Barbizon, went to several auditions, and played around with a stage name. Within three months she found herself in a small six-character comedy off-Broadway at the Cherry Lane Theater. It was the first play by a young man from Michigan. Lisa might have fallen in love with him. He was handsome, sandy-haired, and sensitive. But he was also incurably homosexual, which went a long way toward wrecking their relationship. Nonetheless, Lisa had the only female role in his play. She made the best of it.

Two other roles followed for Lisa Pennington. Neither play lasted long, but her name appeared favorably in *Variety* and in the daily press. By February 1948 she had her first Broadway role—all forty-three lines of it as a saucy, impertinent, leggy French maid— in a sprawling musical comedy entitled *Halfway to Heaven.* There were sixty-eight new productions on Broadway that buoyant postwar year. Opportunities were there to be had. Sadly it was during her twenty-week run in *Halfway to Heaven,* when everything else seemed to be going right, that she met Jesse Chadwick, the film director.

Chadwick, who'd actually been born in Flatbush under the name of Bernard Cherkasky thirty-seven years earlier, had missed the world war for reasons that were unclear to everyone. His contribution to the Allied victory had been to roam the back lots of RKO, where he churned out three second features a year. Inevitably one would be a western with an admirable moral for boys and girls. The other two were usually contemporary wartime potboilers with some veiled sex and a heavy propaganda message for adults.

Chadwick was coarse and crude, but he was not stupid. Additionally he had a feeling for what would sell to the American public. And in Lisa Pennington he saw—from a business perspective—the woman he'd hoped would come along at least once in his lifetime. With her freshness, her delicately fragile but perfectly formed body, her straightforward, wholesome large-boned blond American beauty, Lisa was to Jesse Chadwick exactly the woman whose appeal could be magnified on film. He was so sure of this that he paid for her transportation by train from New York to the West Coast in July 1948.

He met her on her arrival at Union Station in Los Angeles. Immediately he turned on the charm. He had friends in town that week and arranged for Lisa to take a screen test. Thereafter, he took her on a guided tour of the RKO studios as well as Paramount's. Cashing in a few small favors, and eager to impress her as a man who could get things done, Chadwick arranged for Lisa to briefly meet Robert Donat and Leo Gorcey. He even got a distant nod from the surly, aloof Orson Welles, who would nod to anyone in those days if it meant a debt was removed.

All this time Chadwick kept a tight rein on Lisa. To keep the other Hollywood wolves away from her, he never let her out of his sight. Literally. And to make sure that his can't-miss discovery couldn't jump ship on him, he continued to pour on the rough-hewn charm and tried to knock the girl off her feet. She fell for it. Once smitten, it bothered her little that the consensus in the movie community was that Jesse Chadwick had the eyes of a cobra and morals almost as high. No matter. When he proposed marriage in April 1949, she accepted.

Lisa knew her parents would have hated the very sight of Chadwick. Even less popular would be the thought of her climbing into bed with him. But worst of all would have been the idea of her potentially becoming pregnant with half-Jewish children. For that matter, her father might have enjoyed killing a man like Chadwick for putting his Brooklyn-born paws on his daughter. So for marriage vows, Lisa Pennington insisted on something quick, quiet, and nonsectarian. She'd intentionally never spoken to Chadwick much about her family anyway.

Jesse figured as a matter of course that no respectable parents could possibly like him no matter what he did. Thus, he was just as happy not to have to run the gauntlet of future in-laws. Thus, while both parties remained in the mood, a quick civil ceremony was performed by a justice of the peace in Burbank, California, that same April. A honeymoon followed in Acapulco, spent mostly indoors. After that Chadwick had plans for his discovery.

He took her to France, where the film industry was reawakening after the nightmare of the Occupation years and the somnambulism of the first years of the Fourth Republic. On the beaches of Nice and Monaco, Chadwick shot a low-budget English-language murder mystery complete with American financing, a Brazilian producer, a French cast, a Hungarian cinematographer, an Italian crew, and a Serbo-Croatian director. The film was called, among other things, *A Pretty Time to Kill,* depending on the language in which it was being mentioned. It featured an ample number of shots of Lisa going in and out of the water on the French beaches. Swimwear was gradually disappearing in 1949, one of the happier developments of the postwar era. The suit that Lisa would wear in her husband's film had two pieces, neither of which covered very much by the standards set by Betty Grable.

Lisa was appalled the first time she saw it. "Jesse, I can't do it," she protested.

"You'll be a pinup all over the world," Jesse Chadwick promised his wife.

"I'm not sure I want to be."

"Sure you do."

"I'll feel naked in front of a camera and film crew, Jesse. Really, I—"

"Do it," he said smoothly, "for both of us."

The first time she tried on the suit and had to step out of her dressing room in it, she felt like crying. Her husband nursed her along with a stiff bourbon and water. Out she came, blushing almost crimson, and began eight days of beach shooting. On the final day, in a scene shot in a hotel bedroom, she removed her top before the appreciative leer of the film's male lead. Even though she kept her back to the camera, the scene took more courage than she knew she had. Somehow she lived through that too.

All of this was in June 1949. The film turned out well and was distributed around the world. It drew the predictable Condemned rating from the Roman Catholic church in the United States, which helped it in some markets but limited its American distribution. Thus it made money for both of them, while it didn't exactly make

Lisa the pinup star her husband hoped for. Not yet, anyway. But Lisa didn't blush much anymore, at least not over what she was asked to do in films. And Jesse Chadwick still had plans for her.

They returned to California. Lisa completed a part in one of her husband's final back-lot epics. The talk was that Chadwick, with sexy Lisa under his wing, was about to move up a notch in Hollywood. Jesse's brother, Harry Cherkasky, who operated a talent agency, negotiated a deal with a loathsome, inarticulate, apelike producer named Joe Preston at RKO. Preston was famous in the film colony for cheap, financially successful movies and a legendarily hyperactive libido.

Chadwick would direct three features for Joe Preston over the next eighteen months. The first of them, a light romantic comedy tentatively titled *Hold the Phone!* would star Lisa. Preston's brother-in-law was currently finishing the script. Only a few details remained to be worked out between Chadwick and Preston, mostly of the sort that didn't appear on paper. As soon as those matters were settled, Lisa Pennington and Jesse Chadwick could sign their contracts.

All this accomplished, Jesse Chadwick had a star on his hands, a studio contract almost in his pocket, and a beautiful woman named Lisa Pennington in his bed whenever he so desired. Thus it was a perfect time, from Chadwick's viewpoint, to start hedging his bets for the future.

Nightly Chadwick prowled the nightclubs, bars, and various other meat factories of Hollywood where fellow directors and producers swapped introductions to other young starlets who also wanted to ingratiate their way into films. The first time that Lisa suspected that her husband had slept with another woman she'd been disbelieving. The second time she'd been emotionally shattered. The third time she confronted him.

"Men are men," Chadwick had replied with complete calm. "It's just sex. The other girls don't mean anything to me."

"Please stop it, Jesse," she begged him.

"No," he said. "I don't plan to."

"Then I won't stay married to you," she said.

"I need a lot of girls," he answered. "I don't expect you to understand. But I do expect you to shut up and accept it."

Lisa threatened to leave. That's when Chadwick explained. His brother had her on a professional contract and he had her on a marriage contract. Much time, attention, and money had already been invested in her. If she tried to fight them or desert them, he explained calmly, or even if she persisted with this nonsense about divorcing him, he had some old friends from Bensonhurst who did odd jobs around the movie industry. These men would find her, wherever she was, no matter what sort of protection she thought she had. Then they would go to work on her beautiful face and body. When they were finished mutilating her—Lisa's husband told her—no one, much less the American public, would ever want to look at her again, much less pay to see her. Further, if she ever went to court alleging adultery, he would produce a dozen studio lackeys who would testify that they'd slept with her. She would be publicly branded an ungrateful slut in addition to what she'd receive from the thugs from Bensonhurst.

This was how Jesse Chadwick did business. "Have I made this clear?" he asked.

He had. Lisa was too stunned and terrified to respond.

"Then don't ever again complain," he concluded. He finished the discussion by belting her hard—the first time he'd ever hit her—across the side of the head. He was careful not to hit her in the face. The face might have to be photographed.

It was not long afterward, as her husband spent more and more evenings out and around Los Angeles, that Lisa began to find solace in the bottle of Jack Daniel's. And it was just such an evening in January 1950 that found her lying awake in the garishly decorated bedroom that she shared with her husband, a paperback across her waist, fighting off fatigue and refilling her glass of bourbon and water.

By quarter to three an uneasy sleep began to settle upon her. It grew deeper a few minutes later until finally she dozed. Then it was a quarter past four when she heard the door to the apartment open. She came awake instantly and was conscious of her own heartbeat. She recognized the rattle of her husband's keys, followed by the sound of the door shutting. Several seconds later the overhead light went on in the bedroom. She shielded her eyes.

"Turn it off, would you?" she mumbled. He ignored her. "Where were you this time?" she asked.

"You don't really want to know," he said.

"Tell me anyway."

"I was with Joe Preston," he said. He undid his necktie and began to unbutton his shirt.

"Joe Preston and a couple of the little whores that he surrounds himself with," she said. "Right, Jesse?"

He ignored her again. "That's no way to talk about the man who's going to produce your next film," he said. He turned toward her. "Nor, for that matter, about the man who's going to direct it."

"Screw yourself, Jesse," she said sleepily.

She thought for a moment he might blow into one of his rages and come over and beat her across the arms and head. He did it about once a week now, often late at night, and she was almost used to it. It was like having to screw him. She almost wished that he did it to her while she slept. That way she'd be less conscious of it as it happened.

Instead, his attention settled upon the bourbon. "God almighty," he said. He picked up the bottle that was next to her glass. He tried to remember how full it had been. "How much have you had?"

"Enough," she said. "After eight months of marriage to you, Jesse, getting drunk is the only thing I enjoy."

"Booze and no sleep," he said. "By the time *Hold the Phone!* starts shooting you'll look like you're fifty years old." He looked at her tauntingly as he set aside the liquor bottle. He pulled his shirt off. "Lisa, you're supposed to have that fresh-as-a-daisy never-been-banged aura about you. How are you going to tease the cocks of America if you look like somebody's grandmother?"

"I don't know, Jesse. You have all the answers. You tell me, you bastard."

"Of course, that's *if* there's a production of *Hold the Phone!*" he said. "I can do only so much. You're the one who has to make the deal final with Joe Preston."

"What are you talking about?" she asked, coming awake.

He sat down on the side of her bed. "Lisa," he said, "Joe Preston is doing you a tremendous favor. He's putting you in a role where you'll be noticed. Don't you think that's going to turn into a significant advancement for your career?"

"Jesse, you son of a bitch," she said, sitting up. "Tell me what you're getting at. What did you promise him?"

"I said you'd have dinner with him at his apartment next Friday," he said. "Just the two of you."

She stared at him.

"And I said that I wouldn't expect you back until the next

afternoon." He paused, then continued. "I'd advise you to wear your diaphragm," he concluded. "Joe thinks rubbers are unmanly."

For a moment their eyes locked, his completely calm, hers in horror. What kind of man bartered away his own wife's body and dignity for a step up in a world of celluloid? Before Lisa could fully comprehend that she had married just that sort of man, he rose and walked to the chair upon which he'd draped his shirt. He routinely removed the gold cuff links from the sleeve.

Lisa rose from the bed and walked to him. She was beyond tears now, but not beyond rage and indignation, at least for the moment. He turned and faced her squarely.

"Yes?" he asked.

With all her force she slapped him across the side of the face. The sound of the contact filled the room but barely fazed him.

"I won't do it," she said. "Never!"

"Yes, you will," he answered. Then suddenly he grabbed her arm and became very angry with her. "Listen, Lisa! If you had any schoolgirl prudery bottled up in you, you should have left it back home in Michigan. There's a film contract involved here. There's money. There's a career for you and me. Los Angeles is filled with girls who want to be stars! How the hell do you think one girl breaks away from the pack?"

"I will not screw Joe Preston," she said between clenched teeth. She yanked her arm and broke free.

He let her go. She broke from him, charged drunkenly away, and knocked over a night table as she fled. She stomped through their living room and locked herself into the guest bedroom.

Friday was five days away. There was plenty of time, Jesse Chadwick reasoned, for his wife to come to further understand the world beyond her irritating middle class values. What, he wondered, was one night of compromise in exchange for the opportunity of a lifetime? The city was filled with starlets who'd have their panties down around one ankle in two seconds, he told himself, were they only lucky enough to be presented with such an offer.

For her part, Lisa tried to cry herself back to sleep, this time with deep, sobbing gasps. The moment was finally upon her when she had to admit to herself exactly what kind of man her husband was. But she also understood the choices before her as well as the utmost seriousness of the threats of physical violence if she disobeyed Jesse Chadwick.

Somehow she managed to pass out. Somehow she managed to

sleep. When she woke up shortly before noon the next morning, she felt sick to her stomach. Then, for the first time in her life, she genuinely felt like killing herself.

She rose from the sofa where she'd slept and walked to the guestroom door. She was about to unlock it and come out, when she heard the telephone. Her husband picked it up after two rings. She stood and listened, realizing very quickly that he was talking with Joe Preston. She could tell because Jesse called him by his name and assured him that everything was fine.

The contracts could be signed, he said, and Lisa would be his dinner companion that following Friday night.

"Ah, Fred Castelli," said Bernie Gedmon, looking up from the examining table. "Am I glad to see you."

"What's going on, Bernie?" Castelli asked.

It was a Sunday morning in Philadelphia. Bernie Gedmon was a young pathologist from Arkansas who worked the weekend shifts at the medical examiner's office. Gedmon was rail-thin with shaggy reddish hair, glasses, and a volcanic complexion. Gedmon was the keeper of the dead, Castelli frequently observed, and he didn't look too healthy himself.

"I called your office 'cause we got a chance to deal with something right away," Gedmon said. "You got a few minutes?"

Gedmon walked away from the corpse before him. The men were in Examination Room C at the M.E.'s office on Spring Garden Street at Eighth, around the corner from the police headquarters.

"I got a few minutes as long as it's good," Castelli said. "If this ain't good, I'm pissed off at you."

"For what?"

"Calling me on a Sunday morning, that's what!" Castelli snapped. "My desk sergeant called me at my girlfriend's house. Didn't even try my own place first."

"So he knows you're a man of the world. What can I do about that?" Gedmon asked. "Would you be happier if he'd looked for you at some after-hours bar for pansies?"

"Don't get cute, Bernie. Just tell me what this is about," Castelli said.

The pathologist tried to lead the detective from the examination room into a warmer hallway. "It's about the guy who got broiled on New Year's Eve," Gedmon said.

Castelli stopped in the doorway. "What about him?"

"Someone wants to claim the body," Gedmon says. "He's here right now."

"What?"

"There's a Mr. Lee here in the waiting room," Gedmon said. "He came in about two hours ago. Six-thirty A.M. on a Sunday. Can you believe that? He says that the dead man was probably his traveling companion from Taiwan. He says they were touring the United States. This guy, Lee, was in New York while his pal came down here to see the Liberty Bell and sample pretzels or something. His buddy disappeared on New Year's Day."

"By the river?" Castelli was skeptical. He followed Gedmon into a washroom.

"Well, I asked him about that. He said his friend liked to look at boats. Particularly navy boats. So I guess he went down to the yard and got in a little trouble with some bad guys."

Gedmon paused to wash his hands. "Like I said, this just happened, Freddie," Gedmon said. "I called you right away. That's why I said it was urgent. I know how you feel about this case."

"Yeah? How do I feel about it?"

"You'd like to get rid of it."

Castelli stared at Gedmon for a moment, then started to chuckle. Gedmon was right. Then Castelli considered the circumstances.

"There's a problem, Bernie," Castelli said. "This makes no sense. The body's torched beyond recognition. *We* don't know who the dead guy is. How does someone show up here and identify the body?"

"Like I said. He knew where his friend went last."

"So how did he know his friend was dead?"

"He didn't. He went to missing persons first. Missing persons sent him over."

"Where was this Lee guy on New Year's Eve while his pal was getting snuffed?"

"He says he was in Times Square in New York with ten friends. He says he has pictures and witnesses."

Castelli's mind was churning. "So how's Mr. Lee so sure this is his pal?" Faintly, in the background, Hank Williams sang on Gedmon's Zenith table radio.

"He identified all the jewelry the dead guy was wearing. That and the eyeglasses," said Gedmon. "He even told me about the coat. Black wool, with a collar made out of monkey fur. There were particles left after the fire.

"*What?*"

"I said, there were particles left—"

"No. Before that. What kind of fur collar?"

"Monkey fur," Gedmon repeated. "Hong Kong. Latest thing according to the Chinaman."

"What Chinaman? Jesus Christ, Bernie. I know it's friggin' Sunday morning, but would you make some sense?"

"Lee. The guy who wants to claim the body. Lee's Chinese. And so was the dead guy."

For several seconds Castelli let it sink in. Then, "Show me," he said at last.

Gedmon brought Castelli to a waiting area in the Philadelphia city morgue. There was a slight, politely mannered Asian man sitting there. He didn't speak much English but he was able to explain that his name was Lee Huong. He produced a British passport. When Castelli opened it, the passport appeared to contain Lee's likeness.

Lee spoke in fractured syntax. He said his friend, the dead man, and he were touring America. Mr. Lee had stayed in New York while the deceased, who's name was Chin, came to Philadelphia. Mr. Chin liked to walk along rivers and look at ships, as he'd previously explained to Gedmon. "The navy yard probably attract him," Lee suggested.

"Even in winter?"

"Very cold where he come from in Nanking," Mr. Lee answered.

"Yeah," said Castelli. "But what bothers me is that it's such a long fucking walk from Nanking. Know what I mean?"

Mr. Lee grinned amiably, appearing to barely understand. "Sir, yes?" he said. "Very honorable."

Gedmon turned away to suppress a schoolboy grin.

"Oh, great," muttered Castelli.

Mr. Lee bowed slightly.

"I figured, Fred," Gedmon said, maintaining a serious expression, "that you might want to handle this in your own way."

Castelli thought about it for another moment. "Yeah. Damn right," he agreed.

Mr. Lee continued to smile.

Castelli looked at the small Oriental. "Can I borrow this, pal?"

he finally asked. He reached for the passport. Again the little man nodded.

Castelli found a telephone in Bernie Gedmon's office. He called the British Consulate in New York. Given the passport number, the consulate confirmed that yes, there was a gentleman named Lee in the United States on a tourist visa. The address Lee gave even checked with consular records.

Next, Castelli called Captain Heintz, taking great pleasure in waking him up at home. Heintz had served in the Second World War and didn't like Asians much anyway. The fact that the victim seemed to be one greatly lessened the importance of the case in his estimation, as Castelli had known it would.

"I just want to give my permission to get this guy buried," Castelli said. "I just want to sign, Cap. Were not getting anywhere on the Chinaman anyway, and if he's a foreign Chinese, we're not likely to. This way we can get him off the active file and go on to something else."

"That's what you'd like to do, isn't it?" Heintz asked accusingly.

"This smells like a dead-end case, Cap," Castelli said. "We spend too much time on one of these and it'll louse our productivity charts. But it's your choice, Captain."

Heintz did see the logic. "Ask him the routine questions," Heintz said. "You got some identification for the live Chinaman you have there?"

"British passport," Castelli said.

"Get an address in the U.S. Get a statement. Cover our asses. Make it look like we were thorough. Sign the papers so that the M.E. can get the stiff out of the morgue. In a couple of days contact this Lee guy again and do a little follow-up. Then dump the case. You're right. I got other stuff for you and Mike."

"Yes, sir!" Castelli said. He came back to Mr. Lee and returned the passport. "Yeah. I can sign," he said to Gedmon.

And he felt some relief doing it. The deceased had probably been an innocent in the ways of American cities and had then wandered off course near the navy yard, Castelli reasoned. There were some bad people in the neighborhood who'd rob him and burn him. Deplorable as these things were, they happened in any city a few times each year.

"Just keep the coroner's report in case we ever need it," said Castelli to Gedmon. "Then get this guy out of here."

"Very obliged," said Lee. He bowed again and shook the policeman's hand. His perfect manners were starting to get on Castelli's nerves. Then Lee said that he'd make arrangements with a funeral home immediately so that his friend could be buried.

"All the Chinese funeral places are on Race and Vine streets," Castelli offered. "I don't think anyone will embalm a Chinese guy except a Chinese funeral parlor."

"Already make arrangements," Mr. Lee said very clearly.

Castelli was working on a bad joke about checking for Chinese funeral parlors in the yellow pages. He laid off, even though he knew it would have split up Gedmon. Instead, he sent the young pathologist for the necessary papers to clear the body for the interment.

Frankly, Castelli was relieved. A dead Chinaman, and a foreigner to boot, was a case with no sex appeal. And now, with the burning victim at least identified and buried, Castelli and Mike Proley could dismiss the whole incident and get on with cases nearer to home.

EIGHT

Given the influence of the F.B.I. in Washington, and having been entrusted to run an investigation sanctioned by J. Edgar Hoover himself, Buchanan had a wide range of investigative powers at his disposal. Some were official, others unofficial. He had every intention of using all of them.

Mary Doyle, his new secretary and assistant, was a trim, graying woman in her fifties. She was a law-enforcement lifer. Her father had been the chief of police in Olney, Pennsylvania, during the First World War, and she'd married a Pennsylvania state trooper in 1923. Together they had two sons and two daughters. In 1941, when manpower shortages beset critical government offices, she'd gone to work at the Philadelphia field office of the F.B.I. as a file clerk. She'd been there since. She was articulate, dedicated, and, above all, trustworthy.

On Wednesday Mary cleaned her desk of all previous business

and cases. On Thursday morning she moved to a location outside of Special Agent Buchanan's office. There she oversaw the connection of two direct telephone lines from the outside to her desk as well as to his. When this was done, Thomas presented her with a condensed file of the case on which she would be assisting him.

"Read it thoroughly," he told her. "Take your time with it. Then come back into my office."

Mary took it to her desk and read it without looking up. At a few minutes after eleven that morning she buzzed Thomas on the intercom.

"Finished," she said.

"Good. Come on in. Ring Bill Roth also. See if he can join us."

Two minutes later Mary came through the door to Thomas Buchanan's office. She had the foresight to arrive with a pad and pencil. She seated herself to the left of his desk. Bill Roth materialized a few minutes later.

"Mary, you've read the briefing report on John Garrett?" Thomas asked.

"Yes, sir," she said.

"Any questions before we start?"

"No, sir."

Buchanan turned toward Roth. "You're the head of this field office," he began. "I want you to know the direction in which I'm starting in case you have any suggestions."

Roth nodded and lit a cigarette.

Buchanan turned back to his assistant. "Mary, the first thing I want to know is the location of each of the four members of the Garrett family. Whatever John Taylor Garrett is involved in, by all indications it has affected his private life."

He turned toward Roth for a moment. "May I have the use of at least two clerical researchers?" Buchanan asked. "I'll need at least two to get started."

Roth nodded. "I'll give you Valenti and Schafft, unless something more urgent comes up. They're two of our best."

"Thank you. Mary, tell them to put aside whatever else they're working on. They can have today to get their desks in order. I want to locate the Garrett daughters first. If they had a falling out with their father, they may be inclined to talk to us. But we have to find them first. Our report says they disappeared." Thomas tossed his next question to Roth. "How thoroughly has the Bureau looked for them?"

"Not as thoroughly as you'll be able to," Roth answered.

Buchanan turned back to Mary. "Tell Valenti and Schafft that I'll brief them together in this office at six this evening. In the meantime prepare a memo for them on the two daughters. Give Ann Garrett to Valenti, give Laura to Schafft. I want them to trace the girls through school records and previous employers. Have them get copies of university alumni bulletins. See if there are any notes there. Have them put calls in to their school and university registrars. Tell the schools we're running an employment security check. Tell them anything that works, but don't tip the investigation. See what the schools know. Also, our files don't even confirm whether or not either girl ever married. Have Valenti and Schafft check the newspapers for that also. Finally, have our two researchers find out everything they can about Garrett's divorce from his wife. The decree should be public record. Get me a copy of it. Also, get me the name of the attorneys for each side."

"Yes, sir," she said.

Buchanan watched Mary write, remarking at the speed of her fingers. Had Mary set out to be a cardsharp, she might have been a great one.

"Now, Mary," he continued, "this is for you to check: Give the Pennsylvania Department of Motor Vehicles the names of all four Garretts. See if any cars are registered to them. If so, get the addresses. Similarly contact Social Security in Washington. See if we can find their social security numbers. If we can, let me know. But also contact the Internal Revenue Service right away. Maybe we can get an address that way. If any of these women are working, I want to know where. If anyone has that information, I.R.S. does." Buchanan paused for a moment, then continued. "Now, for some reason, no one has thought to review John Garrett's income tax records. Tell I.R.S. I want to see as many years of his records as they have."

"Sir?" she questioned.

"What?"

She shook her head, indicating that it couldn't be done.

"Illegal, you know," Roth said. "I.R.S. won't cooperate without a court order."

"That's your experience with them?" Buchanan asked.

Roth nodded. So did Mary. "They're stubborn," Roth warned.

"I.R.S. and Social Security cooperate with our Washington office all the time," Buchanan said.

"That's Washington, Tom."

"So what's the problem here?"

"This is Philadelphia."

Buchanan thought for a moment. "Try both of them anyway, Mary. When you encounter the first suggestion of resistance, put in a person-to-person call for me to the top man in each agency. They'll come around."

"Certainly, sir," she said. She sounded skeptical. Mary flipped her pad onto a second page of shorthand notes. "What else?" she asked.

Buchanan looked back at Roth. "Garrett did intelligence work during the war. What sort? Army? Navy? O.S.S.?"

"No one admits he was theirs," Roth answered.

Buchanan thought for a moment. "That's peculiar, isn't it?"

Roth nodded.

"Who's the senator who plays golf with Frank Lerrick?"

"Russell. Georgia."

"He's on the Senate Armed Services Committee, isn't he?" Buchanan looked back to his secretary. "Mary, call Assistant Director Frank Lerrick at F.B.I. headquarters in Washington. Tell him I need the home telephone number of Senator Richard Russell. Don't make the call to Senator Russell though. Just get me the number."

Buchanan waited until Mary Doyle finished writing and looked up. "Anything else?" she asked.

Buchanan paused for a moment before he answered. "Yes," he said. "Two more things. First, contact the Bureau's Chicago office. Find out how soon I can contact any special agent who might have been involved in an investigation touching upon John Taylor Garrett or Commonwealth Penn. Second, do we have any entree to the Mayflower Club here in Philadelphia?"

"Garrett's club?" Roth asked.

Buchanan nodded. "My uncle used to belong also. I'd like to have a working lunch there today. But without my name being immediately recognized."

Roth considered it for a moment. "A friend of mine is chairman of the Republican Club of Philadelphia. The club would be happy to host one of his guests."

"Perfect," Buchanan said. "Mary, book a table for one at lunch at the latest possible time."

"I have only one question," Roth concluded.

Buchanan nodded.

"How do you have a working lunch by yourself?"

"How else do you get people to talk to you," Buchanan answered, "unless you *are* by yourself?"

NINE

As Special Agent Thomas Buchanan walked from his Chestnut Street office toward the Mayflower Club early that same afternoon, he reminded himself again of one of the simple truths of his profession. The key element in any federal investigation—in fact ninety percent of the job, if not more—is routine, unspectacular inquiry. Cases were not solved by magic and they were rarely solved by luck. They were, however, frequently cracked by a diligent reassembly of every available fact involved, and an arduous gathering of all the parts of a case. Eventually one single clue might stand out and lead in the proper direction. Alternatively all of the parts will become a whole. And the whole will become the truth that the investigation sought.

It was with this philosophy that Buchanan had made his first moves on the Garrett case that same morning. Despite the swashbuckling image of the Bureau, little of the F.B.I.'s positive public image had been created by the Bureau leadership, which rarely left the safety of its Washington offices. Rather, the routine, painstaking investigations of dedicated agents in the field had gone a long way toward building the Bureau's reputation.

Buchanan had been around the Bureau long enough to have spoken to many of the veterans who had worked on a case seventeen years earlier which had become part of F.B.I. folklore. As he walked westward on a cold Chestnut Street and pulled his coat close to him to ward off the blustery January wind, he couldn't help but recall it.

A millionaire oilman named Charles Urschel had been abducted from the front porch of his Oklahoma City mansion on the steamy Saturday night of July 23, 1933. Masked gunmen blindfolded him and drove him by car to a remote ranch in the Southwest. The kidnappers then demanded $200,000 in ransom from Urschel's family. The money was to be paid immediately in old unmarked twenty-dollar bills or Urschel would be blown into the next dimension.

For his first week as a prisoner, Urschel heard little more than the sound of pigs outside the building where he was held, a farm sound that didn't come as much of a surprise, considering his captors fed him ham at every meal. The only other sounds of note were the distant muffled voices of his captors and, reliably at 9:45 each morning, the sound of an aircraft passing overhead. Another airplane, sounding remarkably similar, passed overhead in the opposite direction at 5:45 each afternoon.

On the eighth day of his captivity, however, a terrific Sunday morning rainstorm lashed Oklahoma and western Texas. Urschel didn't hear the airplane. He wondered whether the noise of the storm had drowned it out, if the flight had been canceled, or if it wasn't scheduled on the Sabbath. Then, at 5:45 in the afternoon, a few minutes before his evening plate of ham, he heard it again. The date was July 30.

On the ninth day Urschel's family paid the $200,000 ransom. The captors, who at least had some sense of ethics, packed their unharmed prey into the murderously hot trunk of a 1931 Chevrolet, drove him several hours over bumpy roads, then dumped him on the outskirts of Oklahoma City. By this time the F.B.I. was already on the case.

Agents listened for hours to Urschel's account of his captivity. They quickly focused on the farm, the pigs, and the sound of the airplane. Dozens of agents descended on airline offices throughout the Southwest, poring over schedules and meticulously comparing flight records with the listings of cancellations and diversions for July 30. The search was long, tedious, unglamorous, and plodding.

But it was also thorough. Agents determined that on the day of the downpour an American Airlines flight from Fort Worth, Texas, to Amarillo had detoured around Wise County, Texas, the center of the storm. The aircraft had landed safely in Amarillo, however, and, when the storm cleared, made its return flight over its normal route that afternoon.

Agents chartered their own plane and traveled the same air corridor. They determined that at 9:45 each morning the flight would be directly above two adjacent farms in the town of Paradise, Texas. One of the farms raised chickens. The other raised pigs. Its

owner, R. G. Shannon, cured hams. Shannon's name rang a loud
bell among federal agents. His daughter, Kathryn Shannon, was
married to a big-time bad boy named George Kelly. Kelly was
better known throughout America by his tabloid nickname, "Machine Gun" Kelly. Kelly was currently holding down the position
of public enemy number two on Hoover's much-publicized charts,
while John Dillinger remained in the top spot. But one clue led to
another in the Urschel case and created a trail. Two months later in
Memphis, F.B.I. agents cornered Kelly and a confederate.

"Don't shoot, G-men!" Kelly screamed, thus creating a nickname and helping to manufacture a legend. Reporters on the scene
would make the incident famous—complete with bold, heroic, gun-
toting agents surrounding the apparently humiliated criminal.

J. Edgar Hoover and the F.B.I. rarely let the public forget the
Bureau's success in the Urschel kidnapping. But Special Agent
Thomas Buchanan never lost sight of the larger lesson. It had been
a relentless questioning of witnesses, investigation of facts, and examination of detail that had solved the case. Not gunfire. In that
respect he anticipated that the investigation of John Taylor Garrett
and the Commonwealth Bank of Pennsylvania to be no different.

Thomas Buchanan, as he sat by himself at a table in the dining
room of the Mayflower Club on Walnut Street, dawdled over a
ginger ale and observed the room.

There were times in his past when he might have felt his youth
beckoning to him from this club. After his father's death, his uncle
had often brought him and other members of his family to lunch
here on Saturdays, frequently followed by a football game at Franklin Field. Then the world war came along. His uncle passed away in
1946, his aunt had dropped her membership, and Thomas had
never gone back.

It was in 1941, he decided. In the fall of that year he had last
visited the Mayflower Club. He was working for a brokerage house
that had a seat on the Philadelphia stock exchange. He was putting
some money together, making plans to enter graduate architectural
school in Boston and, now that he recalled it, was a month away
from working up the courage to ask Ann Garrett to marry him.
Today, as an adult and studying the place carefully, Thomas could
see things that were never visible when he was a boy. Much of the
furniture was the same as it had been in the 1930s. The ubiquitous

green carpeting was a little more worn than he'd remembered it, and so were a few of the white tablecloths. But the oil paintings on the walls had survived virtually intact, and so, apparently, had the institution's membership. If the Mayflower Club had been a cross-section of America, Thomas Dewey would have been president. Buchanan suppressed a smile. His uncle, one of the club's few Democrats, used to joke that there were members who'd had the pleasure of voting against Franklin Roosevelt four times.

Thomas watched three middle-aged waiters in black jackets hurry between the kitchen door and the dining tables. Busboys in white service jackets followed in their wake. A quartet of bankers sat near him and lingered over coffee. Buchanan's attention tuned in and out of their discussion of prime interest rates. At the next closest table three ladies in their forties picked at their lunches. Idly he looked for a beautiful woman to occupy his attentions, but he found none. A few moments later his waiter delivered his entree, half of a roasted chicken.

By ten minutes after three the dining room was nearly empty. The three women near him assembled their purses and shopping bags and made a slow exit toward the club's main lobby. The bankers had long since vanished. Thomas signed a guest check and looked across the quiet room. Perfect, he thought to himself.

Paul Evans had been the club's maître d' since just after the Depression. Evans was a fair-complexioned man, squarely built. His hair was sandy, though thinner than Tom remembered it.

Evans was seated at a table near the kitchen when Buchanan approached him. The maître d' had loosened his collar and tie very slightly, and had settled into some staff schedules on the table before him. Thomas moved closer.

Buchanan arrived at Evans's table and placed a hand on an empty chair. "May I join you?" Buchanan asked.

Paul Evans looked up with a start. "Sir?" Evans began, not knowing whether he was about to book a banquet for one hundred or field a complaint surrounding the cuisine. Then a moment passed as Evans tried to determine what was familiar about the young man before him. Another moment passed before recognition.

"Tommy Buchanan!" Evans exclaimed, standing.

"Hello, Paul," Buchanan said. He offered his hand, and the maître d' took it. Then Evans's expression resolutely gave way to a pleased, astonished smile. "By God! It *is,* isn't it? Young Tommy

Buchanan all grown up!" He set aside his paperwork and placed his hands on the younger man's shoulders.

Evans's touch was firm. In his earlier years at St. Joseph's University he'd been a fair athlete, rowing in lightweight fours when springtime came to the Schuylkill. But then the evil October of 1929 had arrived. Evans had barely been able to put the money together to finish college, and, once graduated, had entered the hotel business. He'd destroyed his right knee in a car accident late in 1934, which kept him out of the war. But he still rowed a bulky scull twice a week and his touch still showed it. Yet there were other aspects of Evans's deportment—the putting back of his head at a certain angle, the repeated brushing aside of a troublesome forelock —that pointed in a direction that was less than totally masculine.

"Let me get a look at you! By God!" Evans repeated. "Wouldn't your dad be proud, God rest his soul. And your poor uncle, too, bless him! Sit down, Tommy. Have a beer with me."

Buchanan eased into the extra chair while Evans reclaimed his own. Evans's right hand was aloft, signaling to the bar for a couple of bottles of beer and, since this was the Mayflower Club, a pair of pilsner glasses to match.

"Tell me everything," Evans insisted. "How did the war treat you?" he asked, turning suddenly serious.

Buchanan told him, taking a minute or two as the bottled beer arrived.

"And now?" Evans wanted to know. "Where are you working?"

Buchanan reached to his inside jacket pocket for his Bureau credentials. He laid them on the table without speaking. It took a moment for Paul Evans to digest what he was seeing.

"The F.B.I.," he said. "Well, I'll be . . ." He looked up and his eyes met Buchanan's. "I've got to tell you, son. I'm damned impressed." He shook his head slowly to indicate just how impressed a man had to be to be damned. "J. Edgar Hoover is my personal hero," Evans said. "One of the two finest Americans alive. Him and General Eisenhower, I'd say. I just don't see how Hoover does it. There he is in Chicago to see that John Dillinger gets what he deserves. The next thing you know he's right there in New Jersey to arrest that kraut bastard who killed the Lindbergh kid. Then he's got you G-men taking care of Pretty Boy Floyd and then—that creepy one. Karpis? Is that his name?"

"I think that's who you mean," Thomas said.

"Hoover's right there when the handcuffs are put on Alvin Karpis," Evans continued. "He's *always* right there when the handcuffs are put in place. Incredible man!"

No, Thomas thought. He's always right there when the photographs are being taken. "Well, there are others in the Bureau," Thomas tried modestly.

"Do you ever see J. Edgar Hoover yourself? To speak to?"

"Very rarely."

"Well, you tell him he's got a fan right here in Philadelphia," Evans said.

"I'll try to tell him," Buchanan lied graciously.

"Oh, please do. I'd appreciate it. Cheers," he said. Evans raised his glass and drank to the health of the Director and the Bureau. Buchanan took a sip at the same moment. Then Thomas steered the conversation to a quarter hour's discussion of intercollegiate football, rowing against the current at the Great Falls bend of the Schuylkill, and whether or not eighty-six-year-old Connie Mack would sell the Philadelphia Athletics as rumored.

"What are you doing back in Philly?" Evans asked at length.

"A little bit of work," Buchanan said. "Investigating a land swindle. Boring stuff, really. A bunch of small investors done out of a few bucks. But the federal laws have to be enforced."

"Damned right," Evans agreed patriotically.

Thomas looked around and gave Evans a conspiratorial grin. "Can I ask you a personal question on the QT?" Buchanan asked.

"Shoot."

"Ever see old John Garrett or any of his family?"

"Funny you should ask," Evans said.

"What's funny?"

"Oh, Mr. Garrett's in fine shape," Evans said. "He's a bit of a hermit these days, you know. Puts in an occasional appearance at his own bank. Fewer appearances in public." Evans toyed with a gold cuff link for a moment. "I saw him not so long ago."

"Did you? Where?"

"Why, right *here,*" said Evans, motioning to a table at center stage of his dining room. Evans spoke as if everything were self-evident. "It was within the last month," Evans remembered halfway through a second beer. "During that Christmas–New Year's stretch." Evans was then struck with a revelation. "Say, you used to be pretty sweet on the younger Garrett daughter, weren't you, Tommy? Seems I remember that."

"I rather liked both of them," said Buchanan.

"I remember something more specific than that," said Evans.

Buchanan grinned. "If you must recall it," he said good-naturedly, "I dated both of them. First Laura, the older daughter. She was closer to my age. Through her I met Ann."

"And you were engaged to Ann, weren't you?"

"I'm afraid I lost out on that one," Thomas allowed. "Long time ago. During the war she got tired of waiting. I assume she met someone else."

"What a shame. Would have made a handsome couple, you and Ann. Did you ever marry?"

"No."

"Me neither. Not the type, some of us, are we?"

Buchanan let the remark pass with a consoling roll of the eyes.

"Ah! I'm right, aren't I?" Evans persisted coyly. "And that's why you're asking a veiled question here and there? Still thinking about the delectable Ann?"

"Paul, you got me," said Buchanan with the air of a confession. "But keep it between us, okay?"

"Mum's the word." Evans raised his right hand in a scout's salute. The gesture made him look preposterous: he sipped from the beer glass in his left hand at the same time.

"You've a world-class memory, Paul," Buchanan said.

"Beautiful girl, Ann," Evans said, his tone changing slightly. "Not that both the girls weren't knockouts. I suppose every red-blooded male in the city was chasing the two Garrett kittens."

Buchanan let Evans ramble until the conversation began to drift. Then, "Have you seen any of the Garrett women recently?" Thomas asked eventually.

"None of them, Tommy," Evans answered. "Not for a long while."

"Where are they?

"Well, Mrs. Garrett divorced John a few years ago."

"I'd heard that. Why did they divorce?"

"Who knows? It took everyone by surprise. It happened right before Christmas. It was so sudden that the hot rumor was that there would be a new Mrs. Garrett right after the holidays were over. But it never happened."

"Where did Mrs. Garrett go?"

Evans looked at the younger man strangely for a few seconds. "She died. Didn't you know?"

It was Buchanan's moment to return the astonished stare. "No. I didn't," he said.

"Poor old girl died of cancer about a year ago," Evans said. "Moved out to Illinois after the divorce. Lived in Lake Forest, I think, with a sister."

"Now that you mention it, I do remember that her family was from out there, right?"

Evans nodded.

"What about Laura? And Ann?" Buchanan asked next.

Evans began to grin. "Ah, Tommy, I hate to disappoint you. But the girls moved away. I hear it was to Europe. Or maybe it was just Laura to Europe. Again, Tommy, it's funny you should bring it up. I was in New York a year or two ago and I saw this girl who was the spitting image of Ann Garrett ducking into a checker cab outside of Henri Bendel's. But who knows? A flash of blond hair, a rustle of skirt, and a glimpse of two beautiful stockinged legs. Could have been Ann, could have been a thousand other young girls in New York. Somebody's daughter, somebody's wife, or somebody's mistress. Who knows where girls go these days? I honestly can't say for sure where Ann and Laura went. I'd tell you if I knew, Tommy, for whatever use it might be to you."

"Where in Europe?" Buchanan asked.

Evans shrugged. "I don't know."

"Well, what did you hear?"

"London, maybe. Paris, maybe. The Garrett sisters were big-city girls, if you know what I mean."

Buchanan knew. "And John Garrett never remarried?"

"Not yet," Evans answered. "But a man of his standing doesn't lack for female companionship, you understand."

"Who was with him when you saw him last?" Thomas asked. It was at that question that Evans fell silent.

"It was an unusual evening. That's all I'll say." Evans finally was adamant.

"Oh, Paul. Come on." Buchanan laughed. "I'm just bringing myself up-to-date on some lost acquaintances."

Evans took a long look at his visitor. "We *are* talking off the record, right?"

"We're old friends, Paul. Aren't we?" Buchanan asked, carefully sidestepping Evans's question. "How old was I when my uncle Hugh first brought me here? Was I twelve years old? Please tell me about Mr. Garrett and his guests."

"It was a party of three," Evans remembered very clearly. "Not what we usually get in here."

"So Mr. Garrett was one. Who were the other two?"

Evans opened his mouth to speak, then stopped as if he'd been stabbed. A different expression altogether came across his face. Resentment. Mystification. Fear. Buchanan knew what he was seeing. He'd seen it before.

"You little bastard," Evans said, his voice barely audible and conveying shock. His neck was reddening and one hand shook very slightly. "This isn't a social call! And these aren't friendly questions!" His words rushed out in a furious whisper.

It was Buchanan's turn to remain silent.

"But your credentials are real, aren't they?" Evans asked.

Buchanan nodded. "Just tell me about Mr. Garrett. I'm not here to complicate your life. I just want answers."

A thin film of sweat had broken out on Evans's brow. His jauntiness had vanished. "One of the men at the table was Jerry DeStefano," he said. "Do you know the name?"

"Should I?"

"Well, I'm sure he's in your files somewhere. Look him up. Everyone in South Philadelphia knows him. He owns a meat-packing concern and a funeral home. Sometimes the two enterprises overlap. Do I make myself clear?"

"Organized crime, right?"

"Check your files. That's all I'll say."

"What sort of business would Garrett have with a man like that?"

"Maybe Mr. DeStefano wants to open a checking account at Commonwealth Penn," Evans answered petulantly. "How would I know?"

"Who was the other man?"

"An Oriental."

"Ever seen him before?"

Again Evans was quiet. He seemed very cross. "Why do you want to know?" he asked.

Buchanan didn't feel like giving reasons. "Had you ever seen the Oriental man before?" he repeated.

"We have tea at the Barclay all the time."

"Do I have to lean on you, Paul?"

"Yes, I'd met him before."

"How? Where?"

"He's some sort of business contact that Mr. Garrett has with the Orient," Evans said. "He looks to me like a full-blood Chinese. His name is Sammy Wong."

"Are you sure?"

"Sure of what?"

"His name?"

"I couldn't *not* be sure!" Evans snapped. "Especially that night."

"Why?"

"First, like I said, I'd met him through Mr. Garrett before. Same as Mr. DeStefano. Second, Mr. Garrett made a big point of reintroducing me to both men that night. By name. And it is my business to remember names. They were all in high spirits. 'This is Mr. DeStefano,' Mr. Garrett said. 'And this is my good friend Sammy Wong. You've seen Sammy here with me before though, haven't you, Paul?' The little Chinese man sort of bowed to me. 'We've just concluded a wonderful business deal, Paul,' Mr. Garrett continued, 'so bring us a bottle of your best French champagne. Something prewar. We're having a celebration.' "

"And did they? Celebrate?" Buchanan asked.

"Yes."

"And did you have something prewar?"

"They guzzled our last three bottles of Moët," Evans answered, not without irritation. "One bottle to each of them. The little Chinaman was putting away his own fair share, too, I might add. In fact, we had complaints from some of our regulars. Mr. Garrett and his new friends made a spectacle of themselves for the whole evening. You know what a conservative place this is. The whole room was staring at them."

"A lot of witnesses, in other words."

"If you want to phrase it that way, yes," Paul Evans said. "Can you imagine this? There was even a newspaper photographer outside the club that evening. Just snapping some pictures. Took a shot of Mr. Garrett leaving with Wong and DeStefano. It was in the *Inquirer* the next day."

Buchanan was already working on the scene, picturing it and trying to understand it. He knew too little to put it in its place, yet already the image before him was out of focus.

"Didn't you find all of this a little strange?" Buchanan asked Evans. "For example, why does an elusive, reclusive man suddenly make a spectacle of himself? Unless we're imagining it, Mr. Garrett seemed to *want* witnesses on this particular evening. Wouldn't it seem that way to you?"

"I'm paid," Evans said guardedly, "to see that guests have a pleasant time in our club. I'm not here to analyze their behavior."

"No," Buchanan said in a tone of conclusion. "Of course you're not."

Evans had little else to add. A few minutes later Buchanan rose. He thanked the maître d', who was in no mood to accept his gratitude.

"No more questions?" Evans asked.

"Not today."

"Then two things," Evans said.

Buchanan waited.

"You're a cocksucker," Evans snapped. "And the beers are fifty cents each. Pay as you leave."

■

TEN

■

Casa Granada wasn't in Granada at all, and for that matter wasn't even in Spain. Instead, somewhat incongruously, it was perched on a cliff in Malibu, nestled on stilts and poles upon a myriad of levels of rock overlooking the Pacific Ocean.

The building was white stucco with red tiles on the roof and was a maze of Spanish arches and turrets. Even in the middle of January it sparkled in the sunlight of the American West Coast. On its grounds, set back away from the cliffs, were a tennis court, a croquet course, a swimming pool, and an array of lawn furniture. This might have been the home of any American millionaire whose financial triumphs had run far out in front of his cultivation. But instead of anyone, this year Casa Granada belonged to Joe Preston, aging satyr and producer of motion pictures.

Jesse Chadwick turned his Cadillac into Joe Preston's domain at seven-thirty that Friday evening. His wife, Lisa Pennington, sat quietly beside him. The car rolled smoothly down the palm-tree-lined driveway that curved across a green lawn to Joe Preston's front door. The Cadillac slowed to a halt. Jesse Chadwick turned and looked at his wife.

"Be nice tonight," he said. It was half a sincere request, half a warning. "Joe can help both of us."

"I hate you for this, Jesse," she said. She turned and looked him squarely in the eye. "Up until now I merely disliked you. Now I hate you."

"This will never happen again," he said. "How about if I promise you that?"

"Jesse," she said. "If you came into a house soaking wet in a raincoat, shaking out an umbrella and told me it was raining, you know what? I'd still look out the window to check."

Chadwick thought about that for a moment. "Know what? I like that," he said.

Lisa would have continued, but a boy in a dark jacket spotted their car from within Casa Granada. He burst quickly from the front door. He was well scrubbed and grinning. His features were clearly Mexican and he introduced himself as Miguel, Mr. Preston's houseboy. He greeted Mr. and Mrs. Chadwick by name and led them to the front door. Then he disappeared to park their car.

Joe Preston had been ready for his guests for an hour, but made an entrance anyway into the living room of Casa Granada. He was a small, compact man in a dark silk suit. His face was angular, but his shoulders were wide and muscular. His hairline was receding and his eyebrows, which were dark and thick, had a downward slant to them, giving him a perpetually mean appearance. Whenever he smiled, which he did when he saw his visitors for the evening, he looked as if he'd just evicted a widow.

Preston greeted his guests before a huge brick fireplace which was flanked by two floral-print sofas.

"Jesse! Great to see you!" Joe Preston boomed from a few feet away. He came to Jesse Chadwick and pumped his hand. "And Lisa, you too!" he boomed next. He leaned to her and kissed her on the cheek. It was an awkward gesture. Preston and Lisa Pennington were the same height. Preston had to stretch himself on his toes slightly to reach her.

In turn, Lisa stiffened at his touch. The prospect of having to go to bed with him seemed all the more repellent as the prospect grew more real. Preston held both of his guests' hands as he continued to talk.

"Speaking of great-looking girls," said Preston, meaning it as a compliment, "I got someone else here for you to meet. Sally?"

Preston motioned to the floral-print sofa nearer the hearth. On it sat a girl with auburn hair. She was very young and very pretty. She held in her hand a clear drink that had been punctuated with a twist of lime. She smiled when she heard her name.

"Sally's a model, but she's gonna be in films too," Joe Preston announced. "I foresee a big break for her in 1950." When it came to casting, Joe Preston and his libido had a remarkable clairvoyance for big breaks.

Lisa felt a slight sense of relief sweep across her. She was, it now seemed, not the only female in the room. With another young woman present, she reasoned, she might have misunderstood the devious purpose for the evening.

"Hi," Sally said. She was clearly ill at ease with Joe Preston, but appeared to enjoy the lavish, wolfish attention paid to her by Jesse Chadwick.

"Let's all have a drink," Preston said next. "Hey, Mike!" he bellowed. He clapped his hands. Seconds later young Miguel reappeared and took requests for liquor.

They seated themselves around the fireplace, which the house-boy fueled with an extra pair of logs. The room, as Lisa had a chance to glance around it, was aggressively decorated, with large swatches of bold colors colliding with each other. Scattered across the wall were minor canvases by several major modern artists. Several matching objets d'art in metal or clay stood in small spotlights on tables where no visitor could miss them.

The two women remained quiet as Chadwick and Joe Preston talked business. Lisa gradually tuned them out, though she was unable to keep from catching pieces of their conversation.

"I gave that broad her first role, you know that?" Preston said of an actress whose face had recently adorned the cover of *Life* magazine. "She was broke at the time and sleeping with a muscle-bound auto mechanic from Pasadena."

Then he added, "If we get a halfway decent script for *Hold the Phone!* we can do one million dollars worth of business worldwide, I'm telling ya."

This was followed by a discussion of a certain handsome leading man whose sexual proclivities were somewhat less than traditional. His studio spent thousands of dollars building up a romantic he-man image and surrounding him with starlets on the beach.

Meanwhile, the man's lawyers were quietly fighting off a messy suit brought against him by the parents of a fourteen-year-old schoolboy who'd been in a recent film with him. Joe Preston hated the actor and took great relish in repeating the story. "Not only is Henry a fag," Joe Preston chortled, "but he's a dumb fag as well. That's unusual. Most fairies in this town are brilliant."

Preston then shared with his audience the inside account of one of Hollywood's more dubious recent triumphs. The previous year, Preston had refused to make a final $2250 payment to a well-known novelist who'd written a film script for him. Preston had held out until the writer was forced to share the screen credit with him. Then the writer, a two-pack-a-day smoker all his adult life, had contracted lung cancer and died. That left Joe Preston nominated for an Academy Award when the film became a critical success.

"Am I a bastard or what?" Joe Preston exulted. "I knew the guy was dying and couldn't fight me for long. You know, Jesse, I couldn't write an effective extortion note, yet I got myself nominated for an Oscar. That's hustling!" With a laugh Preston drained his glass. "Hey, where's the Mexican kid? We need more drinks here." Neither Lisa nor Sally were halfway through theirs.

"Did you win it?" Sally asked suddenly. It was the first time she'd spoken in twenty minutes.

Joe Preston's eyes narrowed. "Win what?" he asked.

"The Oscar."

"If I had, sweetheart, don't you think the little fucking statue would be sitting out here with bells on it where the world could see it?"

"Oh," she said.

"The academy doesn't like me, honey," he said. "They think I'm a crude meshugganah from Brooklyn. They wouldn't give me an award if I'd written the Torah."

Jesse Chadwick laughed. Sally was lost. Lisa was silent. Joe Preston was on a roll.

In the kitchen a professional chef labored over a Pacific salmon. Dinner was served at nine. The chef made the presentation and Miguel served. Joe Preston talked business with Jesse Chadwick for most of the meal. Miguel circulated frequently, quiet as a breeze, and poured chilled California rosé wine even when none was needed. Seeking solace, Lisa fell into a conversation with Sally as the wine began to tiptoe up on both of them.

Sally said she was from Minnesota. Her modeling career had been limited so far to a some nonpaid shots in a department store catalog in St. Paul. Nonetheless, there she was in Los Angeles, seeking her fortune like everyone else and working at a perfume shop in Beverly Hills in the meantime. She was nineteen, gullible, compliant, and had never finished high school. She'd also never taken an acting class. But Joe Preston had said that she'd do just fine if she just stayed in tight with the right people.

"I can believe Joe, can't I?" Sally asked her after dessert.

Lisa looked her straight in the eye. "No," she answered. "You can't."

The remark seemed to cast a pall over their conversation. But just then Joe Preston, who must have been listening to their whole conversation while carrying on his own, broke in.

"Time to go into the lounge, girls," he said. He had an unlit Cuban cigar in his hand. He offered a second one to Jesse Chadwick, who accepted it. Preston then guided his guests to the next room.

In another twenty minutes the cigar smoke drove Lisa into a first floor powder room. She stood there before the mirror and stared into it. So this was what it had come to, she said to herself, and these were the people among whom she circulated.

She was disgusted with herself and demoralized by her lifestyle. The desire to flee was again very strong. But where would she go? Whom could she turn to? And who would protect her from Jesse Chadwick's thugs?

Well, she told herself, she had one or two ideas. She knew one devastating way she could get back at all of them. From her purse she pulled a vial of laudanum. There were thirty in the vial, one powerful sedative for each day of the month.

But she hadn't been taking them recently. Instead, she'd been saving them. Twice recently she'd renewed the prescription her husband had gotten for her from the quack in West Hollywood, the man who dispensed anything the stars wanted, from mescaline to morphine, if the price was right. Lisa had about ninety of these pills. More than enough, if taken all at once, to end things completely. Suicide was an option for Lisa that had appeared increasingly attractive in recent weeks. But if she did it, she told herself, or *when* she did it, she would choose the time perfectly. She would time it to—

There was a tentative knock on the bathroom door. "Lisa?"

asked a female voice on the other side. It was Sally. "Can I come in?" Sally asked.

The door opened before Lisa could answer. Lisa hid the vial of laudanum capsules in her hand. She turned to the other girl. "Yes?" she asked with some annoyance.

"Lisa?" Sally seemed upset. "I got to ask someone tonight. There's nobody else and I got to know something."

Lisa looked at her blankly and slipped the prescription back into her purse. "What is it?" she asked.

Sally didn't appear to know how to phrase the question. Lisa asked again.

"Do you know if I could get pregnant on the third day of my period?"

"What?"

Sally repeated the question. For another moment Lisa only stared.

"Don't get mad at me for asking, Lisa, please," she said. "But I need to know."

"Do you think you're pregnant?" Lisa asked, missing the point.

Sally smiled. "I just don't want to *get* pregnant," she said.

"If you don't want to get pregnant, don't get in bed with anyone." Lisa was almost embarrassed by her moralistic tone, on this night above all.

Sally looked away. "Lisa, help me. That's not what I'm asking."

"You probably won't. But you should see a doctor."

"Thank you." Sally turned back toward the door. "Your husband," Sally said, sounding as if she were trying to be gracious. "He's very handsome."

"Unfortunately, he knows," Lisa replied.

It was Sally's turn to miss the point. She nodded, smiled, and left. Lisa took the laudanum back out of her purse.

Lisa Pennington drew a deep breath. Then she stood perfectly still. Through the haze of too much rosé wine, she tried to put Sally in perspective. Where did the nineteen-year-old fit into Joe Preston's plans for the evening? Where indeed, if she, Lisa, was expected to end the evening in bed with him?

The thought crossed her mind that Preston might have plans for two sexual conquests at the same time. Or maybe Sally was a live-in, something to pick up the slack when Preston wasn't busy chasing another man's wife.

Lisa blew out a long breath. She stared at the vial of laudanum in her hand. Drugs at least made things less painful when they occurred. Like when her husband beat her. Like the times she had to appear with barely any clothes in front of a camera and a dozen leering stagehands. Like tonight, when obnoxious little Joe . . .

A strong urge was brewing within her to go out there and tell them she wasn't going to do it. But whenever she got up the nerve to do something like that, the specter of Jesse Chadwick's goon squad appeared before her.

She opened the vial. One of these normally knocked her right out. Two would numb the sensibilities of anyone. Three would . . .

The very idea of Joe Preston entering her body! . . . She wondered how many other women he'd violated this way. . . . She trembled. . . . Her hand was unsteady. . . . She poured out three capsules, then threw them down her throat with some water. . . .

Three hits of a strong sedative to get into bed with Joe Preston. Three capsules and a total loss of dignity. And what the hell was Sally talking about anyway?

She gazed at herself in the mirror. She stared long and hard until she began to feel the drugs mix with the wine. She didn't know whether to throw up or cheer.

No, she decided. No, dammit, no. She hadn't any idea where she would go or where she would hide, but she would not have this rodent of a man forced upon her! The deal was off. Her career was off! They could go to hell with their film! She would hide out from Jesse Chadwick's goons for the rest of her life if need be. But she wasn't going to screw Joe Preston tonight.

She weaved slightly as she turned. Too much wine. Then there was a big rush from the laudanum. She listened carefully to her body.

Here in the laudanum was a vice that preceded Jesse Chadwick. Here was something that went back a few years. Three capsules at once and she could have sworn she felt the slow stroking of angels' feathers starting at the base of her spine. A dormant snake seemed to uncoil in the small of her back. It wrapped itself warmly and cozily around her stomach and up to her lungs and breasts. Her senses seemed open, but she felt more friendly toward herself. Everything looked as if it would be all right after all.

She wondered if she'd be able to drive her husband's car if she could get the keys. Well, she decided, might as well make a try for it.

She steadied herself. Her head seemed to be moving in circles already.

She opened the door and walked tentatively back to the living room. She stopped short when she saw Joe Preston sitting on the floral sofa, a drink in one hand, the half-smoked cigar in the other. Joe was alone.

"Where's Jesse?" she asked softly.

"I was hoping you'd be undressed."

"Where's Jesse?" she asked again.

"Gone." Joe Preston blew out a long puff of expensive smoke. Lisa eyed the room. "Where's Sally?" she asked.

"She left with Jesse," he said. He sipped his drink. "Don't tell me that your husband didn't explain the sleeping arrangements for the evening."

She allowed it to sink in for a moment. So that's what it was. An even-up swap by her husband: My wife for your starlet. And Lisa hadn't even recognized the logistics of it while it was happening.

"Well?" Joe Preston asked.

"Only half of the arrangements," she said.

"Yeah? Which ones did you know about?"

"You and me."

The producer grinned and thought about it for a minute. "Well, as far as I'm concerned, this is the more important half," he said. "Come sit next to me."

"I'm not doing it, Joe. You can take your film and stuff it."

Preston was unmoved. "Know something, sugar?" he asked. "There are two types of girl that I screw. The first type can't wait to get her panties down for me so that I can put her in a film. The second type protests for maybe half an hour to prove that she's really a good girl. Then I grab her and hump her anyway." He took a long draw on his cigar, then blew out a stream of smoke that might have done justice to a factory. "Know something? I like the second type better. I even like it when a girl fights a little when I'm on top of her. More fun."

"I mean it, Joe. Let me out of here."

"Not a wise position, Lisa. You be nice to me this one night, and I can help you more ways than you can count. You refuse to play along, you get hurt worse than you could imagine. Have another drink."

"Drink . . . ?" she asked blearily. "No drink . . ."

Oh, those pills! Three, she knew now, was a mistake. A big mistake. She took a step toward the door, wobbled, and caught herself against the side of a chair. The chair started to slide on the hardwood floor, and Lisa grabbed a lamp. Her head swam. The lamp gave way and she stumbled forward.

Joe was up off his sofa like a bear. He caught her and pushed her toward the other sofa facing the fireplace.

"Too much to drink, huh, Lisa? Well, have it however you like it."

"No, Joe," she said softly. "Don't do it."

Her head felt as if it were floating away from her body. Everything was bright, as if she were about to faint. One thing about three shots of laudanum: break your wrist and you'll know it hurts, but the hurt won't seem important. It worked the same way for mental pain.

Joe's paws were all over her, reaching under her clothes, undoing buttons, exploring her breasts and under her skirt.

She tried to push him off. But he was strong, much stronger than he looked. And her head! Lisa felt as if she were on another planet.

"Joe!" she moaned. She knew what was happening. "Jesus Christ, Joe . . . have some decency . . . no!"

He laughed again. His hands overpowered her. She was pinned onto the sofa and her clothes were coming off piece by piece. She thought it would be a good idea to scream, and tried to. But whatever came out of her throat sounded distant and weak. And who would stop this anyway? The houseboy?

She wished to God that she would black out. But unconsciousness wouldn't come. She was aware of everything that happened as Joe Preston undid his own clothing just enough so that he could get at her.

Then, as always seemed to be the case for Joe Preston, the producer got what he wanted, as opposed to what he deserved.

Special Agent Thomas Buchanan sat unhappily in his superior's office in Philadelphia. The first steps of his investigation of John T. Garrett and Commonwealth Penn were turning into dust.

It was ten A.M. on Saturday morning, January 21. Bill Roth sat at his desk and smoked. Thomas Buchanan spoke.

"Motor Vehicles hasn't found anything for us," Buchanan began. "There's no operator's license or vehicle registration anywhere in Pennsylvania for John Garrett's wife. Same for Ann Garrett. Laura Garrett had a driver's license until 1948, but then let it lapse."

"And John Garrett?" Roth asked.

"License and two vehicles registered to his home in Devon. But he's never there and never at the bank."

"Where are the cars?"

"In his garage. They never move."

"Think he's alive?" asked Roth.

"He was alive at the Mayflower Club two or three weeks ago. Remember?"

"That's right. Of course." Pensively Roth tapped a forefinger on his desk.

"As of two days ago," Buchanan continued, "I've placed surveillance teams on the house and the bank headquarters. They're to call immediately if they see anything."

Roth nodded. "I hope he turns up sometime soon. We'll have to justify the manpower expense."

"Rosemary Garrett, John's wife, died of cancer in 1949. I found out from the maître d' at the Mayflower Club, then reconfirmed it with the attorney who represented her during her divorce. There are no extenuating circumstances in her divorce or death that would help us, though I'm still checking into both."

"Why didn't *she* keep the house and stay in the area? That would have been more normal."

"The house has always been in the Garrett family. She took a very good cash settlement and moved back to Illinois to be with her own family. She's buried there. Again, I checked."

"And the daughters?" Roth asked.

"Ann lived in New York in 1946. She worked at Saks Fifth Avenue for a very short time. Rented a small apartment on East Fifty-second Street. But no forwarding address after that and no inquiries at Saks from future employers. No marriage name and no one still in the little apartment building who knew much about her. She disappeared, in other words. Or at least her name did. The trail is completely cold."

"And Laura?"

"No trail at all. No employment record in the United States. No tax returns either." Buchanan paused for a moment. "I was able to invoke Mr. Hoover's name to Social Security and Internal Revenue. They wouldn't show me records, but they checked them for me. No leads there. As far as John Garrett is concerned, he draws a routine salary from Commonwealth Penn and takes a standard personal deduction. That doesn't tell us anything either."

Buchanan studied some notes that were across his lap. "One angle that our investigators Valenti and Schafft are still trying is through the girls' schools and colleges. They've made inquiries with the registrars' offices, which have yielded only old addresses. But we're trying to find alumni bulletins to see if we can find a lead there. One source suggested that both sisters may have moved to Europe. I'm starting to believe that might be the case. So I'm attempting to follow that up."

"Grasping at straws already, are we?" Roth asked sourly.

"Let's just say I'm working every angle."

Roth extinguished his cigarette. Saturday-morning briefings drove him to distraction. He particularly hated being briefed on an investigator's lack of success.

"What about the U.S. Army?" Roth asked.

"They sent me a copy of Garrett's record. Standard stuff. Senator Russell's office speeded things along for us. Garrett was an exemplary soldier, in fact. A major in intelligence, as you know. But there's nothing in the file that's extraordinary."

"Where was he in the war?"

"France. Italy. Germany."

"What about the O.S.S.?" Roth suggested. "Was Garrett in it?"

"The C.I.A. has those files. But so far they don't return my calls. I'm going to contact Senator Russell again over the weekend. We may have to go that route."

Roth nodded. "Be careful with that one. C.I.A. is touchy. Hoover hates them and vice versa. I wouldn't even put it past them to give us a bum steer. Send us around chasing our ass."

"I'll be careful," Buchanan said.

"Can you do it today?"

The question surprised Buchanan. "If I can get Senator Russell at home. Why today?"

"You might be traveling tomorrow," Roth said.

"Where?"

"Mark O'Connell," said Roth. "Special agent in Chicago when you were there, right?"

"Yes. Of course."

"You knew him, didn't you?"

"I knew him very well."

"A friend of yours?"

"I considered him a good friend," Buchanan said. "He was also a good agent. Why? What the hell are you talking about, Bill?"

"Special Agent O'Connell did some preliminary investigation into Commonwealth Penn last year. Then the investigation was dropped." Roth paused. "O'Connell retired from the Bureau a few months ago. On Christmas Eve he took four bullets in the stomach."

"Oh, God . . ." Buchanan muttered. For a moment the room seemed suspended in silence.

Roth indicated a folder on his desk. "The full report came in last night before midnight. You can read it. The shooting looks like a setup to me."

Roth started another smoke. He handed the folder to Buchanan, who took it speechlessly. Whenever a law enforcement official in the United States was shot, the F.B.I. received a report. Roth had been scanning names within the last twenty-four hours, he said, had recognized O'Connell's name and asked for a file.

"I don't believe there's such a thing as coincidence, Tom," Roth said. "I'd strongly suggest that you get yourself out to Oregon to see what happened."

■
ELEVEN
■

President Harry S. Truman sat at his desk in the Oval Office of the White House and tilted back in his swivel chair. Truman's gray hair was neatly parted and his mouth was tight with tension. Behind the round lenses of his glasses, his eyes glistened with anger. He was reading the seventh page of an eight-page report brought to him by a White House attaché named John J. Malone.

Malone was a veteran member of the United States Secret Service and was second in command of White House security. But to the President, Malone also fulfilled a critical function as a liaison officer with the National Security Council. Malone, a dark-haired, quiet Missourian from Kansas City, was fifty-one years old and had been with Harry Truman since Truman's second term in the U.S. Senate. Almost everywhere in Washington, Malone was perceived as a die-hard Truman loyalist. The President trusted him totally, and Malone served as the President's unseen eyes and ears in many matters of consequence.

Malone had stayed up till two A.M. writing the report now before the President and had brought it to Mr. Truman's attention at eight-thirty A.M. that same morning. Now it was Malone who was still seated in the Oval Office before the President as Truman held the report in his lap and read it. And, inevitably, it was also Malone who watched uncomfortably as the President's cheeks grew florid with rage.

And why wouldn't they? The report contained nothing except material that would enrage the President. The F.B.I., it appeared, was diligently building an espionage case against a Pennsylvania banker named John Taylor Garrett. If established, the case would prove to be of considerable embarrassment to the White House. And clearly J. Edgar Hoover's people were building the case against Garrett regardless of whether or not the banker was guilty.

Truman finished reading, set the report on his desk, and looked up to Malone.

"What's your source on this, Jack?" the President asked.

"Since 1946, as you know Mr. President, C.I.A. and F.B.I. have been busy spying on each other. It's almost impossible for one agency to embark on a project without the other knowing. In this case, I have friends at Central Intelligence who alerted us."

Ever since the creation of the Central Intelligence Agency, as everyone knew, Hoover had been looking for ways to one-up the C.I.A. or to otherwise discredit it. His motivation was again clear. By building a spy case that he could dump at the White House gates, Hoover reaped a triple benefit. He enhanced his own credibility as the nation's top cop and spy catcher, he embarrassed the President—who'd created the C.I.A. against Hoover's wishes—and he discredited the C.I.A., who were made to look incompetent for missing the same case. With or without evidence, as soon as Hoover had enough he'd leak the story to friendly journalists and conservative legislators. It was the type of political masterstroke for which Hoover had become famous—or at least notorious—in Washington.

"Hoover can't lose, in other words," said Truman.

Malone nodded. "There are a few things we can do," Malone advised thoughtfully. "We could attempt to sabotage the F.B.I.'s investigation. We could fabricate some faulty information which would send them in the wrong direction. We could try to take over the investigation ourselves. We could—"

"No, no, no." Truman's response was quiet and impatient. "I want to do the right thing, Jack," he said. "If we're dealing with a security breach, let's find out about and plug it up."

"We could make some sort of accommodation with Hoover," Malone suggested next. "Give him something he wants."

"What he wants is his own private gestapo," snapped Truman. "Well, that's one thing the lousy son of a bitch won't get from me. We'll just make damned well sure that he doesn't have a way to use this case against us. *If* he even has a case."

"Yes, sir," Malone said.

"Do you think he has something or not?"

"No way of knowing. *He* certainly seems to think he does."

Truman thought for a few moments. "Who's running the investigation for Hoover?" the President asked. "Anyone we've dealt with before?"

"The F.B.I. appears to have assigned it to a relatively young agent named Thomas C. Buchanan. Hoover has him operating with relative independence. Obviously J. Edgar doesn't want any part of the investigation leaking outside the F.B.I. before he's ready to use it."

"What do we know about this Buchanan?" the President asked. "Who is he?"

"From Pennsylvania. Solid career as an army officer before the F.B.I. Single. No hint of corruption or political bias. A 'good American,' you might say."

"I have no problems with good Americans," Truman said. "A good American is an honest man. You can appeal to reason and a sense of fair play with an honest man."

"Yes, sir."

Several more seconds passed as Truman tried to apply common sense to the situation. Then he spoke again.

"Get me a complete report on Buchanan," Truman requested. "That's the only way we'll know what we're dealing with. Can you do that?"

"No problem at all, Mr. President," Malone said.

"Then do it today," Truman said, concluding the meeting. "I'll look at it tonight."

Malone rose and departed, leaving the report in Truman's possession. The President picked it up and angrily began to reread.

Henry Walters, one of the five American foreign service political officers assigned to London, had spent half of that same day in an isolated soundproof office of the United States Embassy. There he had carefully written and retyped a report of his own. Walters's work would be submitted to U.S. Ambassador John Fitzroy the next morning. If it met Fitzroy's approval, it would be returned by diplomatic pouch to the State Department in Washington the following evening.

The report was Walters's most significant piece of work since joining the foreign service. It summarized an American intelligence operation about to be launched from Austria against the People's Republic of Germany. Transport and backup systems for the operation were to be provided by Britain's Special Intelligence Service, which was why the report was being passed through London.

Walters hated the menial task of typing. Yet, he had written the report three times and retyped it painfully in each version. Sensitive material could be a nuisance. Even the secretaries weren't allowed to see it.

Walters was meticulously careful about his own phraseology. To him, the purpose of the operation was questionable at best. The previous summer the C.I.A. had set a trap for an East German diplomat named Hans Zolling, a graying, divorced undersecretary in the East German politburo. The bait was a perky Danish-born stenographer named Lili, who was actually a citizen of the United States. Lili had met the East German diplomat in July 1949 while both had vacationed on the cheap in Dubrovnik. The diplomat was set to defect and join the girl, who was half his age, in West Germany if only someone in the West could bring him out. With him he would bring an insider's knowledge of the East German defense ministry, an attractive commodity in the first year of N.A.T.O.'s existence.

Walters took a cautiously skeptical view of the whole arrangement, however. In the wording of the report, he obliquely indicated this. Without actually criticizing the operation, he questioned how valuable the defector could be. At age fifty-two, Zolling had the lack of self-discipline to lose his head over a twenty-five-year-old secretary. If a man couldn't see a simple woman in clear perspective, Henry Walters suggested, how good a perspective would he have on armaments, defense procedures, weapons systems, and the like? Similarly how much could anyone believe a man who was ready to turn his whole life around over a few tumbles in the sack?

Walters's questions were rhetorical and phrased more delicately. He had no answers either. But when he posed a few of the questions to the senior American diplomats in London, no one had taken them seriously.

"Henry," Ambassador Fitzroy had even said in private, "I appreciate your concern. But when you're fifty-two-years-old yourself, you'll realize that *any* twenty-five-year-old secretary is worth a scramble across barbed wire. People have betrayed their country to foreign intelligence services for a lot less. What are this Danish girl's legs like, by the way?" The ambassador, who was fifty-eight, seemed to speak from experience.

Well, Walters concluded, if the operation crashed he could point to his own report as having questioned its wisdom from the start. If the operation succeeded, and if the tone of his report were ever brought before him for explanation, he could reasonably explain that he had been cautious and prudent in a matter of national security. How could anyone take him to task for that? He believed he had, in other words, maneuvered himself where he could not lose.

And why not? Clearly he was on the rise within the scheme of things within the U.S. Embassy. An exception had recently been made in his posting assignment, for example. His tour in London had been extended from two years to five. Why should he start taking risks with other people's operations? Why, when those in power in the government were actually starting to trust him with security decisions?

Walters finished the report, reread it, and placed it in a sealed envelope. He personally took it to the ambassador's office and placed it on the ambassador's desk, where it would be read first thing in the morning. Now, finally, Henry Walters could be on his way.

Henry might have positioned himself well in diplomatic circles that day, but in romantic considerations he'd been less skillful. He had promised to take Laura out to dinner. He was two hours late, hadn't bothered to call, and Laura Garrett was steaming by the time he arrived at her apartment in Mayfair.

"Hi," he said as she opened the door.

"Henry," she said. "It's ten o'clock." She looked angrily at her watch. "Sorry," she corrected herself. "It's ten-nineteen."

"I'm sorry," he said. "Something really urgent came up at work. I didn't leave until twenty minutes ago."

"You've used that excuse before," she said.

"It's happened before. It will probably happen again."

"Not in this relationship," Laura said. "Good-bye, Henry." She attempted to close the door. He stopped the door with his hand.

"Can I come in at least?" he asked.

"No," she said. She glared at him. "Ann will be home any minute," she added.

"Good. Then I finally get to meet her."

Laura held the door in its place. "That's not what I meant, Henry," she said.

"Oh. Well, then, come on over to my place. Get your stuff. I'll wait." His romance with such a beautiful woman had emboldened him, as had his quick ascent within the American diplomatic corps. A few months ago he would never have had the self-confidence to make such a response.

And clearly Laura didn't appear to care for it. "You show up here two hours late!" she snapped. "And I'm just supposed to leave and jump into bed with you?"

"Laura . . ."

"Good night, Henry," she said. "Don't bother to come by again."

"Laura! Please!" he begged. He caught the door just before it closed. "Can't we talk at least?" The evening's momentum had shifted in her direction.

"There's nothing to say," she said. "Now, leave!"

"How," he asked aloud with mock melodrama, "can I just walk away from a woman I love?"

"Oh, brother . . ." she said. She rolled her eyes in dismay.

"I'm going to stand out here and scream until you let me in," he said in a louder voice.

"Henry, be quiet. Or I'll call the constables."

"They'll sympathize with me and knock the door in," he said. "Plus, I have diplomatic immunity."

She started to laugh, but still looked mad. Another few minutes of pleading by Henry did the trick, however. Laura said he could come in. But only for twenty minutes, she made him promise, and one cup of coffee. Or until Ann returned home, whichever came first. Considering Laura's mood when he arrived, this, too, was a triumph of diplomacy.

Half an hour later, after much small talk, Ann still had not walked through the door, Laura was calmer, and Henry was drinking a second cup of coffee.

Laura stifled a yawn. "You might at least do two things," she said to Henry Walters.

"And they are?" he asked.

"Promise me dinner tomorrow. No matter what."

"Promise," he said, but with a moment's hesitation.

"I'll starve myself between now and then," she said. "So we'll make it the Café Royale or the Savoy Grill."

"Laura! I struggle along on a diplomat's salary."

"Then it's a Dutch treat. I have money."

He opened his hands in amazement. "What can I say? I'm cornered." Clearly he loved this.

"Don't say anything," she said. "Just answer my second question."

"You have to ask it first."

"Since something similar may happen again, what happened tonight?"

"Nothing," he said, "that you should worry about."

She made a distasteful expression. "Henry? Do we trust each other or not?" Laura pulled away from him.

"Embassy business," he said.

"Not good enough, Henry," she countered with an arch tone of voice. "There's embassy business every day."

"Not like this."

"Don't tease me," she said in mock anger. "Or I'll tease you." She ran her hand from his knee to his crotch. She patted him gently and felt his penis react.

"Hey!" he said.

"See what I mean?"

"You're pumping me for information," he accused her.

She pulled her hand away. "Henry. I grew up in America the same as you did. You and I go to bed together. I count the time between the days that I see you. If you really want to know what I'm angry about, I was waiting all day to have a few hours alone with you. I wanted to go out, have a nice dinner, then go back to your flat and make love. I'd like to be your wife someday. But tonight something was more important to you than me. I want to know what it was, because maybe I'm wrong about us. Maybe we shouldn't see each other anymore." As a speech, it had been brewing for a while.

He looked away from her. She had a way of intimidating him, not the least by suggesting an end to their relationship on one hand and undying affection on the other.

He spoke softly. He tried to make what followed sound as important as possible. "If I tell you," he said, "you can't mention it to a soul."

"Who would I tell?" she answered sarcastically. "We don't know any of the same people."

"You have to promise."

"I promise."

"The U.S. is trying to get a man named Hans Zolling out of East Germany," he said. "The C.I.A. is sending a transit team from Vienna to Prague on Monday."

She waited for a moment, as if expecting him to come to a more breathtaking point. He didn't. "So?" she finally asked.

"So it's important," he said, mildly exasperated. "Zolling is an important defection. The transit team has Italian passports. They were outfitted here in the U.K. and we're using a British contact network in Czechoslovakia."

"All this for one man?" She shrugged.

"Take my word for it. It's important. It's not the type of thing that females understand. But it's import—" He stopped in mid-sentence. "What did you say?"

"About what?"

He paused awkwardly, not knowing whether or not to mention it. "About being my wife someday."

"Uh-oh. Shouldn't I have said that?"

"Well . . ." he stammered. "I don't know."

"Haven't you had some thoughts along the same lines?"

"Well, yes, but—"

Laura leaned to him and kissed him. Her whole personality seemed to change. Her indignation evaporated. "I'm sorry," she said. "I shouldn't assume anything."

"No, no," he said quickly. "It's all right. I—"

"Just forget it," she said indulgently. "Then maybe someday when the time is right you'll want to ask me. Then it can be a surprise. Okay?"

"Okay," he agreed after a moment's thought.

He kissed her in return. Laura glanced at the door and still didn't see her sister. She pushed her hand back to his crotch and teased him again.

"I think Ann's making a late night of it again," she said. "Another naughty American girl abroad." Laura giggled.

He picked up on her tone. "What are we coming to," he asked in amusement, "in terms of contemporary morality?"

She felt his penis pushing beneath his fly. "Maybe we have a little bit of time," she said. "Want to lock the door?"

Silly question. "Uh-huh," he agreed.

"Let's do it quickly," she said. "I'll show you what you could come home to every night if we *were* married."

Henry said he'd like that quite a bit. He undressed as Laura put a bolt latch across the door. And Ann Garrett, reliable Ann Garrett, had the good sense to stay away once again.

Then again, Henry Walters would have been pleased if Ann stayed away forever.

■
TWELVE
■

Helen O'Connell sat in the kitchen of the Oregon home she'd shared with her husband when she heard the knock at the front door. She jumped in alarm. She'd been reading a movie magazine. She'd been thoroughly engrossed by an article about Jane Wyman when the knocking jarred her back to reality.

She set down the magazine and remained perfectly still. She felt her heart pound in her chest.

God damn them all, she thought to herself. God damn the people who had shot her husband and left her alone with two young children. God damn the people in Washington Mark had worked for. And God damn whoever was at her door.

She barely breathed. She listened. She stood, careful not to be visible from any window, and moved slowly to the second drawer of a kitchen cabinet a few feet from her stove.

She pulled the drawer open. The knock came again. Helen's hand pushed its way past the tableware to a pile of paper napkins. From beneath the napkins she pulled one of her husband's thirty-eight-caliber pistols. Helen kept it loaded now, and always in the same room where she was.

The house had been broken into once already since Mark had been shot. It was clear to Helen that whoever had been after her husband wasn't finished. Well, so be it. The next person who threatened her or her family would catch a bullet. Mark would be proud of her.

She moved from the kitchen to the living room, the pistol in her hand. Whoever was knocking was still there. She moved stealthily through the front hall. She heard a male voice call.

"Hello? Anyone there?"

The chain was on the front door. All right. She held the gun aloft. She'd open the door and have a look.

Her hand was on the knob. She turned it, expecting the worse. So help her, if someone slammed a shoulder into the door, she'd shoot. Her palm was soaking against the handle of the gun.

She opened the door two inches. She stared blankly at the handsome man who stood before her in a hat and trench coat.

"Helen?" he asked. "Is that you?"

She blinked once, then recognized him. "Oh, God," she said in relief. "Tom? Tom Buchanan!" Her voice cracked.

"Helen, open up," he said consolingly. "It's only me. I'm alone."

"Oh, Lord! I don't believe it!"

She fumbled with the chain, unlocked the door, and pushed the pistol onto a side table. When Buchanan stepped into the house, Helen broke down into long, lamenting sobs and fell into his arms.

"They shot him, Tom," she cried. "They shot poor Mark and they broke into our home last week. I'm petrified. . . ."

Her voice then disintegrated into tears. Buchanan pushed the door shut behind him and kept Helen under an arm. He saw the pistol, locked the safety catch, and pushed it into his pocket.

"No one's going to do anything more to you," he reassured her. "Come on. Come sit down. Let's talk. The worst is over. We're going to make things better now."

Buchanan sat Helen in an armchair in her living room. When she calmed herself again, he went to the kitchen and found some tea. It was Earl Grey, and Thomas recalled from Chicago that this was what Mark O'Connell and his wife always favored. He brewed it and put the lights on in the house to dispense some of the gloom.

When he served the tea, she had stopped crying. A pile of tissues was in her lap. She dried her eyes and wrung her hands. The fingers of her left hand played with the wedding ring on her right.

"I can't tell you how happy I am to see a friendly face," she said. "It's tremendous that they let you come."

"I read the report Saturday morning," Buchanan said. "It was horrible."

"I didn't think anyone back east would care much about Mark. The Bureau drove him to quit, you know."

"That's what I figured. I can read between the lines of a Bureau document as well as anyone."

She looked at him strangely for a moment. "Are you here officially or on your own time, Tom?" she asked.

He answered diplomatically. "Both," he said. "Mark was my

mentor on my first assignment in Chicago, Helen. You remember that."

The memory of nicer days elicited a smile from her. "Indeed I do. Long, long ago. You were fresh out of the army. A child."

"It was only four years ago," he corrected her, but went along with her joke. "And I was twenty-nine years old."

She laughed and sipped her tea. Her hand was steady again. "My husband always said you were the best young agent in the Bureau. Everyone was heartbroken when they transferred you back east. But they send all their best men back east, don't they?"

"They sent me here today, didn't they?" he answered. "All the way from Philadelphia."

"Point," she said. "I'd forgotten how good you were with words too, Tom."

"If I remember," Buchanan said, "you're not bad with words either. That's why I thought I'd come by and talk."

"Three thousand miles? Just to talk?"

"I want to know who shot Mark," he said. "I'd want to know no matter what the circumstances were. But it also might break a case for me."

Helen nodded.

"Do you know who did it?" he asked.

She shook her head.

"Did Mark know?"

"He suspected something, Tom," she said, "even if he didn't completely understand it. The last cases he worked on didn't make sense to him. He had this instinct. This feeling that he'd been on to something."

Buchanan knew all about that instinct.

"He used to sit down in the basement late at night talking onto tapes," Helen told him. "He wanted to get everything down on record. In case something . . ."

Her voice trailed off.

"In case something happened to him," he said.

She nodded. "He sealed the tapes in a panel in the basement wall," she said. "I didn't even think much about them. Then"—her voice broke again, but she forged on—"three days after the shooting, someone broke in. Knew just where to go. Took the panel off the wall and stole every tape." That, she said, was when she sent her children away also. The two kids were staying with a brother and sister-in-law in Eugene.

"And you don't know what was on those tapes?" Buchanan asked. He stood and picked up the teapot. He poured more for both of them.

"Only Mark could tell you that," she said.

"But surely he told you things," Tom said. "I know he always used to. He used to sound you out on cases. He told me that in Chicago."

"Your memory is excellent," she said.

"Know what? Yours is probably just as good, Helen. Tell me what you remember. Then I'm going to tell you about a plan I have. I have an idea that might help everyone."

That was all the prodding Helen needed. Braced with a second cup of Earl Grey, she began to recount her husband's fall from grace within the Federal Bureau of Investigation.

He'd joined the Bureau in late 1936, she recalled, having put in two years before that with the Massachusetts state police. Thereafter, Special Agent O'Connell had put together a sterling record at every office to which he'd been assigned. In one year alone, 1938, he'd received three letters of commendation from the Director himself. Meritorious pay increases had come his way every six months, almost as regularly as clockwork. He'd done prewar tours of duty in Washington, D.C., Atlanta, and San Francisco, then went into the United States Marine Corps in 1942. He'd gone in as a second lieutenant. He'd come out a major with a fistful of medals. The bureau hired him back immediately and made him assistant SAC in Chicago, which is how he knew Tom Buchanan.

"It was after the war," Helen said, "that my husband went to 'sound school.' I encouraged it." She twisted her hands slightly. "I thought it would be safer than some other field work."

"Sound school" was a euphemism. Wiretapping and bugging was what it was, legal and otherwise. In the days after the war, particularly in the late 1940s, J. Edgar Hoover's personal radar began to intuit Commies, pinkos, lefties, and various fellow travelers under every bed. Eavesdropping was the "in" doctrine. The bureau used to watch, interrogate, and deduce; now it listened.

Mark O'Connell was one of the best listeners. Trouble was, he was also an independent thinker.

In Chicago the remnants of the Capone organization as well as several rival groups still ran lucrative businesses in gambling, prostitution, loan sharking, burglary, and hijacking. For sport, O'Connell invaded a few telephone junction boxes on both the north and south sides of the city. Had anyone wished to act, O'Connell had enough material after one week to break the biggest crime organization in the city. And since most of the crime was of an interstate nature, enforcement was clearly within the province of the F.B.I.

"But it was against Bureau policy, Tom," Helen said. "Mark couldn't believe it. But as far as the Bureau was concerned, the Mob didn't exist and the Mafia was a lurid figment of his imagination."

The orders came directly from Washington, she recalled. "Stop wiretapping guinea gangsters!" Hoover had roared into the phone to Bill St. Clair, the Special Agent in Charge in Chicago. "And give that O'Connell man a departmental rebuke for planting bugs we don't need."

It was O'Connell's first official chastisement in thirteen years. It would not be his last. O'Connell had spent his adult life fighting corruption as a civilian and fighting fascism as a soldier. He was one of those old-fashioned American Irishmen who combined conservative personal values with a keen sense of fair play and justice. It was why he and the younger Thomas Buchanan had seen eye to eye on so many things. They understood each other and shared the same view of the world.

"Chicago was a sewer," Helen said, emboldened for a moment. "Corrupt cops. Dishonest judges. We even wondered about the U.S. Attorney's office sometimes. You're lucky you didn't stay there, Tom."

"No city has a monopoly on corruption," he offered. "But please continue."

What Hoover really wanted was "glamour" stuff, big-time kidnappers and bank robbers, Helen remembered. Or at least, that was the first thing he coveted. "But what he wanted even more, Tom," she explained, "was statistics."

Buchanan felt a sinking sensation in his stomach. He knew exactly how the F.B.I.'s numbers game worked. "Shame on them all," he muttered.

Toward the end of each fiscal year, the gun would sound to start the new statistics race in each office. Hoover needed to petition Congress for a bigger budget every year and liked to display what he referred to as "new peaks of achievement." He was talking here of quantity, not quality. Heaven help the Bureau office that hadn't increased its numbers from the previous twelve months.

"They called Mark in the middle of the night once in February 1948," she said. "I was pregnant at the time. I was sick and I needed him. But Bill St. Clair was a Hoover crony and obviously wanted to be seen as disciplining Mark soundly. So he had my husband away for three nights straight planting microphones in the Chicago offices of the Progressive Labor Party. Do you know who they are, Tom?"

Buchanan nodded. "A bunch of homegrown socialists," he said.

Helen kept explaining. A few days later, she said, eleven members of the party were arrested for advocating the overthrow of the United States government. "Tom, these were a bunch of University of Chicago students and professors having their own little intellectual debate. They eventually pleaded guilty to some misdemeanor charge."

"But the Chicago office had eleven more arrests and convictions," Buchanan said.

That was the whole point, Helen agreed. And her husband let his feelings be known loud and clear what a waste of Bureau time this all seemed to be. It was not as if there was no real work to be done in the Windy City.

"These wop gangsters on the South Side have a piece of every truck and every crate of liquor that moves through this city," O'Connell had ranted. "And we're arresting college students."

"Don't buck Hoover," Bill St. Clair had warned, "and don't duck his instructions. The Director is all-powerful and he knows what he wants."

Unfortunately O'Connell had a trace of Gaelic irreverence within him, as well as a touch of the poet. "Buck him, duck him, and fuck him," O'Connell had retorted. That earned a second letter of rebuke for his personnel file, though he was fast becoming a living legend among other agents throughout the Midwest. O'Connell was not alone in wanting to do constructive law enforcement work.

O'Connell's views traveled quickly through the local F.B.I. bureaucrats who reported directly to Hoover. O'Connell thus received an official letter of censure from Washington. It was above the Director's own signature and left Mark O'Connell just a few more smart remarks away from being dismissed with prejudice. Then Bill St. Clair, who didn't like letters of censure arriving for anyone in his office, tried to defuse the situation. He instigated Mark O'Connell's transfer to Seattle, Washington. But there was a bit of spite to it:

The transfer was immediate, so that O'Connell would miss the birth of his second child. That, or he could resign.

"We were in no financial position for Mark to quit," Helen said. "Yet, we knew at that point he'd never get an honorable discharge from the Bureau."

But in a way, O'Connell and his wife welcomed the move to Washington State. The Chicago nonsense would be over. Their new location was pretty and peaceful. The pay was the same, but the hours were shorter and the money went farther. Things might have turned out all right, after all, had the Seattle office not been every bit as hell-bent for statistics as Chicago had been.

That led first to what many of the Seattle agents disparagingly called the Great Handsaw Caper.

Near the Krieger-McGhie army base just north of Seattle there was a government warehouse that stored used or obsolete carpentry tools. The warehouse was left over from the W.P.A. days. Security wasn't just lax, it was nonexistent. For one period of several weeks in the late spring of 1949, the main door was unlocked. It swung open and shut at will with the May breezes of the Pacific Northwest.

A number of people who lived in the area were in the habit of occasionally helping themselves to tools. A handsaw here. A screwdriver there. An odd wrench, crowbar, or wirecutter vanished into the night. It was not the type of thing that was going to make the republic fall. No one thought much about it. The warehouse was something of a free store, provided by Uncle Sam.

But then a couple of corporals at Krieger-McGhie began helping themselves to greater quantities of tools and selling them cheap to private establishments in Seattle. The tools were so old that they weren't even recognizable as government property, though the soldiers did represent them as legal military surplus. The Seattle police, almost as an afterthought, sent a memo about this to the local F.B.I. office. Mark O'Connell was put in charge of a squad of agents assigned to track the stolen goods.

"More bullshit" was how Mark O'Connell had described the assignment to Helen. But for a while he quietly set about his assignment. He went to several gas stations, mechanics, hardware stores, and carpentry outlets that had unwittingly received the filched goods. From each O'Connell took witness statements. O'Connell had twelve names of witness/recipients. None were considered by the investigating agents as culpable of any crime. Everyone involved, in fact, agreed to quickly return what he'd bought and to be helpful to the F.B.I.

"They *were* helpful to the F.B.I.," Helen said. "The head of the Seattle office was under pressure for big numbers, same as Chicago. So when he turned the names of the witnesses over to the Assistant U.S. Attorney, he authorized prosecution for receiving stolen property."

Buchanan listened with his lower jaw hanging open. But the story grew even worse. O'Connell was asked to form an apprehension team, complete with rifles and flak jackets to look good for the newspapers. This, to bust a dozen shopkeepers. But O'Connell was further told to wait to make arrests so that the twelve witnesses/recipients could be officially declared fugitives. Seattle was low on arrests of "fleeing felons" also.

Eventually ten of the twelve were convicted of relatively minor charges. None did jail time, though the two soldiers who'd resold the tools did six months apiece. And all contributed to some gorgeously inflated crime statistics issued by the Seattle office in 1949.

The Great Handsaw Caper was an operation rivaled locally only by what Mark called the Great Wobbly Witch Hunt. There was a domestic security division in the Seattle office and here again they needed wiretaps. Hoover wanted to know whether waterfront unions were being "infiltrated by Communists." And what better place to start than Seattle, where there resided dozens of veteran CPUSA members and aging "Wobblies," members of the Industrial Workers of the World who still clung to their rose-tinted memories of the 1930s.

No fewer than thirty-six agents from the Seattle office were assigned to the security squad. They spent their days shadowing a bunch of enfeebled, aging old Marxists, filling out surveillance forms, tapping private phones, reading mail the day before the addressee received it, and bugging their homes. Out of this came twenty-eight arrests for "security threats to the United States of America." Out of this also, Helen explained in great detail as she concluded, came Mark O'Connell's final and total disillusionment of the F.B.I. If this was what federal law enforcement was going to be in the 1950s, he wanted no part of it. He had two children to raise. O'Connell was a man who looked ahead in moral terms. Someday, when his kids were adults, he wanted to be able to look them in the eye.

Mark concluded the Wobbly investigation with a trip to San

Francisco. "There he stumbled across something that he referred to as Morning Glory," Helen said. "But he never told me anything about it. Shortly afterward, the police chief's job opened in Peterton, Oregon. He asked me if he should take it. I urged him to. We were sick of the Bureau and its politics. So Mark resigned from the Bureau. I had no idea, Tom, that the past would follow him. How would I know that he'd be shot? How could anyone know that? Yet somehow Mark must have suspected it. But how?"

"Instinct," Buchanan guessed.

"Instinct," Mark O'Connell's grieving wife concurred. Here was something else that she understood but couldn't explain.

It was past six in the evening. It was dark outside now. Helen and Thomas Buchanan had been talking for three hours.

"What I can't get over," Buchanan finally said, "is how lucky Mark was. I can't believe he survived the shooting."

"Have you been to the hospital yet?" she said.

Buchanan nodded. "I stopped there first," he said. "I wanted to say hello and wish him well. I met his doctor also." The surgeon bore the unlikely name of Sigmund Alan Hamburger. He was a southerner who'd studied at Emory University in Atlanta before taking his practice north. It had been Dr. Hamburger who had stitched the fallen Mark O'Connell back together on the Christmas Eve when he had been shot.

"A man name Walt Kowell saved Mark's life," said Helen. "Kowell drove a truck along the highway where the shooting took place. Apparently, when the truck's headlights came around the bend, the man and the woman who'd shot my husband fled right away. Otherwise . . ."

"Otherwise they would have finished what they'd begun," Buchanan said. "Particularly if they were there specifically to kill Mark." The coup de grâce—a final bullet in the brain—was all that was missing from the scenario. "And I think that's exactly why they were there. Whoever they were."

She nodded, then lowered her gaze.

"Helen," he said, "I want you to think about something. I have a plan that's going to seem very elaborate and very unorthodox. But I believe it will make your husband's life more secure, and yours as well. Similarly it may lead to the capture of the people who attempted to kill Mark—as well as whoever directed them."

Helen stared at her visitor. Her eyes were very tired, and pinkish from crying.

"Will you listen to my plan and consider it?" he asked. "I already have Dr. Hamburger's approval, as well as that of the state police and the F.B.I."

"Tom," she said. "I trust you more than any of them. Do you believe in what you're about to suggest? Or are these some crazy motions that you have to put all of us through?"

"I believe in this," he said.

"Then I'll go along with it too."

"Thank you," he said. "Let's go somewhere for dinner. Someplace quiet. We'll get a table away from everyone else and I'll tell you all about it."

"Oh, Tom. I couldn't. Not tonight."

But he was standing and insistent, offering his hand for her to rise as well as his moral support. "Come on, you must," he said. "It will do you good to get out. Mark would tell you so himself."

Faced with such logic, Helen agreed.

■
THIRTEEN
■

For a day in late January the sun was warm, even by the standards of southern California. For the first morning in more than a week—it had been that long since the horrendous evening with Joe Preston—Lisa had started a day without a drink or a pill, or both.

She reclined on a cloth-and-aluminum beach chair, the long type that allowed her to stretch out her legs. She wore a cotton sweater and a pair of blue shorts. She hid her eyes beneath dark glasses and a straw hat. For a few moments, as she felt the warmth of the sun against her skin, she almost felt at peace with herself.

She was on an isolated stretch of sand at Redondo Beach. It was a Sunday morning, and her husband was scouting locations nearby for his upcoming film. Lisa was mercifully alone, listening to the waves break and the occasional squawk of gulls. She was alone and thinking.

Recently Lisa had spent a lot of time reexamining her life, She thought about her school days back east and about her choice of acting as a career. She wondered how things would have gone if she'd stayed in New York and remained on the stage. She'd drop everything and go back there in an instant now, were it not for Jesse Chadwick and his threats. Everything, it seemed, from the movie she was about to shoot to the sex Joe Preston had forced upon her, now somehow emanated from her brutalizing husband.

And yet he had the nerve to be quoted in the newspapers on the subject of "cinema." What a filthy man. What a filthy life. What a filthy feeling Lisa had inside her.

The sun rose a little higher. She closed her eyes. Sleep at home was an occasional thing these days. Often Jesse interfered with that too. So this stretch of beach that she came to was a bit of a respite, even if her husband knew exactly where she was. Lisa stared out across the blue waves and saw a steamer on the horizon. She wished she were on it, no matter where it was going. Its destination looked more tranquil than hers.

Lisa had decided that she would kill herself. It was harder to come to grips with the fact that she would soon be dead. But that was the way it would be. Being dead would surely be less painful than living. It was just a matter of how she would do it. And when. She looked at those waves and wondered what it would be like to swim out as far as she could, until fatigue overtook her and the currents of the Pacific swallowed her.

Drowning. She didn't like the idea that her body might never be found. She wanted a good burial. And she wanted to leave a letter behind explaining why she had killed herself and who was to blame. And then there was the matter of timing. When would she do it? When would the effect be maximum?

Or, she wondered, should she kill Jesse first? Maybe she should get a gun, shoot her husband, and then go murder Joe Preston before turning the gun on herself.

The problem was putting the nose of a pistol to her head. She wasn't sure she could really pull the trigger. Same with murdering Jesse or Joe. The thought, horrendous as murder was, appealed to her. But could she really do it?

No, she decided, there was really only one way. She would write out her suicide note, send copies to the appropriate people, lock herself in a hotel room, and take every one of the laudanum capsules.

That would do it. She'd been checking the medical texts in the library recently. Fifty capsules would do the job. Fifty capsules would have her dead in an hour.

Lisa looked at her legs. She raised one and then the other, examining them critically. Years ago, when she was seventeen, a stocking manufacturer wanted her to model for his advertisements. Perfect legs, the man said she had. He wasn't a wolf or a playboy or anything. He had seen her legs on an afternoon when she'd been playing tennis. He had introduced himself and left a business card. Her father, however, would hear none of it. No modeling for any daughter of his. No acting either. Undignified, he said. Tasteless. Not worthy of his family.

Dad, if you could see me now, she thought to herself. The slave of a boorish movie director, swapped to an animal of a producer, lying on a California beach contemplating the most effective manner of suicide. She felt like dirt.

Contemplating the end of her life returned Lisa to thoughts of earlier, happier times. Childhood, in retrospect, had seemed idyllic for a while. The family was happy and well off. There had been no deprivation, no abuse. Just a family that loved each other. Mom, Dad, and kids. It had been that way for many years until—

Lisa Pennington glanced down the beach. Two hundred yards away there was a figure walking in her direction. At first, with alarm, she thought it was Jesse. It would have been just like him to follow her here, to intrude on the little corner of the world that remained as her sanctuary. Then, to her considerable relief, she realized that the intruder was a woman.

Yet Lisa knew better than to take her eyes off her. She stared as the woman walked closer. The stranger was wearing a straw hat and a brightly colored striped dress. With one hand the woman held her hat on so that no breeze could take it. With the other arm she seemed to be clutching something against her body. A purse, perhaps. Or a book or a small bag.

Without moving her head Lisa stared for several seconds more. Then she began to relax. She didn't know the woman. Chances were, the stranger just was taking a stroll on the beach, enjoying the California outdoors, same as Lisa.

Lisa set her head back and closed her eyes. Where would she be buried, she wondered. Where would her possessions go? What would death be like? Should she bother to write a will? If heaven existed, who would she see there whom she knew?

Many years ago she'd been engaged to a young man. She'd

given him her virginity and they'd exchanged their vows of love. Then one day he'd disappeared from her life, never to return. Unlike some young women her age, enjoying a new freedom after the war, she hadn't made love to another man until she'd met her husband-to-be. Now that seemed like a mistake too.

Her thoughts floated and drifted. They were as free as she would like to have been. Lisa savored the warmth of the sun upon her bare skin. She was still very pretty. She felt she'd have a lot to give if a decent man were ever interested in her. Why couldn't she just spend time relaxing in the sunlight with a man she loved?

Then she realized again that there would never be such a man. No self-respecting man would even want her considering what had happened to her, and what she'd turned into. And maybe it didn't matter anyway. This, she concluded, was her fate. What did one more premature death mean in a world in which twenty million people had just died in global warfare?

Several minutes passed peacefully. She wondered if she should go to church once again before she died, just in case there was something to that whole Lutheran orthodoxy that she'd grown up with. As she thought, her only sensations were a gently drifting motion that frequently preceded sleep, plus the sound of the ocean and the gentle touch of breezes playing across her skin.

Then she was aware of a shadow crossing her face.

"Hello." A woman spoke from close by.

Lisa's eyes opened. The woman in the brightly colored dress was standing next to her.

"Sorry," the woman said. "Did I startle you?"

Lisa looked carefully at her face but didn't recognize her. "I was asleep," Lisa said. "Or almost asleep."

"Sorry again," the woman said. "You're Lisa, aren't you?"

"That depends. Who are you?"

The woman smiled weakly. "I've been looking for you. Your husband said I'd find you here."

"Who are you and what do you want?"

"Well, Lisa," she said with labored intimacy, "I just want to talk to you for a moment. I have a job to do. Mind if I sit down?"

Lisa didn't answer. The stranger sat down on the far end of the beach chair. She opened the cloth bag she carried and pulled out a notebook and pencil, setting the bag on the sand.

"I'm Esther Greeb," she said. "I'm a publicist for RKO Studios. I was told the *wonderful* news that *Hold the Phone!* goes into production at our studios in two weeks. That means we need to get together your publicity bio *immediately* so that we can start getting you in the newspapers."

"I don't want to be in the newspapers," Lisa said with contempt.

"The press is a marvelous source of free publicity," Esther said. "And you know what? They *want* to like you."

Lisa leaned back in her chair, a wave of despondency upon her. She slid the hat down over her eyes. "It's a Sunday morning, Esther," she said. "That might not mean anything to you, but it means something to me."

"One of my favorite times to work," the publicist said. "I'm so glad I caught you in a free moment. We can get to know each other better."

Lisa moved the hat from her eyes. "I don't want to know you," she said. "Don't you understand English? I want you to go away."

"I'm afraid I can't."

"Why not?"

"I don't have a salary, Lisa. Nor do I have a contract to become a star like you do. Nor do I have a wealthy husband. I lost my husband in the war, I have two children, and I get paid only if I get your bio sheets together this weekend. I don't loll around on the beach waiting to become a movie star, I fight to make ends meet. Do you understand what I'm saying?"

"I understand you perfectly since you're shouting."

"Lisa, I don't just walk away. I can't. I need this interview."

Lisa moaned. "Fifteen minutes, Esther. Then leave me alone."

Esther had her pad out and began writing. "Where are you from originally, Lisa?"

It took Lisa several seconds to answer. "Wallingford, Connecticut," she said.

"Where's that?"

"Connecticut or Wallingford?"

"Wallingford."

"Near New Haven." She paused to think, then her account of things came more readily. "But I grew up in Michigan. My mother still lives there."

"Is her name Pennington?"

"No. It's Ellison. Mrs. Margaret Ellison."

"Then Ellison is your real name, Lisa?"

Lisa looked askance at Esther. "You're not going to print my real name, are you?"

"Lisa, dear. Some of these questions are for the studio employment records. You'll have a chance to take a good hard look at anything we write before the press sees it."

"Is that a promise?"

"A solemn promise, Lisa dear."

Lisa closed her eyes and imagined as she spoke. "My mother is remarried. Her name now is Ellison. Lisa Pennington is my stage name. I first started using it when I was acting off-Broadway in New York. Before that," she said, "I was Doris Elizabeth Oelsner of Wallingford, Connecticut."

"Doris Elizabeth . . . ?"

"O-e-l-s-n-e-r," Lisa said. "Doris Oelsner. Doesn't have quite the memorable ring as Lisa Pennington, does it?"

Esther was writing furiously.

"Don't print it," Lisa requested again.

"Do you have brothers or sisters?"

"A brother," said Lisa. "He's with the navy. Stationed with the U.S. Sixth Fleet in the Mediterranean."

Esther was writing furiously. "And your parents?" she asked.

"Mom is a third grade schoolteacher back in Michigan," Lisa said. "My father was an electrician. Had his own shop. He died in the war."

"I'm sorry," she said.

"Normandy," Lisa said. "A week after D-Day."

"Terrible," Esther said, her hand not missing a phrase. "Damned Germans."

"Oelsner is a German name," Lisa said very sharply.

"Oh, of course, dear!" Esther looked up, on the defensive at last. "What I meant was, damned Nazis!"

"Don't confuse the two," Lisa said.

"I won't. What do you like to do, Lisa?" she asked, not missing a beat. "You like to act, obviously. Sports?"

"I play tennis."

"You look like a smart girl too. Let's put down that you like to read also. Let's make this good," she said thoughtfully. She knew what she needed. "What books shall we say you've read recently? How about *The Sound and the Fury* by F. Scott Fitzgerald?"

"That's William Faulkner."

Esther paused. "Are you sure?"

"He won the Nobel Prize this past year. I'm sure."

"Fitzgerald did? He worked on some scripts at RKO before the war."

"Faulkner did," Lisa said. "*Faulkner* won the Nobel Prize."

"Oh. Well," she said, starting to scribble again, "let's put a Fitzgerald book in too. He's popular. Can you think of one?"

"How about *Gatsby*?"

"That's a good choice, Lisa. It's well-known." She stopped writing. "What's the full title again?"

On it went for far longer than fifteen minutes. Lisa talked freely thereafter and Esther wrote everything in her notebook. The sun rose higher in the sky and the day grew warmer. Lisa pushed up her sleeves and tilted back her hat. A winter tan made anyone feel better. And in a weird sort of way, Lisa enjoyed the bubble-headed banter back and forth, fraudulent and insincere as it all was. Sly, mendacious Esther wouldn't be confused with an atomic scientist, but her companionship wasn't all that bad either. It took Lisa's mind off everything else.

The publicist felt she had enough by a few minutes after noon. She thanked Lisa, closed her notepad, and dropped it and her pencils back into her tote bag. "See you soon," she said when the interview was over. She gave a faint wave.

"Yeah," Lisa answered. "See you," she agreed, knowing she wouldn't. She watched Esther turn and walk down the beach. The publicist retreated faster than she'd advanced.

Esther turned in the biographical material to RKO two days later. The publicity people in Hollywood rewrote it, added whatever they felt would appeal to the public, and coupled it with a still photograph of Lisa that had been taken on the beach in France the previous summer. RKO's intention was to get some newspaper space as soon as possible for Lisa, to build her into a future star before *Hold the Phone!* was even in motion before Jesse Chadwick's cameras. A pretty face, a nice figure, and familiarity before the public were key ingredients.

As for the press release that followed—picture, bio, and all— no one ran it past Lisa. No one showed her anything that it contained. Out it went to 215 newspapers and magazines.

Of course Esther Greeb had known that the studio system worked this way. Esther was married to one of RKO's armada of creative accountants. Esther Greeb dabbled in writing press releases only for some extra dollars. She had one child, a chubby little boy named Jason, and he was well supported by his father. They lived in Pacific Palisades and had no struggle at all to make ends meet. So much for truth in the acquisition of an interview.

Then again, Lisa had been around long enough to know what to expect as well. She'd told a self-serving fib here and there, and had believed not a word fed to her by Esther Greeb. In point of fact, Lisa was more concerned with enjoying the early afternoon sunlight than with the contents of a puff piece for the newspapers.

The biographical notes probably wouldn't appear until after she was dead, Lisa reasoned. And what difference would they make to anyone—most of all her—at that point?

■

FOURTEEN

■

Unlike southern California, the states of Oregon and Washington sat under a layer of clouds and heavy drizzle. Thomas Buchanan used an F.B.I. car on loan from the Portland, Oregon, office to drive Helen to Good Samaritan Hospital, where her husband lay. Dr. Hamburger had called an hour earlier that morning. The news was not good.

The emergency care unit was on the hospital's second floor. Thomas and Helen rode up in the main elevator. Somehow, two reporters from the Portland newspapers who had been covering the case had caught wind of a change in the patient's condition. They were seated in a visitor's lounge when Thomas and Helen came out of the elevator.

"Mrs. O'Connell . . . ?" one of them called.

Thomas glanced at them. One of the men was removing his hat. News of the patient's fate had traveled fast. Fast and unofficially.

"Not now," Buchanan said, waving them away. "Keep walking," he said to Helen. Helen looked as if she were starting to sense the worst.

Dr. Hamburger was stepping out of his office when he looked up and saw the F.B.I. agent with the wife of his patient. His expression never changed. Hamburger was an imposing, authoritative figure in a white lab coat and stethoscope. He was in his early forties, thick but muscular and handsome. He was also all-business, though he appeared sad.

"Doctor . . . ?" Helen said.

"Why don't you come into my office?" the surgeon said consolingly.

"Doctor. Tell me now," she said.

The reporters stood nearby. Thomas took Helen's hand. Dr. Hamburger looked her squarely in the eye. "I'm sorry," he said. "Your husband went into an abrupt cardiac arrest this morning at six-thirty. He passed away half an hour ago."

Buchanan was watching Helen's face as the news hit her. "Oh, God . . ." she said. Her expression disintegrated with sadness. She swayed and Buchanan steadied her.

"I'm sorry," Dr. Hamburger said. "Everything that could have been done was."

Helen started to cry. "I thought he was pulling through," she said.

"He was a strong, brave man," Hamburger said. "He fought like hell for his life and to stay here with you and your family. He's with God now, Mrs. O'Connell. Again, I'm sorry."

The staff nurses went on their way. An older nurse, stocky with gray hair, came to Helen's side to assist her.

"Maybe we could sit down in private," Thomas suggested.

"There's a Catholic chapel on the first floor," the nurse said.

"Thank you," Buchanan said softly. "I know that will be of comfort."

"Please," said Dr. Hamburger. "Use my office."

Buchanan led Helen to the doctor's office, where he sat her down. Her husband's body had already been removed, Hamburger said. He was awaiting further instructions.

"I can make the proper arrangements through the F.B.I.," Buchanan said.

"That would be excellent," Hamburger answered.

Helen sat quietly. Hamburger dropped his sturdy frame into a swivel chair behind his desk.

"You have to realize," he said, "most patients don't have the visibility that we've had in this case."

"I understand," Buchanan said. "Most patients aren't former F.B.I. agents gunned down on state highways."

"Thank God for that," Hamburger said. He turned to Helen.

"I'm sure Mr. Buchanan explained the situation to you, Mrs. O'Connell," Hamburger said. "I was on loan to this hospital from the military facility in Shannon, Washington. I was covering a shortage of surgeons for two weeks at the time when your husband was brought in."

Helen nodded.

"I'll be returning to Shannon tonight," Hamburger said. "And I'll be resuming my assignment to the Veterans' Hospital there starting Monday morning at eight."

Helen understood. She turned to Buchanan. "Can we do the funeral tomorrow?" she asked. "I'd like to have this over with. I'm going to leave the children with my sister. No point in getting everyone worked up."

Buchanan nodded again. He had two or three trusted friends from Washington and Chicago who would be arriving in Oregon later that day. They would take care of everything, as well as assist in the continuing investigation.

Helen said that sounded acceptable to her. From her point of view, she just wanted what was best for her husband. That, and she wanted this to be over.

The funeral service for Chief of Police Mark O'Connell was held in Peterton, Oregon. The Mass was celebrated at St. Mary's Roman Catholic Church and the coffin was closed. The town could remember how her husband looked in life, Helen said. There were representatives of the Oregon state police as well as O'Connell's two deputies. Bill Lucy, the former Peterton chief of police, was there also. He looked stunned. Most of the adult citizens of the town of Peterton were present. Many wept openly.

A few of Mark O'Connell's relatives from back east were expected, but none came. O'Connell had a brother in Natick, Massachusetts, who cited the difficulty and expense of traveling in the winter. A sister who lived in Arkansas couldn't be reached. Mark's only other brother had died in Germany during the war. Thomas Buchanan and three other agents who had flown west to assist represented the Federal Bureau of Investigation.

The burial was at a new Catholic cemetery on the east end of Peterton. The service was held in a steady rain beneath a canopy of wet black umbrellas. A young priest named Father Raley from St. Mary's Parish conducted the final part of the service at the graveside. Fortunately the temperature was above freezing and the interment was not delayed by frozen earth, as many January burials are.

Afterward, Thomas Buchanan made a brief statement to some of the reporters present. He said that while the F.B.I. remained active in the case, Mark O'Connell's failure to survive his wounds left police with few clues. Chief O'Connell had remained unconscious from the time of the shooting until his death, said Buchanan. The statements, for what they were worth, were reported in the newspapers on the West Coast that still followed the case. The Oregon State Sheriff's Association also posted a reward of $2500 for information leading to the capture and conviction of the killers.

Later that same day Buchanan helped Helen temporarily close the O'Connell house. As she packed some of her possessions— clothes, jewelry, cosmetics, and even some of her movie and film magazines—Buchanan nailed the ground floor windows shut, drained the pipes, and shut down the furnace. He also installed alarms at the doors. Chief Lucy and his deputies said they'd drive by a few times a day, just to keep an eye on things.

Helen told friends in town that she'd be going back east for a short time, better to get over the shock of the loss. She'd be taking a bus to Portland, then flying to Chicago. There her sister would meet her and she would be reunited with her children. As for staying in Peterton in the future, she hoped to. It was a nice community, she said.

All of that made perfect sense to everyone. Yet, Walt Kowell, the truck driver who'd been credited with saving Mark O'Connell's life—temporarily at least—might have had an inkling that something was amiss, had he thought about it.

Toward four-thirty that afternoon, Thomas Buchanan packed Helen and several of her suitcases into his car, the Ford that he had on loan from the Portland field office. Kowell and his twelve-wheel diesel rig came to a stop sign at the same moment on the state highway leading out of town, not too far from the lumber company. It was just before dusk. Kowell had spent a few hours with Buchanan; the F.B.I. agent had meticulously taken a lengthy statement from the trucker as to what he'd observed at the scene of the shooting. So the two men knew each other.

Kowell gave a friendly, respectful wave to Thomas and Helen. They reciprocated. Then Kowell continued on his way. It never occurred to him for a second that Buchanan, despite all of Helen's suitcases in the back of the Ford, couldn't possibly have been taking her to the bus depot. The terminal was on the south side of Peterton. And the F.B.I. vehicle was on the state highway heading north. In point of fact, the car was going in the direction of Washington State.

But Walt Kowell didn't think much about that at all. Buchanan, the F.B.I. agent, had seemed like a straightforward type, sort of an everyday stand-up guy. He'd be incapable of deceiving a town of good Americans. In fact, Kowell held the opinion shared by most Americans. The members of the F.B.I. were all pretty unimpeachable types, from J. Edgar Hoover right on down. So he attached no significance at all to what he'd seen.

But forgetting the events of that day would not be as easy for Thomas Buchanan. He would, in the years that followed, look back upon that dreary day in early February as a turning point in the investigation of John Garrett and Commonwealth Penn.

Before leaving Oregon, Buchanan had placed a long distance call back to Philadelphia. Across a static-ridden telephone line, he learned that Bill Roth had been eagerly waiting for the call.

Bill Schafft, one of the clerical researchers assigned to the Garrett case, had managed to obtain all the recent Smith College alumni bulletins. Listed in a spring 1949 bulletin was a notice on Laura Garrett. It said she was enjoying living in London and working for a jewelry concern.

"London what?" Buchanan asked.

"London, England, Tom. Ever been there?"

"After the war," he said.

"Lovely country. Wonderful people. Terrible food, just like here. You'll enjoy your visit."

"What are you talking about?" Buchanan asked. "England?"

"Correct. We checked with the British Consulate in New York. Laura has a visa to be in the United Kingdom. We even have an address."

"What about her sister?" The static crackled heavily again across the long distance line.

"Nothing on Ann yet," Roth said.

Buchanan considered it. "I'm not finished here yet," he said. "I still have one key witness to talk to."

"Can you get him today?"

"No. Not for several more days."

"Then you'll have to go back," Roth instructed. "Now, listen closely. We'll have a passport ready for you by Wednesday. But don't come back to Philadelphia. Get a plane to Washington as soon as you can."

"Why Washington?"

"Someone near the top wants to talk to you directly. Do I need to name names?"

"Hoover?"

"You said it. I didn't."

Buchanan felt a surge of anxiety. Rarely were agents called before the Director in person. And when they were, the circumstances were always extreme, good or bad.

"I have to tell you, Tom," Roth concluded, "I don't know what you might have accomplished out there in America's rain forest, but all hell looks like it's about to break out on this case. For your own sake and everyone else's, you better have something positive to report damned soon. I think there's a war party brewing at headquarters."

Buchanan set down the phone. He looked at it for several seconds and pondered the silence. What could Hoover have to say? Why were things heating up in Washington? And for that matter, what would he, Tom Buchanan, have to say to Laura Garrett after all these years?

He exuded a long sigh and stepped away from the telephone. Then another wave of anxiety started to come over him, knowing as he did that if Laura could be located, he was that much closer to her father. And for that matter, though he tried to push the thought away, he was that much closer to Ann Garrett also.

■
FIFTEEN
■

Detective Fred Castelli of the Philadelphia police department slammed down his telephone and stared straight ahead. "Son of a bitch," he snarled to himself. He felt outright pain rising from the center of his chest.

For several minutes he stared out the dirty window of his office. Then he picked up the file in front of him, left his desk, and walked down the corridor to Captain Heintz's office. He found Heintz's door ajar. The captain was standing at his desk staring at his own paperwork.

"Hey, Cap," Castelli said, knocking. "Got a minute?"

Heintz said he did. Castelli entered and sat down.

"What's bothering you?" Heintz said.

"That Chinaman," he said. "Barrier Point. New Year's morning."

It took Heintz a moment. "Oh, yeah. What about him?"

"I was writing the final report," Castelli said. "I wanted to put in the name and address of the Chinese who claimed the body. I couldn't find the address he gave me at the M.E.'s office, but I had the passport number. So I called the British Consulate in New York. Like we did last time."

"And?"

"His passport was a forgery. And the address he gave was a fake."

Now it was Heintz's turn to stare for a moment. Castelli expanded. He had called the British Consulate in New York. But when he mentioned the name and passport again, he was put through to a security officer. After Castelli had called previously, someone noticed something familiar about the passport number. It had been reported stolen the previous week. A cursory check at the time would have revealed this, but on a Sunday morning no one was empowered to do much of anything. And no one had called the Philadelphia police back because the police hadn't left a number. The British did make one follow-up inquiry on Monday, but the query went to the wrong division in Philadelphia. That had been the end of it.

"Sloppy all around," said Heintz.

Castelli nodded. "Yes, sir." The implications hung in the air and taunted them both.

"Shit!" Heintz muttered. "That means the identification of the body is suspect also."

Castelli nodded. "*More* than suspect," he said.

"What happened to the body?" Heintz asked.

"It was released to 'Mr. Lee.' From there I don't know."

"Did you ever check in our own Chinatown?" Heintz asked.

"We never knew he was Chinese until the body was claimed, Cap," Castelli said. "If we canvas Chinatown, we'll get the usual results. As soon as you show a shield they don't speak English."

"Yeah. Of course." Heintz rubbed his eyes. "I hate walking away from a murder case," he said. "Even if it's a chink murder case."

"Hey, Cap, look," Castelli said. "Mike and me can stay on it, but Jesus Christ, talk about being at square one. No witnesses. No identification. No dental records. No legitimate missing person's report."

Heintz lit a Chesterfield and considered his squad's options. "Write up what you can," he decided. "Mark it John Doe, but you'll have to keep it on your desk for a few months. How many other cases do you and Mike have?"

"Five. We normally carry six."

"Okay. You get the next thing that comes from South Philly or Center City. Put the Chinaman on the back burner. But keep your eyes open in case any other Chinese turn up torched. It might be the chinky way of welcoming in the new year."

"They have a different new year, Cap."

"I meant it as a joke."

"Oh." He laughed.

"Get out of here. Would you?"

"Yes, sir."

Castelli was on his feet and quickly out the door. But as he trudged back to his own office, he felt his anger building. The body of an unidentified man had been claimed by a second unidentified man. Further, the second Chinaman had played him for a fool. Castelli knew he should have known there was something amiss when the claimant showed up early on a Sunday morning. In a decade and a half as a homicide detective, no one had ever turned up on a Sunday morning two weeks after the fact to claim a corpse. It was his job to notice what was out of the ordinary and to note its significance. Now, unlike before, he realized that there probably was nothing random about the slaying at Barrier Point.

Castelli spent the first week of February immersed in his work. A man turned up dead in a bathtub at the Bellevue Stratford Hotel on February 6. Castelli and Proley drew the case. They had the victim, an attorney from New York, traced to a pair of hookers within twenty-four hours and had busted the girls' pimp for murder within another forty-eight.

He should have been pleased, but wasn't. The more he thought about the Barrier Point case, the larger it loomed. Once, toward dusk, he drove to Barrier Point and walked the area by himself, seeking inspiration.

Then, later that same week, other thoughts of a more global nature started to unsettle him.

The Communists, entrenched in Soviet Russia for a third of a century, had set off an atomic bomb the previous September. And just the previous week the Russians had boycotted a meeting of the United Nations Security Council because their atheistic pals, the Red Chinese, had been denied admission to the world body.

But there had also been much in the news recently about Communists in America and how, according to some, the Red Menace was chewing away at the fabric of the nation. While Joe Doe was more concerned with new cars, low mortgage rates, and the booming postwar prosperity, there was apparently serious Communist infiltration into labor unions, newspaper publishing, and broadcasting. And everyone knew that universities were filled with Communists, particularly history, English and poli sci departments. As if to prove the point, eleven Marxists had been convicted in New York in 1949 for conspiring to overthrow the government, and Alger Hiss had been convicted of perjury just that January, a scant three weeks after the burning at Barrier Point.

Castelli searched for a method in these events, a pattern that he could carry over into his personal life. But he couldn't find one. He couldn't see one, that is, until the tenth of February, a Friday.

On that afternoon the detective read a story on the front page of the Philadelphia *Inquirer*. The previous evening in Wheeling, West Virginia, Senator Joseph McCarthy had addressed a Republican women's club. In his speech McCarthy maintained that he had a list of 205 "card-carrying" members of the Communist Party who were employed in the State Department of the United States. McCarthy's speech, and the allegations therein, catapulted the Wisconsin senator to national prominence. He was on every radio, appeared on television for those lucky Americans who had one, and was on the front page of every newspaper. He gave voice to fears that every good American entertained. And if nothing else, Fred Castelli was a good American.

In the days that followed, as the senator and his aides scurried around Washington trying to find documentation for their charges, Detective Fred Castelli began to look upon the Communist threat to the United States with a new seriousness. And, pledged to never again overlook a curious circumstance, he began to sense a strange design in the murder at Barrier Point. The Chinese were Communists these days, weren't they? Communists were infiltrating America, weren't they? The Reds were spying on Americans, weren't they? The man who had been torched had been found right next to a U.S. Navy yard, hadn't he? And he was Chinese, wasn't he?

"Coincidence maybe," answered Mike Proley when Castelli began to concoct his new perception of things.

"Coincidence, horseshit!" Castelli snapped. The dead man, he was sure, had been a Red agent of some sort.

"Uh-huh," said Proley, gently indulging his partner.

But Castelli pulled the case from the rear of his desk and began to carry it with him everywhere he went. It was off the back burner and onto the front. This business of Communists took on a new urgency for him, and he had Senator McCarthy to thank.

His only problem was the one he'd had all along. He had no angle on the case and nowhere to go with it.

"Just a bunch of halfwit theories," Mike Proley taunted him on the morning of Lincoln's birthday, 1950. "Enough to have you chasing your own ass for months. Then again, who else would chase your ass?"

"Fuck you, Proley," Castelli answered. "Fuck all of you. This case I'm going to solve."

J. Edgar Hoover had the blood of martyrs in his eye.

Special Agent Buchanan was shown into Hoover's private office in F.B.I. headquarters by Assistant Director Frank Lerrick. Hoover stared at the special agent as Buchanan took his place at the other side of a small round table. Lerrick seated himself in a chair away from the table behind Hoover.

"Good morning," Hoover snapped.

"Good morning, sir."

"Give me an update on the Garrett investigation. I want to hear everything."

Methodically Buchanan began a detailed recapitulation of his entire investigation, starting with the initial inquiries in D.C. and Philadelphia, and leading to Oregon and Washington. As he spoke, conscious of the sound of his own voice reverberating off the bare walls in the sparse conference room, he was aware that Hoover was listening not so much to what he said as for what he didn't say. Yet Buchanan knew better than to elaborate. Hoover had a way of jumping all over any small detail.

Hoover wore a gray suit with white pinstripes. A handkerchief was positioned perfectly in his breast pocket. His shirt was white and crisply starched, his tie red and striped. The Director sat quietly, staring intently at the young agent in his employ. Hoover's hair was slicked back, and his dark crescent eyebrows were frowning downward. The features of his face were contorted into a belligerent scowl. In the midst of his monologue, Buchanan was struck by the observation that Hoover resembled an angry version of Mr. Toad of Toad Hall. Buchanan came to the conclusion of his report.

"So you have no definitive break in the case yet?" Hoover asked.

"No, sir." Mentally Buchanan was ready for trouble.

Hoover pursed his lips. "When do you think you might have one?"

Buchanan stuck by his instincts. "I couldn't promise, Mr. Director."

Hoover tapped a finger on the conference table. Buchanan knew it was a less-than-friendly gesture. "I'm told that you've requisitioned hundreds of dollars for a trip to England."

"That's correct, sir."

Hoover looked as if he were about to explode. "Using Bureau money for a trip to a foreign land?" he snorted. "Suppose you were hauled in front of Congress, young man! How the living hell would you justify an expense like that? Tell me that!" he roared suddenly. "Right now!" The Director's face was crimson.

"I'd justify it by the merits of this investigation, Mr. Director," Buchanan answered. His voice was calm and unhesitant, but beneath his suit jacket his shirt was soaking wet. "This is an investigation which may have overtones beyond the boundaries of the United States, and may involve national security. Given that situation, we have to follow where our investigation leads us. I have no apologies."

Hoover drew back in his wooden armchair. He turned to Lerrick and smiled. "That's perfect," he said. "That's just what Congress should hear."

For a moment Buchanan thought the remark was sarcastic. Then he realized that Hoover meant it.

The Director moved around to face Buchanan again.

"Have you been following the newspapers, Special Agent Buchanan?"

"I try to, sir."

"It's important that you do," Hoover said. "Senator Joseph McCarthy is a close personal friend of mine. He made a very important speech the other night in West Virginia. The senator is alarmed —as we all are—about the infiltration of Communist agents into our political system. The fact is, the senator used the number of two hundred five as the total number of agents he feels are currently in the State Department. Now some of the left wing press is taking him to task for an exact count. The number here isn't really important, Mr. Buchanan. What's important is that Communists are seeking to overthrow our government and Senator McCarthy is standing up to them."

Buchanan remained silent. He sensed he knew where the conversation was headed.

"These are difficult times," the Director resumed. "Enemies of this country are everywhere. Its friends must stick together." He paused for what seemed like an hour. It was probably closer to twenty seconds. "John Taylor Garrett has been a generous benefactor to the Democratic Party both nationally and within the state of Pennsylvania for at least a dozen years. Pictures exist of Garrett with Roosevelt and Truman. Imagine the embarrassment of the political left in this country," Hoover suggested, "if it were revealed that Garrett was a Soviet sympathizer."

Hoover clearly relished the idea. He let it hang in the air. Buchanan managed to stifle his disgust for Hoover's partisan instincts. Frank Lerrick looked as if he were seated at a poker table. No expression whatsoever.

Hoover felt he'd made his point. He was on to the next one.

"Similarly, Mr. Buchanan," said Hoover. "This Bureau has received some criticism in certain congressional quarters about operations outside of the United States. There have even been suggestions that the bureau is incapable of handling foreign intelligence as well as domestic."

Frank Lerrick always knew when to add a sentence in support of the Boss. "Truman wants to permit this new Central Intelligence Agency to handle *all* foreign work," Lerrick intoned. "Nothing for us, in other words. We're suppose to sit by while the C.I.A. allows subversives to take over the country." The disdain in his voice was clear.

"The last thing we need, or this country needs, is a rival intelligence service," Hoover said. "But what we do need, right now," he said with rising emphasis, "is the revelation of a Communist agent close to the Truman administration. That would be perfect. And if the case were made by virtue of work abroad, so much the better. It would show that the F.B.I. can and should operate anywhere in the world." Hoover studied the special agent before him. "When do you leave for England?" he asked in conclusion.

"Tomorrow, sir."

The Director's tone of voice softened strangely. "And what are your thoughts? About this case, I mean? Is this a big-league case or midget potatoes? Are we after a spy or not?"

"Sir, I've spent almost a month on nothing else," Buchanan said. "And I don't know yet. I'm not sure, either way."

Hoover grinned. "You're on a hot trail, son," he said indulgently. "It's just a matter of time. Go to England. Do your best, but for God's sake, *come home convinced*! Understand?"

"Yes, sir."

"Also, be sure to check your weapon before you leave. The Brits are squishy about letting our people bring guns into the country. What do you carry?"

"A Colt thirty-eight, sir. Standard issue."

"Ever had to use it?"

"No, sir."

"The day will come," Hoover said. "Thank you. Get moving and good luck."

The Director didn't shake hands. Instead, he lowered his gaze to a series of files before him. In more ways than one, Buchanan knew it was time to leave.

SIXTEEN

isa Pennington sat by herself on the edge of a living room set in RKO Studio Number 6. Across her lap were the most recent script revisions for *Hold the Phone!* If there was one thing that Lisa was not in the mood for today, it was light comedy. If there was a second thing she was not in the mood for, it was her husband. If there was a third, it was Joe Preston. Unfortunately the day would be filled with all three.

Her co-star was an aging leading man who'd been a matinee idol in the late 1930s but whose celebrity had faded during the war. His real name was Damon Forbes. His friends and acquaintances called him by that name, but the public knew him by something more famous and more memorable. He worked less frequently now but took any job offered. Worldwide he still had a reputation, meaning a producer such as Joe Preston was that much closer to several foreign sales by employing him, as long as the actor stayed sober. Lisa had met Damon for the first time the previous weekend.

"I always have an affair with my leading lady," he announced two minutes into their acquaintanceship.

"This time will be an exception, Damon," she said.

"I'll talk to Jesse about it," he said. She knew what he meant. Inside, she burned. The stories about her and Joe Preston had already made the rounds, promulgated primarily by Preston.

"When you do," Lisa replied sweetly, "tell him he can screw himself too."

"I wouldn't say anything like that to Jesse," the actor said. "Not with his connections back in New York."

"Then don't say anything to him at all," she said. "And aside from when we're shooting, don't say anything to me either."

Sitting on the edge of the set on this, the first day of principal photography, she watched the same man make his entrance. She knew he'd probably never read the script and would need cue cards stapled to props in order to remember his lines. Yet fan magazines still carried his picture, gossip columns tittered with his name, and when he seated himself at a prominent, visible table at the Brown

Derby, autograph seekers from the prairie states, mostly middle-aged women, would form lines. Damon Forbes flirted with them all, and sometimes managed to take some of the younger ones home. This morning, however, Damon had appeared on the set with his latest squeeze, a seventeen-year-old blond girl who'd recently dropped out of Santa Barbara High School.

"Like her?" Jesse Chadwick asked his wife as he eased into a frame chair next to her. "Her name is Cindy. Joe Preston supplied her to keep Damon happy."

"I'm so glad," Lisa said.

"You should be. That means Damon stays sober and keeps his hands to himself on the set. That's the deal. If he screws up, Joe sends Cindy home."

"Joe's got real talent for management, doesn't he?"

"Stop being a bitch. Do you know your lines?"

"Would it matter if I didn't?"

Chadwick looked at her with contempt and anger. "Lisa," he said. "I could fight with you for the two weeks of this shoot. I could take you aside and beat the daylights out of you. I could dump you and give your role to someone else and delay the film by only half a day. Instead, I'm going to be nice."

"I'm so pleased."

Chadwick reached within his shirt pocket and pulled out an envelope. He opened it in front of her. It was stuffed with money, mostly $100 or $500 bills.

"The completion insurance on this film would have cost $9850," he said. "But think about it. There's only four major cast members and ten minor. Everyone's in good health except for Damon, and he's not going to drink himself to death for another few years. So we didn't take the insurance."

She turned to him. "You what?" she said. "That makes you and Joe Preston financially liable for the whole production."

"Joe and I paid an insurance agent $1000 to fill out the forms. The forms we filed with RKO. The agent processed a check for $9850, kept his money, and tossed the other $8850 back to us." Proudly he motioned to the envelope.

"You are absolutely crazy," she said. "You and Joe would be ruined if the studio found that out."

"No one would ever believe it." He laughed. "And you're not going to tell anyone. Plus, we have an insurance contract we can dummy up after the fact. It's just a two-week shoot. Joe and I pocket an extra four grand apiece out of it."

"You're even dumber to tell me about it," she said.

"No," he said. "That's kind of the point. You look like hell. You hate everything that's going on. So I'm going to make it worth your while to put on a happy face and act like you're a cat in heat whenever the camera starts to roll." She folded her arms in front of her. "Eight hundred dollars," he said. "Right off the top. Cash. Just to cooperate."

"Go away, Jesse."

"I'm serious."

"You think you can buy your way in and out of everything, don't you?" Lisa asked.

"Honey," he boasted. "I *know* I can." He took the money from the envelope, rolled it, then snapped a rubber band around it. He picked up her purse from the floor and dropped in the money.

"There," he said. "My gift to you. Now you've accepted it. So no trouble from you until this film is over. Understand?"

She turned toward him and stared. "Sure, Jesse," she said coldly. "You'll have no trouble at all."

There was a cynical tone to her voice, but Chadwick didn't know how to interpret it. He also had other matters to deal with. Even a film like this didn't direct itself.

"Good," he said. He leaned over and kissed Lisa on the cheek. She pulled away from him. Then he stood and walked away.

Marvelous, she thought to herself. Jesse had now indicated how she could ruin him. The time to commit suicide was twelve days hence, with most of the film complete but with key scenes not yet recorded. Jesse's budget would be shot, he would have no way of completing the movie, the studio would sue him, the press would crucify him, and no one in the future would hire him. To make it all perfect, Joe Preston would be dragged down too.

A strange inner peace came over her. She knew that she had ten days to live. But moreover, she had regained her mastery over her life as well as over two of the most vile men she'd ever met.

Robert Sayre, the chief intelligence officer of the United States Embassy in London, looked across his desk at his visitor and thought things over. "F.B.I., huh?" said Sayre. "Jesus Christ. We could use you around here. How long are you staying?"

"Not very long, I'm afraid," Thomas Buchanan answered. "Maybe only a day or so."

"Hell of a trip for such a short stay. Are you a detective?"

"Sometimes," Buchanan said.

"What if I get Ambassador Fitzroy on the phone to Washington?" Sayre inquired. "Do you think Mr. Hoover could spare you for a few weeks?"

Buchanan laughed. "As much as I'd like to stay, I assure you I'm in the midst of a lengthy investigation. Mr. Hoover would say no." Buchanan paused. "What exactly is the problem?"

"What's *always* the problem? Security. A leak somewhere. What's your government security clearance?"

"One-AAB," Buchanan replied.

"Good," said Sayre. "That means we can talk."

Sayre was a chunky man with closely cropped brown hair. He wore glasses and looked worried. He went on to describe an intelligence operation that had emanated out of the U.S. Embassy in London the previous week. Five American operatives, former soldiers, were picked up at the central railway station in Prague right when they stepped from an Austrian train. Then Czech intelligence had shipped them off to Moscow for questioning.

Buchanan cringed. Questioning: He knew what that meant under the circumstances. "We had a defector all lined up," said Sayre. "East German named Zolling. Important man. Ready to talk."

"About what?"

Sayre rubbed his chin. "He was an expert on Soviet policy and military strategy in Africa and Asia. I'm told he was going to give us the Russian military blueprint for the 1950s." Bob Sayre shrugged. "That's presupposing Ivan Russkie *has* a blueprint."

"Ivan might not," said Buchanan, seeking to lighten the tone a trifle, "but I'm sure Joe Stalin does."

Sayre nodded.

"What happened to Zolling?" Buchanan asked. "Anyone know?"

"Tortured. Then shot. A lesson to others who'd be so foolish as to try to leave the East German workers' paradise."

Buchanan winced.

"Well," Sayre continued, "if you can't help me, maybe I can help you. Why are you here?"

"I'm looking for resident Americans in London with the last

name of Garrett," he said. "I wonder if you could check the current visa files."

"Well, I know of one offhand. Laura Garrett."

Buchanan appeared pleased. "You know her personally?"

"I've met her. Very pretty. Very intelligent girl."

"That's the one. How do you know her?"

"She's the fiancée, if that's not too strong a word, of a member of our political staff."

"Is that a fact?" Buchanan remarked.

"A man named Henry Walters," Sayre said. "Just bought her an engagement ring, unless I'm mistaken. One of those things. Supposed to be a secret, so only a hundred of his closet friends know about it."

Buchanan laughed.

"No one could ever have imagined that an egghead like Henry would land such a beautiful woman."

"Have they known each other long?"

"Whirlwind romance," said Sayre with a touch of envy. "Just since November."

"November? That recently? How did they meet?"

"Chance meeting in a pub," Sayre said. "Don't tell anyone, but it happens all the time. Young Americans abroad. They hear each other's accent, they start to chat. You know how these thing snowball."

"Who talked to who first?"

Sayre shrugged. "Who knows? Who cares?" He thought for a moment. "Henry's here today. Would you like to meet him?" Sayre moved a hand toward his intercom.

Buchanan raised a hand to stop Sayre. "In a few minutes," he answered.

Sayre shook his head. "Henry's in the political department. They could use some cheering up. That's the team that took the beating on the defection."

"Beating, how?"

"This is between you and me and the four walls, right?"

"I hope so," Buchanan answered.

"There are five political officers here. They and they alone determined the route our people would take into Czechoslovakia to bring Zolling out. Conventional wisdom says therefore that the leak has to be there. Yet it *can't* be there. All five have the highest possible security clearance."

"With all due respect," Buchanan said, "one's country is rarely betrayed by people with *low* security clearances."

Sayre looked at his visitor with a stricken expression for several seconds. After several moments of thought, Buchanan continued with a more positive tone. "If I come up with any theories, I'll let you know," he said.

"Would you?"

"And I'll mention your request to Mr. Hoover himself. He'll be thrilled. You might even consider writing to him."

"Okay. I'll do that."

"In the meantime, maybe you could check the visa files or any listing you have for Americans in the United Kingdom. Specifically I'm looking for Ann Garrett, Laura's sister. Or John Taylor Garrett, her father. This on the QT, of course. Don't even alarm Mr. Walters with the knowledge of this."

"Of course."

Sayre left the room and reappeared five minutes later. There was no listing for any related Garrett anywhere in England, Scotland, or Wales. Nor was there any record of an entry or exit for John or Ann into or out of the U.K. within the last year. There was just the single visa and work permit for Laura.

Buchanan thanked Sayre, then asked if he might now be introduced to Laura's fiancé. Sayre reached to his intercom immediately and summoned Walters.

It was late the same afternoon in London on a chilly February day. It was not the ideal time to call on a woman he hadn't seen for a decade, the older sister of a former fiancée, but there was no luxury of choice.

Laura's flat was in a yellowish sandstone building on Brook Street, half a block from Claridge's toward Grosvenor Square. He was about to ring her bell in the entrance foyer on the ground floor when the door opened from within. A plump woman with black hair and very fair skin held the door open and admitted him to the building. Then Buchanan mounted two flights of steps and rang the bell at Laura Garrett's flat.

A few moments later Laura opened the door. "Yes . . . ?" she said.

"Hello, Laura," he said.

It took several seconds, then she recognized him. "My God! A ghost!" she said with what he almost thought to be horror. "Tommy Buchanan."

"I know it's rude to just drop in," he said. "But I'm in London for a day or two. And I thought—"

"Don't say another word," she said. "Come in. How long has it been since I've seen you? Five years? Seven?"

"Closer to ten."

She was still very beautiful, he noted, and as she closed the door she reminded him painfully of Ann. Her movements and carriage were the same.

She stood back a pace or two and assessed him. "How extraordinary!" she said. "It's not every day that a man who asked me out ten years ago drops by to say hello."

"I don't suppose it is."

"Make yourself comfortable," she said. She motioned to her living room. He entered and sat on her sofa. In response to her questions of why he was in London, he said he had a government job now and a piece of important business had brought him here. As he spoke, he studied her eyes carefully. And he was sure he detected something he didn't like.

"Can I get you something cold to drink? Or hot?" she asked at length. "Just tell me what, Tom, and we'll have it."

He settled on ginger ale. While she went for it, he used the washroom. On his way back he glanced at the array of clothes in an open closet in the hallway, the only closet in an otherwise spacious flat. When he came back and sat down, she drank some ginger ale too.

They talked for almost half an hour. She'd been working in London for a few years, she said, just to get out and see the world. She was an occasional buyer for a jewelry dealer, she said, and had most recently fallen in love. This she glossed over quickly, almost as if embarrassed, giggling like a schoolgirl.

"And your family?" he asked.

"They're well."

"Tell me about them," he said.

"Dad's back in America. He still operates Commonwealth Penn, of course."

"Seen him recently?"

She answered cautiously. "About three months ago."

"Is that right?" he asked genially. "November?"

"I think it was. Yes."

"Then you've been back home very recently?"

"No. I saw him here."

"In London?"

"Why, yes." She produced a snapshot of the two of them. It was of recent vintage, taken on Westminster Bridge.

"How nice," he said. "Did Ann take this?" he asked, glancing up. "I noticed the name 'A. Garrett' next to the name 'L. Garrett' downstairs."

"No. A friend took the picture."

"Does your father get here often?"

"No. Not at all."

"It sounds as if his business is doing well." Buchanan handed the snapshot back to her.

"I'm sure it is," she said. "We have father-daughter talks. Not business talks. I only assume the bank is doing well. He doesn't discuss it with me."

"Well, that's genteel of him, isn't it?"

Laura thought for a moment. "Yes," she said, as if slightly irritated. "I think it is." Then she stood and moved to the mantel. She pulled down the family pictures in the two silver frames. She showed them to Buchanan.

He stared at the photograph of her parents and expressed his sorrow over the death of her mother. He guessed that the photograph might be five years old. Then he moved his attention to the picture of Ann and Laura together. This was of similar vintage. Circa 1945, he guessed, and obviously taken at home in Pennsylvania.

Then his attention drifted and he tried to imagine what Ann might have been doing at that point in her life, two years after stepping out of his. Whatever it was, however, it seemed to have treated her well. Ann was as beautiful as he remembered her. And no matter how life had been treating her at the time, she was smiling in the photograph.

"And how *is* Ann?" he asked. "Your equally beautiful sister?"

Laura started to laugh. "Oh, Tom," she chided him. "You're not here chasing that old flame, are you? Tell me honestly."

He lied smoothly. "Not in the slightest," he said. "I'd just like to be remembered. Where is she?"

"She lives here," Laura said. "With me."

"Then I'll get to see her?"

"No. I'm sorry. She's out of London right now."

"What a shame. For how long?"

"Indefinitely."

"But she's normally here?" Buchanan asked.

"Usually, yes," Laura answered.

In the next room the telephone rang twice. "Excuse me," Laura said. She stood and hurried to the phone. It was in the front hallway and out of his sight.

He turned the photographs over, hoping he'd find the photographer's name. But he found none. When his attention returned to the shot of the Garrett sisters, however, he noticed how thick the picture seemed in its glass-and-silver frame.

He examined the frame. Then, with Laura still on the telephone, he opened it. Within, he discovered a second photograph beneath the first. It was a smaller-sized portrait of the two girls, identical to the photograph on top. He stared at it as he tuned in to her voice from the front hall.

An impulse was upon him. His hands worked quickly. Then he heard Laura sign off the telephone and hang up. Buchanan had closed the frame again by the time Laura reentered the room.

"My fiancé just called," she said. "He's on his way over."

Buchanan handed the frames back to her. She took them carefully and held them.

"Let me guess," he said. "He's a banker. Like your dad."

"Who?"

"Your boyfriend."

"Wrong. He's an attorney," she said after a pause.

"Really?" he said. "What type of law?"

She lied poorly. She was not quick enough. "International," she said after a beat. "Anglo-American business."

"Fascinating field. I'd love to meet him. What firm did you say he was with?"

"Tom," she said, "I'm getting engaged today. I'm not even supposed to know, but my boyfriend's bringing me a ring. I found out through friends."

"That's wonderful," he said. "Congratulations! What's the lucky fellow's name?"

She stood and returned the framed portraits to the mantel. For a moment she looked unnerved. "McClintock," she said. "Bruce McClintock."

"So you'll be Laura McClintock," he mused.

"That's correct," she said. She set the pictures back in place on the mantel.

"And what firm did you say he was with?"

"I didn't say," she said.

"May I ask again?"

"It's a small English firm," she replied in a terse monotone. "You've never heard of them."

"Try me."

"It's getting late, Tom. And it might be a little awkward if he found you here."

"I simply asked the name of your fiancé's firm."

A moment passed. "Gaskin, Greeley, and Brown, Limited," she finally said. "They have offices in Regent Street."

"You're right. I've never heard of them."

"Why would you have? You live in America. You're not in that line of work, I assume." She was growing angry.

"Oh, I've been around the world a little bit," he said. "I've heard a few names. I've seen a few things. But I doubt if I move around God's green earth quite as deftly as your father."

He studied her reaction. He could see that the sudden mention of John Taylor Garrett had set her further on edge.

"What makes you say that?"

"It's just an impression I get," he said. "John Taylor Garrett is such a busy man that he never seems to be at his office."

"So?"

"I tried to contact him recently. I had a banking contact who wanted to do some business in Pennsylvania. I couldn't find him at all."

"He travels a lot," she said easily. "You could just leave a message with any of his senior vice presidents."

"I'll remember that in the future," Buchanan promised. His tone shifted slowly. "I'm sure the three of you must have a wonderful time together last fall," Buchanan said.

"What three of us?"

"You, Ann, and your father, of course," he said. "You said your father was in London."

"Yes. So?"

"I simply suggested that the three of you must have spent some time together. Did you?"

She hesitated half a second. "Why are you asking me that?"

"Just being friendly, Laura. I don't understand why you seem to be groping for an answer. It's either yes or no."

"Frankly," she said sharply, "it's none of your business."

"It would seem strange to me," he continued evenly, "that a man like John Garrett would visit London and not want to see *both* of his girls. And you just said she was usually here."

"I'm sorry, Tom," she said flatly. "Okay. I fibbed to you a bit because it's really a family matter. None of your business at all. Ann and Dad had a rather vehement disagreement several months ago. She took off one night. Didn't even say good-bye. The truth is, she has a boyfriend in Rome. I'd expect that she's staying there."

"What a damned shame. I would love to have said hello."

"Well, you won't be able to."

"Will she be there long?"

"Probably."

"Then maybe you could give me the address."

Laura answered icily. "I don't have it."

"Then maybe you could give me her boyfriend's name. I'm excellent at locating people. As you can see."

She glared at him and said nothing.

"I see," he said, noting her silence. "Still," he continued in polite tones, "it strikes me as so very strange: Ann has a disagreement with your father and departs her flat *here.* If your father is so rarely in London, why leave?"

"I sided with my father," Laura said. She was no longer smiling. "Ann is furious with me."

"What a loyal daughter," said Buchanan. "And I don't doubt for a moment that you're on your father's side. But I have a hunch that the break in your family came much sooner. Say, about 1947. I'd further theorize that Ann has been nowhere near this apartment for quite some time. Tell me, what was the dispute over that it could drive a family apart like that?"

For a moment she stared at him awkwardly, completely at a loss for words.

"Laura," he said, "I don't want this to become unpleasant. But you're lying to me about practically everything."

"Am I?"

He nodded. "I looked in your medicine cabinet. Women don't share their creams or their makeup or their lipsticks. I saw only those things that belong to you. And you wouldn't have disposed of all of Ann's things so quickly. Same with the clothes in the closet.

Ann was smaller than you. Those are your clothes, plus a smatter-
ing of items to make it *look* like someone else lives here."

"You're a snoop, Tom. Always were."

"Further," he said, "I know your father is a remarkable man.
But among the most remarkable things about him would be this
recent visit to the U.K., the one you just mentioned."

"What about it?"

"He *was* here?" he pressed again.

"Yes." Her response was adamant. "You saw the picture."

"Then what passport did he travel on?" Buchanan asked. "The
United States Embassy here keeps track of all Americans who have
come and gone. No John Taylor Garrett ever entered England. At
least, not officially. So what name does he travel under? And what
passport might he be using, Laura?"

Buchanan's eyes were riveted upon her. Laura's face turned
crimson in anger.

"Similarly I learn that you have a visa to be in the U.K., but
Ann does not. That would seem strange, too, were it not for the fact
that she has probably never been here anyway."

"Anything else?" she asked.

"Now that you ask, yes. I had the foresight to stop at the U.S.
Embassy before coming by here. I met a young man named Henry
Walters. He seems to be quite smitten with you. Hopelessly in love,
I would say. Well, that's understandable. But I assume that you
don't have two suitors at once. So I would further deduce that the
nonsense you gave me a few minutes ago about an attorney named
Bruce McClintock was as false as everything else you've told me."

She stared at him furiously. "You have no damned right to—"

"And, of course, to add to the general atmosphere of confusion," Buchanan resumed, "Mr. Walters says that he's never met
Ann, though he thinks she's here all the time. So which is it, Laura?
Even *I* am a little baffled. *Is* she here? Or have you simply used her
as a device to dismiss the occasional male visitor at your conven-
ience?"

"What do you want from me?" she asked angrily.

"A few honest answers," he said, "to the questions I've already
asked."

"Look," Laura said, "I knew as soon as I saw you that this
isn't a social call. You're employed by the F.B.I. and you're after
my father."

"And how would you know that?"

She was silent again. He waited a moment.

"Thank you," he said. "You just confirmed how. Paul Evans from the Mayflower Club alerted your father. And your father alerted you."

"Why ask me any questions?" she asked. "You seem to know all the answers."

"Oh, but I don't," he said. "You know many more answers than I do."

"I'll tell you what I know. I know that my father is completely innocent of any wrongdoing. But people like you who work for J. Edgar Hoover run around compiling files on innocent Americans. Then, if their politics aren't quite right, you start smearing them. I suspect you're after Dad because first he worked for Henry Wallace, then he contributed time and money to Truman's reelection."

"Nothing can be further from the truth, Laura. I'd be more than happy to turn in a report exonerating an innocent man."

"I've seen the way people like you operate, Tom. I don't like it or them. And I'll tell you something else. For exactly that reason I'm damned glad you didn't marry into our family. You're an intellectual flyweight. You're a glorified two-bit cop, a second cousin to the gestapo."

"You're changing the subject."

"So what? I really don't think we have anything more to say to each other."

"No?"

"Tom. You have no jurisdiction in England. Do I have to throw you out? I'll call the police if I have to."

He sighed with disappointment. But she had finished their meeting, though he tried one final time to prolong it.

"Laura," he was almost embarrassed to hear himself say, "everything would be much easier if—"

"Just *leave!*" she said.

He stood and gathered his hat and coat. "If you see Ann, say hello for me, Laura. When you communicate with your father, as I know you will, tell him I'd like to talk to him. Is that fair enough?"

She pointed him toward the entrance hall. "Good-bye, Tom," she said. "I wish I could say it was nice to see you again. But we both know it wasn't. Now, please go."

Down the block of Brook Street later the same evening, standing in the clear window of a pub, Buchanan nursed pints of warm English lager, thirty minutes to a glass, watching the doorway where Ann lived.

At 6:15 Henry Walters arrived, holding what appeared to be a gift-wrapped champagne bottle under his arm. He was upstairs for more than half an hour. Buchanan made note of the time. Laura and her Romeo reappeared a few minutes before seven. Henry raised his arm and flagged a taxi. The couple climbed in. Buchanan watched as the vehicle accelerated noisily toward Hanover Square.

Then Buchanan emerged from the pub and stood in the drizzly London night. One part of him was in open revolt against the rest. All of the excesses of J. Edgar Hoover's F.B.I. repelled him: Illegal wiretaps. Bureau files filled with the dirty laundry of private citizens. Breaking and entering with no warrant. Black-bag jobs. Sound jobs. Perhaps Laura had been right. Perhaps her father had done nothing illegal. Or perhaps—to imagine the unthinkable—whatever he had done, maybe John Taylor Garrett was a lesser evil than those who would prosecute him.

Yet why had Laura lied to him so relentlessly? Why had she singled out a political officer in the United States Embassy for her affections when she could have her pick of men? Why, concurrent to their romance, had an important operation in Prague blown up? And where was Ann? Not Rome, surely. Prague, maybe? Moscow? Why would no one tell him? Why was there no trace of the only woman with whom he'd ever been in love?

The rain intensified as he turned down Duke Street, walking away from Laura's neighborhood. He wondered if Ann was dead, like her mother. He shuddered.

A more troubling question was then upon him. With his disgust of Hoover's methods and motives, why had he just operated in much the same manner? Within his coat pocket was the small photograph of Laura and Ann. On impulse he had stolen it from the silver frame when she was on the telephone. He dipped his hand within his coat to reassure himself that he had it. It was there.

A few minutes later, a few blocks farther away, the rain was torrential. Buchanan took refuge under the canopy of a Persian teahouse and looked hopefully over his shoulder for a taxi. But, simultaneous to the heavier raindrops, the furies had chosen to punish him by removing all cabs from the streets of London. *For which transgression,* he wondered.

Then the worst thought of all seized him. For the first time it was completely credible that John Taylor Garrett was some sort of spy and Laura was his apprentice. A wave of demoralization was upon him when the next logical thought visited. Ann was her father's apprentice, too, only more deeply under cover than her older sister. She was so deeply into her devious role, he imagined, that he would never find her at all.

J. Edgar Hoover's words returned to him: *Come back convinced!* the Boss had ordered. Convinced he now was, even against his most personal wishes. And he was on his way home to boot.

A surge of disgust filled him. Yet in a weird, disgraceful, backhanded way, he was glad he'd stolen the photograph.

■
SEVENTEEN
■

On Saturday morning, February 18, Viktor Milenkin, who worked for the New York Telephone Company under the name of George Mulligan, took his weekly walk under the Williamsburg Bridge. He was accompanied by his dog, part Labrador, part German shepherd. Milenkin had named the dog "O'Dwyer," after the recent mayor, or just "Bad Bill" for short. Friends took this to be a mark of Milenkin's playful sense of humor. They mistook it, however, to be an Irish trait rather than a Russian one.

The wind in New York gusted up the East River the same way as, almost a hundred miles to the south, it swept up the Delaware. Milenkin was chilled to the bone. In the back of his mind he wondered if he might not start making these walks every *other* week instead of each Saturday. There were rarely any messages left for him in the stonework under the bridge. Nothing from Colonel Klisinski, wherever he was, and nothing from Mother Liliya back in Russia.

Recently, however, many other things had gone well for Milenkin. He was a hard worker, as anyone who knew him from the G.R.U. or from the Communist Party of the Soviet Union could have attested. He was dedicated and kept good work habits and hours. His American employers, the New York Telephone Company, observed the same qualities. Before Christmas the company had given him a merit raise. Milenkin still lived very simply on Perry Street in Greenwich Village, but he now banked each week, even after taxes, a full fifty dollars more than he spent. He was also now included in profit-sharing. As part of a Christmas bonus his employer issued him stock in the company.

"Stock? What does that mean?" he asked when he received the certificate.

"It means you own part of the company," someone in Payroll told him. Milenkin took the certificate home and stared at it for hours. Then, in January, one of his superiors had been taken ill and left the company. New York Telephone again promoted the man they knew as George Mulligan, and once again he was presented with a raise. And the best news followed: Within another few months he was scheduled to go into the company's supervisory management training program. That would mean even more money, better working conditions, and increased status with job security. It was not a bad deal at all.

Something else nice was happening also. Milenkin had found a special girl at New York Telephone. She was a typist. Her name was Barbara Litvinov. She was a plain girl from Brooklyn but she'd taken a shine to him for several months. During the December holidays in 1949, she invited him to her family's place in Brooklyn for dinner. To Milenkin's utter amazement, Barbara's mother, Mrs. Ellen Litvinov, had cooked a Russian-Jewish meal that was so good that it almost brought tears to his eyes. In return Milenkin took Barbara dancing at Roseland the next weekend and then to see *All the King's Men* at the Radio City Music Hall the Friday after that.

Focusing on the name Mulligan, Barbara liked to kid him about his Irishness. George didn't seem like Brooklyn Irish at all. He was, for example, the only Irishman she'd ever met who didn't hang out in bars or attend Mass at least once a month, sometimes going directly from one to the other. He answered that saloons didn't appeal to him all that much, and churches didn't either. But secretly her observations gave him pause. Back in Moscow, the name Mulligan had seemed neutral American, with no ethnic implications. In California it might have been. But in New York it was not. So if Milenkin had adopted an Irish name and identity, here were a few tiny flaws in his new cover. Like discovering a painting that is a forgery, Milenkin knew that the unraveling of a fraud often came in small steps, until the smaller inconsistencies gave way to larger ones. At that time the authenticity of the whole canvas would collapse. If Barbara found little incongruities in his persona, Milenkin worried, wouldn't someone who might be investigating him for more serious reasons?

Yet Barbara Litvinov and George Mulligan remained more than friendly, even if it was merely a cordial companionship at the office and then for a very low-key date on Friday night. He was always courteous to her parents and careful to get her home by the time he'd promised. On those occasions when he had to wait for Barbara, he enjoyed conversation with her father, Irving, who liked to share observations and opinions on living in America. ("It's not Canaan, but it will have to do," Irving liked to joke.) For this, and for many other reasons, Mr. and Mrs. Litvinov became fond of George Mulligan too. The irony was that Mrs. Litvinov kept referring to him as a "nice American boy."

Then, sometime in December, one thing led to another, and Barbara went to bed with him at his apartment in the Village. That night Barbara came home to Brooklyn three hours late. Her parents, knowing that she'd been with George Mulligan, said nothing.

Yet, all of this figured into a strange confluence of thoughts for Viktor Milenkin. He had been told in the Soviet Union that workers were relentlessly exploited in the United States. Yet he had been given one promotion after another, had more money than he actually knew how to spend, now owned part of the company, and was being geared to a management position. He had been told that society in the United States was closed and oppressive. Yet he found Greenwich Village to be a cheerful, informal, friendly neighborhood, where he was free to go wherever or do whatever he pleased.

He had been told by officers he respected in Soviet military intelligence that Jews were dishonest, dirty, cabalistic, greedy, and slothful, representing the worst of the capitalist class. Yet he'd seen the living proof that this, too, was a misconception. No—Milenkin had been thinking seriously on this subject—these were not misconceptions, these were lies. The Litvinovs were kind, hardworking, well spoken, thoughtful, literate, joyful people. Their daughter incorporated all of those qualities, and he was falling in love with her.

Then something else extraordinary happened. On the eighteenth of February, the Saturday morning when Milenkin strolled with O'Dwyer under the Williamsburg Bridge, he put his hand along the stones at shoulder level as he always did. On this morning he found a construction pipe.

His heart skipped a beat. After all these weeks and months, finally there was something for him.

He recognized the handwriting. The message was from Colonel Klisinski, his recruiter into the G.R.U. and his control agent in the United States. The message was in English. If Milenkin was certain that he was completely free from any surveillance, he was to place a potted plant visibly in his Perry Street window that same day. Then he was to return to the bridge on Sunday morning for further instructions.

He bought the plant at a Woolworth's on Sixth Avenue that afternoon. He placed it in his window immediately. The next morning by ten Klisinski, or someone, had placed another correspondence in another pipe in the supporting foundation of the bridge.

Milenkin experienced an immediate rush of excitement when he found the second communication. It was sealed in an envelope. He clutched it tightly to him, walked home, and opened it. There was a photograph in it of a man he'd never seen before. And there were instructions which he broke down by use of a pinhole codebook which he'd had with him since his reentry into the United States after the world war.

The message was succinct. Milenkin was to pass along the photograph and a second set of coded instructions to a husband-and-wife team who were currently in the United States. They had a dead-letter drop in the second pew from the rear at St. Peter's Lutheran Church two blocks from Washington Square. There was a loose floorboard which would come up if a pair of nails were worked with a small screwdriver. Milenkin was to get the message into the box by Tuesday evening. The husband and wife would pick it up Wednesday.

For several hours Milenkin forgot about everything in his current life—his job, his dog, his woman friend—and reverted with enthusiasm to the role of a Soviet mole in American society. The glow of actually being able to do something for the Soviet Republic pumped him up to a certain level of excitement. It was only later that same evening, when he was lying in bed trying to sleep, listening to a music student practice her flute downstairs, that some of the inconsistencies of what he was doing began to sink in.

For all of Monday he was troubled. He knew nothing about any Soviet operation that was in progress. And frankly, now he

didn't want to know. After months and months of disappointment
when there was no communication for him beneath the Williamsburg Bridge, he was now sorry that he'd finally received some. Suppose whatever was in progress blew up? Suppose the American police began to roll up the Soviet networks that had been involved?
That midwestern senator had been making news all month about
Communists, and people would probably accuse George Mulligan
—or Viktor Milenkin—of being one. Surely a long, harsh prison
sentence would follow. Surely his life would be in ruins.

Well, he reasoned, he *was* a Soviet agent, after all. Or was he?
Even he didn't know. And what if the current mission were botched
so badly that he had to leave the country fast? He didn't want to
leave the United States. Not fast, not now, and, for that matter, not
at all. For the first time in his adult life, Viktor Milenkin realized he
felt more at home in America than in the Soviet Union.

What should he do? On Tuesday he agonized. He decided,
however, that the odds of being caught and convicted were small,
whereas if he disobeyed his G.R.U. commander, he would surely
endure some brutal repercussions. So he made the drop at St. Peter's, to which the doors were always open. And then on Wednesday
he did something he'd never done before. He called in to work and
told a lie. He said he was sick.

He was, of course, healthy as a race horse. But he wanted to
see who made the pickup from the church. He dressed himself casually that morning and went to the church himself. He took a seat in
a rear pew and appeared to be absorbed in meditation. There he had
a vantage point over the dead-letter drop. He would be able to see
who came in and who worked the floorboards, but he was not at an
angle that would inhibit the pickup team from doing their job.

He waited for hours. Marina Sejna came into the church at
about 3:45 in the afternoon. Milenkin knew who she was. He knew
by the way her eyes swept the building to see if the coast was clear.
She knelt in prayer in the assigned pew. When she didn't leave the
church in ten minutes, her man came in to join her.

Milenkin cringed when he saw Alexandr Filiatov. The Americans might not immediately recognize what he was, but Milenkin
did. He knew a G.R.U.-trained hit man when he saw one—a six-
cylinder Moscow-trained hood.

Milenkin sat perfectly still, as if in silent prayer. He heard the
slight but unmistakable squeak of the floorboard as Filiatov lifted it.

He was careful not to turn around at this time, though he knew that the blond woman was blocking his view.

Milenkin, in fact, kept his eyes straight ahead, focusing on the wall behind the central altar. There a reassuring mural depicted a benign, blue-eyed Jesus ascending to heaven amid harps, doves, and angels. As Milenkin stared, he heard the floorboard go back down with a tiny squeak. Then about a minute later he heard the footsteps of the woman leave the church with the man close behind.

Milenkin was not a man who'd been trained to pray. Had he, he might have spent some time praying right there. The big, thick-browed character who'd made the pickup was clearly and simply an assassin. Obviously the woman was his second or his assistant. And the picture of the man in the envelope was obviously their next assigned victim.

There was nothing Milenkin could do, of course, other than hope that the Soviet hit team proved unsuccessful and fled the country. He wished the whole thing would go away, leaving him to settle down to his job, his home, and his girlfriend. He had the right to these things just like . . . well, to use an expression that he commonly heard, just like any other American citizen.

But it was out of Milenkin's hands now. Alexandr Filiatov and Marina Sejna had their orders and their instructions. And they also had a clear photograph of their next target, the man who'd most recently been snooping around London—Special Agent Thomas Buchanan of the Federal Bureau of Investigation.

Thomas Buchanan tightened his seat belt as the Trans World Constellation climbed into the sky above London and slowly swung an arc that would take it northward. The afternoon was rainy, and the pilot had already warned that some turbulence could be expected. Somehow, the more Buchanan flew, the less he enjoyed the experience.

Below him he saw the highways into London grow smaller as the airplane climbed. Then they were in the clouds and there was no ground at all. There was just the steady groan of the airplane's engines and the rumbling vibrations of its fuselage. Nine hours and home, he mused. Well, he thought to himself, as soon as the stewardess passed down the aisle he'd set himself up with a double scotch and try to decide if he could be satisfied with this trip.

Laura Garrett had lied to him several times. She'd lied about her father and her relationship with him. She'd refused to reveal her sister's whereabouts. Then, for one reason or another, she'd even sought to mislead him about her future husband's employment at the embassy. Why? A thousand times, why?

For several minutes Buchanan stared out the window, hoping to find answers in the billowing clouds in the sky above the north of England and Scotland. There were none. Eventually the stewardess provided a strong drink and Buchanan settled in.

At length he reached to the inside pocket of his jacket and took out the picture that he'd removed from Laura Garrett's frame. He stared at Laura. He stared at Ann. He guessed that the picture had been taken five years previously. The feeling grew more persistent within him that Ann was no longer alive.

He looked at her, pressed the photograph back into his pocket, and leaned back in his seat. Mercifully the aircraft's path had evened out now and the flight was smoother.

He was tired. Sleep began to sneak up on him. He closed his eyes for several moments and could feel himself drifting back to a magical evening in June 1942. . . .

He saw the big green Packard that had belonged to his father. Ann was in her fiery red dress with her shoulders bare. Thomas was twenty-two and she was twenty. The Bucks County Cricket Club had cleared all the tables to the sides of their sprawling dining room and the floor had been waxed for dancing. An orchestra played. Paper Chinese lanterns glowed on the walls and across the ceilings while candles flickered brightly on the tables. By the end of the summer at least two dozen of the young men whose families belonged to the club would be in the armed forces. Seven of them would be lost in Europe or the Pacific. No one said it, but the cotillions and dinner dances of early summer were a way of saying good-bye and wishing the young men good luck. Already fourteen independent nations had fallen in Europe. England stood alone against Hitler. The Japanese held Hong Kong, Burma, Indochina, the Philippines, and Malaya. The Battle of Midway was in full progress. It was unquestionable that thousands of young Americans would have to lay down their lives before this latest installment of tyranny could be banished from the globe—if it ever would be.

Thomas had held her closely as they danced, feeling her in his arms, wanting nothing more than the war to go away so that he might marry her. She'd worn his engagement ring that night, and it had sparkled in the reflected glow from the lanterns and candles. So had Ann Garrett's eyes.

The band played their last dance a few minutes after eleven. Thomas and Ann stayed for a while thereafter and chatted with friends, smoked, and drank champagne punch. Afterward they'd left to go to the Packard, which was parked on the other side of a polo field. Thomas couldn't remember which of them had suggested it, but they'd decided to stop by the lake that was just past the field. They had both had a bit too much to drink. A few minutes later Thomas had pried open the lock on the boathouse and they were upstairs by the big bay windows, overlooking the water and a first quarter moon.

"When I was a boy," he said, "I used to come up here and try to measure the lake. I always wanted to swim across it. Still haven't."

"After the war," she said bravely. "Maybe all the fighting will end and you'll be home by Christmas."

"They thought that in 1914 too," he said.

"We can always hope," she said.

"I just want to live through it and come back to marry you," he said.

"You'd better," she answered.

On the grand sofa in the boathouse meeting room, he pulled her to him and kissed her. Then, as he'd done many times before, he gently pushed Ann backward, until she was reclining. He lay next to her. His hand was on her hip. He kissed her on the lips and then the throat. When she responded by pressing herself against him, his lips worked downward. With his free hand he loosened her dress where it buttoned in the back. The straps at the shoulders came loose. Her breasts were free, and, for the first time, she allowed him to kiss them.

"Tonight?" he asked.

"I don't know," she said.

"Is it a good time of month?"

With a slight hesitation, she nodded.

He looked at her. "Ann, I love you so much. And this might be our last chance for a long time." She rolled away from him and stood up, one arm folded in front of her to keep her dress from falling. Then, because of the war, because of the urgency in his voice, or maybe just because of the longing that she, too, felt, she began to smile.

"I guess a girl doesn't have to be perfect anymore, does she?" she asked.

He shook his head.

"Do you think there's a blanket anywhere?" she asked.

He found one.

"I hope no one walks in on us," she said.

He wedged the back of a chair under the doorknob.

"Promise to be gentle?" she asked.

"Ann, could I be anything else with you?"

No, she agreed, he couldn't be. Together they lost their virginity pleasantly, painlessly, and eagerly. In the months that later passed while he was in the United States Army, never once did he have the courage to reveal that for all the sincerity of his love for her, this had been a planned seduction. Nor did she ever confess to him that she'd known exactly what he'd planned when he'd jimmied the lock on the boathouse door. She'd known and wished that he'd done it a summer earlier. . . .

High above Ireland, thoughts came back to him that he hadn't had in years: Why had Ann broken their engagement? And what, he wondered, had ever happened to their ring? She'd never given it back, and he'd never requested it.

Buchanan nodded off and was asleep, the scotch only half finished. The airliner hit a placid stretch of sky and proceeded smoothly over the north Atlantic. When he awoke several hours later, the flight was only two hours from Washington. On arrival he planned to stop quickly at the Bureau to retrieve his weapon and check his mail. He would then go directly home and crash into bed.

Absently he wondered if the many facets of the Garrett case would ever make sense. Similarly he wondered if certain pieces of his life would ever make sense either. As the airplane began its descent toward the coast of Newfoundland, Buchanan marveled how those two concerns now seemed to dovetail so neatly.

EIGHTEEN

I t was half past seven in the evening when the green and white District of Columbia taxi carrying Thomas Buchanan pulled to a stop in front of the wooden frame house on 7th Street, S.E. Tired as he was from the flight from London, Buchanan was pleased to be back home.

He paid the driver four dollars for the ride from National Airport, then added a dollar as a tip. The driver thanked him. Carrying one small suitcase, Buchanan walked up the steps to the Raffertys' house. As he pulled his key from his pocket, he shivered against the cold of late February in Washington. For some reason, as he stood on the porch and fumbled with the lock, he thought of old Rafferty himself sitting on that same porch in the blazing summer heat, wishing for a breeze, listening to the punchless Washington Senators getting blasted by the New York Yankees. Well, cold or not, Bureau notwithstanding, Buchanan decided it was good to be back in the United States.

Then, as he inserted the key in the lock, he stopped. He turned slowly. He felt eyes upon him from somewhere. He scanned up and down 7th Street, but found it deserted aside from a young woman walking alone. He scanned the cars parked near the curb and saw nothing unusual.

Rubbish, he told himself. This assignment was getting the better of him. He was looking for two people, Ann Garrett and her father, who had turned invisible, and now he imagined invisible people watching him. It was after midnight, London time. A good night's sleep, he hoped, would cure whatever ailed him.

As he entered the house, the Raffertys were nowhere to be seen or heard. That in itself was strange. Normally at this hour the homey smell of dinner still floated in the air and the sound of their console radio frequently came from the parlor. But tonight, nothing. Buchanan wondered if they were out visiting. They sometimes were. He hoped neither had taken sick.

He climbed the first flight of stairs. Again he remarked at the quiet of the house. He mounted the second flight. There was a different feeling in the house, something he hadn't sensed previously. He stopped at the landing before his door and stood perfectly still. He glanced back downstairs and noticed that the lights were on in a pattern different from the one the Raffertys ever used. For that matter, it was odd that so many lights were on if no one was in the house.

He unlocked his own door. He stepped in and reached for the light switch, setting down his suitcase at the same time. Then, in a quick lapse of time that defied any standard of measurement, everything came together at once: the sense of being watched, the stillness of the house, the pattern of lights. He reached for the Colt .38 that he'd placed back on his left hip, but the hand of an unseen man beat him to the light switch. A pair of steel arms came down around his and completely immobilized him. The light flashed on and Buchanan stared into the dark, angular face of a man he had never seen before. Buchanan couldn't see the man behind him. But the man before him wore a dark brown suit, a gray fedora, and stood several inches taller than he. A pistol was upraised and pointed directly into Buchanan's face. From six inches away it was very possible that if the trigger were pulled, the sound of the gunshot and explosive pain of instant death would be simultaneous.

In the breadth of a second, the vision of Mark O'Connell, shot down on an Oregon highway, was before him. This was followed by an image of his own parents when he was a boy, followed inexplicably by one of Ann Garrett, young, radiant, and beautiful, lying next to him naked in the dimly lit attic of the boathouse.

"Don't move!" the gunman said. "Don't fight!"

Buchanan simply stared. His instinct was to stamp on the instep of the man behind him and kick toward the groin of the man in front of him. The business end of the pistol, however, was a convincing argument to the contrary. That, and the fact that if he were to be murdered, it would have been done already.

One of the steel hands from behind reached to Buchanan's hip and stripped him of his weapon. "Stay calm," the man in front of him said. "You're in no danger."

"Who the hell are you?" Buchanan asked.

The gunman retreated a step, then slowly lowered the pistol. The gorilla behind him loosened his grip and freed Buchanan.

"Frederick C. Clark," said the man in front. "United States Secret Service." He put his gun away and showed his Secret Service shield.

"William W. Kirby," said the man from behind. "U.S. Secret Service." Kirby was removing the bullets from Buchanan's revolver. "Nice to meet you." Kirby was at least six feet three, a big, thick six feet three.

"What's the idea? What's going on?" Buchanan asked. His fear subsided. Anger took its place.

"You have an appointment across town. Right away. We're here to pick you up." It was Clark who spoke. He had a drawl and sounded like a Texan.

Buchanan, mystified, looked from one man to the other. "You could have just asked. You didn't need the rough stuff."

"Had to make sure you'd come willingly," Clark said. "You'd be surprised how much resistance we get from rival agencies. Particularly yours. No fucking cooperation at all sometimes."

"Pity," said Buchanan. His heartbeat was just starting to settle down. Clark motioned to the door. He said he had a car waiting outside, which confirmed Buchanan's feeling of being on view.

"Don't forget your keys, but you can leave your suitcase," Kirby said. "You'll be only an hour or so. We'll bring you home later."

Buchanan assessed them a final time. "Can I have my weapon back?" he asked.

Kirby shook his head. "Not till your meeting is finished," he said. "Those are our instructions." Kirby had a deep voice and a slow, easy speech pattern. Buchanan guessed Tennessee or Virginia. "Come on along."

Then, moments later, they were back out in the Washington night. A dark Plymouth sedan was waiting in front of the Raffertys' home, its headlights throwing two bright yellow beams down the block. Its engine was rumbling and its driver was waiting. Clark and Kirby hustled Buchanan into the car. The driver noisily ground a gearshift on the steering column. The sedan began to move. The driver lost no time. And Buchanan noticed that the driver speedily navigated the streets and turns of the capital with a precision born of experience—as well as the knowledge that local traffic ordinances applied to other vehicles but not this one.

The soldier on guard duty at the rear entrance to the White House recognized the Secret Service sedan and waved it through the iron gates. When the vehicle neared the White House itself, Clark and Kirby jumped out even as the car was still moving. They looked in both directions, as if they were expecting an attack on a visitor even within the grounds of the White House. The driver pulled the car to a stop. Buchanan stepped out of the right side. Clark and Kirby led him into a rear entrance of the American President's official residence.

"Just follow," Fred Clark said. "Don't ask questions."

The two Secret Service men led Buchanan through a basement corridor, then into an elevator which was attended by a middle-aged black man. The elevator rose to the building's main floor. Next, Clark and Kirby hustled Buchanan down a light green corridor and into a small room with a fireplace. Their mission accomplished, the two agents almost seemed to relax. Kirby left. Clark spoke.

"Just have a seat," the agent said. "I think he'll be with you in a minute."

"*Who* will?"

"Normally he's getting ready for bed at this hour. I'm sure he's still up tonight, though. He's been waiting for you."

Buchanan would have asked who again, but how many men lived in the White House?

The door closed. Buchanan had the feeling that the two agents were seated close by on the other side. He didn't feel like sitting, so he turned and looked at his surroundings.

He was in a snug conference room with pale beige walls. There was an American flag in one corner, a desk in the center of the room near a window, and a colonial divan with matching chairs. A fire, freshly lit, crackled in the fireplace, and above a mantel hung a picture of Jefferson—the famous portrait that adorned the two-dollar bill. It was a comfortable room with a relaxed atmosphere. It was very traditionally Washington and very American.

Buchanan was still standing, warming himself before the fire when the door swung open. "Good evening, Mr. Buchanan," said the man who entered the room. "Thank you for coming right away."

There was an immeasurably short moment between the time that Buchanan heard the famous nasal Missourian voice and the moment that he was able to turn and have his eyes properly focus. Entering the room wearing a maroon print robe, a sport shirt, casual gray slacks, and navy slippers was the President of the United States.

Buchanan was almost tongue-tied as he gazed at one of the most recognizable men in the world. "Good evening, sir," he managed to say, almost sputtering the words. Buchanan still had no idea what this was about. His eyes fixed upon the five-foot-nine-inch President. Harry S. Truman's gray hair was freshly parted, and his brown eyes were alert and searching. His head was round, and the orbicular eyeglasses dominated his face.

The President spoke clearly and succinctly in crisp clipped tones. "I understand you're just back from a long, important trip," Truman said. "Please sit down. You must be tired. I won't keep you here long." Truman extended a hand to indicate a cherry-wood chair where Buchanan should sit.

"Thank you, sir," Buchanan said. He retreated to the chair and sat.

"I hope the Secret Service didn't manhandle you too badly," Truman apologized. "My instructions were for them to bring you here directly, quickly and without fail. And I told them you were to communicate with no one until I'd spoken to you."

"They carried out your orders to a T."

"How good of them." Banter. Back and forth. Buchanan knew that the President was marking time before starting. Buchanan wished that he would get to the point, whatever it was.

Characteristically Truman stood behind the desk and leaned forward on it, never sitting. He stared at the F.B.I. agent before him. "London, was it?" Truman inquired. He spoke with the flat inflections of the American Midwest.

"Yes, Mr. President."

"Then what? Staying in Washington or back to Philadelphia?"

Buchanan started to catch on. If the President knew his itinerary, he also had to know his current assignment.

"I'll be making a report on my trip tomorrow morning at F.B.I. headquarters," Buchanan said.

"I know. Mr. Hoover told us. That's why I wanted to talk to you in person tonight. What then? After your report?"

"All else being equal, sir, I plan to go back to the West Coast. You're aware of the case I'm working on?"

"Painfully."

"I have an important witness in the Northwest. I wish to interview the witness in person."

"Good luck with it."

"Thank you."

Truman assessed Buchanan for several seconds. "I'm sure you're aware of the speech Senator Joseph McCarthy made in West Virginia on February ninth, Mr. Buchanan. Did you by chance hear it on the radio? Or did you read it in your morning paper?"

"I read part of it, sir."

"And what did you think?"

"Mr. President, as a law enforcement officer, I'm trained to differentiate fact from unsubstantiated charges. I don't think there's much question which category the senator's allegations fall into."

"Bravo!" Truman exulted. "I didn't know John Edgar Hoover was hiring renaissance men over there."

"I can't guarantee that he is either, sir."

Truman smiled for an instant. "The fact remains though, Mr. Buchanan: First McCarthy charges that there are two hundred and five Communists in the State Department. Then the number is fifty-seven. Then it's eighty-one. The undistinguished senator is pulling numbers out of his hat, which is about the only use he has for a hat since he hasn't much of a head to put it on. But he also has a few cronies at your Bureau, including your Director. So right now, as we speak, McCarthy has his friends at the F.B.I. putting together names and dirty files. Then they smuggle them to Senator McCarthy, trying to give some credibility to the reckless charges he's making." Truman paused for an instant. "You're not involved in that, are you, Buchanan?"

"No, sir."

"Good! Know what my friend Senator Lyndon Johnson of Texas says about John Edgar Hoover? He says it's better to have Hoover inside your tent pissing out than outside your tent pissing in."

Buchanan grinned.

"Well, I'd like to have John Edgar Hoover on my side too. But on my terms, not his. And don't think for a moment I don't know what he's doing. Hoover supplies names. Whether a man is guilty or innocent, the F.B.I. supplies names and files of dirt. Don't deny it!" Truman snapped abruptly. "Over on Constitution Avenue they reduce everything to a cheap, partisan issue. Don't argue with me about that either," he said to Buchanan, who hadn't opened his mouth. "In fact, don't even speak until your President asks you a direct question."

Truman was increasingly angry. He paced for a moment. He

pulled his glasses off and used the fat end of his bathrobe sash to polish the lenses.

"Joe McCarthy's a cheat, a troublemaker, a bastard, a drunk, and a goddamned liar," Truman said softly. "But he's a dangerous goddamned liar. With a little bit of substantiation, the public will listen to him. There are a lot of screwball Americans out there with a Nazi streak in them. They're all listening to their radios or reading their yellow Hearst tabloids, waiting for someone to confirm that their worst fears and prejudices have a tiny bit of merit. That's what Senator McCarthy is pandering to. I'm going to fight him with every drop of blood I have." He paused and tucked his lower lip into his mouth in a pensive scowl.

Buchanan was wise enough to remain quiet, not knowing where the conversation was heading next.

"Mr. Buchanan, the F.B.I. is not the only agency that has files," the President said. "The Justice Department has its own files. So does the Defense Department. What would you say if I told you that I have a personnel file on you?"

Truman waited for a response. A direct question! Buchanan answered, "Me, sir?"

"You're the only one in the room I'm talking to, dammit! Yes, you! Scholastic record. Army record. Professional record at the Bureau. You've done well. In fact—and I didn't bring you here to flatter you—I have a feeling you're an honorable man, unlike some of your federal police brethren over on Constitution Avenue. What do you say to that?"

"I'm flattered by your assessment, Mr. President."

"Oh, cut all that damned bullshit! Let's have a real talk!" Truman snapped. "I've done some snooping too. I know that you've been assigned this case in good faith and that you're not one of the Hoover-McCarthy hatchet men at the F.B.I."

The President barely paused for a breath. "Further," he continued, "I have a feeling there's a strong sense of decency in you, as well as some plain old Yankee common sense. So I brought you here to impress upon you one point. I want to tell you myself because I know they've probably told you something else already over at the F.B.I."

Harry Truman paused. It was apparent that he was tired and sleepy, but Buchanan could also see that he was inordinately angry. His adrenaline was pumping.

"I know what's going on in this country," Truman said.

"There's a tide rising. Not a Red tide, but an anti-Red tide. The Republicans and Republicats—that's what I call their Democratic allies in the Congress—are going to try to ride it into this building. Taft or McCarthy or some other Red-baiting Neanderthal. God knows there's enough of them. They seem to breed as fast as cats, and almost as indiscriminately."

Buchanan kept his eyes on Truman and listened, feeling his palms moisten against the arms of his chair.

"Well, I'm telling you something, Mr. Buchanan," the President continued, "and you can report this back to your Director. If this John Taylor Garrett turns out to be a Soviet agent, so be it. I know damned well that Hoover would like nothing more than to have something on John Garrett since Garrett's been a generous Democratic benefactor for many years. But I want you to be god-damned sure of what you're doing. Mistakes won't particularly hurt you or me. But they'll crucify many innocent people. Do you understand me?" Truman glared directly at him.

"I'm not sure I follow completely," Buchanan answered.

The President looked at him with displeasure. Then Truman's mood softened and he grew almost philosophical. "Look at the work there is to be done," he resumed. "The American Negro is tired of hearing about American ideals but not witnessing them. Son, I'm a man from a Jim Crow state with two segregationist senators. I walk a tightrope on civil rights for the colored people. By God, I want to do what's right. The colored race has gotten the shit end of the stick for too long in the United States. But if I push too hard, the South deserts me on Capitol Hill and the Negroes get nothing. If I don't push hard enough, the Negroes blast me, and Mrs. Roosevelt sends me letters. Not to mention what those professional bubbleheads in the American left say about me."

Buchanan didn't twitch an eyelash. The President stared at the fire for several seconds, then kept speaking.

"And how about the American Jews?" he asked. "They want a homeland for their European relatives, and I can't blame them. But I can't see how a partition of Palestine will work without a war. So how do you keep the Jews happy? Jesus Christ here on earth couldn't please them, so how am I suppose to do it?"

"I don't know, sir."

"Suppose the next world war breaks out through the Middle East. Without Saudi oil, every American tank in the world will grind to a halt. On top of this, Mr. Buchanan, the Soviets have the atomic bomb, plus four million Red Army troops in Europe ready to roll west. And all hell is ready to break out again in Asia. But those are my burdens. Let's get to the point of why you're here. I want to talk to you about your own area of expertise and how you can best serve your country. Are you following me?"

"I'm trying to, Mr. President."

"Is John Taylor Garrett some sort of Soviet agent?"

"I don't know yet, sir."

"Don't talk hogwash to the President of the United States, young man. Is there any possibility?"

"Yes. A considerable one."

The Chief Executive was clearly irked by the answer. "What makes you think so?" he snapped.

Buchanan drew a breath. "As you know, sir, I just returned from London. There was an intelligence operation launched there against the East German defense ministry. We might have gained a defector who could have informed us of impending Soviet strategies in Africa and Asia. Unfortunately the plan failed."

"I have a defense secretary named Louis Johnson. He informed me about it. So? A lot of these harebrained spy schemes fail."

"Only the five members of the political division in London knew the exact train route our agents in Europe were taking. Ambassador Fitzroy believes the leak was right there."

"Leaks can be anywhere. Fitzroy's a political hack. I'd love to sack him. But the English like him. They think he's a typical American buffoon. Fitzroy can be wrong. Usually is."

"Well, perhaps it's only a coincidence," said Buchanan, "but one of the younger political officers is about to marry one of John Garrett's daughters. I further learned that she pursued him rather arduously. She singled him out, then chased him while letting him think he was chasing her."

Truman blinked. "Good God, Buchanan! All women do that!"

"Certainly, Mr. President. But if one wanted to draw suppositions about exactly where the leak might have occurred . . ."

"All right, all right! I see your point." Truman cut Buchanan off with a wave of his hand. "Did you bring this to the attention of anyone at the London embassy?"

"No, sir. I wanted to wait for instructions when I returned to Washington."

"Good." The President was thoughtful. He removed his glasses and pressed a thumb and forefinger to his eyes, rubbing them fiercely. Again the President was distant in thought.

"Can you imagine?" Truman resumed at length. "I slept for eight and a half hours last night. And I'm still exhausted. As you'll remember, I was vice president for only two months and twenty-two days before Franklin Roosevelt died. I've been tired ever since. I'm looking forward to the day when I can go back to normal living."

Truman gave Buchanan a wry grin. Buchanan responded in kind. "Unless I'm mistaken, sir, you recently ran for reelection. You campaigned hard and you won."

"There are days when I think I should have asked for a recount. Today is one of them."

Both men laughed.

Truman pushed his glasses back into place. "Mr. Buchanan, it's getting late. Let's finish. What if John Garrett is a spy or a Soviet agent? Then what?"

"Well, first we'd have to find him."

Truman responded sarcastically. "Have you tried his home?"

"It's not an easy matter. His bank, Commonwealth Penn, now seems to run itself. We've been trying to locate Mr. Garrett for several weeks, but we've been unable."

"This is not directed at you personally, son," Truman said, "but sometimes I don't think some of John Edgar Hoover's people could locate the Pacific Ocean from underneath the Golden Gate Bridge."

"We've been working on Commonwealth Penn quite hard."

"I'm sure you have," Truman said. "But suppose you have some evidence against John Taylor Garrett. Not some trumped-up case like the ones Joe McCarthy's people are trying to fabricate. But suppose you have something real. Presupposing that you can find Garrett, what then?"

"I imagine we'd have him arrested. And placed on trial."

"No," Truman said. "That's just the point. A trial would turn into another carnival like the Lindbergh case. Every screwball columnist like Drew Pearson, Westbrook Pegler, and Walter Winchell would use Garrett's existence as proof that another thousand Communists are somewhere in the government. It would set off a tidal wave of persecutions of innocent people of moderate and liberal politics."

"Then what are you suggesting?"

"This is the part of our meeting that I hope you will *not* report to your Bureau: When you leave here," Truman said, "you'll be given a telephone number. Take it, memorize it immediately, and then destroy it. If you establish Garrett's guilt, report it to the White House first. Justice can be dispensed quietly in this case. Believe me, it will be in the best interests of the United States."

Buchanan sat before the President for several seconds. "In other words, you're asking me to bypass my superiors at the F.B.I."

"For two or three days, yes. Then you can file your standard report. Too many American lives were spent fighting fascism in Europe to let it take hold here," Truman said. "John Taylor Garrett as a political case will only hurt the United States. But we can do something positive with it."

"Such as?"

"For starters, we could trade him to the damned Russians for the five of our people who were arrested in Prague. Joe Stalin may be a murdering, dishonest, conniving bastard, but he'll also make deals. Sometimes he even keeps his end of them. Garrett has no value to us in any other way."

Buchanan studied the President and considered the proposition. "In other words," Buchanan said, "if there's to be a major spy scandal, you'd like it kept out of the newspapers."

"Yes," said Truman. "It would do the country no good."

"Nor your administration," Buchanan continued.

"My administration?" Truman scoffed. "As far as I'm concerned, Alban Barclay can come over and claim this job right now. No man in his right mind would want it. I'm interested in what's right, Mr. Buchanan." The President pursed his lips and thought for a moment. "Do you recall what went on in the Soviet Union in the 1930s, Mr. Buchanan? The purge trials?"

"Yes, sir."

"Well, with a few more highly visible spy cases, that's the sort of atmosphere we'll have right here in America: Witch hunts and political inquisitions in every court in the country. We can't have that. It would risk propelling a yahoo like Senator McCarthy into the White House. How would you sleep at night, Special Agent Buchanan, with a Cro-Magnon like Joseph McCarthy dealing with the issues of the hydrogen bomb, Palestine, North Atlantic defense treaties, the United Nations, civil rights, and China?"

"I suspect that I'd feel the same way about it as you do, Mr. President."

"Good! Because I can't force you to do this for me," the President said. "And I wouldn't dare try. God knows, for all the power of this office, the President is rarely nothing more than a public relations man trying to talk people into doing things they ought to do anyway. But for you, Mr. Buchanan, I'll simply appeal to your reason. And I'll let it drop at that." Truman toyed with the sash of his robe again. "That's all," he said. "You can go now."

Buchanan stood and offered his hand to the President. The two men shook. On Buchanan's way out the door, Truman spoke to him once again, this time while reading something on the desk and without looking up.

"There's nothing much at stake here," the President said. "Civil liberties. The future of our democracy for the next few years. The lives and careers of scores—maybe hundreds—of individual Americans. Think about that while you make your decision."

"I've already made my decision," said Buchanan, standing by the open door. Agent Kirby of the Secret Service loomed on the other side of him.

The President waited and finally did raise his eyes. His gaze settled upon Buchanan.

"I'll do what I feel is in the best interests of the country."

Tired as he was, Harry Truman managed a slight smile. "I was hopeful that you might," he said. "God bless you, Mr. Buchanan. And thank you."

The Secret Service agents escorted Buchanan back toward the rear exit of the White House. Halfway down the corridor leading from the President's study, however, Clark and Kirby led Buchanan into a small lounge beneath the rear portico.

When Buchanan entered the room, a man in a navy blue suit stood. He offered his hand. "I'm Jack Malone, United States Secret Service," the man said. "I believe the President mentioned that you'd have a contact here."

"He did," Buchanan said.

"That's me," Malone said. He pulled a pad of paper from a side table and began to write. "I'm going to give you a telephone number," Malone said. "It will put you directly in touch with me if you have any problems or need any assistance. Memorize it. Destroy it before you get home tonight. And don't hesitate to use it if you need to."

Buchanan watched Malone write. Malone handed Buchanan the number printed boldly on a sheet of paper.

"Thank you," Buchanan said. He folded it but kept it in his hand.

Clark and Kirby led their guest back to the Plymouth in the rear driveway. Buchanan settled into the backseat. Clark drove, turning over the engine with a heavy foot. A minute later the sedan rolled past the marine guard at the rear gates of the White House.

Clark and Kirby seemed in less of a hurry now. The car moved languidly across the wet, quiet streets of the capital. In the occasional light from a streetlamp Buchanan read the number off the sheet of paper. He memorized it. Then, during the drive back to 7th Street, S.E. in the back of the sedan, Buchanan borrowed Agent Kirby's cigarette lighter. In the car's rear seat ashtray he burned the sheet of paper, putting an end to the most extraordinary evening of his life.

PART
TWO
■

NINETEEN

The wheels of American Airlines Flight 437 touched the ground with a gentle thump on the Seattle runway, bounced aloft several yards, then touched down again as the flight crew applied brakes and lifted the wing flaps of the DC-3. For Thomas Buchanan, the trip from the East Coast had seemed endless. He'd flown from Washington to Chicago with a two-hour layover at Midway before catching his connection to Seattle. The smooth landing had seemed almost too much to hope for. But smooth it was, and twenty-five minutes later Buchanan walked through the debarkation portal to the main terminal.

He searched the crowd of those waiting to meet passengers. It took a few seconds to spot the woman in the tan raincoat who was waiting for him. He had spoken to Helen by telephone the previous day. He knew she would be there.

She lifted an arm and waved to him. She was alone, but looked more relaxed than when he'd seen her last. She even smiled. He walked to her.

"Hello," she said. She took his arm.

"Hello. How are things going?" he answered.

"Much better than last time," she said. "I really can't believe any of this. Come along. I have a car outside."

She asked if he was tired. He said he was, but preferred to see his witness as soon as possible anyway.

"How is Dr. Hamburger treating you?" Buchanan asked.

"Perfectly."

"And the patient? 'Braverman'? Is that what we're calling him?"

Helen laughed. "Dr. Hamburger said he'd never seen a *braver man*. So the name sort of stuck."

They arrived at Helen's car, a blue Nash. "How far is the V.A. Hospital from here?" he asked.

"Thirty minutes."

"Let's go now."

She said they would. They climbed into the car. Buchanan tossed his single suitcase into the backseat and Helen drove.

The military facility at Shannon, Washington, was the home of the 52nd Infantry Division, a unit that had borne more than its share of casualties during the fighting in the Pacific. Thus it was not unrelated that a new Veterans Administration hospital had been constructed on the unit's grounds in the dark days of 1943. The hospital remained busy seven years later.

They drove along a new highway south from Seattle. Helen knew the route perfectly. When they arrived at the army base, Helen showed a pass to a sentry and drove through the gates of the compound. She parked the car before the hospital. She pulled the key out of the ignition and turned toward Thomas.

"He can't seem to walk," she said. "The doctors say it's in his head. There's no neurological reason for it, but he won't get up on his feet."

Buchanan had heard some strange things in the last month, but this was something new. "You mean it's a mental problem?" he asked.

Helen shrugged. "I don't know. Maybe it's the medication. We'll solve the big problems first, then go on to the next ones."

She led him into the hospital and up six flights in an elevator. They walked to the end of a quiet, unguarded corridor. Helen knocked on the door of a private room in the farthest corner. The patient's sign said BRAVERMAN, JOHN EDGAR. Cute, Buchanan thought, particularly the first and middle names.

"Who is it?" called a voice from within.

"It's me," Helen called back. She stepped away from the door. "Unlock. I brought you a visitor."

Buchanan listened to the squeak of a wheelchair's rubber tires on the linoleum floor of the hospital. He glanced to Helen, who offered a hopeful smile. Buchanan rolled his eyes and tried to present the best of spirits. Meanwhile, there was a fumbling with a bolt on the other side of the door.

Then the door swung open. A man in a wheelchair rolled away from the door and stared at his visitors. His head was bandaged and his left arm was in a sling. He wore blue and red striped pajamas beneath a white hospital gown. He stared at his visitors, and Thomas saw the man's eyes take a quick, sharp look behind them to make sure that they were alone.

Then a wide smile creased the face of Mark O'Connell, the man in the wheelchair.

"Son of a bitch," O'Connell said. "Tommy, you bastard! I love you!"

He offered his hand. Buchanan stepped forward. The two men didn't shake hands so much as they embraced. O'Connell reached up with two robed arms and Buchanan leaned over to reciprocate with a hug for his former partner.

Helen closed the door. Thomas stepped away from his friend and assessed him.

"You don't look so bad for a guy who was buried less than two weeks ago," he said.

"I don't feel so bad either," O'Connell said. "The worst thing is the life insurance money. It'd be one hell of a nice thing to collect it. But we can't."

Buchanan laughed. "That's the price you pay for being alive," he said. Even Helen was mildly amused.

"I'll tell you something, Tommy," O'Connell said. "This being-given-up-for-dead stuff is for the birds. Bolt the damned door and sit down, will you?"

O'Connell motioned to a chair. Helen sat on a bench near the window. Buchanan threw the bolt on the door and sat in a chair.

"Nice room," said Buchanan, looking around.

"We installed the door bolt ourselves," O'Connell said. "Dr. Hamburger gave us permission. You wearing your piece?" O'Connell asked. It was a strange way to start.

Buchanan pushed away his jacket for a moment to show the thirty-eight-caliber Colt pistol on his left hip. "These days I don't travel without it," he said.

"Me neither," said O'Connell. "He lifted up the left leg of his pajamas and showed Buchanan the snub-nosed revolver in an inside ankle holster. "This drives the nurses into a sexual frenzy," he said.

"It drives *me* crazy," Helen shot back.

"You can go into a sexual frenzy anytime you want, sweetheart," O'Connell said to his wife, who blushed. "We'll just have Tommy leave the room for a few minutes."

"I think he's recovering," Buchanan said to Helen.

All three laughed. "What about the wheelchair?" Buchanan finally asked.

"I don't know," said O'Connell. "I just can't seem to stand up. Funny, huh?"

"No."

O'Connell shrugged. "What's the doc say to you, honey?" he asked his wife. "Says I got screws loose? That's why I don't stand up yet?"

"You'll walk again soon," Helen said to him. "You're not paralyzed. It's just a matter of when you're mentally ready."

"Yeah?" O'Connell answered. He looked as if he were searching for a flip response.

For some reason Buchanan felt compelled to intercede. "I talked to your physician yesterday by phone," he said. "Dr. Hamburger didn't say anything about walking. But he did say you took four bullets in the upper torso. One hit muscle in the upper shoulder and exited. A second nicked your collarbone. That's why you have an arm in a sling."

O'Connell's spirits seemed high, perhaps partially due to medication. He jerked the sling as if to show off.

"A third passed through your left lung. A fourth just missed your heart. You're alive by about an inch."

"I know. I looked at the scars. The luck of the Irish on Christmas Eve." O'Connell grinned. "Now. Tommy. Talk to me. Where am I and why am I here?"

"No one's told you?"

"You were the architect of this. I want to hear it from you."

"I didn't feel they were taking your security seriously enough down in Oregon," said Buchanan. "Anyone who wanted you dead could have walked into that hospital and finished the job. I didn't care for that. So I spoke to Dr. Hamburger. I told him that there were, shall we say, extenuating circumstances surrounding your shooting. And so, for your own safety, he agreed to declare you dead. I got permission from Washington, and the F.B.I. moved you here in our own ambulance so that you could remain in Dr. Hamburger's care."

"Hamburger's from Georgia, you know," O'Connell said. "He even seems bright for a southerner. Gets on fine with the colored people on the staff here too. Ty Cobb was from Georgia. My father was a Boston Red Sox fan. Hated Ty Cobb."

"Is that right?"

"I grew up with the Braves though, Tommy. Remember how I used to drag you out to Wrigley Field in 1946 whenever my Braves came into Chicago?"

"I remember."

"I'll tell you, my life was complete when I married the woman I loved, had two beautiful children, survived the war, and got to see the Boston Braves win the pennant two years ago. So what that Tom Dewey lost the election if the Braves finished first? Who's your team again, Tommy?"

"The Philadelphia A's."

O'Connell laughed. "You'd best stick to your work and stay away from Shibe Park. These are dark days."

Buchanan allowed that O'Connell had a point. Then there was an awkward pause.

"Know what else, Tommy?" O'Connell said, turning suddenly serious.

"No. What?"

"It's damned good to be alive," he said. "The doc says it's a matter of time before everything works right again. Even the legs."

He offered his hand again. Buchanan accepted it and held it for several seconds. O'Connell's eyes misted and his chin quivered. His mood darkened. "I don't know, Tom," he said. "So damned many things don't make sense." He winced and tried to control some pain that seemed to come up out of the floor. "See, Tom," he said. "I've paid dearly. I'm not sure what I've bought for it, but I've paid." He gave Buchanan a wink. "Don't lie to me: Are you here official or unofficial?"

"Both."

"Let's get to business, then," O'Connell finally said. "I know you're not here just to chat."

"I want to know who shot you. And why."

"Well, I'd be interested myself. The Oregon state police seem to think I got plugged because I was about to write a speeding ticket. Or because I surprised some bank robbers. But no one was speeding and no bank had been robbed anywhere within five hundred miles. Ah, no one listened to the details. A woman. Then a man. Two cars. One in front, one behind. Blinding headlights. Come on. I know a professional hit when I receive one."

Helen had heard the story enough times and cringed at having to relive it again. O'Connell suggested that she treat herself to a movie. Helen accepted the offer.

Buchanan stood and let her out, then bolted the door and settled back into his chair. He took out a notepad and a pen.

"Whatever you're working on, Tommy," O'Connell said after Helen had left, "it must be damned important."

"It looks increasingly that way. I even met with Hoover the other day."

"Yeah?" O'Connell managed a wry smile. "The old man, huh?"

"Himself."

"Do you think he's a fairy?"

"What?"

"You heard me. You saw him live and in person. Do you think Hoover's queer?"

"Mark, those stories have been around for years. Not one has ever been substantiated."

"Has anyone ever proved God exists?" O'Connell retorted. "But I'll bet you believe that too."

Buchanan experienced a sinking feeling as this subject came up. He had forgotten, but O'Connell and several of the other agents in the Chicago field office had been obsessed with the character of their Director. They speculated and hypothesized among themselves until stories about their suggestions circulated back to Washington. Several received letters of rebuke in their personnel files. O'Connell was apparently still fixed upon the topic, Buchanan was sorry to learn.

"What about Hoover and Tolson?" O'Connell mused. "Constant companions. Clyde calls Hoover 'Speed,' and Hoover calls Clyde 'Junior.' Both bachelors, both a little on the priggish and dandified side—right, Tom?—with their boutonnieres, their crisp white shirts, and their snap-brim fedoras. You know, Tolson made assistant Director within three years of joining the Bureau. Does that strike you as normal?"

"That was back in the twenties," Buchanan said. "Things worked differently then."

"They arrive for work together, lunch together, and have dinner together at the Mayflower Hotel in Washington. What else do they do together, Tom? Got a guess?"

Buchanan was silent.

"Did you ever hear about the Guy Hottell incident?" O'Connell continued. "Hottell was a big, handsome fellow. Enormously gifted athlete. Football player at George Washington University. He moved right into Hoover's inner circle, remember? Hottell, Tolson, and Hoover used to take their vacations together down south. Never any women, of course. Remember how jealous Tolson would get? And remember how Hoover used to walk right out of the spas and hotels where the three of them had stayed together? Hoover never paid any of the bills."

"I heard those stories too, Mark. It's a free country, so you can draw whatever conclusion you want."

"But what conclusion do you, draw, Tommy? You just saw Hoover in person."

"I conclude that I know why you're an *ex*-agent."

"If J. Edgar Hoover's not queer, then he's pretty weird," O'Connell said. "Know something else? Hottell also was Tolson's roommate at George Washington." He looked at Buchanan again, hoping for a response.

"Come on, Mark," Buchanan finally said. "Character assassination is only going to get you in trouble. Hoover will have you crucified if he learns you're saying stuff like that."

O'Connell grimaced, looked at his friend, and at length began to laugh. "Okay, you win," O'Connell said. "Let's get to business. There's a cute little nurse on this floor named Maryann. A blonde with black stockings. She specializes at tossing visitors out. Talk to me before she comes in and chases you. What's this case you're working on?"

"It began as a bank investigation," Buchanan said. "I now believe it's much more than that."

"What bank?"

"The Second Commonwealth Bank of Pennsylvania."

"Yeah. I've heard of it. Small and independent, right?" O'Connell asked. Buchanan nodded in response. "The only people who usually get shot during bank investigations," O'Connell continued, "are senior vice presidents. And they do the job themselves if the auditors come on an unexpected day."

"In particular, I'm investigating a man named John Taylor Garrett," said Buchanan. "He's the chief officer of Commonwealth Penn."

O'Connell didn't move a muscle as he thought. His arms rested on the wooden arms of his chair. He sat comfortably but at attention. "Seems his name came up in something I was working on in Chicago," he said. "Nothing dirty by itself. I know what it was. The

Bureau was studying some currency speculation between the United States and Europe. Looking to see if anyone had broken the law."

"I took the liberty of requesting your report from Chicago, Mark. There's mention of Garrett and Commonwealth Penn. But there was never an indictment."

"Never any substantial case. That's why," O'Connell said. "Other banks, yes. Commonwealth Penn, no. Maybe they just covered their tracks better than the others. I remember that we had enough indictments to make our time worthwhile."

"Was there anything you recall that wasn't in your report?"

O'Connell thought hard. "No," he said. "I tend to remember the stuff we leave out." He pondered it for another moment. "So what does Commonwealth Penn have to do with me?"

"Mark, I'm trying to resolve my own case," he said. "But I also want to know who shot you. There may be a correlation."

"How the hell do you arrive at that?"

"Maybe through Morning Glory," Buchanan said. "But you have to tell me."

O'Connell rubbed his eyes. He kept his hand in his face. Then he looked back up. "Helen, right?" he said. "She told you about Morning Glory? Or did you listen to the tapes I made?"

"The tapes were stolen," Buchanan reminded him gently. "I never heard them. So let's go back to the beginning," Buchanan said. "Helen told me about the Great Handsaw Caper. She also told me about the Wobbly Witch Hunt. And I talked to a few of your friends in the Seattle field office."

"You didn't talk to that prick Dick Fletcher, did you? He's the special agent in charge in Seattle."

"I had a feeling that wouldn't have been productive," Buchanan said.

"I'm sure he wasn't terribly upset. About my being killed, I mean. Dick's a high-grade moron. Know what his own men say about him? 'Frequently wrong, but never in doubt.'"

"Mark, I want to focus on those three cases. Handsaw. Wobbly. And Morning Glory."

O'Connell looked away, as if the mere mention of any of them brought him considerable pain. "I don't want to seem obstinate, Tom," he said. "But if you want information on either of the first two, read the files. I put everything in the reports."

"I read them," Buchanan said. "Bill Roth at the Philadelphia office obtained them for me."

"Did you read between the lines?"

"I know they were bullshit cases," Buchanan said. "But what else was there, Mark? I know how reports have to be written from a certain perspective. A certain tone to keep the Bureau panjandrums happy."

"You can say that again."

"Please reach back. Think as hard as you can. Was there anything in either that didn't appear in your final report?"

"No," O'Connell answered. "It was straightforward stuff. It's just that those cases depressed me. Imagine, wasting agents' time and attention just for the Bureau's bullshit arrest-conviction ratios. Imagine going after a bunch of broken-down old lefties and trying to take their social security away. I liked to think of the Bureau as a pretty serious operation, Tom. Then they get me hung up with crap like that. Oh, man. It turned my fucking stomach."

"Helen told me," he said. "And I read your file, as you suggested. There's always the possibility that something was missed on Handsaw and Wobbly. But I'm willing to presuppose that there wasn't anything else. That's why I want to know about what you called Morning Glory."

O'Connell seemed to gaze angrily off into the middle distance for several seconds. Buchanan waited. "Did you make tapes on Morning Glory?" Buchanan pressed gently.

O'Connell nodded. "Eight of them." He stared at Buchanan. "All gone?" he asked.

"All eight. Stolen."

O'Connell grimaced. "Poor Helen must be terrified," he said.

"Your wife is a very brave woman," he said. "And a very bright one. You're a lucky man."

O'Connell nodded. For a few seconds Buchanan waited patiently. "I must ask you these questions," Buchanan pressed gently. "Please try hard, Mark.

O'Connell nodded with a grunt.

"I looked all through your personnel file for something called Morning Glory, Mark. I spoke with a few of your friends. I couldn't find any file that might have been the Morning Glory case. Do you have any idea why it might be missing? Did someone mark it Do Not File and send it to Washington?"

"There is no Morning Glory file," O'Connell said. "I never wrote a report."

"But why?"

"It wasn't an assigned case, Tom," O'Connell said. "It was something that I stumbled across. I was still involved in it when I finally had my fill of the Bureau and resigned. As far as the F.B.I. was concerned, I was still on the Wobblies."

"And you reasoned . . ." Buchanan began, instantly starting to understand.

"I was pissed at the Bureau. And I didn't want to put my name on something half baked. Also, they were shoving me down the shaft, so why should I do them any favors? Why give them a big lead, in other words. That and the fact that a Morning Glory file would have created more questions than it answered."

"But you spoke to at least two other agents about it. In San Francisco. Larry Herter and Jim Meadley."

"How did you know that?" O'Connell snapped.

"I made some phone calls. After your 'death.' "

"And what did they tell you?" O'Connell suddenly sounded very defensive.

"Nothing. They said that you and they were trying to put together an extracurricular project. But nothing came of it. You used the code name Morning Glory."

"They're good men, those two. Don't let them get their asses in Hoover's charcoal."

"I won't," Buchanan promised.

"Herter and Meadley helped me," O'Connell said. "They covered my back. Provided me with extra eyes and a couple of guns. If Morning Glory surfaces again, they could be brilliant."

"What about Seattle?" Buchanan asked. "Did you talk to anyone there?"

"About what?"

"Morning Glory."

"No. Didn't trust anyone there." His brow furrowed and he looked at Buchanan with considerable displeasure. "What are you implying? Why are you asking me that?"

"Well, for God's sake, Mark, you were shot for a reason. And there are only two scenarios. One, someone picked you up in the midst of your investigation and figured you had to be silenced for what you might know. *Or* two, there was some sort of leak within the Bureau. And since you were working out of Seattle, the leak may have been there."

It was O'Connell's turn to sit without speaking as he pondered the implications.

"Well, we have to consider that possibility," Buchanan continued. "We infiltrate the other side during investigations. Someday the other side might infiltrate us."

"Tom, things like that don't happen in criminal investigations. You and I were both in the war. That's more the type of thing that happens in an intelligence operation. Spies and the like. Foreign governments."

"Yes," Buchanan said flatly. "I know. I'm just back from London, Mark. And a foreign intelligence operation is perhaps what we're dealing with here."

The astonishment broadened on O'Connell's face. "How the *hell* do you get to that conclusion?" he barked indignantly.

"I don't want to color your own memory," Buchanan said. "So you tell me about Morning Glory before I say anything else. Who else knew about it, for example?"

"There was Herter and Meadley in San Francisco," he said. "They knew I was on a trail, but they didn't know exactly what I was doing. All they knew was that I'd drawn a bead on someone. I left the Bureau before I could tell them much. And there was no one else. And that includes Helen. I *mentioned* the name of the case to her once or twice. Eventually I might have told her. But—you're not married currently, are you, Tom?"

"No."

"Ever been married?"

"No."

"Well, a man's wife does enough worrying. Why give her anything extra?"

"I quite understand. And agree," Buchanan said. "But could anyone have broken into your home and listened to your tapes?"

"No," O'Connell answered. "Impossible." Not only had he sealed the box of tapes in the wall, he explained, but he'd put his own signature on the paneling. That is, with the cellar window sealed by the cardboard, he'd put a pair of bent staples into the space between the panels. No one saw him do that. If anyone had disturbed the panels, O'Connell would have picked up the intrusion immediately. Buchanan awarded him points on that move. O'Connell was right. No one else in the Bureau could have known the full story of Morning Glory.

"And you realize the implications of that, don't you?" Buchanan said. "That's reason enough for someone to go to considerable trouble to have you shot."

"That's occurred to me," said O'Connell.

"Morning Glory," Buchanan prodded gently.

This time O'Connell was ready to talk. In fact, he seemed to draw strength from the story he had to tell. His eyes were suddenly keen, and he rose up a bit in his wheelchair as he spoke.

"This is the story of a smuggler, Tom," said O'Connell. "Does a lot of business with the Orient." A strange look of realization passed across O'Connell's face. "Come to think of it, Tom, he also does a bit of business with your neck of the woods. Philadelphia. Of course, it still doesn't make any sense that he'd hunt down an ex-agent and have me shot just because I caught a suspicious whiff of him once." Then it was Buchanan's turn to be struck in the chest and knocked cold, as if by bullets.

"Who is he?" Buchanan asked.

"The man's a Chinaman," O'Connell said. "His name is Sammy Wong. Why are you looking at me like that, Tommy? Heard of him?"

Several seconds transpired before Buchanan could verbalize his response. "If it's the same Sammy Wong," Buchanan said, "he was one of John Garrett's dinner guests the last time Garrett was seen in public."

"Is that a fact?"

"It's more than a fact, Mark. It's probably the reason I'm here." Buchanan sat quietly and listened. Calmly Mark O'Connell held court in his wheelchair and unraveled for the first time to any human listener the full account of Morning Glory.

TWENTY

O'Connell took Buchanan on a journey through his unlovely past, which called for a confession or two on his own.

It had been in San Francisco in 1949, Buchanan said. O'Connell was still in the midst of the Wobbly—or I.W.W. —fiasco, spreading nets all over the Pacific Northwest trying to catch a bunch of broken-down old radicals and, if possible, clap them into jail for expressing their opinions.

"Really foul stuff, Tom," O'Connell said again. He spoke not so much to excuse himself, but rather to convey the acrid taste that remained in his mouth, even after a year. "I despised it particularly coming on the heels of the Handsaw case. Half of the Seattle office hated to come to work each morning." Yet there was Dick Fletcher, the special agent in charge, with orders from Hoover on his desk. Fletcher was screaming like a banshee for arrests, convictions, and quotas. So in to work they came and out they went to wage war on the Wobblies.

"Dick Fletcher had some travel money plus the authorization for it on the Wobbly case. Fletcher got a further directive from Hoover," O'Connell explained. "Hoover's own handwriting: 'How far up and down the West Coast have these Communists been infiltrating American unions?' Hoover asked. Fletcher wanted a man to go to San Francisco to check the situation. He asked me. I had no objections. I figured it was a fishing trip, wouldn't come back with much, but, frankly, I wanted out of Seattle for a few days."

"Why?"

"I was burned out on the Wobbly case. I wanted a change of scenery for a few hours at least."

"Why didn't Seattle just asked the San Francisco office to run a few local checks?" Buchanan asked. "That would have more closely resembled the official procedure."

"Sure it would have," O'Connell said. "But Dick Fletcher had this hatred of the San Francisco office. Claimed they would run the entire northern stretch of the West Coast if allowed to. And you know what the *unofficial* procedure always turns into, Tom. Small office like Seattle asks big office like San Francisco to snoop. If the big guys pick up a scent, they grab your whole investigation. You've put in hundreds of man-hours, they run away with the arrests and convictions, and your own charts look like everyone's been busy picking toenails all year. Bureaus get closed, agents get dismissed, and bureau chiefs get retired at age forty over such things."

"Of course," Buchanan answered. "So you went to San Francisco on the Wobbly case, Mark. What happened when you got there?"

"*Nothing* happened," Mark O'Connell explained. "At least nothing having to do with the Wobblies. The I.W.W. contingents in the longshore unions had been taken over by rival unions during the war. The new boys on the piers were lead-pipe punch-in-the-mouth guys. The only liberal causes they took a shine to were salary increases for their men, particularly the leadership."

The ex-agent's memory was sharp now. "The new locals came in with some heavy-hitting Italian types and some Jew labor lawyers from New York back around 1947," O'Connell said. "They ran all the old-time F.D.R.-thirties liberals straight into the Bay. Sometimes literally. The piers were always a tough place, and they were tougher still when the stevedores, the maritime unions, and the guys who unloaded the fish and the freight organized new locals. Forget about those old bleeding-heart Socialists, Tom," O'Connell said. "They were gone. And any Red who came in and tried to start organizing would probably end up in the Oakland side of the Bay wearing concrete boots."

Buchanan said he understood.

O'Connell spent four days there, reaching that conclusion. His work was solid and he covered himself by conferring with a couple of local Feebees at the San Francisco office. That was where Larry Herter and Jim Meadley came in. They had worked with O'Connell in Chicago. O'Connell knew he could trust them. He ran a check on the local unions through them and they confirmed that his information was good.

O'Connell seemed a little uneasy with what he came to next. "Well, I was alone in the city," he said. "So, you know, I wanted to amuse myself one evening. Boys' night out, know what I mean?"

"I'm getting the idea," Buchanan said.

Not surprisingly the idea revolved around an establishment not unknown to single men traveling alone. It was called the Candid Camera Artists' Models Studio and was left over from the San Francisco World's Fair of 1940. Men could rent a camera for a few dollars at the door. In a lounge they could buy a drink or two. And in an adjacent "studio" they could take their cameras and snap pictures of—or just gaze at—several experts at pulchritude who were sitting or standing around, posing in the nude. Most of the male customers had no previous experience in photography. But that was beside the point.

"The owner of the place was a former actor named Blake Warren," O'Connell said. O'Connell described Warren as an alert-looking character with sharp dark eyes and a trim mustache. He wore a tuxedo each evening to give his strip joint a touch of class. He also lived in an apartment right upstairs, where O'Connell said he also kept his records.

At one time Warren had been known as the King of the Robots. He had performed in vaudeville and a few films, including one with Charlie Chaplin. But he had also made a good living in—of all places—department store windows. He possessed remarkable control over all his muscles, both voluntary and involuntary. For hours on end he could stand completely motionless in a store window, usually alongside a dummy dressed exactly the same way. The idea was to draw a crowd, some of whom would end up going into the store. The crowd tried to decide which was Blake Warren and which was the dummy. It wasn't an easy matter.

"Blake did some work for us in Chicago during the war," O'Connell said. "I won't go into it, but you can imagine how useful a man like that can be in a surveillance situation."

Buchanan said he could conjure up a whole vista of possibilities.

"Anyway, Blake ran the place. I used to drop in now and then. Yeah, you know, I liked to have a drink with him and look at his girls. I admit that. I couldn't put it in my report though. That's another reason why I never wrote anything on Morning Glory. How do I explain how I was in the Candid Camera Artists' Models Studio to start with? By lying? Bad idea."

"Bad idea, indeed," Buchanan agreed. "What else did the girls do beside pose?"

"After a girl had put in half an hour on the stage, she was free to come out to the lounge and circulate. She could let an enthusiastic fan buy her a drink. Blake Warren encouraged that much, you understand," O'Connell said. "His business was renting cameras and selling drinks."

"Mark," Buchanan asked, experiencing a slightly sinking feeling, "you're telling me this place was a brothel, right?"

"Sort of," O'Connell said.

" 'Sort of'? It either was or it wasn't."

"Warren didn't pay the girls to be there. Didn't pay them a nickel. And they didn't pay him anything either."

"They just sat there nude for the fun of it?"

O'Connell paused for several seconds before making the setup clear. "Look," he finally said, "like I said, Blake Warren made his money on the cameras and the refreshments. The girls could meet a date there, maybe . . . ."

"And if the girl left arm in arm with a man and conducted some sort of business elsewhere," Buchanan said, "that wasn't anything Warren had anything to do with?"

"Not monetarily. So he was within the law." O'Connell

paused. "He helped the local police frequently, and he'd assisted the Bureau a number of times in the past. So the law left him alone."

"I get it," Buchanan said.

"I rarely talked to Blake's girls myself," O'Connell said. Thinking, he stopped and corrected himself. "Maybe once or twice, okay. But that was all. I'm like any other man. I like to look at women without clothes. There's no crime in that. No sin, either, in my opinion. I'm just looking. I wouldn't dream of touching." Momentarily O'Connell seemed uneasy. "But look, though. Don't even breathe a word about this part to Helen, okay?" he asked. "About me going to look at Blake's stable. A wife doesn't understand why a man needs to do stuff like that every once in a while. A girl gives you what you want when you ask for it; she doesn't understand why you might just want to take a peek somewhere else. No touching, just a peek."

Buchanan said it would never come up, either to Helen or to anyone in the Bureau. O'Connell looked relieved.

"This is where we get to Sammy Wong," the wounded police chief of Peterton, Oregon, said next.

As long as he was in the establishment, O'Connell recalled, he figured he might as well take a good look at its denizens, girls and boys both. "Some of the girls who'd been posing had made their way out to the bar. They were passing around among the audience. I took up a position at the far end of the rail. That's when I saw this Chinese guy come in, Tom," O'Connell said. "He was smoking a cigarette and his hat brim was pulled low over his eyes as if he didn't want anyone to recognize him. I was watching this carefully. Most white bar girls down in California won't go to bed with Oriental men, you know. The Orientals have a bad reputation, especially the ones just off the boat. They want to tie the girls up or do it through the ass. Funny stuff, you know?"

Buchanan stifled a wry smile. O'Connell saw it and reacted defensively. "That's not just my opinion or upbringing, Tom. That's the reputation the Chinese have."

Buchanan said he knew, which was at least partially a lie. "Uh-huh," he said.

"So I'm watching this guy," O'Connell said. "I'm waiting for him to go rent a camera and enter the studio. But he doesn't. He just checks out the crowd, buys a brandy, and goes over to a table by the south wall. He puts his hat on the edge of a chair, sits, and smiles. I figure, this guy's just going to talk to any girl and leave with the first one who'll fuck a Chinaman. I look at his suit and it's expensive silk. I can see the shine on his tie clear across the room. And he's got a diamond on his little finger that could choke a horse. But then he confuses me again," O'Connell said.

"How?"

"He doesn't even make a play for any of the girls. So what's he there for? I'm watching him in the mirror behind the bar now and I'm wondering: Why is this man here at all? You can drink a lot cheaper somewhere else. Then I realize what I'm watching. This guy's a professional gangster, Hong Kong- or Peking-style. I didn't recognize it right away because back in Chicago or up in Washington State you don't see the Chinese all that often. I watched him pick up his drink and reach for his wallet. He was right-handed, and he was covered by a left-handed wall. He had a choice of twenty tables, yet he took the only one that gave him a view of the entire room, plus both doors, the bar, and a set of service stairs that led down to Blake Warren's storage room. I can tell: the man's watching the room. He's making sure that no one's got surveillance on him. He honed in on me in a couple of seconds since I wasn't making time with any of the females. So I started talking to this little dark-haired girl who'd been nude in the studio a few minutes earlier. She was dressed now. She talked a blue streak. She said she was a college student and needed the money. Must have been about nineteen. Very pretty. She said her name was Kim and she'd obviously taking a liking to me. She kept asking me if I wanted to leave with her and I kept putting her off. Finally she figured I was dense or something, and didn't catch on. She came right out and whispered in my ear. 'For twenty dollars you can fuck me,' she said. 'That, or I'll take you in my mouth.' That put me on the spot. I can't leave with her and I sure can't tell her I'm a Fed. So I said I liked her. But I'd come to admire, not to touch. She looked kind of disappointed and went right on to some other guy in a suit. She left with him about five minutes later, and I got to tell you, I felt a little jealous. I mean, I was talking to her first, but this other guy left with her. But I had to talk with her, or the Chinaman would have made me as a cop within five minutes."

"But you kept watching him?"

"Through the mirror behind the bar," O'Connell said again. "I watched him as best I could. See, when Kim started bargaining with me I had to pay some attention to her too. She was distracting me. I know another man came in and sat down next to Wong. I believe he handed him something. An envelope, maybe, under the table. Then the man left. A few minutes later Wong got up, popped his hat back on his head, and walked out also."

"And you followed?"

"I figured I'd give him a tail, yes. Just for the hell of it, if nothing else. Or at least I would have," said O'Connell. "But Blake caught my arm as I was halfway to the door. 'Blake, I have to be going now,' I said to him. 'Not a good idea,' he answers. 'But Blake, I have to—'

" 'The Chinaman's name is Sammy Wong,' Blake Warren said to me. " 'And you go out that door and he'll have you made in two seconds.'

" 'So you know him?' I asked Blake.

" 'I know enough,' Warren answered, 'to suggest that you stay away from him.'

" 'Then you talk to me about him,' I said to Warren. He said he would."

Plain and simple, Sammy Wong was an opium dealer. No, that was like saying Henry Ford was a car dealer. Sammy Wong *was* opium in San Francisco. "Try not to hold his profession against him, old boy," Blake Warren said to O'Connell, "and for God's sake don't drag a federal case into my camera shop. Make me those promises, and I'll tell you all you want to know."

O'Connell made that promise, not knowing whether or not he intended to keep it.

Wong was from a good family in China, Blake Warren explained. "Good" meant wealthy and non-Communist before the civil war began in the 1930s. A rumor in the West Coast underworld had it that Wong had studied to be a doctor when he was a young man, which may have been where he gained an introduction to pharmaceuticals. There'd also been a reference here and there to a Madame Wong, suggesting that he'd been married. But he wasn't practicing anything that would be considered legally sanctioned medicine anywhere in the world, and he was known to have a few mistresses scattered around Asia, the Philippines, and Hawaii. "Mostly American and European girls," Blake Warren said. "Heaven knows, the man can afford it. It's as if he has a permit to print money." Then again, at forty dollars a gram for opium, his business was better than printing money—though his cover was that of an importer of inexpensive toys and novelties from Formosa.

Any business that was better than printing money had to be illegal, immoral, or both, so Buchanan's ears perked doubly.

"I couldn't just let it go at that, Tom," O'Connell said. "So I started to lean on Warren for a little extra information. I wanted to know where Wong stayed in San Francisco. Was he a resident? Did he maintain an apartment? What about a company?"

Warren wasn't immediately forthcoming with that information. But he did provide enough. "He told me to try S.W. Imports, which was a one-flight-up job above a restaurant in Chinatown. And he also suggested that Wong sometimes stayed at the California Pacific Hotel."

That was good enough for O'Connell. The next morning he dropped in on Herter and Meadley again and asked if they would cover his back while he visited the hotel. They said they'd be delighted. All three chipped in ten dollars and Herter rented a $29.95 room in the California Pacific for the night of April 30. O'Connell brought along a little Minox spy camera for the occasion. He visited the hotel and sat in Herter's room. Meadley worked the sidewalk across the street and waited till Wong went out in the evening. Then he called Herter's room from an outside telephone.

"The Chinaman's gone," he said.

Herter and O'Connell went to Wong's floor while Meadley took a position in the hotel lobby, watching for the Chinaman to come back. "Herter maintained a vigil on the elevators while I broke into the Chinaman's room," O'Connell said. "Meadley had all the angles covered in the lobby. If Wong reappeared, he'd dial Wong's room on the house phone, give it one ring, hang up fast, and I'd be out. If for some reason this failed and Wong arrived back on the floor unexpectedly, Herter would noisily delay him at the elevator banks. The elevators were around two corners from his room."

"How did you get entrance to Wong's room?" Buchanan asked.

O'Connell smiled. "The California Pacific is kind of a casual place. It's also old. The locks practically fainted when they saw three Feebees coming."

"How much time did you have in Wong's room?"

"I took twenty minutes and tossed the place thoroughly," said O'Connell. "Let me tell you. Wong was a sly little bastard. The room was pristine. Almost as if no one were staying in it. Just his suitcase."

"I suppose you broke into that too."

"Didn't have to. Wong left it open, almost as if he didn't care who snooped. Only one thing of interest in it. A tiny ledger in Chinese, sort of a notebook version of an abacus, all tight with his spidery handwriting. Chinese write real small, as if they got microscopes for eyes, or as if they're going to run out of paper." O'Connell stared at Buchanan for a moment. "Well, I didn't steal it. That way Wong would know someone was on to him. So I photographed it."

Meadley and Herter had the photographs developed the next day. The San Francisco F.B.I. office was pretty much of a white-bread operation. No blacks, no Jews, and, even more important on this occasion, no Chinese. Nothing more exotic, actually, than an Irish Protestant, so no one in the Bureau could read the pages.

Meadley passed them along to a contact in the San Francisco police department who managed to have them read. All of that put the agents back at square one. The ledgers suggested a vast flow of cash, but the figures were coded. Without reading Wong's mind there was no way of knowing which amount flowed through which account in which financial institution and in which company. Like criminal geniuses such as Arnold Rothstein or Meyer Lansky before him, Wong kept his figures in his head. There was, in fact, nothing within the figures to even suggest a criminal activity or the dealing in opium. Nor was there anything else in Wong's possession to suggest it. For all the trouble that O'Connell had gone to, he had nothing more than some hearsay against an importer of cheap toys.

Just for the hell of it, O'Connell continued, they resumed on Wong's trail that same day. O'Connell had to be getting back to Seattle and was increasingly at a loss to explain what he was doing in San Francisco. But there was always the chance of scoring a major case quickly, the kind of thing that could make an agent's career. So he couldn't bring himself to drop Wong. Not just yet.

Here Meadley got innovative. O'Connell pulled the address for S.W. Imports straight out of the San Francisco telephone directory. With virtually the same ease, Meadley checked a telescope out of the F.B.I.'s equipment room. Then they set up their own observation nest in a warehouse two blocks from S.W. Imports' office. All this time the San Francisco police agreed to lend them a stakeout team for two days, just to monitor Wong's movements from the California Pacific Hotel.

The telescope was trained directly into the window of Wong's office. O'Connell, Meadley, and Herter took turns watching while

Wong was in residence. The Chinaman's office was a single room with two large single-panel windows. It was awash in papers, books, and correspondence, files that overflowed and steel bookcases that sagged. "That office was cluttered to the rafters, Tom," O'Connell recalled. "Our little Asian dynamo needed nothing quite so much as he needed a secretary and some extra office space."

But the watchers saw more than clutter. They observed an industrious little man who poured relentlessly over books and papers at his desk. He smoked Lucky Strikes all day and ate no more than an apple at lunch. He worked on the telephone for very short periods of time, also, but mostly he went over the reams and reams of correspondence in his office. The vision made sense. Blake Warren said Wong was in town only a week every few months, and the man seemed like he was doing months worth of bookkeeping and correspondence all in one sitting. Meadley watched Wong make some of his telephone calls, and the special agent made noises about invading the junction box in the basement of the building. Never mind a court order; they would just make some recordings.

Wong worked there from ten A.M. without a break. "You'd think the little fucker would leave to take a piss," Herter observed. But he didn't, except for one time at two in the afternoon. Then Wong flipped a light on toward five in the afternoon and gave the watchers an even clearer view of what he was doing.

Shortly before ten P.M. that night, Wong began to tidy up. He pushed things from his desk and shoved papers into folders. O'Connell was watching at the time and couldn't believe the casualness with which the man stuffed his files.

"Here we thought we'd hit paydirt, Tom," O'Connell recalled. "Now we figured we knew where his records were. From here it would be simple. We'd maintain a stakeout, make sure Wong was far away, and then do a black-bag job on his office one night." By black bag he meant an illegal entry, one of the specialties of the West Coast F.B.I. field offices in 1950. "Wong left his shades up, left that packed little office all a-clutter, stood up, and walked out. He went to the Shanghai Inn for some late dinner. He held his waiter in a long conversation, then ate almost nothing. Then he went back to the hotel. He spoke to no one, Tom, other than the waiter in the restaurant along the way. Not a soul. Then he was back to his hotel by midnight. Didn't even stop off at the Artists' Models Studio," O'Connell added wryly. "And I didn't either."

"I assume," Buchanan said, "that you watched him all the way back to the hotel."

"All the way back and up the elevator to the fifth floor. From the street we even saw the light go on in his room."

O'Connell was suddenly in some discomfort from his bullet wounds. He fidgeted uncomfortably in his wheelchair. But he was even more ill at ease with what he had to say next.

"He never came out of the hotel the next day," O'Connell said.

"What?"

And that, O'Connell resumed, wasn't even the most astounding part.

O'Connell, Meadley, and Herter spent the entire next day waiting for Wong to appear. O'Connell had the street covered and Meadley had the lobby. Herter alternated on the stakeout team with the San Francisco police who manned the telescope. But the telescope itself wasn't picking up much of a picture that next day. The glass windows in Wong's office were blocked by a big black shade that hadn't been drawn the night before.

O'Connell left Herter at the hotel and drove to Chinatown. He parked his car two blocks from Wong's office and walked the rest of the way to the telescope point. There he peered at the black shade and cursed violently. Where was Wong? And who had been in and out of his office?

"I want to go into both places," O'Connell had said. "The hotel room and the office."

"When?" Meadley asked.

"Now."

They drove back to the hotel. Meadley and Herter waited down below. O'Connell admitted that he had been losing his composure by this point. He inquired at the front desk for Wong, but no one was registered at the hotel by that name. He rudely grabbed the reservation book and searched out Wong's entry. Not only was it not there, it had never been there.

O'Connell turned and forged into the elevator. He went up to the fifth floor and rapped sharply on Wong's door. There was no answer. He gave serious consideration to kicking the door in. Then a man showed up in the hallway who introduced himself as Roger Lund. "Lund was the house dick," O'Connell said.

"What's the problem?" Lund asked.

O'Connell stared at him. "You got a set of keys?" he asked.

"It depends who you are," Lund answered.

"I couldn't decide whether to smash the bastard or just flash him the F.B.I. shield," said O'Connell. But then the door opened. A middle-aged couple stood before them. They had little trouble convincing the F.B.I. agent and the house detective that they were in fact a vacationing couple named Albert and Mary Nunzio from Bridgeport, Connecticut. The previous guest, an Asian businessman, was long gone.

By his own admission, O'Connell stormed out of the hotel in a blind rage. He joined Herter and Meadley in their car. They drove back to Chinatown. There the warehouse was closed, but they bribed the night porter into letting them take the freight elevator up.

"I went to the door of S.W. Imports myself," O'Connell said. "I didn't know what I'd find. I knocked. No answer. So what the hell? There was a fire ax in the hall. I used it. The door was wooden and didn't pose much of a problem. I knocked in the lock with the dull end of the ax."

Then O'Connell stood at the door he'd broken open. He stood and stared. Like the smile of the Cheshire cat, Wong managed to recede the closer anyone approached. The office was empty.

"Just the desk and a chair remained, Tom. Sometime, somehow, overnight, into thin air. Everything was gone from the office. The shelves were neat and clean. There wasn't a paper clip on the floor or a scrap of paper anywhere in a drawer or basket." It was as if it had been cleaned hermetically.

"Practically before my very eyes, Tom," O'Connell concluded, "Wong had slipped his leash. We practically had a saddle on him the whole time, yet he vanished. All his clothes. All his records. Everything. *Everything!* Right before our eyes." In a way, O'Connell concluded, it was eerie. Wong had carefully and instantaneously obliterated every trace of himself.

It was as if, O'Connell observed, for the last four days the three F.B.I. men had been watching a ghost. Now that the sun had risen, the nocturnal vision had vanished. It was as if, they concluded, Sammy Wong had never existed at all.

"To this day, Tom," O'Connell said, "I can't figure it. Wong made it some way. But I don't know how. Further, we didn't even have anything on him. All I had were empty time sheets when I went back to Seattle."

For a moment Buchanan fell completely silent, trying to lend some order to the chaos of O'Connell's story. For his part, in the uneasy silence of the hospital room O'Connell felt his flesh crawl uncomfortably. He also felt his energy wane. Buchanan could see both from the drained expression on the man's face.

From there O'Connell took a final breath and moved for the next forty-five minutes nonstop to the present—from his resignation from the Bureau in Seattle, to Peterton, to the memorable Christmas Eve when he lay in the snow with four bullets in his chest.

"You know, Tom," O'Connell said when it was over, "I was hit four times. One went on each side of my heart. It would have been enough to make a religious man out of me, except I already was one."

Buchanan allowed that such an incident would easily have that sort of effect on a sane individual. Then someone tried the door and, finding it bolted, knocked loudly. Moments later Buchanan admitted the nurse named Maryann to the hospital chamber. She brought with her Mark O'Connell's dinner and instructions for Buchanan to leave her patient in peace for the next hour.

"She's beautiful," O'Connell warned, "but she's tough. Better obey."

Understanding where power resides in any hospital, Buchanan politely did obey. He withdrew to the hospital's cafeteria for coffee, taking with him a myriad of impressions and suspicions engendered by Mark O'Connell's meticulous and unimpaired memory.

TWENTY-ONE

Buchanan glanced at his watch. It was 7:25 in the evening, or 10:25 in the East, where Buchanan's day had begun at six A.M. O'Connell was back in bed now and Buchanan was seated in a chair across from him. Helen was at the nursing station raving about *Twelve O'Clock High,* which she'd just caught up with earlier that day. Gregory Peck and Dean Jagger were two of Helen's passions.

"Mark, you've been very generous with your time and energy today. I have a few more minutes before visitors have to leave. Tomorrow, unless plans change overnight, I have to return to either

Philadelphia or Washington. That, or I'll have to go down to California for a few days. So in the minutes that remain, I'd like to put a hypothesis to you about what you've observed and what you've experienced. May I?"

"Go ahead," said O'Connell.

"I don't have all the answers yet or all the details," Buchanan said, "so I can't give them to you. But I can speak in general terms. First, there's little mystery *why* you were shot. You knew something you shouldn't. Or you saw something you weren't meant to. We both know that much. But let's work Morning Glory in reverse. Take your own story and play it backward."

"Backward how?"

"I want to take a reverse look at everything you told me. For example, Mark, think back of the moments when you were shot, just before you lost consciousness. You said that the man and the woman spoke to each other. You said their speech was unintelligible to you. Am I correct?"

"Yes."

"At the time you thought you weren't hearing correctly. Or that your mind was going. But actually, could they have been speaking Russian?"

A frown, a grimace, a scratch of the head. "I don't know. They could have been," said O'Connell. "I wouldn't necessarily recognize Russian."

"Fine. Now let's go back to San Francisco: The hotel. Wong's office. I suspect that you were so angry, Mark, and so emotionally burned out, that you missed the obvious. Wong probably moved from one hotel room to another within the California Pacific. He had a confederate there just in case he did acquire a surveillance team. He was never registered under his own name and he moved to his confederate's room as soon as you visited his. He was a small man too, correct?"

"Yes. That's right."

"So couldn't his confederate have removed him from the hotel in a trunk if necessary? A trunk with the proper airholes punched into it for breathing? This, of course, if he didn't just walk out by himself a week later."

"Maybe."

"Something similar happened at the warehouse, Mark. Wong left. He gave a signal to accomplices in San Francisco on the way home. They came into his office that night when there was no surveillance and moved everything of his to another office within the same building. From there, over the next few days, or maybe two weeks later, they moved all his records out, piece by piece."

"There's a problem," said O'Connell. "We watched Wong all the way to the hotel. How did he tip his accomplices? He wouldn't use the telephone for that, even in Chinese in his office."

"That's right," Buchanan said. "But what about the waiter in the Shanghai Inn? You said yourself that Wong didn't eat much, and that he and the waiter talked more than briefly. So why was he at the Shanghai Inn? I checked a San Francisco map downstairs. That restaurant was way out of his way, and Wong wasn't even hungry. Why not any chop suey joint on the way home? Why did he happen to stop at this one?"

O'Connell's eyes were riveted upon Buchanan. "All right. Go on," he said.

"That takes us back to the so-called models' studio," Buchanan resumed. "You mentioned that he had a brief exchange with a man while you were talking to the bar girl. That's what you said, isn't it?"

O'Connell nodded.

"What did the man look like? No, don't tell me. Let me guess. Maybe in his very early fifties. Nicely dressed in a suit, perhaps. Very Anglo-Saxon features. Fair complexion. Sandy hair, though he probably wore a hat. Thin. Good-looking in a classically American way. Eyeglasses. Was that him, Mark?"

O'Connell replied in mild amazement. "Well, it was dark. But that fits what I saw."

"That was John Taylor Garrett," Buchanan said. "I would bet anything on it. And what you witnessed was not just another connection between them, but a transaction as well. Something was handed from Garrett to Wong. Now, it's one thing for a banker to be carrying accounts of dirty or laundered money. But it's quite another to be exchanging parcels in a strip joint in a red light district. Right, Mark? It suggests more than a banker-client relationship, doesn't it? As, I might add, does the fact that you were gunned down by a Soviet male-and-female hit team *precisely* because of what you witnessed."

"But what did I see?"

"How else do all the pieces fit together?" Buchanan asked. "You witnessed a drop in a Soviet intelligence operation."

"But I didn't know that at the time."

"And they didn't wish to wait until you, or someone who could use you as a witness, could figure it out. So you became a target."

O'Connell turned it over relentlessly in his mind. Buchanan glanced at his watch. It was five minutes of eight.

"It doesn't work, Tom," O'Connell said.

"Why?"

"How did they 'make' me, Tom? How did they know who I was? There was no preexisting surveillance on either of them, and they didn't pick me up as a Fed while I was at the bar."

"That's right," Buchanan said. "They didn't have to. Someone was in the habit of covering for them in that studio. So they were tipped off immediately."

"Who? Dammit, Tom, who?"

"Come on, Mark. You can figure that one out."

When the conclusion was upon him, O'Connell almost looked as if he would bolt from his hospital bed. "Jesus Christ!" he snarled. "Blake Warren."

"I'm not suggesting Warren is a Soviet agent," Buchanan concluded, "but if Wong trades opium, he wouldn't go into an establishment for an important drop without having someone watching for him. Who else in that studio would know all the cops, local and federal? It had to be Blake Warren."

"Some friend," O'Connell mused.

"In fairness, Warren did try to talk you off the case, remember? But he was protecting himself from both sides. He not only warned you, but he warned Sammy Wong as well."

There was a quick knock, and the door swung open. Buchanan had left it unbolted. Helen came in, accompanied by Nurse Maryann, who seemed to be working a double shift. Buchanan turned to the two of them.

"Thank you," he said. He rose and reached for his coat. "We've had a wonderful talk. I know it's time to leave."

Helen, as wife of the patient, was allowed to stay. Buchanan excused himself and thanked O'Connell. For the first time in the case, however, looking at the former F.B.I. agent incapacitated by gunshot wounds, he had a sense of the basest aspects of the crime he was investigating. There was no jubilation over his hypothesis. There was only a sense of disgust and a bewildering number of doubts over how to proceed.

Buchanan pulled on his coat. He thanked both Mark and Helen. "I'll wait for you downstairs," he said to her. It was Mark

O'Connell, however, who stopped him as he was halfway out the door.

"Tommy," he said, raising his good hand. "Everything you said makes sense. So watch your back."

"I already am," he said.

"Promise me something else," O'Connell said.

Buchanan waited.

"A couple of bullets does a lot to wet a man's curiosity," he said. "Let me know what you're doing, as much as you can."

Buchanan nodded and said he would. Then he was gone.

It was ten-thirty P.M. Pacific time, one-thirty in the morning back in Washington. With his eyes red and heavy with fatigue, Thomas Buchanan sat at a table in the coffee shop of his motel.

Helen sat across the table from him, finishing a cup of coffee. In Thomas's eyes, she looked tired in the harsh overhead light. Her face was lined, and there were more gray streaks in her hair than he previously remembered. He looked out a window and stared across a parking lot. There were three cars and a pair of trucks sitting idly, their lights off.

"Have you decided where you're going yet?" Helen asked. "What time's your flight tomorrow?"

"Nine-fifty," he answered. "I talked to Washington tonight. I'm going to San Francisco."

"San Francisco? What for?" She set down her cup.

"I'm retracing Mark's steps," he said. "I want to see everything with my own eyes. Instinct counts for a lot in this line of work."

"Mark used to say that too," she said. "It's amazing. The two of you. Sometimes you think like brothers."

Buchanan smiled. And that's what Mark was thinking too: travel the same road, come to the same end, he concluded. That's why he warned me. Doesn't want me to get shot same as he did.

"I always liked Mark," Buchanan said, not really addressing the point. "You know that? We had the same style. The same approach to a case."

His gaze shifted from the parking lot and settled into her eyes. Why, he wondered, was she looking at him this way? Helen had once been very pretty, but she had suffered too much along with her husband. Now her hazel eyes were drawn and sad. Her mouth was tinged with anxiety.

"Know something, Tom?" she asked. "It doesn't pay to be a Feebee wife. You devote yourself to a good man, then Hoover's people run him out of the Bureau. Just when you think you're ready to enjoy a few of the pleasures in life, someone guns him down and, if you're lucky enough not to be a widow, your life revolves around hospital wards."

Buchanan wanted to say something to cheer her. But because of the hour, because of his fatigue, he couldn't find anything. Or maybe there wasn't anything.

"Why do you think he won't walk?" she asked.

" 'Won't'?" he asked. "Or can't?"

"Won't," she said again. "I know that man pretty well. Something's in his head. Something he hasn't told you or me."

"Like what?" Buchanan asked.

"For once, I couldn't even guess," Helen answered. "I just know there's something there."

Buchanan considered this for several seconds. But in his increasing fatigue, he drew a blank here too.

"Maybe we're both tired," he said. "Imagining things." He summoned the waitress. She wore a tag that said her name was Sylvia. She had red hair, wore a tight blue uniform, and was forty pounds overweight. She presented Buchanan with the bill for sandwiches and coffee. Thomas paid and placed a tip on the table.

"Thirteen years," Helen said, the thought apparently coming out of nowhere. "That's how long Mark and I have been married. That's not much time to spend with the right person, an eternity with the wrong one." She paused. "Can I ask you a question?"

He knew what was coming. "Go ahead," he said.

"I can't believe you've never been married," she said.

"That's not a question," he answered.

"To me it is."

He smiled. "It almost happened once," he said graciously. "The war interfered."

"You had a girl before Pearl Harbor?"

"The wedding date was already set. I suppose I should have moved faster," he said, suppressing a yawn. "I lost her when I was away in the army."

"I'm sorry," said Helen.

He shrugged. "It's eight years ago now. Seems like much longer." He wondered why she was asking.

"She was married when you came home in 1945?"

"So I'm told," he said. "To tell you the truth, I've heard conflicting stories. I don't know what ever happened to her."

"Ever tried to look her up?"

"Unsuccessfully," he said.

"Oh."

Helen watched him for a few seconds, then looked away. Then an impulse was upon him. "As it happened," he said, "a friend found this picture of her the other day. Sent it on to me. Want to see her?"

"Sure," Helen said.

He reached within his jacket pocket. He pulled out the photograph he'd stolen from Laura Garrett. "She's the younger one," he said, showing it. "The one on the left."

He watched Helen intently as she looked. "She's very pretty," he said. "What's her name?"

"Ann," he said. He took the picture back.

"Just Ann?" she asked.

"Ann Who-knows-what these days," he said. "It barely matters. When I get back to Washington I have to remind myself to bury the picture in the bottom of a desk drawer. Then I can throw it away when I do find the right girl to marry."

"Good idea," she said.

"Time to go."

They stood and walked to the door. Thomas held the door for her and they stepped outside into the chilly winter night. He suppressed a shiver.

"Button your coat," she said. "It's cold." Helen was someone's wife and someone's mother. She couldn't stop being either, he reasoned. But the advice was sound. He buttoned his trench coat and pulled his hat tight.

Behind him somewhere in the parking lot a truck turned over its engine with a clank and a growl that clashed with the cold and quiet of the evening.

They walked several feet, and Buchanan led Helen to the door of her motel room. "I'll see you at breakfast," she said. "I'll drive you to the airport."

"That would be nice," he said. "We should leave by eight-thirty."

She leaned to him and kissed him on the cheek. For a moment an urge was upon him, an urge that existed outside the boundaries of loyalty to Mark. It had been so long since he'd made love to a woman, and he was sure that he'd caught something in Helen's eye a little earlier. Something that told him that she'd be receptive. He raised his hands and was about to embrace her. Then she pulled away from him, another man's woman.

"Good night," she said.

"Good night, Helen."

He watched her go into her room and close the door. He heard the lock fall. Behind him the truck began to move. Then a whole canvas of deceit was upon him:

Helen was in league with all of them. He'd talked to her too much. She'd set her husband up and set Buchanan up too. Now they'd kill Thomas right there in that parking lot and they'd finish Mark at the hospital.

He whirled. The truck was coming straight at him, its headlights in his eyes. Exactly the same way Mark had gotten it, he thought. He looked to his left, then to the right. There was no cover at all. And Helen had bolted her door.

The truck's engine roared. Thomas reached beneath his jacket for his pistol. The truck moved toward him. Damn Helen, he thought, and damn all who sailed with her. The front of his coat was buttoned—just as she'd asked—and his cuff caught between the buttons. He was as good as dead. He plunged his fist beneath the coat, ripped a button off and still couldn't get a palm on the pistol.

The truck swerved slightly on the slick asphalt. Its wheels cut away from him and Thomas could see the driver from a space of about twenty feet. There was nowhere to dive, nowhere to hide. The truck window rolled down. Buchanan's palm reached the handle of his pistol, but the safety strap held the gun in the holster.

The truck was just a few feet away. Thomas was riveted in place, frozen into his shoes and waiting to be shot down.

The driver of the truck flipped a cigarette out the window and gave Thomas a congenial wave of the hand. The truck turned, accelerated, and barreled toward the exit of the parking lot, its exhaust white against the cold mist, its big wheels kicking up a cloud of moisture, and its heavy engine clanking.

And in Buchanan's throat his heart clanked also. He was grossly overtired, he told himself. His sense of reason was disintegrating into morbid fantasy. No one was following him, no one had marked him for assassination, and Helen had been Mark O'Connell's devoted wife since 1937. Tonight that was all there was to anything.

He walked the next few feet to his own door, unlocked it, and went in, almost ashamed of himself.

But he slept with the back of a chair lodged underneath the door handle and with his pistol loaded on the night table, an arm's length away. And for the foreseeable future he would dispense with the safety straps on his holster, he decided. Nor, until his nerves had stabilized, would he button his coat.

■

TWENTY-TWO
■

On the day when she was scheduled to die, Lisa Pennington anxiously came awake at a few minutes before five in the morning.

Her head hurt. Her back ached. Her stomach was a mass of jitters. The time had come to face up to her own execution.

She looked at the bed next to her. Her husband's place was empty and untouched. Once again Jesse had not come home. There was something about the times when he was shooting a picture that made Jesse Chadwick an even bigger louse than he was on ordinary days. When he had a film in production he behaved like a prince of the city, from bed to bed, from starlet to fading star. "Some damned famous broads don't push your hand away" was a frequent Jesse Chadwick boast. While he had a film before the cameras, Jesse seemed to want to prove his aphorism as many times as possible.

Well, Lisa told herself, it would barely matter much longer. At least, not to her. She would undergo one more day of filming. That way every bit of his production budget would be spent. She would leave by herself after filming that day. That would be maybe about five o'clock. Then she would . . . she would . . .

Well, yes. She realized now that she had the courage to do it. She'd saved more than sixty laudanum tablets. She would wash them down all at once with a solid belt of bourbon. That would be easily enough to kill her.

She lay very still in bed, imagining what it would be like to be dead. The morning was gray. Dawn hadn't broken yet. She had the sensation of floating, of looking at herself from a great distance. She envisioned her obituary in the Hollywood papers as well as the papers back home. She envisioned her own tombstone with her dates on it. How terribly short her life seemed to be.

Her head pounded. Her nightgown was soaked with sweat. She was terrified of living like this, but equally frightened of dying.

The horrible truth was that she hadn't even decided on the proper place to die. Somewhere in public, she wondered, where her body would be scooped up by strangers? In private, where her husband would find her?

In a hotel room? In a car? How important that final detail seemed. For several minutes she pondered it until the first glimmer of a bluish dawn filtered through her window, accompanied by a rustle of a curtain and a breeze.

For a moment she flirted again with the idea of fleeing. Maybe she'd run off to Europe. To South America. But what would she live on? Fantasy pursued itself. She would become a courtesan, she told herself with a deliciously naughty tingle. She was a retired actress, American, and blond. Why, of course! She could demand top money from attractive men—men of means and influence. The only difference was she could choose her partners and she could charge them money. No more of the meat-rack bartering that her husband subjected her to in this city.

Her husband. Jesse. Again she shuddered. Everything came back to Jesse Chadwick. Jesse and his films. Jesse and his studio whores. Jesse and his goons from Brooklyn, who would inevitably track her down and maim her if she ran out on his film and fled the country.

It was the same old circular chain of logic. She was better off dead. At least she'd die knowing she had some measure of revenge.

The previous night she'd written a stack of letters. She had addressed them to the local newspapers and to a few papers back east. She described what she'd been through, the type of man her husband was, and exactly why she was killing herself. Ah, would the press ever murder Jesse Chadwick! This *was* delicious, just thinking how she could ruin the man's life and career. It would take years before the scandal died. She would ruin him financially and ruin him socially. No one would ever go to see a Jesse Chadwick film again. In fact, there would be no Jesse Chadwick films again. In that she felt she was doing a public service. The man had no talent anyway. Only nerve and mendacity.

Lisa rose from bed. She went to her purse. She reassured herself that the letters were in the purse and in one packet, just as she'd left them. Her fingers trembled slightly as she flicked through them. There were eleven. After this day's shoot, she would even take the precaution of mailing them from different mailboxes around the city.

Then she would go somewhere and take her poison. Where? Oh, hell, it barely mattered. She could decide at the time. In her purse, brushing against the letters, was her vial of death. Sixty-four pills, all set and waiting for her. The funny thing was, since she'd been saving up the pills, she was drug free for the first time since before her marriage. Life was filled with strange ironies: finally drug free, she would soon die of an overdose.

Her day—her final day—was all charted out. She would dress and be on the set by eight A.M. Shooting should wrap for the day at four-thirty or five. She would skip the dailies that evening, would go somewhere and ingest her poison.

A marvelous thought occurred to her. Why not do it at someplace famous? The Beverly Hills Hotel. The Brown Derby. Ciro's. A perfect bit of theatrics after all. She would bring even more publicity upon herself when she fell over dead at the Beverly Wilshire Hotel. She even managed a smile.

It would be a difficult task to finally do. But the real hell to pay would befall her husband in the days that followed. Crucial scenes in his film would be impossible without her. His fraud with the completion insurance would be apparent. Well, he would have earned it, every bit.

She moved to the window. She loosened her nightgown and pulled it off. From her window she could see dawn breaking clearly above the Hollywood Hills. Naked, just as she'd come into the world, she sat down for a moment to watch the sunrise.

She felt oddly poetical. She had never paid much attention to the sunrise before, but felt she should savor it today. It would be her last chance, so why miss it? Men and women close to death have such different perspectives from everyone else.

The Candid Camera Artists' Models Studio was much as Thomas Buchanan expected it to be, particularly in the harsh light of day. It was located on a gritty San Francisco street not far from Treasure Island, a street of tacky souvenir shops, a pair of untidy grocery stores, a book shop across the street that boldly dealt print versions of what patrons could view live at Blake Warren's, a couple of ominous-looking places that seemed to do some sort of import-export trade with the Orient, and a hotel that rented rooms by the hour. Passing the hotel, Buchanan saw an enormously fat woman with bright red lipstick sitting at the front desk, knitting. She smiled to him, and he nodded in return.

The studio was locked when Buchanan tried the front door at a few minutes before noon. The establishment had one window, but it was curtained. A hand-painted sign upon it simply said: BAR/LIVE MODELS!

Patrons were not stumbling into this establishment by accident.

Buchanan stepped back from the front door and eyed the studio up and down. There was no movement from within, no activity on the street. Recalling his conversation with Mark O'Connell, Buchanan looked in both directions. Somewhere there was an alley, he remembered, which led both to the studio's rear exit as well as to Blake Warren's domicile upstairs.

Buchanan saw an alley to the left and walked toward it. Buchanan did not plan to be terribly gentle with Blake Warren this afternoon. Warren was a former actor and a consort of major criminals. Warren dealt with corrupt local police. Under the circumstances, questions posed by police officers—even federal agents— would be nothing new to him. The gentle, reasonable approach never worked with such men. If necessary, Buchanan told himself, he might have to be extremely rough with the King of the Robots. To a man trained to remain motionless in store windows or onstage for several hours, it would be easy work to remain silent or maintain a lie indefinitely.

Buchanan found the doorway in the alley. There were a pair of overflowing stainless-steel garbage cans near Warren's private entrance door. The alley itself was an assault upon the senses and common decency. It smelled of urine. Buchanan had to step carefully around broken beer and liquor bottles. There were used condoms scattered about. Presumably some of the "artists' models" who worked at Blake Warren's were in the habit of saving travel time. They simply stepped into this alley at night, raised their skirts, put their buttocks to the brick wall, and plied their private business. That, or they went quickly to their knees.

Such activities always provoked a Puritan streak in Buchanan, and each time he struggled to suppress it. He stood in this alley from circumstances, he reminded himself, stemming from a bank investigation. A bank investigation which had already branched into espionage and attempted murder, or so he thought. He could not allow himself to get bogged down in moral judgments on sexual behavior. Then he had to stifle a grin. He wondered how these rates with the girls' buttocks against the wall compared to the hotel across the street.

Buchanan stepped through an outer doorway and found himself in a locked vestibule. Now he faced two more doors, one of which opened only from the inside. There were three locks on one door and two on the other. Very likely there would be a chain or a bolt across each from the inside. The door frames had been reinforced with steel strips. Obviously Blake Warren was not a man who liked unexpected visitors. Probably with good reason.

Through a crack in one door Buchanan could see steps leading upward. Buchanan reasoned that these led to Blake Warren's residence. It was the other door which had no knob to the outside. It made sense that this was the rear exit from the studio.

Beside the door to Warren's apartment was a single bell. Buchanan rang it. When there was no answer, Buchanan leaned heavily upon it. He was not about to accept a nonresponse from Blake Warren. Warren, wittingly or not, had been a party to the shooting of Mark O'Connell. Warren also operated an establishment within the gray area of the law. There were pressures that could be brought to bear on Warren if and when he proved uncooperative. But silence was the only response to the doorbell.

Buchanan stepped back into the alley. Above the studio was a single row of windows. Warren's living quarters, no doubt. One of the windows was open very slightly, and not too far from it was a drainpipe. He estimated that the height of the window was thirteen feet above the alley.

Buchanan thought it strange that a man who had three locks on steel-reinforced doors would leave a second-story window open. But there it was. And he had seen enough of human nature to know that people could be notoriously inconsistent. But at this juncture, the partially open window seemed as good as a written invitation.

Buchanan walked back to the alley to check for pedestrians.

There were none. He walked back to the garbage cans, poured excess bottles off the top of each, and fastened the lids securely. He steadied the first can against the drainpipe and wedged it in place with a piece of lumber. He put the second can on top of the first and held it till it balanced evenly.

Then he began to climb. He placed a foot firmly on the first can and braced himself against the drainpipe. He pulled himself upward onto the second garbage can. For one unsure instant the cans felt as if they would give way. Then the pipe broke free from one of its bolts and rattled and trembled. For almost a full second Buchanan wildly waved one arm to steady himself.

But then all the play from the pipe was gone. Buchanan was steady. Leaning against the bricks of the building to brace himself, Buchanan moved his hands upward. He could easily reach the windowsill. It was splintery and poised upon old bricks. For a moment it felt like either the wooden sill or the bricks beneath it would collapse. But Buchanan pulled himself upward. Now it was as easy as a single chin-up.

He muscled himself to the window. Peering in, he looked into what appeared to be a living area. He saw no one. Maybe, he decided, he would enter and wait for Warren. In the meantime he would have the benefit of a look around.

He muscled himself forward and drove an elbow between the edge of the window and its frame. He pushed the frame upward, and with a final effort he pulled himself into Warren's residence. Intentionally he pushed off on the garbage cans and forced them to topple behind him.

He came to his feet in a hurry, listening to the echo of the crashing garbage cans. He stood very still and drew his pistol. There was no sound within the apartment. Without taking his eyes away from the room in front of him, he reached back to the window. He lowered it to the position where he'd found it.

If Warren returned, the garbage cans would look as if dogs had knocked them over and the window would be as he'd left it. Warren was undoubtedly too clever to miss the implications of two cans standing on each other beneath his window.

Buchanan stood very quietly in Blake Warren's living room, listening to the pounding of his own heart. It was an ordinary living area, with a worn green sofa bracketed by two end tables, each with a pink lamp. There were a pair of stuffed chairs around a fireplace. There was a coffee table, a desk in a corner, and a pair of standing lamps. It almost looked like a modest hotel room. There were no books or personal items at all.

From where he stood, Thomas Buchanan could see two doorways. One was to a kitchen. He could see the entire space. There was no one there. The other door led to a bedroom.

Buchanan stood perfectly still for a full minute. His pistol was pointed in the direction of the bedroom. He had the terrible sense of another human presence somewhere in the apartment. But where? He could feel his hands sweat and his neck sweat. His legs even felt a trifle weak. It was the same feeling he remembered from the war, just before combat. Just as he thought the truck driver was going to try to kill him in Washington State the previous evening, he now had the sense that someone was going to come out shooting.

He walked slowly toward the bedroom. Then he stopped. "Blake?" he said. "I'm a friend. We need to talk."

Again silence. Still holding the gun, Buchanan checked a closet in the entrance hall. He checked a flight of steps leading down to the doorway. He could see the stairwell cleanly, and no one was there. Then his eyes settled on something else and he felt a chilly tremor take over his body.

The door downstairs was bolted from the inside.

He whirled, half expecting to see a figure moving toward him. But again there was nothing. But how could a door be bolted from within? Someone had to be there somewhere.

Again he stood so quietly that he could hear himself breathe. Then he began to move toward the bedroom. He took one step, then another. He moved at an angle, holding his pistol aloft in case he needed to shoot.

"Blake?" he said again.

But no answer. He reached the door. He looked into the bedroom and scanned at eye level. There was no one there.

It was an ordinary bedroom. There was a double bed and a dresser, a pair of lamps, side tables, and a large easy chair with big, thick arms. Above the bed was a framed reproduction of *September Morn*. It was a curious bit of decoration for a man in Warren's line of work: tasteful nudity upstairs, tawdry nakedness downstairs. But as Huey Long had said, every man a king.

Buchanan moved through the center of the room, past Warren's bed, and went to the room's single closet. He lunged to it and threw open the door. Again nothing. Only clothes, mostly men's, but, curiously, a few women's. He glanced to the bathroom. No one there either. The conclusion was overwhelming that he was alone. Yet he couldn't shake the feeling of a presence somewhere.

Slowly he pushed back his jacket and eased his pistol into its holster. He calmed. His breathing slackened. He moved from the bedroom. Then he began to see the little things that he'd missed the first time.

In the living room there was a desk. None of the drawers was neatly closed. Buchanan walked to the desk and looked at it. The top of it was clear. In some drawers there was writing equipment: pencils, blank pads, envelopes, and tape. But several drawers were completely empty. So was the wastebasket. The contents of both, he concluded, had been removed.

Buchanan turned. His eye traveled around the room and settled upon the fireplace. There his gaze froze again. Next to the hearth there was a basket piled high with logs. But the fireplace itself overflowed with ashes, the particular feathery sort of ashes left by papers. Very recently someone had burned or removed every bit of Warren's correspondence.

Had it been Warren himself? Or someone more ominous? Again Buchanan sensed a presence.

Mentally Thomas began to calculate. Burning papers was a long job. It could take hours. He held his hand to the fireplace, and the ashes were cold. He stepped back. Then he saw he had left a partial footprint on the lightly colored floorboards before the marble of the fireplace.

He stared down at it. With sudden shock he realized what he was looking at. A bloodstain! And he'd freshly tracked it there himself. Somewhere in that apartment he'd stepped in blood.

When he turned he could see very faintly on the dark green carpet a set of partial footprints made by his shoe. He looked back to the bedroom. There was no question that he'd picked it up there.

Buchanan stood at the bedroom door and studied the carpet. Now he easily observed what he'd missed the first time. The carpet was a dark maroon imitation Persian, with a navy, black, green, and gold pattern woven in. It was, conveniently, not the type of design that would reveal a bloodstain unless a man were looking for it. But now that Buchanan looked carefully, the fresh stains were unmistakable, right in the center of the room. He had missed them the first time because his gaze, in more ways than one, had not been low enough.

He walked to the stains. Very clearly now the series of clues unfurled themselves into a story. Someone—Blake Warren, he guessed—had been shot in the center of the room. He had been shot and had fallen. There was a large stain, perhaps from where a bullet had hit a man in the chest. With the heart still pumping, much blood had obviously come out. Someone had made an attempt to clean up some of it.

Then there was a second stain, a large, thick one, bounded by a smaller one, one which stemmed from an explosion of bone and red mist. To Buchanan there was little question surrounding this too. After the victim had fallen, the killer had pumped another shot into his skull, blowing his brains out and killing him instantly. Then, most ominous of all, both stains gave an indication that something heavy had been dragged through them. The body of the victim, Buchanan presumed, since a man shot in the chest and head didn't normally rise up and trot away.

Buchanan looked in the direction where the body might have been dragged. His eyes settled on a large wardrobe trunk, the type used in a previous age by touring actors and vaudevillians such as Blake Warren. The trunk was against the room's far wall.

"Oh, Christ," he said to himself.

Buchanan walked to the wardrobe. There was a linen mat on the top of it. Buchanan removed it. He tried to lift the top but found it locked. A foul smell started to assault his nostrils and he knew—from the war, from his days in the pathology lab at the National Police Academy—what he was about to discover.

Reassuring himself again that he was alone, he removed the bullets from his Colt. With two powerful blows from the butt end of the gun, he smashed the latching mechanism on the trunk.

He then drew a breath and lifted the lid.

Against his will, against all his years as a soldier and as an agent of the law, he let out a gasp of horror. From Mark O'Connell's description, Buchanan recognized the body in the trunk as that of Blake Warren. But today the King of the Robots was motionless in a way he had never been while living. And there was no mistaking this for a performance.

Blake Warren's head was leaning heavily against his shoulder. His legs were folded up against his chest. As Buchanan grimaced, he could see that his assessment of the bloodstains on the rug had been frightfully accurate. And, in a macabre sort of way, so had his sense of another presence in the apartment.

An initial shot had pierced Warren's chest. The wound had

been grave, but probably not mortal by itself. But then there had been a second shot. This one had been an executioner's coup de grâce. It had entered the crown of the victim's head, presumably from close range, and had traveled downward. The bullet, Buchanan saw, was probably still in Warren's stomach. There was a huge reddish-brown blotch of dried blood beneath Warren's right arm. As for Warren's head, it had been smashed in from the top by the bullet fired at close range. The hair and the left eye were drowned and caked in blood. The right eye had a star fracture in the lens. Yet, in a final ironic touch, Warren was wearing the formal suit that he wore for operating his club. Probably no man had ever been better attired for a date with death.

Buchanan stepped back from the wardrobe trunk. He gently allowed the lid to close. He walked into the next room and helped himself to a tumbler of scotch from Warren's kitchen cabinet. Then he sat down in the living room and thought.

Whoever had killed Warren had been someone the victim had known: No break-in, no struggle. It had been someone he'd trusted to even enter his bedroom. Someone like John Garrett. Or Sammy Wong. Or even the two of them. For several minutes he thought of them. Trying to picture the genteel Pennsylvania banker as a gunman was difficult, though less difficult than it used to be. Seeing Sammy Wong as an assassin was easier to Buchanan, based only on what Mark O'Connell had told him.

The mystery of the bolted door and the open window was, to his mind, solved. Whoever had done it, however, had intended to buy several days before the body was discovered. Hence the door had been left bolted from within. The killer had left via the window, pulling it shut and letting himself down the drainpipe or some makeshift ladder. Most likely, Buchanan ruminated, this was done in darkness.

Buchanan stood again and went to the window. There were no streetlamps anywhere in or near the alley. All the more reason to believe it was done in darkness, probably an hour or two after Warren's studio had closed. Clearly the killer had left this way, the reverse of the way Buchanan had entered. It was the only method possible. Buchanan looked for other exits from the apartment, but there were none. Every other window was locked. He even examined closets for false passages and found none.

But there were other answers that Buchanan needed. He walked back to the wardrobe and distastefully opened it again. Grimacing, he pulled the body of the dead man slightly upward. The bullet hole beneath the front right arm was matched by a larger exit wound in the topmost portion of Warren's back. Again the wound was serious, though it probably wouldn't have been fatal. Yet it had been more than sufficient to drop him. Most likely Warren had been standing in the center of the room and had been turning when the gunman fired. Buchanan examined the angle of the wound again. From the location on the rib cage, Buchanan could see that Warren's arm had been upraised when the bullet had been fired.

Warren had known at the last minute that his visitor was going to shoot him. He'd raised his hand at the final second in an instinctive—yet futile—effort to survive.

Buchanan closed the trunk. He pictured the upward flight of the bullet. The killer, he realized, had seated himself in the armchair in the corner of Warren's bedroom. And he'd fired from about five feet away.

Buchanan looked at the chair. Then he turned and looked at the wall behind him. If the bullet left an exit wound, it had to hit something else. Simple physics. Buchanan searched for the bullet hole. With considerable effort he found it. The killer had repositioned the print of *September Morn* to conceal the hole.

Buchanan removed the print and borrowed a knife from Warren's kitchen. He dug the slug out of the wall. There was still a bit of bone and flesh clinging to the bullet, as well as plaster and a bit of Warren's suit jacket. Buchanan wrapped the bullet in a handkerchief and saved it.

Then Buchanan walked back to the center of the small room. From there it was easy to discern the trajectory of the first shot. It had come from six to eight inches in front of the left armrest of the chair, and an equal distance above and to the right of that same armrest. This told Buchanan something critical. The killer was left-handed as well as a good shot. A right-handed killer would have put a hole in the wall fifteen feet in the other direction.

There was one other clue Buchanan wished to take from the death scene. He walked to the trunk a final time. He felt the blood to see if it was tacky. He pressed his hand to Warren's chest to feel for warmth. There was none. He touched Warren's shoes. There was a give to the dead man's ankles. The feet were always the last to stiffen. He estimated that Warren had been dead for twelve hours.

The situation above the Candid Camera Artists' Models Studio now read to Buchanan like an open book. Warren had had a rendezvous with a killer or killers the previous evening after the studio closed. They went upstairs together. It had been someone Warren knew well and trusted, as he allowed his killer to follow him into the bedroom and sit down in a chair. At some subsequent moment the visitor drew a pistol. Warren realized what was happening, turned, and raised an arm to protect himself. But the executioner fired. Warren fell. Then the killer stepped forward and finished him off with a bullet through the crown of the head.

Thereupon, the papers in Warren's desk were ransacked and burned. All books, particularly those pertaining to the business downstairs, were removed. More than likely the killer wished to remove any written record of contact with Blake Warren.

The killer managed to lift the dead man up and put him into the trunk. To Buchanan's way of thinking, that ruled out a small Oriental like Sammy Wong. But it did not eliminate John Garrett. Nor did it point against a male-female hit team, such as the one that had attempted to kill Mark O'Connell. But Buchanan sensed that there had been one killer there alone. Otherwise the body would have been carried to the trunk, not dragged.

It was possible that Warren had been murdered for reasons having nothing to do with Commonwealth Penn and the ensuing investigation. But Buchanan quickly dismissed them. One of Warren's "models" could have done it, he theorized. But this didn't seem like a woman's sort of crime. Similarly members of the underworld, wanting a piece of Warren's business, could have killed him. But Warren wouldn't have admitted an underworld assassin to his bedroom. Nor would a professional killer have gone there. An underworld gunman would have nailed Warren in the alley, a single shot to the back of the head. Like most murder victims in America, Warren knew his killer well. What Buchanan wondered was whether he knew him too.

■
TWENTY-THREE
■

Buchanan spent another half hour prowling through Warren's apartment, finding nothing that shed further light on his investigation. His initial assessment of the situation seemed correct. Every piece of paper or correspondence had been removed from Warren's residence or fed into the fire.

He found a set of keys to Warren's door. He walked down the front stairs and went through the door. He closed it and pushed a wood splinter taken from the windowsill into the tiny aperture between the top of the door and the door frame. If the splinter was not exactly as he left it when he returned, he would know that someone else had been through the door.

He left the building, passed through the alley, and walked down the street. From a public telephone at the end of the block he reached a long distance operator. Thereupon, he called Shannon, Washington. His call was transferred by a Shannon operator to the local hospital, then kicked through to the room of the patient known as Braverman.

Buchanan told Mark O'Connell what he had found when he'd visited Warren. O'Connell was silent, but expressed no surprise. Both men agreed that the death of Warren enhanced Buchanan's interpretation of recent events.

Buchanan spoke to O'Connell for several minutes. He asked for contacts of trustworthy local police in San Francisco, but O'Connell had none. O'Connell instead suggested contacting Meadley and Herter, his two F.B.I. associates out of the San Francisco field office. Buchanan said he would. Someone would have to do a reliable follow-up, complete with proper fingerprinting of the apartment and official autopsy. Nothing could be left to error; sloppiness was unacceptable. O'Connell said that Meadley and Herter had good contacts within the S.F.P.D. While Buchanan's concerns were legitimate, O'Connell said, the proper procedures could be expected.

"And by the way," Buchanan asked in conclusion, "it might be a small point, but can you envision when you were watching Wong through the telescope? Can you picture him the way you saw him?"

O'Connell said he could.

"Good. What hand did he write with?"

O'Connell thought for a moment. Then he recalled the little Chinaman pulling all his records from the right side of his desk and setting to work with them with a pen on the same side.

"The right hand," O'Connell said. "Why?"

"Just a small point," Buchanan said. "I'll let you know. You walking around yet?"

"Don't feel up to it," O'Connell said.

"Better get up soon," Buchanan teased. "You got a damned fine woman there. Someone might run off with her."

O'Connell laughed and appreciated the remark. "Which reminds me," he said. "Helen wants to say something."

Helen had been there all the time, waiting patiently for her moment. Buchanan heard her voice come on the line. He'd left her only five hours earlier when she'd dropped him at the airport.

"Hello, Tom," she said. "You being careful?"

"I'm trying to." He stood in the booth watching the access to the alley adjacent to the Artists' Models Studio. No one came. No one left.

"You're a sly character, Special Agent Thomas Buchanan," she said to him with mock indignation. "Either that or you're missing something obvious."

"What are you talking about, Helen?"

"Do you get any of the Los Angeles newspapers?" she asked.

"Not usually."

"Do it today," she said. "Page twenty-four of today's Los Angeles *Times*. As if you don't know, Tom."

"I *don't* know," he answered.

"Then you should. And so should I. You know how I am about movies. And you know how I am about actors and actresses. You coy man, you. Why didn't you tell me?"

"Helen . . . ?"

"Page twenty-four, Tom. Bye!" She giggled. "I know your secret."

Buchanan was starting to lose patience, but then Mark was back on the phone. He reassured Buchanan that Herter and Meadley should do just fine. O'Connell gave him the two agents' home telephone numbers. Then he was off the line.

For a moment Buchanan stood and stared across the street at Blake Warren's nightspot. Then, from the same phone booth, he called Herter and Meadley and summoned them.

As he waited, he remained on the street for a few minutes. He stood in the breeze on an overcast San Francisco day and looked down the block. He saw a newspaper kiosk. He walked to it, pondering the implications of Blake Warren's death.

At the kiosk he purchased a Los Angeles *Times*. He folded it under his arm and walked back toward the dead man's apartment. Fortunately it was still early in the afternoon and the studio was an evening enterprise. There was no crowd growing. At the door that led up to Warren's apartment the splinter was still in place. Good, he thought. No visitors.

Warren's death, Buchanan decided, fit into the current wisdom. Warren had worked for Wong. But he had also witnessed something he shouldn't have, same as Mark O'Connell. Whoever employed Warren—Wong or maybe even John Garrett—knew the most rudimentary aspects of Warren's character and his career. That was, he was a man who always had his price. And as a man with a price, he was not to be trusted: somewhere there could always be a higher bidder. So whatever Blake Warren knew, whatever he had seen, it was so explosive that his silence had to be assured. A bullet to the temple purchases silence at economy rates.

Buchanan went downstairs and used Warren's keys to enter the Artists' Models Studio. He walked through the place, which seemed grim and ordinary in the glare of daylight and bare sixty-watt bulbs. He searched again for business records, paperwork, or even a safe. He found none. He found several hundred dollars in a strongbox bolted to the underside of Warren's desk in the rear room, however. Any robber could have taken it, pushing Buchanan further in the direction of his own theories of Warren's demise.

Eventually he sat down at the bar. The telephone rang once. One of Blake's girls wanted to know if she'd be needed that night. Buchanan told her Mr. Warren was ailing and the establishment might not open. There was a silence and the girl hung up.

Buchanan opened the newspaper. He had forgotten what page Helen had mentioned. So he started in the sports section, glancing once or twice at his watch, wondering what was keeping Meadley and Herter. Time passed.

He scanned the movie page, which also carried the radio listings. He read stories that bored him. He looked to see what was playing at the local grind houses. His eyes wandered down the page, then settled upon a publicity photograph of a film in production. Immediately he froze. For Thomas Buchanan this was a moment made up of many emotions.

The film in production was called *Hold the Phone!* It was directed by Jesse Chadwick, a New York-born director whom Buchanan had heard of only vaguely. It starred fulsome old Damon Forbes and a newcomer named Lisa Pennington. Buchanan stared at their pictures until his face was hot and flush and his hands soaked with sweat.

He read the story beneath the photographs. Mostly it was the claptrap assembled by Esther Greeb, the R.K.O. publicist, rewritten by a *Times* staffer. Buchanan read how Jesse Chadwick had studied filmmaking in Europe and was going to emerge as one of Hollywood's hottest directors in the optimistic postwar years—this miracle to occur under the tutelage of that great humanitarian and producer, Joe Preston.

Buchanan read how starlet Lisa Pennington had grown up in Wallingford, Connecticut, had changed her name from Doris Oelsner, and had a mother named Mrs. Ellison who taught school back in Michigan. And he read how Damon Forbes was entering his third decade of stardom. Buchanan read all of this over and over. He stared at the studio photographs and he wondered how people could print such things, much less believe it.

"What bullshit!" he said aloud.

But his palms were wet. And he knew he'd moved a crucial step closer to John Taylor Garrett.

There was a sharp knocking on the front door of the studio. Buchanan was jolted for a moment. Then he turned and walked to the door. He admitted Herter and Meadley. He identified himself as F.B.I. out of Washington, D.C., following up an investigation that touched upon the shooting of Mark O'Connell, their friend and one-time associate.

Buchanan next led the two agents around the corner and upstairs to the trunk that contained the remains of Blake Warren. Methodically Buchanan ran through everything. If O'Connell had trusted these men, Buchanan did too.

"I'm working directly beneath J. Edgar Hoover," Buchanan said. "If anyone in your field office gives you a problem, refer them to the Director's office in Washington. Assistant Director Frank Lerrick will expedite anything for you."

They got the message.

"Mark O'Connell was one of my closest friends in the Bureau," Buchanan continued. "He told me everything before he died. Wong. Morning Glory. The hotel. The stakeout."

Herter and Meadley barely blinked.

Thereupon Buchanan described how he came to the studio that day and how he'd found the corpse. He then placed the San Francisco part of the case into their hands.

"I'd strongly suggest keeping the studio closed tonight," Buchanan said. "But when the girls arrive for work, have them questioned. See who was here last night. See if anyone was hanging around late. We want to know who Blake Warren went upstairs with. And I think a complete toss of the place would be in order. I'd suggest that the Bureau do it before the local police. A safety consideration, I'd say."

They agreed.

"I want a complete workup of the murder room," he said. "I want fingerprints and I want the weapon identified. Two shots were fired. I have one bullet. The other's in the dead man's stomach. I also want an estimate of the time of death."

Herter and Meadley were amenable. Buchanan walked to the street, feeling his pulse quicken as he walked. He took a taxi to the airport, and bought a ticket for the next flight to Los Angeles. Nervously he waited forty-five minutes, took a drink in the airport bar, and boarded a southbound Western Airlines flight via San Jose. The flight took off at two-fifty in the afternoon.

Buchanan knew that a day's filming might wrap as early as three or four in the afternoon, depending on the behavior and sobriety of all involved. Or, if the producer were trying to beat a schedule, photography could go well into the evening. He arrived in Los Angeles at four-thirty.

He picked up a car at Los Angeles International Airport and drove at a mad speed across La Cienega. There he picked up the Santa Monica Freeway and drove toward Hollywood. He found Universal Studios easily and from there found R.K.O. His F.B.I. credentials got him through the gates. J. Edgar Hoover had more than one friend as a studio mogul. It didn't hurt, for example, that Max Wolberg, the pleasantly profane head of R.K.O., liked to go to the Santa Anita racetrack with Hoover when the F.B.I. Director was in Los Angeles. Wolberg also slipped Hoover sexual information about his studio's most famous actors and actresses for J. Edgar's private bedtime reading.

"Is *Hold the Phone!* still shooting today?" he asked the security guard at the gate.

"As far as I know."

"Can you tell me where?"

The guard consulted a clipboard and gave Buchanan a back-lot location. Buchanan drove to it, his heartbeat quickening.

About a hundred yards from the location, a set manager stopped him and indicated where he should park his car. Buchanan politely put the vehicle where the man had designated. Then Buchanan was asked again his business on the set.

"Seeing a friend," he said. He showed his F.B.I. credentials again. "Where's *Hold the Phone!* shooting?" he asked.

The manager indicated an outdoor set about two hundred feet down a brick path. The set purported to be the backyard of an American home. From the angle from which Buchanan viewed it, however, the house was clearly a shell.

When he arrived on the set, no one took much notice of him. There were several dozen people present, most of them milling around, attending to microphones, props, electrical cables, the one camera, the script, or a table of food and drink. The crew, to the extent that they appeared to be doing anything, looked to be setting up the next scene. Buchanan recognized Damon Forbes, sitting in a director's chair, his hand lecherously poised on the knee of a teenage girl next to him. He recognized Jesse Chadwick also. Chadwick was a man in motion, obscenely chewing out a pair of prop men for their tardiness in preparing a scene.

Sitting to one side, on a canvas director's chair, was the actress known as Lisa Pennington. To Buchanan's eye, she looked tired, drawn, and tense, as if she were greatly preoccupied with some event distant from the film. She wore dark glasses over her eyes and a royal blue scarf around her hair, presumably to keep it fresh for the cameras. Buchanan noted that she looked very bored and angry with the proceedings. He wondered if she was always like that now but was able to loosen up when a camera was on her. He had no way of knowing.

He studied her for several seconds. She almost seemed like an outcast on the set. No one was seated near her. One arm was folded across her lap, her head rested on the other as her elbow was on the arm of her chair. The F.B.I. agent wondered what was wrong with the actress.

There were two chairs empty on each side of her. Clearly Jesse Chadwick's chair was next to the camera. So, attracting as little attention to himself as possible, Buchanan casually walked through the technicians and propmen and moved in the direction of Lisa Pennington.

He settled into the chair next to her. She refused to turn toward him. He faced her. Her profile was very pretty, even with the scarf and the glasses and even with her absent, angry expression. He wondered what Hollywood had done to her.

Doris Oelsner. What a name!

Wallingford, Connecticut. What a lie!

A mother named Mrs. Ellison teaching school in Michigan. What a farce!

He looked at her for several seconds, almost waiting for her to turn toward him. Then he realized that she knew someone was next to her. This was her way of avoiding small talk.

That meant he had to speak first. For the first time since he'd entered the Commonwealth Penn case, his composure almost disintegrated. Words threatened to fail him. He had to remind himself that he was a professional with a job to do. He was there on work, no matter what other feelings he might have. But then the words just came out, unplanned and unrehearsed.

"I can honestly say, Ann," he said, "that if you'd married me you wouldn't be here today."

Slowly Ann Garrett turned toward him. Buchanan saw an expression of total shock come across her face. For several seconds she stared in growing disbelief. He saw her mood, whatever it was— anger, boredom, he didn't know—give way to something else: total incredulity. She removed the sunglasses as if she were trying to dispel a hallucination.

Uncovered, her eyes went wide as saucers. "I do not believe this," she said. "Not today of all days."

"Please believe it, Miss 'Pennington,'" he said. He grinned nervously and offered his hand to her.

"My God," she said quietly but emphatically.

"How are you, Ann?" he asked. "No hard feelings, I hope. Not after all these years."

She stared and stared, just as he had stared at her photograph in the Los Angeles *Times* a few hours earlier. "No. None, Tom," she said softly. Her expression was completely flat. "None at all."

Then Jesse Chadwick appeared suddenly. He was in his usual mood. "Who the fuck are you?" he asked.

A belligerent approach always angered Buchanan. He eased back in his chair. "My name is Thomas Buchanan," he said. Then, adding an insult too subtle for Chadwick, he added. "Who are you?"

"How'd you get on the set? What are you doing here?"

Pressed, Buchanan was about to invoke the name of Max Wolberg, R.K.O.'s chief. At the same time he reached for his F.B.I. identification. But Ann Garrett held out her hand and stayed Thomas's.

"He's an old friend. I invited him, Jesse," she snapped defiantly.

"I want him out of here."

"You invite your friends, Jesse, I invite mine."

"He goes."

It was just the confrontation that Ann Garrett wanted. "He goes, I go," she said. "And see if you finish your film on time."

She stood. Heads on the set began to turn. The background talk lessened, turned to a murmur, then ceased completely. Chadwick glared at his wife and the intruder, then roughly grabbed Ann by her shoulder. He was about to slam her back down into her chair. But as things transpired, Chadwick never knew what hit him.

In one swift, strong motion, Buchanan sprung upward from his chair and caught Chadwick with two palms against the chest. He shoved with the same force he'd use bench-pressing a barbell of twice Chadwick's weight.

Chadwick panicked at the touch of Buchanan and released his wife. But following through with his instinctive reaction, Buchanan hit Chadwick so hard that he lifted the director cleanly off his feet and sent him reeling backward several yards until he sprawled clumsily onto his back.

"Sorry," Buchanan said. "I'll leave when I want to."

The crew gawked at what happened. Ann sat down again. Buchanan sat next to her. Mortified, Chadwick climbed to his feet. Behind his back, much of the crew was grinning or looking away to conceal smiles.

Joe Preston hulked over from somewhere nearby. "What the fucking hell's going on?" he ranted.

"We got a troublemaker on the set, Joe," Chadwick said. "Call the goddamned police."

"Jesse tripped," Ann said. "This is Mr. Buchanan. He's a friend of mine, Joe. Friends are permitted on the set. He stays or I walk off, Joe, and you've got an unfinished project."

"She wouldn't do that," Chadwick said.

"No?" Ann asked.

"She knows what would happen to her."

"You don't scare me anymore, Jesse," Ann Garrett said.

"What would happen to her?" Buchanan asked.

"What would happen, pal?" Chadwick snorted. "Same as is going to happen to you, shitface. I got some friends back east and around L.A. that make a career out of busting heads. Normally they do it for pay. For me they'd do it for fun."

"Oh?" Buchanan asked.

"Yeah!" snapped Chadwick. He couldn't figure out why Buchanan wasn't intimidated.

"That's fascinating," said Buchanan. "Maybe I could meet them someday."

Chadwick stared at him without comprehension. He was burning. Buchanan said nothing. Chadwick's assistant director appeared and informed him the set was ready. Preston angrily looked at all the parties involved and, in his inimitable way, reduced it all to finances.

"Sort out your personal shit later, Jesse," Joe Preston snarled. "I want this film finished on schedule or I'll see that the R.K.O. flagpole is shoved sideways up your ass. Get it?"

"Hey, but, Joe—?"

"Just get the friggin' film done. That's all." Preston stalked away. Furiously Chadwick ordered his assistant director to ready the crew for the next take. Then he walked back to Buchanan.

"You and I aren't finished," he said.

"That's up to you," Buchanan answered. He knew a physical coward when he saw one.

Chadwick glared at him, turned, and walked away. Buchanan waited till he was out of earshot.

"Sorry," he said to Ann.

"For what?" she asked.

"I just came by to say hello. To see if you'd talk to me for a few minutes. I wanted to catch up on old times a bit."

"Just like that. Out of the blue?"

He shrugged. "Why not?" He didn't say he was investigating her father. Not yet.

"I'd love to do that," she said.

He was not about to let her out of his sight. "I'll wait for you," Buchanan said. "After you're finished shooting today."

"That would be fine."

"Can I wait here?"

"You're my guest, remember?" She smiled for the first time. "I have two more scenes. We'll be here till six o'clock. We can go somewhere afterward."

"I seem to have caused you some trouble," he said.

"Not in the slightest," Ann Garrett said. "That man. Jesse Chadwick. He's my husband."

"Your *husband*?"

She nodded.

"He doesn't seem very affectionate. He must be having a bad day."

"Every day is a bad day for Jesse," she said.

"I wasn't planning to include him," Buchanan said. "But I'm not trying to make long-term trouble for you."

" 'Long term'?" She laughed. He didn't understand why. "Don't worry about that," she said. "With me there is no 'long term.' "

Ann's attention seemed to disappear for a moment. It went somewhere and then came back. She pulled her scarf off. A dresser came to her and ran a brush through her hair.

"Do you know how long it's been," she asked Buchanan at length, "since anyone has called me Ann?" She stopped for another moment, and Buchanan thought he saw an curious mistiness in her eyes. Then she turned and looked him squarely eye to eye. "I liked the way that sounded, Tom. I liked it a lot. Know what? You just changed my life. I really think you did."

TWENTY-FOUR

"I can't believe you found me," she said.

He mentioned the photograph in the newspaper and, with some sheepishness, confessed that a man didn't forget the face of the first woman with whom he'd fallen in love.

"You're very kind," she said. "You always were."

They sat in one of the better-known restaurants in Beverly Hills, a place of white tablecloths, expensive potted palms, and hushed conversations. Yet Ann had insisted on going there. It was an exciting place, she said, the type where, if anything interesting happened, it would turn up the next day in all the papers.

"But what I can't figure out," she said next, "is how you got past the studio gates."

"Ex-servicemen have their ways," he said, deflecting the question.

"Oh, tell me," she said.

"Soon enough," he promised. "Not now."

Then, as they ordered dinner, he moved the conversation to several amiable minutes of small talk, time to catch up on the years gone by.

Neither brought up the subject of their broken engagement. Thomas lured Ann into doing most of the talking. She mentioned that her mother had died and that she wasn't on the best of terms with the other two members of her family. Her sister was off in Europe, she said, and she barely had any idea where her father might be. The bank made money and he trotted around the globe, she said, presumably showing the flag for his bank in international circles. "He's unorthodox," she said. Thomas agreed that he was. He tried several questions about her father, and she sidestepped each of them, intentionally, Buchanan quickly concluded. She either wished to conceal something or avoid the subject altogether. And he was in no position to press the issue until she came around to the subject again.

She'd had a falling out with her family, she went on to say, and much of it had to do with her desire to go into acting. After college she'd done some stage work in New York, and there she'd met her husband. She didn't belabor the details, but she spoke of Jesse Chadwick with so little enthusiasm that Thomas didn't have to be a genius to know it was a bad marriage. Not from what she'd said, and not from what he'd seen on the set.

He asked if she enjoyed acting and the life-style it brought her. Her answer was no, and her voice suddenly turned very sad.

Dinner was served. A bottle of California white wine arrived at the same moment. More time went by in conversation. Eventually Buchanan mentioned that he'd recently seen Laura Garrett in England.

"You've seen my sister?" she asked, almost incredulous.

"About two weeks ago."

"Where?"

"In London," he said. "She said that you'd been living there with her."

"Me? In London with Laura?" She let a silence answer her own rhetorical question.

"That's what she told me."

Ann remained quiet. "Ann, forgive me," he said, "but I didn't believe it at the time either. Why would she have so specifically told me something that wasn't true?"

"Sounds like Laura was just fibbing to you a bit," Ann said.

"I take a slightly more serious view of it," he said.

"Why is that?"

"Well, I'd traveled a long way to speak to a member of the Garrett family," he said. "I was in the mood for straightforward answers."

"Tom," she said, catching on and looking at him in a different light. "Why are you in Los Angeles?"

He drew a breath. In any interrogation of a witness there is a moment when the investigation can go either way. The witness will either fall silent or proceed. With Ann Garrett, Thomas Buchanan had reached that point. Yet deceit would only backfire.

"Ann, wouldn't you be happier if I just asked the questions? Afterward, I'll tell you why I want to know."

"I don't like that system," she said. Then she repeated, "Why are you in Los Angeles? Tell me!"

He gave it considerable final thought. Then he reached into his inside jacket pocket. "I'd greatly appreciate it if you would keep this between us," she said. "At least for now."

On the table in front of her he laid the case containing his F.B.I. shield and identification. At first she didn't understand what it was.

"Early this year," he said with steadfast politeness, "I was in Washington, having just concluded another case. The Director of the F.B.I. determined that an"—here he chose his words carefully again—"an *inquiry* might be made into the affairs of the Commonwealth Bank of Pennsylvania. Your father's bank. There appeared to be irregularities in some of their financing, anonymous sources for large foreign deposits, and—"

"Tom," she said slowly, stopping him. She stared at him for several seconds. "You son of a bitch!" she finally said.

"Ann, please listen to me. I would like nothing more than to completely vindicate your father of any—"

"I can't believe you!" she snapped. "You come onto the set. You sit down next to me. You talk politely. And all the time, all you're doing is plying me for information! You're trying to put my father in jail, aren't you?"

And she knows the reason why, he thought immediately. *She knows and snow will fall in hell before she will ever tell me!*

"No," he said. "If he hasn't done anything, no, I'm not. We do not put innocent people in—"

But she was barely listening. "Whatever he's done," she said, "whatever he may be guilty of, I'm sure not telling you or anyone else. I may not speak to him, I may not get along with him, I may not even like him, but so help me, Tom Buchanan—"

She lost control of her words. She stood, picked up her wine, and splashed it onto his face and shirt. She lunged for her purse, but he put his hand on it.

"Ann, sit down. We're not finished yet," he said, calm but wet.

"You're not finished," she said, starting to cry, "but I am. You people are all alike!"

She pulled at her purse, but he kept his hand on it. When he wouldn't release it, she shoved her hand into it, knocking loose a bunch of letters. He tried to grab her wrist, but she pulled away. She held a vial of pills, he could easily see, and once she had those in her grasp, she stepped back.

"Good-bye!" she said with a solemn finality. The entire restaurant was watching, just as the entire crew had watched him knock over Jesse Chadwick a few hours earlier.

He was going to stop her from leaving, but she walked in the wrong direction. She went back toward the washrooms rather than the front door. So he sat for a moment, watching her go. A waiter appeared with a towel.

"Sir?" the man offered.

"Thank you," he said, taking it.

"Happen often, this sort of thing?" he asked, trying to make light of it. Conversation resumed at other tables.

"Once a week," the waiter said, "but not usually on week-nights. Usually it's people from New York."

"Thank you," Buchanan said again. He handed the towel back. The waiter departed.

Lying next to Buchanan was a handful of letters, all uniform in size with Ann's handwriting on their front. Two of them were un-sealed. Most were addressed to newspapers. Buchanan couldn't help himself. Watching for her to return, he pulled one open and began to read.

He had a habit of scanning text quickly, of picking up key words, blending them together, and coming rapidly to a sense of what he was reading. The words "commit suicide" leapt out at him, followed a half a second later by mention of sixty-two laudanum capsules. Comprehension of what was happening came upon him in a flash. Less than a second thereafter, he sprung up from the table and ran in the direction she had gone, in the process almost knock-ing over a waiter carrying a full tray of food.

He raced back toward the washrooms, leapt down a short flight of stairs, bolted past the men's room, and stopped when he saw the door to the ladies' washroom. Then he crashed through it, greatly startling a pair of young women leaving together, one of whom shrieked.

But he saw Ann at the sink. She'd been waiting for a moment of privacy. This was it. He wouldn't give it to her. There were tears, he could see, streaming down her cheeks. In one hand she held a glass of water and in the other, inevitably, a fistful of pills.

Praise God, he thought, he was still in time! He lunged toward her as she shoved the pills toward her mouth.

As he came forward he hit her arm hard and from underneath. Her arm flew upward and her fist broke open. Pills flew into the air in every direction, and he pushed a hand to her mouth, forcing it open and roughly shoving his fingers inside.

None. Not one pill had found its way to her lips. She bit at him and he withdrew his fingers.

"Let me go!" she screamed. Behind him one of the two women excitedly summoned the management. *"Let me go, damn you!"* Ann screamed again. But he wouldn't.

The water was running. He pushed her away from the sink. He swept every pill he could see into the flow of the running water and watched as her tablets of death were washed away. She cried uncontrollably, leaning against the washroom wall, until, her face in her hands, she'd slid down to the floor. There was no more battle, no struggle at all. He looked to the floor and picked up the few pills that had fallen. These, too, he threw away. "Where do you get those things? Through your husband?" he asked.

She was silent, except for the sobs.

"Answer me, Ann." His voice was remarkably calm and reassuring. "I want to help you."

She didn't say anything, but she nodded.

"Might have known," he said. "What the hell does Jesse care if he kills you, right? He can always get someone else."

"And what the hell do you care?" she snapped. She turned at him and screamed. *"And what the hell do you care? Huh? Tell me that! Tell me what the hell do you care!"*

He faced her sympathetically and sat down on the floor next to her. He placed an arm on her, not as an ex-lover would, nor as a man would trying to rekindle an old romance. Rather, as a protector. Someone who did care.

"Enough to run in here and stop you," he said. "That's more than anyone else did, isn't it? Isn't that worth something?"

She looked at him, first in anger, then in desperation. She was quiet.

"Ann, probably not more than a day or two has gone by since 1943 when I didn't think of you and wonder how you were. Your life is your own business. But I was not about to sit in an overpriced restaurant in Beverly Hills and preside over your suicide."

At first she gave no reaction. Then, before he knew what had happened, she was sobbing anew, telling him how scared she was, how her whole life had gone wrong and how, no matter what he might think now, no, she didn't want to die. All she wanted, she cried, was one person to trust.

While all this was happening, the restaurant manager appeared at the door. Behind him was one of the larger waiters. The manager made a semithreatening remark about calling the police. The statement was still hanging in the air, however, when Buchanan used a free hand to show them his shield.

"F.B.I.," he said. "It's all under control now. We're sorry about the disturbance."

The manager blinked. Then he and the waiter backed off.

Minutes later Buchanan led Ann to his car. He told her whatever the problems, whatever the danger she felt she was in, she would have protection. She didn't have to tell him anything or talk about her father. He simply wanted her safe from anyone who might harm her and far away from any more vials of pills.

She had, he reminded her, a film to complete. When she made noises about not finishing it, he insisted.

He refused to take her home that night. Instead, he took her to the Commodore Hotel, where he registered. He booked his own room, then installed Ann in a single room directly across the hall.

There, not completely understanding what he had precipitated, he left his own door partly open for the night. Against it on the inside he propped a lamp and a wastebasket in such a position that both would fall and crash if anyone nudged the door. The noise would bring him quickly awake, he reasoned. But for several hours he sat up wide awake, trying to make sense of the Garrett family. On this he again failed.

Then, toward three A.M., still in a hotel armchair, a loaded pistol tucked under his arm, he nodded off to sleep. If he dreamed, he didn't remember it when his wake-up call came at seven A.M. What he did remember was that Ann Garrett was across the hall and they'd slept under the same roof for the first time in seven years. In his line of work, he mused to himself, such small victories were important.

The nearby attic was long, low, and stuffy, and its one window looked toward Hollywood. The wallpaper was at least twenty years old—flocked, discolored pink, and disgusting. There was a single light overhead, but the instructions were to never turn it on, day or night. Alexandr Filiatov sat a few feet back from the window, reclining in a wooden straight-back chair, occasionally glancing through his binoculars at the rear of a house a quarter mile away.

Inside the Soviet safe house in North Hollywood, the state of restlessness was constant. Filiatov and his wife, Marina, traveling through the western United States, had hit what they thought was their final stop.

After shooting the Oregon policeman, they had burned the passports that gave their name as Mr. and Mrs. Gregory Abelow. They, as well as Colonel Klisinski, were convinced that their backs were clean and that no one was on their trail. But the colonel had personally provided them with new American passports anyway, following the receipt of their new assignment at St. Peter's Church in New York.

Now Filiatov and Sejna were Mr. and Mrs. Samuel Melkevy, but their cover story was the same, as they'd not yet had to use it. Their instructions were continuing, and whatever they were involved in, they both knew it was important. Klisinski himself had twice made a rendezvous with them in California. This persistent member of the American secret police had made a pest of himself in both London and San Francisco, Klisinski had complained. He was to be silenced before he compromised a critical Soviet network.

Through binoculars, at two-hour shifts, they watched the rear of another Soviet safe house where Klisinski was temporarily staying. The colonel would give the signal. There were three yellow shades on the top floor of the distant house. If all three were to be pulled down, Filiatov and Sejna were to proceed against their target at the first possible moment. They were to shoot the F.B.I. agent named Buchanan, then leave Los Angeles and drive on the highway leading south.

They were to use the Melkevy passports, cross the border at El Paso, and rendezvous at the Soviet Embassy in Mexico City. From there they would pass from Klisinski's command to the G.R.U. station chief in the Mexican capital. A Soviet steamer would start them immediately back to Moscow and a heroic reception at Dzerzhinski Place.

Filiatov smoked endless cigarettes. The entire attic smelled like an ashtray. Filiatov lit one cigarette from another, snuffed the butt out on the side of his chair, and raised the glasses to his eyes again. Downstairs Marina sat alone, combating her own form of boredom. She listened to a radio that was playing an American singer named Perry Como. Idly she wondered if she could smuggle a Perry Como record back to Moscow.

Filiatov even knew where his target was. Thomas Buchanan was staying at the Commodore. All Filiatov wanted was a sign. Over and over he repeated the possible variations: Three shades down, proceed immediately. Two shades down, assignment canceled, return to New York for further instructions. One shade down, leave U.S. immediately. No shades moving, remain in place.

Filiatov kept looking. He barely cared which sign he received. He just wanted movement. Sitting and waiting, feeling the tedium mount, went against his personal deportment.

■ TWENTY-FIVE ■

Miraculously Ann was on the set at eight A.M. the next morning, still overwhelmed by the events of the previous day. In many ways she was surprised to be alive. She knew that without intervention she would have killed herself. And in some ways being alive left her in a quandary. How now was she to proceed with her life?

But an old love stepping back into her life lifted her spirits. Somehow it seemed that all things were possible and all problems were solvable. Maybe, she told herself, this was a delusion. But if so, it was a nice one, and it would get her through the next days . . . as long as nothing happened to Thomas Buchanan.

The scenes that were to be filmed that day revolved around a cocktail party. There were thirty extras. The set had been rearranged from the day before to look like a different suburban house, this one with a swimming pool. That meant that the first scene of the day, which was to begin photography at eight-thirty in the morning, called for a black cocktail dress for Ann's character and suits for all the men.

The script called for one of the supporting actors, a blustery but likably rotund man in his fifties, to playfully pursue Ann, with whom he is hopelessly smitten, onto a diving board. Thereupon, following their dialogue, she would give him a peck on the cheek and step past him. He would forget where he was, take a step backward, and plunge into the pool in front of the other guests. This was Jesse Chadwick's concept of high comedy. Yet the scene went smoothly and worked. Thereafter, Ann shot a scene with Damon Forbes, one in which he, playing her husband, followed her around the backyard, complaining about his wife's inattention to him. The scene was made technically more difficult by the fact that Damon Forbes stood only five feet six and Ann stood five seven. A miniature catwalk had to be specially constructed along Forbes's route which would add four inches to his height. Chadwick would shoot the scene never showing Forbes from the knees down. He would also film from an angle that would allow propmen to crawl on their stomachs to retrieve pieces of the catwalk immediately after Forbes had passed over them. For Forbes this was nothing new. The catwalk consideration had even been written into his contract. For two decades in Hollywood, Damon Forbes had never appeared full-length with another actor above the height of five feet two.

In the afternoon Buchanan again visited the set, this time as Ann Garrett's guest. Jesse Chadwick was irritated to see him and conferred with Joe Preston. The producer attempted immediately to talk Buchanan into leaving.

"Jesse's afraid you'll get Lisa all agitated up," Joe Preston said. "I don't know how much you know about our businesses, but we got to get the best shot in the fastest time."

Disregarding the violence Joe Preston inflicted on the English language, Buchanan answered. "Your leading lady says she'd feel better with me here," he said.

"I could force you to leave," Joe Preston said.

"No," Buchanan answered, "I don't think so. I had a nice chat with Max Wolberg this morning. Max said I could make myself right at home. If you don't believe me, call him."

When it came to an even match, Joe Preston had the same attitude on physical violence as Jesse Chadwick. Bullying actors was fine, so was knocking around women or screaming at studio underlings. But an able-bodied man with friends in the R.K.O. hierarchy was to be avoided. He backed off, flirted with the idea of calling out some studio goons just for show, then retreated from that idea too. What did he care, Preston decided, who another man's wife invited onto the set as long as the day's shoot was completed smoothly?

"Sorry, Jesse. He stays," Preston said to Chadwick. And Buchanan did.

In the evening Ann avoided her husband again. The last twenty-four hours, since the failure of her suicide attempt, had been the most placid of the last year. She hooked her arm on to Thomas's as soon as they were off the set. Thomas initially felt awkward about it, Ann being married to another man. She was easily triggering all the old emotions he had for her. Yet the gesture seemed both gracious and platonic. Plus, he told himself, he might never have an opportunity to spend time with her again.

He was, after all, an employee of the United States government who worked in Washington. She was an actress living in southern California. Despite a bad marriage, she would probably stay there. It would have to be enough, he told himself, just to have seen her again.

He'd read about a little French bistro named Chez Jacques on Ventura Boulevard and he invited her there for dinner.

This time, halfway through a bottle of wine, Ann let loose. She told him about the depths to which her marriage had descended and told Buchanan about Jesse Chadwick's treatment of her. Without naming names she told him of how she'd been pawned off to another man for the night, filmed in positions she found compromising, and, gradually, over the months of her marriage, had her dignity eroded by her husband's incessant womanizing.

Buchanan found himself listening with increasing anger. "Do you still love him?" he finally asked.

She looked at him strangely, as if the question were an insult. "No. How could I?" she asked.

"So why don't you divorce him?" he asked.

She cited the professional contract she was hooked into with Jesse Chadwick's brother, as well as the not-so-subtle threats surrounding Chadwick's hoodlum friends.

"Are you really that afraid of him?" Buchanan asked. "You think he'd really carry those threats out?"

"You don't know Jesse," she said. "I'm sure he would. Same way he has it in for you."

"You haven't mentioned I'm employed by the F.B.I., have you?" he asked.

"No," she said.

"Do you really want to be protected from him?"

"Yes."

"Can you get some money on your own? Enough to tide you through for a few weeks?"

She nodded. She was filming now. Half her fee had been paid to her.

"Then go somewhere safe as soon as the filming is over. Wait there. Keep in touch with me. I'll do the rest."

"What are you going to do?" she asked.

"Nothing that shouldn't have been done already," he said. "No one should have to live in fear like that."

"Tom. Tell me what you're going to do. Before I get too deeply into this."

"At the very least," he said, "I can offer you full protection under the law. Taking things a little further, I could help you get out of the marriage."

"Did I say I wanted that?" she asked.

"What else could you be talking about?"

Her attention settled on something across the room, then returned. "Why would you do that for me?" she asked.

"Because you look unhappy," he said. "Call it a favor for an old friend."

"We were more than friends, Tom."

"I remember," he said.

"Any other reason?" she asked.

"Yes," he admitted. "I suppose you know what it is."

She looked away. "This shouldn't happen yet. I'm still a married woman," she said. "I appreciate everything you're doing. I really do. But I can't take on extra troubles on top of everything else."

"Come on, Ann," he said. "We're trying to be honest, aren't we? I didn't come here to revive a romance that left off many years ago. I came here because I was assigned a case. If you're wondering if I've ever fallen in love with anyone else, the answer is no. I always wanted to marry you. But I didn't and you met other people. Well, that's done now. And I've worked things out in my mind." He spoke with such dispassion that he amazed himself. "If I can help you, and you go on your way, at least I'll have had that satisfaction. I didn't want to take this case, investigating your father and his bank, for exactly these personal reasons. But I've made peace with the situation."

She considered his response. "I understand," she said.

"Is that the answer you were looking for?" he asked.

She smiled in a relaxed way. "No," she said. "But it's an answer I can live with."

He didn't understand what she meant and was about to ask. Then she spoke again.

"I'm going to do you a favor," she said. "I'm going to tell you a story about Dad. It might make you understand him better."

Buchanan was all ears.

In the late thirties, she said, her family had gone on a driving tour through the American Midwest. Her father spent time in each city they visited, trying to rustle up some corresponding business with local bankers.

They were stopped in Indianapolis, she remembered, and her father looked for some entertainment for the family. It was a blazing hot summer day, she said, and her father bought them tickets to the local music hall for that evening. John T. Garrett had always been a fan of the stage. Vaudeville was in its dying days, but a few acts, especially those of local interest, still managed to make a living.

Of course, many of the acts on vaudeville bills weren't really acts at all. They were personal appearances, opportunities for the audience to see a famous person up close. On the bill on this particular night was John Dillinger, Sr., father of the notorious gunman, murderer, and native Hoosier bank robber. It was this appearance that Garrett wanted his family to see.

Buchanan wondered where this story was going. He listened quietly.

"Old man Dillinger didn't have much of an act," Ann said. "All he did was come out and talk about his son, 'Johnny.' "

The old man came out in shirt-sleeves, suspenders, and a pair of blue serge slacks, Ann recounted. He stood there in the evening heat of the American Midwest in 1939, ran his hands up and down his suspenders, and talked about his son. It wasn't memorable stuff, except for the wrap-up.

The old man glanced at his shoes, then his face looked up toward the audience. "They say my son Johnny was a pretty bad man," he concluded. "But you know," he went on, "after what them banks done to all of us during the Depression, maybe my boy Johnny wasn't so bad after all."

There was a moment of a silence. Then the hall erupted with a roar of approval. People were on their feet applauding the old man. They even brought him back for an extra bow, Ann remembered.

Garrett led his wife and daughters out of the show after Dillinger was finished. They quietly drove back to the inn where they were registered.

"We had a lot of discussions about that night in later years," Ann said. "But I'll never forget what Dad said first. 'Don't ever forget,' he said. 'That's what most people think of bankers.' "

Buchanan paid at Chez Jacques. He walked with Ann through
the parking lot to their car. She said she would be safe that night,
and didn't need to be guarded at the hotel again. He asked if she
was sure and she said yes. Her husband hadn't been home for a
week, she said, and he was already making his post-production
plans. These included a trip to Las Vegas with a pair of fifteen-year-
old girls.

"Is that a fact?" he said, barely looking up.

It was, she said. Joe Preston had many talents endemic to the
industry, and one of them was procuring star-struck girls from the
local high schools. He provided them for his stars and his friends,
but only after trying them out firsthand himself.

"That's where Jesse is tonight," she said sourly. "On a talent
hunt with Joe Preston."

Buchanan drove her to the door of her apartment house. "I
understand a lot of things," he said when the car stopped. "I understand why people steal, I understand why people kill. I know why
people betray their country and I know why people crave power.
What I don't understand," he said, "is why a man married to you
would treat you like dirt and then leave you alone."

"Thank you, Tom," Ann Garrett said. She shrugged. "That
makes two of us. I don't understand it either."

She leaned to him and kissed him gently on the lips. Then she
pulled away. "I'll see you tomorrow," she said. She opened the car
door and was out in a second, disappearing into the entrance foyer
of her building.

He sat in the car and raised his eyes. He didn't move until he
saw the lights go on in her apartment, and until Ann had waved to
him from her window to indicate that she was safe.

He drove back across Los Angeles to the Commodore. As
much as he enjoyed seeing her again, he was somehow troubled. All
that had happened in the last day still mystified him. He wondered
how it put anything in perspective with Commonwealth Penn.
Worse, it threatened to lead him off on an endless tangent. It was a
matter of time before Hoover was on his back. And, for that matter,
he'd now interviewed both Garrett daughters and seemed—for all
that he could see—barely any closer to John Taylor Garrett than
he'd been at the outset.

He parked in the Commodore parking lot. He rode a quiet

elevator back to his room. He was still evaluating the events of the evening, and pondering his next move, when he unlocked the door to his room, stepped in, and was surprised to find the light on.

His initial thought was that the cleaning staff had entered to make down the bed. That, of course, was true, and they would have left the light on also. But then from the peripheral ranges of his vision he perceived the figure of a man seated in the corner of his room.

It passed through his mind that he might be in the wrong room. But just as quickly it recurred to him that he had turned his own key in his own door, meaning that the man—of whom the legs lazily unfolded as Buchanan raised his sight—was waiting for him, and wished to conduct whatever was to follow in private.

Again Buchanan's next instinct was to expect to be shot. He jumped slightly, pulled at his weapon, and drew it cleanly. But by that moment Buchanan's eyes had focused on the intruder.

The man was seated peaceably in a hotel chair, his hat and coat on a side table. He was a handsome man in his fifties, graying gracefully, with features that might just have easily fit upon an Episcopalian minister. He wore a dark suit, much befitting a place of prestige within the banking community, and he even offered Buchanan an ironic smile as his eyes met Buchanan's.

"There's no need for a gun," the man said. "I'm quite unarmed."

Buchanan's eyes scanned the rest of the chamber as well as the bathroom before he was convinced.

"I'd say your nerves are getting the best of you," the man said. "Can't imagine why."

Buchanan slowly holstered his weapon. The man reached to a cigar that he'd placed next to his hat on the side table. "I'm getting a little tired of what's going on," the visitor said, unwrapping the cellophane around the cigar. "I thought maybe we should talk person to person. Man to man, if you're capable of it."

"Fine with me," Buchanan said, using his foot to push the door closed behind him.

"Mind if I smoke?"

"I hate cigars."

The man used a small smoker's knife to clip the end of the cigar. He moistened the smoking end of the tobacco and lit it, creating a large bluish-gray cloud that surrounded him.

"This is a fine cigar," the man in the suit said. "No one culti-vated objects to the aroma of a quality smoke."

He puffed again.

"Then again," the intruder said, "I never took you much for a man of cultivation. And, judging by the crude investigation you're running, I dare say you haven't changed much."

The man raised his eyebrows and grinned sarcastically. "Care to chat?" he asked.

A moment passed before Buchanan gave an answer. Then, "More than anything else in the world," he said.

Buchanan reached behind him and placed the chain on the door, never for an instant taking his eyes off his uninvited guest, John Taylor Garrett.

■
TWENTY-SIX
■

"**H**ow did you know I was looking for you?" Buchanan asked. settling into an armchair.

Garrett laughed. "It's not much of a secret, is it? You've been asking questions on two continents. Are you ready to talk to me, or do you have other questions to pose behind my back?"

"I'm ready to talk to you."

"So here I am. Talk." John Taylor Garrett made an expansive, mocking gesture with his open arms. He waited with exaggerated impatience.

"You could begin by answering my first question," Buchanan said. "How did you know?"

"Paul Evans told me," Garrett said in condescending tones. "Paul Evans, the maître d' at the Mayflower Club in Philadelphia. And if you must know," he nodded haughtily, "my daughter told me too."

"Which one?"

"The smart one. The only one I talk to. Laura."

"I think they're both bright young women."

"And I think, Thomas Buchanan," he said abruptly and with

rising anger, "that you've got your head shoved up your ass! Who the hell do you think you are, trying to spy on me or intimidate my family or friends? I know immediately when some damned fool is asking after me! Do you know what you're dealing with?"

"Why don't you tell me?"

"I might as well. You'll never find out by yourself. In fact"—here Garrett seemed to think about it, "—I'm going to do you a favor, not that I owe you one. I'll tell you exactly what you're dealing with and I'll give you a good hard one-time-only warning to keep your nose out of my business. Otherwise, you'll find—"

"Cut the threats! You don't scare me!" Buchanan shot back, allowing anger to come to his rescue also. He stood up. "It's not *me* who's running an irregular bank and whose whereabouts are a perpetual mystery. So you give me a one-time-only talk, and I'll give you a one-time-only listen."

He stepped to Garrett and with a detachment that astonished even him, reached to the cigar, pulled it from Garrett's hand, and snuffed it into the ashtray.

Garrett stared at him furiously but made no movement other than to bring his hands together, the fingers making a steeple for a moment. Then he set his hands to his lap as Buchanan sat down again.

"What would you like to talk about?" Garrett asked, his tone softening.

"Your bank. Your financing. Where it comes from. What you do with it." He paused. "Any illegal activity you happen to be engaged in. It would save us both a lot of time."

Garrett looked at him coldly, then began to chuckle. "Oh, God," he said, shaking his head. "You've been set up, son. You, your incompetent F.B.I., and your spineless F.B.I. Director have been played perfectly by the President and the Central Intelligence Agency. Can't you see that?"

Buchanan was quiet. "I want specifics if you're bothering to talk at all," he said finally.

"I went into intelligence work during the war, Buchanan. I was in the O.S.S. You know that much. Won a few medals. Did my share of work in Europe."

"And Eastern Europe. And in the Soviet Union."

"I did exactly as I was assigned," said Garrett. "Probably the same as you. I came out of there with a fistful of medals and a presidential commendation."

"Yeah. So?"

"After the war I went back to banking. You know that much too. I had contacts overseas. I used them because my bank, Commonwealth Penn, had been poorly administered during the war. I don't mind telling you that my service to my country, which I do not regret, cost my family millions of dollars in lost earnings."

"Which you've now more than made up in foreign deposits."

"Is there a law against that?"

"If the money's laundered, yes. If the money is financing illegal activities, yes."

"And do you have a shred of evidence that any of it is?"

"I thought you were going to talk," Buchanan reminded him.

"Here's another basic principle of banking, Thomas Buchanan," Garrett said. "When you've used up the supply of business in one area, in order to survive you have to have an influx of business from somewhere else. I applied that principle when I first went into banking in the 1930s. I applied it after the war to save Commonwealth Penn again. Most bankers can't see out of their own backyards. I bring money from all over the world into Commonwealth Penn. That's the name of the game, isn't it? It benefits my employees and my community."

"As well as yourself."

"I admit it. As well as myself." He fingered the cigar as if deciding whether or not to light it again. "After all," he said silkily, "I'm a capitalist."

"Are you?" Buchanan let the question hang in the air.

"Now, what the hell does that mean?" Garrett snapped angrily.

"You have some odd contacts for a banker," Buchanan countered. "It's hard to figure out exactly what you are. Your guests at the Mayflower Club, for example: Sammy Wong, an opium pusher. Jerry DeStefano, a south Philadelphia hoodlum. These are not men cut from a bolt of traditional banker's cloth."

"No, they're not. But if I were a traditional banker, Commonwealth Penn would have failed in 1933."

"That's fine. What I want to know is where men like Wong and DeStefano fit into your business."

"They're major depositors of my bank."

"And that doesn't bother you?"

"Why should it?" Here his face became one of philosophical introspection. "Money is amoral as soon as it goes through a teller's window, Mr. Buchanan. I don't doubt that some wealthy men may have gained their station in life through questionable activities. Know what Balzac wrote in *Père Goriot*? 'Behind every great fortune there is a crime.' Rockefeller, Carnegie, Ford, Morgan. These men were pirates by modern day morality. But they left foundations behind them to square the ledgers a bit. With men like Wong and DeStefano, the process—I'm happy to report—is more direct. I use their deposits to finance mortgages and home constructions in Bucks County. Because of deposits like that, people in my community are able to qualify for car loans, college loans, and home improvements that other banks might refuse. If Mr. Wong and DeStefano have made money illegally—which is their business, not mine —then I've played Robin Hood. How does that merit an F.B.I. investigation?"

"I think you're involved in something else."

"Like what?"

"I don't know the whole picture yet. Only pieces. And I'm not going to talk until I can prove it."

Garrett laughed, his mood changing again. "You don't have anything on me, you little moron."

"No?"

"No. And I'm going on my way," Garrett said. "I'm tired of wasting time." He gathered his hat and coat. He stood. "But if you've got anything to say to me in the future, or if you've some serious questions, be an adult. Come ask me in person." He pulled on his coat and reached into his inside pocket. He wrote something in a notebook, ripped the page out, and handed it to Buchanan.

"This is my home address and business address," Garrett said. "I'm on my way back to Pennsylvania. You can look me up there."

Buchanan took the paper. "How about a telephone number too?" he asked.

Garrett had taken one step toward the door. With irritation, he stopped.

"If you don't mind?" Buchanan asked. He held out his hand, seeking to borrow Garrett's silver fountain pen.

"You don't carry anything to write with?"

"I like yours."

Garrett handed him his pen. He gave his telephone number in Devon.

"I think you arranged to have Mark O'Connell, a former F.B.I. agent, murdered," Buchanan said as he wrote. "And I think you murdered a San Francisco nightclub owner named Blake Warren also."

Garrett remained perfectly in place for a moment. His gaze remained straight ahead, then roamed the room and settled back upon Buchanan.

"I don't think I heard you properly," Garrett said.

"Sure you did." Thomas set down the pen next to him.

"I've never in my life seen or heard of either of the men you named."

"You met Sammy Wong at Blake Warren's strip joint in San Francisco," Buchanan said. "You transacted some sort of business. Warren was your point man, but Mark O'Connell saw you. As a result, you sought to eliminate both Warren and O'Connell. My theory is that whatever business contact you had with Wong, it would be enough to send you to prison for a long time. That's why you were willing to have two murders committed."

"And what makes you so sure?"

"I have a witness."

"Who?"

"I'll tell you at the appropriate time," Buchanan said. "But my witness is excellent. I even have a description of your hit team. Big thick man. Blond woman, on the pretty side. Probably Soviets, both of them."

Garrett barely drew a breath. Buchanan studied the reaction on Garrett's face. Buchanan saw a hesitation. Then, for half a second he thought he saw what he wanted: uncertainty that he just might be able to prove he was right and link it all to Garrett. In any case, Garrett removed his hat and coat again.

"All right, Mr. Buchanan," said Garrett. "Let me tell what's going to happen to you. It's clear you and I will have to speak on a, shall we say, 'more advanced' level."

"I don't suppose you're admitting to murder?"

"I'm admitting only to what I'm about to tell you. So listen up. And keep a man like Sammy Wong in perspective. Yes, I was in the O.S.S. during the war. And yes, I operate a family bank. The bank has some foreign resources which some people—yourself included, as well as the infantile Mr. Hoover, I assume—would refer to as questionable. But now I'll tell you something else."

Buchanan waited.

"After the war the President of the United States, whom I have known personally for many years, asked me to stay on in a certain capacity. He was furious at some of the recent rudimentary failures of the U.S. intelligence community, and he was not sure how to structure the new centralized intelligence services. He wanted to be sure some of the men he trusted would be in his new C.I.A. He asked me to participate. I agreed. The work I'm doing, the activities for which you have me under investigation, is directly for the President and the C.I.A."

"Uh-huh," Buchanan said skeptically.

"Well, do I need to spell it out even more blatantly?" Garrett snapped. "Where were American troops fighting between 1941 and 1945? Didn't they teach you anything in those schools you went to? In the Orient, for example. In Italy, right in through Sicily and up the leg of the boot."

"So?"

"So did it ever occur to you that the much-maligned Sammy Wong and the even more maligned Jerry DeStefano might have done a few favors for the American government based on their knowledge of the homeland of their respective youths?"

Buchanan stared at him. In an awful kind of way, it made perfect sense. Even a career gangster like Lucky Luciano, with his lifetime of murder, extortion, gambling, and prostitution, won a pardon and a trip back home to Sicily courtesy of Uncle Sam in 1948. Luciano's knowledge of the southern Italian coastline—as well as the contribution of a gang of local partisan gunmen in Calabria to soften up the local fascisti—had immeasurably aided the invasion of Italy from Africa in 1943. Now Garrett maintained that Wong and DeStefano had struck similar deals.

"And now I'll tell you something else," Garrett continued. "Your F.B.I. has been positioned beautifully for a public embarrassment, and you're going to be the fall guy. Hoover's made a lot of enemies in Washington with his secret files and his overt blackmail. Well, the White House wants to be rid of Hoover, and this investigation is how it's going to happen. The F.B.I. has been goaded into investigating me. You'll file a report. Next Hoover will go public with some charge about me being a spy or a Communist or something. Know what happens then? The Central Intelligence Agency acknowledges me as one of their own. Hoover will be crucified in the press for blowing a spy investigation and ruining the credentials of a good agent. Hoover will take the public blame and he'll take it straight in the nuts. He and his Bureau will be discredited for the fiasco. The next day President Truman can fire him. Good riddance to a bad man."

"And where does that leave you if you're so eager to continue your work in the C.I.A.?"

"Exactly where I want to be," Garrett said. "I'm *not* eager to continue. I'm fifty-eight years old. I want to retire after being of one final service to my country. If that service is retiring a corrupt old crypto-Nazi like Hoover, then I'll be damned proud to go home, run my bank, and call it a career."

Buchanan was silent.

"The problem for you is that Hoover stuck you with this case precisely because it might go wrong. You're going to look even worse, investigating a man whose daughter dumped you. When the case blows up in Hoover's fat, effeminate jowls, my boy, he'll pass the blame along to you. In his unsuccessful attempt to save himself, you, too, will be fired. You'll find you have no job and no friends. Maybe, if you're lucky and come ask me nicely, I'll make you a teller in one of my branches." Garrett paused and, as was his habit, twisted the knife a little harder. "I think you'll find Commonwealth Penn a pleasant place to work if you don't mind spending the day counting the money of richer, more worldly, and altogether smarter men."

Garrett assembled his belongings again. This time he would be undeterred. He even picked up the cigar.

"I suppose," said Buchanan, "it wouldn't surprise you if I told you I'd met with the President personally on this already."

"Good Lord, no!" Garrett laughed, actually intrigued. "That wouldn't surprise me at all. Harry Truman is one clever little S.O.B. Everyone underestimates his shrewdness. He must have doped out from you exactly how you were doing on the case. You're being set up even more thoroughly than I thought. And you were probably foolish enough to tell him, right? What a laugh! Harry even got the opposition to tell him how they were doing."

Garrett shook his head in amusement and poked the unlit cigar back between his teeth.

Buchanan was silent.

Garrett pulled his coat on. "You know something, Thomas Buchanan? If you examine it, you've just answered for yourself something you may always have wondered about. Why my daughter dropped you."

He paused. Without looking at Buchanan, he straightened his

tie in the hotel room's mirror and adjusted the lapels of his coat as he spoke.

"We have a saying in certain privileged circles. 'Every wealthy American family has three sons. The best of the three becomes a professional man—a doctor or a lawyer. The second best, if he doesn't go into the clergy, runs the family business. The third goes to an Ivy League university, then comes home to become an officer in the local bank.' "

Garrett paused. He patted his hat onto his head. "That third son is usually personable, well educated, nicely mannered, and pleasant. He is also uncourageous and unimaginative. Through my banking career I've made it a point to avoid the employment of such individuals. And you are exactly that type of young man. So you see, I wouldn't tolerate that type marrying into my family either. I made that clear to Ann, and she came to agree with me. If you'll excuse the expression, that's why you were so unceremoniously dumped in 1943." He paused for a moment before concluding. "If only you'd been killed in the war. You could have gone out a hero instead."

Garrett took a final glance at himself in the mirror. "Good day, Buchanan. I've spent enough time here. And, by the way, when this case blows up in your face, forget about the teller's job at Commonwealth Penn. Heaven knows, I was only kidding."

Garrett moved toward the door. Buchanan stood in the room, seething, his face burning with anger. Yet he was amazed how outwardly calm he was. He watched Garrett walk to the door, stop, light the cigar, and exhale a cloud of smoke.

"Forgetting something, aren't you?" Buchanan asked.

Garrett turned. "What's that?"

Buchanan motioned to Garrett's fountain pen, where it lay on a writing table.

"Oh. Thank you," Garrett said.

Buchanan picked it up and held it for a moment. Then he tossed it across the room to the man at the door. Garrett froze for a moment. Then, instinctively, he reached out and caught it perfectly with his left hand.

Recently many of Viktor Milenkin's free hours had been spent in the reading room of the New York Public Library. He was, by the end of February 1950, a tortured man. Raised as a boy in California and a teenager in Moscow, his soul was torn in two, his allegiance pledged to two masters.

As George Mulligan, the employee of New York Telephone, he had been placed in a management internship, as promised. He had a secure job and a girl he wanted to marry. He had an adoptive family in Brooklyn. But now what he wanted most was truth.

In the reading room and the periodicals room of the Astor Branch of the New York Public Library, he sought to find it. He read everything he could concerning Soviet Russia, the war, and the United States. Increasingly he realized that things were not as he had been told back in Moscow from 1939 until 1948.

Milenkin had been a Soviet resident in February 1946 when Stalin had made his famous speech dropping "the front of cooperative and agreeable meeting of the minds" between East and West. Stalin had reaffirmed the traditional Communist teaching on the causes of capitalist wars, blamed the United States and England for World War II, dropped the pretense that the defeat of Germany eliminated the danger of more war, lauded the new Soviet order as "the greatest, most mighty" in the world, and called for greater sacrifice by the Soviet people to "claim the rest of the century for the Soviet Union."

At the time Viktor Milenkin had bought every word of the speech. His own sacrifice was having been talked by Colonel Klisinski to go to the West as a mole. And when Winston Churchill made his famous "Iron Curtain" speech in Fulton, Missouri, less than a month later, Viktor had agreed with Stalin that Churchill was "a foolish old warmonger" like all other Western diplomats.

Hadn't the Americans and the British allowed the war to go on for two extra years to wear down the Soviets? Hadn't the western powers plus their Chinese allies geographically encircled the Soviet Union by 1945? Hadn't the great Stalin been *forced* by strategic necessity to leave Red Army divisions in Eastern Europe as a barrier against Western aggression?

But as Milenkin spent time in the library, no one took notes over what he read. No book, pamphlet, or foreign journal was denied to him. His opinions began to change. He saw the Marshall Plan in a new light, for example. The Soviet Union had denounced the plan as "the American blueprint for the economic subjugation of Europe." Yet Milenkin learned for the first time that the Americans had promised to bolster the economies of all European countries—including the U.S.S.R.—that had been ruined by the war.

The Soviets originally accepted aid from the plan, then withdrew in 1947, coercing the Poles and the Czechs to withdraw as well. Further, Communist opposition to the Marshall Plan in Italy and France led to violent strikes. And to actively and overtly combat the Marshall Plan, the Soviet Union formed COMECO, an agency structured primarily to assure that all Communist parties in the West obediently toed the Moscow line.

Added to this was the news of the terrible purge trials which were resuming in the Soviet Union with much of the savagery of the 1930s. In terms of magnitude, according to reports even in the journals from the nonaligned West, thousands of victims were again being jailed, shot, or locked in mental hospitals. Hundreds of top party functionaries, names Milenkin remembered from the war and immediately afterward, had vanished for reasons real and imagined. Included were many Communists who had sought asylum in the Soviet Union during the war. The only members of the party who seemed able to ride out the storm were the trusted, faithful old Bolsheviks—Khrushchev, Malenkov, Mikoyan, Molotov, Beria, and Voroshilov—Stalin's longtime comrades in arms.

Still, the man now known as George Mulligan might never have believed it had he not received a shock in his own mailbox on the twenty-fifth day of February.

There was an envelope for him with a foreign postmark. When he examined it, he saw that the letter was postmarked from Stockholm. Even more incredibly, however, the envelope was addressed to him in the unmistakable handwriting of his mother.

Mulligan was initially overjoyed to receive it. He walked upstairs to his neat Perry Street apartment, smiling broadly to himself. He opened it. Surely now the lines of communication had been fixed and the letter would brim with joyful news. He sat and felt his heart pound as he read it. Then he felt sweat soak into his shirt as his soaring joy turned into agony.

The letter was in English. It read:

My dear son,

I do not know if this letter will reach you, but I do know that I may never again have a chance to write. I will give this letter to a foreign man who is visiting Moscow and Leningrad. He is a Swede, a friend who is well positioned in the diplomatic corps and will return to the West soon. He says he will post this for me.

I have been an hour ago arrested for anti-Soviet activity. I think this is because the man I have been seeing from the trade ministry was arrested in October. I am told that he will be executed. In these cases, often the woman's fate follows the man's. This is the way things are in the Soviet Union today.

I know I have done nothing to warrant prison or a labor camp or death. I have been a good woman all my life and a dedicated worker of the Soviet State. But there are terrible criminals in power now, men who promote their own personal glory and not the interests of the great Russian Republic. I sincerely hope that you are safe and well. But above all, I caution you to sever any link you have with the Soviet government, and in particular the deceitful Colonel Klisinski. I believe this "Colonel" romanced me only to gain your trust so he could employ you as his agent in the West.

I have given Klisinski many letters to mail to you but I feel he does not mail them. Otherwise you would write to me in return, I know. But through a friend I learned your new name and address. I am overjoyed to know that you are safe in America, and will stay there.

If I am ever free again to travel, I will try to find you. But do not try to find me, as it may sacrifice your own safety. If we do not see each other again, please understand, my dear son, that I love you with more than my heart could ever bear. Know also about Klisinski . . .

I must go now. I love you.

Your mother,
Liliya Milenkinova

Mulligan read the letter three times, each in ever-mounting disbelief. When he finished, tears flooded his eyes. He ripped at the paper, crumpled it, and flung it on the floor. He let go with a wail of agony so intense and so horrible that it brought O'Dwyer, his faithful mongrel, whimpering to his side, and Mr. LoBianco, his downstairs neighbor, to his door.

He put on a brave face and dismissed LoBianco. Then he went to his bedroom, closed the door, and cried like a little boy for several hours until he fell asleep.

For the next days he was quiet to friends at work. He did not seek companionship. When he spoke to Barbara Litvinov, his lover, he spoke very formally and with great preoccupation. Yet he did this with much difficulty. He needed her warmth and affection more than ever. Yet even to her he dared not confide his darkest secrets as to his identity. Nor could he reveal his purpose in the United States.

Then something else happened. On March 2, a Thursday, there was a story in the New York *Times* that riveted his attention. It concerned a man named Klaus Fuchs. Fuchs's life had, in many ways, paralleled Milenkin's.

Fuchs had been born in Germany in 1911. As a young man he joined the German Communist Party in reaction to the barbaric excesses of the Nazis. In 1933, when Hitler came to power, Fuchs fled first to France, then to England. There, as a naturalized Briton, he resumed his studies in the academic field in which he had demonstrated his brilliance: physics.

Even his detractors admitted that Fuchs was a gifted young scientist. Eventually he was offered a professorship at the University of Birmingham. His work would encompass atomic physics. That was in late 1941. In early 1942 he was contacted by Soviet agents and asked to give them access to whatever scientific information to which he was a party. Still a good Communist, he agreed.

In 1943 Fuchs was sent to work in the United States, first in New York, then at Los Alamos, where research on the first atomic bomb was in progress. During the years that followed, he continued to smuggle atomic information to his Soviet contacts. When President Truman told Soviet leader Joseph Stalin that the Americans had exploded their first atomic device, Stalin already knew— through Fuchs.

The physicist returned to England in 1946 and became head of the theoretical physics division of the new British atomic energy research station at Harwell. There he continued to pass atomic secrets to Moscow, though his infatuation with Marxism had cooled dramatically. He was, in fact, skeptical of communism, at least the way it was practiced by the Soviet Union. And, just as Viktor Milenkin would grow to respect his American peers a few years later, Fuchs had also acquired an affinity for the resolute, steadfast British and the work they were doing at Harwell.

But for Klaus Fuchs there would be no pleasant road back, even though he stopped passing secrets in 1948. An American Communist named Harry Gold was arrested by the F.B.I. in early 1949.

Gold, attempting to save his own skin, ratted on many fellow travelers, including Fuchs. Fuchs was questioned by MI5. Voluntarily he confessed. On March 1, 1950, his arrest was made public. Now he stood to draw a sentence of fifteen to twenty years in prison in the United Kingdom.

Viktor Milenkin, sitting in Washington Square Park on an mild late-winter day, shook all over when he read this story. Here was his life, the past, present, and future. Twenty years in prison! Where could he run? Where could he hide? What kind of life could he ever lead?

At work he now became sullen and quick-tempered. To Barbara he was short, then moody, then wildly emotional, breaking down twice into tears over seemingly petty little events. Surely she knew something was wrong. She couldn't be in love with a man as she was and not notice or not care. She asked him what was bothering him. He wouldn't tell her. She retreated. She thought she knew because she'd seen it happen to her girlfriends. George had another woman.

"Do you want out of our relationship?" she asked him one night in the stairwell of his building. "Is that it, George?"

No, he said. That wasn't it. He held her tight, hugged her, and cried again. "And my name isn't George. It's Viktor."

"What?" she said.

"It's Viktor Milenkin," he said.

She looked him straight in the eye for several seconds. "So?" she asked. "Jack Benny's real name is Benjamin Kubelski."

She maintained her hand on his shoulder. She leaned to him and kissed him on the side of the face. With that gesture of love, however, on an unswept set of steps in a lower Manhattan walk-up, she changed the course of several lives. For she encouraged him to keep talking.

"I'm in terrible trouble, Barbara," he said. "I could go to jail."

She never took her arm from him. She never hesitated in her support. "Did you steal something?" she asked.

"No."

"Did you hurt anyone or kill anyone?"

"No."

"Then how bad could it be?"

"Very bad."

"I don't care. I love you."

"You better hear it all first," he said.

"I'll stick by you all the way, George," she said. "And so will my family. You're one of us."

He was dumbfounded by her reaction. Americans, real Americans, never ceased to amaze him. New Yorkers in particular baffled him. Every time he thought he had them figured out, they stunned him again.

She led him onto the BMT and they took a subway train to Brooklyn. They walked hand in hand to her home. They came in unannounced. Mrs. Litvinov was pleasantly surprised to see him, so she set an extra place for dinner. Milenkin could hardly comprehend that this was happening. His fear from reading about Klaus Fuchs had given way to a strange bewilderment. From the reaction of Barbara so far, his spirits were almost buoyed. Then again, he hadn't confessed anything yet.

Barbara sat him down at their dinner table. Mrs. Litvinov, with her worrisome, motherly eyes, brought him a glass of hot tea. Barbara's father sat down too. So did Barbara. Dinner stayed on the stove for a few extra minutes.

"George has a problem," Barbara said. "I told him there's nothing we can't solve. Right, Daddy?"

"Right, angel," said Barbara's father, Irving Litvinov.

Viktor Milenkin surveyed the table, calmer now but still incredulous. He squeezed a wedge of lemon into his tea, then sipped. Truly, he had no idea how these kind people would react if he told them the whole truth.

But he had a feeling. So he drew a deep breath and tried to stop trembling. Only then did Colonel Klisinski's conduit man in the United States begin to talk.

TWENTY-SEVEN

■

n the rear lobby of his hotel, Thomas Buchanan dialed a long distance operator and asked for the number in Washington, D.C., given him by Jack Malone, his Secret Service contact at the White House. At this hour it was Malone's home phone. ". . . *If you have any problems or need any assistance . . ."* Malone had promised.

Yes, Jack, now is the time, Buchanan thought to himself. *So what if it's past ten p.m., Pacific Time?*

Malone answered the phone on the third ring, coming instantly awake. No, he didn't want to talk on this line, he said. He would have to move to a line that he felt was more secure. Where was Buchanan calling from?

"The rear lobby of the Los Angeles Commodore," Buchanan answered.

No good, said Malone. The operators listen in on all those phones, hoping to catch a bit of gossip from a movie star which they can then sell to a scandal sheet for five bucks. Could Buchanan move to someplace more anonymous? Buchanan said he could. Malone gave him a White House number to call in forty-five minutes and instructed him to be prepared to give a call-back number. That would be at exactly eleven o'clock California time, two A.M. back east, where Malone would be moving through the dark streets of the American capital.

"Remember the date we met?" Malone asked. "Don't say it aloud. Remember which day of February it was?"

It had been the twenty-first of the month, Buchanan recalled. "Yes," he said. Easy to pinpoint: it was the date he had returned from England.

"Add the number of the date to the telephone number my assistant will give you. Then call that number and we'll talk."

Malone hung up.

Buchanan went to his car. He drove to Vine Street. First he found an all-night diner, but considered it too noisy. Shortly thereafter he found a drugstore with a midnight closing. He bought a ham salad sandwich and a Coca-Cola at the lunch counter and staked out one of the two phones in the rear. He took the stool at the far end of the counter.

He kept his eyes upon the door. White House or no White House, Secret Service or no Secret Service, he trusted no one now. It occurred to him that Jack Malone could have been jerking him around late-evening Los Angeles for a reason. A Notre Dame alumnus used to say at the Bureau, out of Hoover's earshot, "Jesus Christ had twelve who he trusted and one of them betrayed Him too." Moral: Never drop your guard. Always cover your back. The Feebee parable of Jesus: Always keep your weapon loaded and within reach. Follow the Savior but pack the ammunition.

Buchanan turned the whole intrigue over and over in his mind. Garrett had insisted that Hoover was to be deposed and he, Buchanan, was to be a fallen pawn in the game. Yet Malone at the White House and President Truman himself had—right before Buchanan's eyes—questioned Garrett's ultimate allegiance. And if the trail that Buchanan was following indicated anything, it was that Garrett was in league with the Soviets.

And yet, Buchanan ruminated, how did it fit together? Who was telling the truth? Garrett? Malone? Truman? What was at stake? And most important, whom could Buchanan trust?

He dwelt upon this final question for too long a time, then arrived at a decision. He would have to trust the White House. At least when Truman had been before him, he had been direct and forthright.

At eleven Buchanan went to the telephone again and dialed. A duty officer at the Secret Service quarters in the White House gave Buchanan a forwarding number, then hung up. Buchanan used the 21 additive and reached Jack Malone seven minutes later.

Almost an hour after he had first tried, Buchanan was ready to speak. "Got a pencil?" he asked.

"I've got two in case I wear out the first one," Malone said. "Start talking."

Buchanan spoke in a low voice and kept his eyes on the door. "I want any file you can find—C.I.A., O.S.S., or whatever—on John Garrett, a smuggler named Sammy Wong, and a South Philly hood named Jerry DeStefano. We've been through this before, Jack, but this time shake the trees. See what else we can find." Specifically Buchanan wanted to know what wartime work they may or may not have been doing.

That done, Buchanan asked Malone to get in touch with London. Find out about an effort against the East Germans that had recently gone awry. The operative name was Zolling, he said. Did security there, such as the C.I.A. station that worked out of an office that overlooked the Russian Consulate, have any further idea what had happened? For that matter, did the English?

Malone said he'd get on it right away.

Buchanan rang off. Next he dialed the F.B.I. in Washington, around the corner from the White House. Leave a message for Frank Lerrick, he asked. He wanted a file, if any existed, on a film producer named Joe Preston and a director named Jesse Chadwick. He knew damned well that Max Wolberg, the head of R.K.O., had been leaking information to Hoover like a sieve. Maybe some of it could be put to good use. And oh yes, he concluded, most important: Preston and Chadwick would be arriving in Las Vegas within the next few days. They always stayed at Bugsy Siegel's hotel. Or at least it belonged to the infamous Bugsy before some anonymous sorehead stuck a shotgun through his window one night in 1947 and blasted him into the next dimension.

"I want a surveillance unit on both Preston and Chadwick," Buchanan said. "It's important. I want to know who they arrive with, who they see, where they go, and what they do."

The F.B.I. already had a sizable presence in Las Vegas and were always scouting for ways to justify an assignment that had them hanging around whores and slot machines. But watching film people was often even more entertaining than watching their films. So maybe, Buchanan reasoned, that presence could be put to good use in the Commonwealth Penn investigation too.

Buchanan hung up. He drew a long breath and felt that some progress had been achieved.

Outside on Vine Street a new Cadillac skidded to a sudden stop and a banged-up Studebaker crashed into it from the rear. This was followed, not surprisingly, by a noisy profane argument; two men, two women, both screaming at each other. One of the men was dressed entirely in orange. Passersby stopped, gathered, and gawked. Ever since the war Buchanan had held a theory about southern California: Someone had tipped the country one night and everything loose rolled to the southwest corner.

"Mister?" someone asked Buchanan. To his right the staff of the pharmacy was preparing to close down the lunch counter and sweep the floors. They asked him if he wanted anything more.

He drank another Coke. Then, on his way back to the hotel he stopped off at a neighborhood bar and enjoyed something stronger.

A few hours later in North Hollywood it was dawn. From the street outside the Russian safe house there was a fragment of laughter and some muffled conversation. Two teenagers, a boy and a girl, passed on foot on their way to high school. Marina Sejna lifted the binoculars to her eyes and peered the quarter mile through the morning haze. Someone had finally adjusted the yellow window shades that she and her husband had watched for days.

She walked downstairs quickly and roused Filiatov. He came up to the attic, put the field glasses to his own eyes, and saw for himself.

Three yellow shades, all pulled down overnight, as if the cover of darkness had somehow added to the mystique. Had Colonel Klisinski been there to draw the shades himself? Or had someone called the location and given the instructions?

Filiatov and Sejna didn't know. Nor did they care. Fact was, they didn't even wonder.

They packed the two suitcases that each of them had lived out of for these many months. Filiatov had more than memorized Buchanan's appearance. He had stalked him enough to know that his proposed victim was constantly back and forth between his hotel and some woman whom he saw at a film studio. Waiting along his route would not be difficult. The only complication was the fact that Buchanan was armed. To Filiatov, that meant ambush was essential.

At least this will complete things in America, Filiatov thought. And he set to work, finishing the packing of his bag, removing any trace of himself from the apartment, and stripping down, cleaning, and reassembling a Walther .38 that he would now wear beneath his left arm.

Twenty-four hours from now he could be on his way to Mexico, and after that, home. He could, he mused, be on the Soviet steamer in the Gulf of Mexico, making love to Marina. He had a violent, aggressive way that he liked to have sex with her, tying her hands, then leaping upon her. In recent days, when he wasn't too rough, she'd come to like it a bit herself. It amused Filiatov to think that while the funeral plans for the American federal police agent were still being set, he could be sailing home, pleasantly ravishing his wife on his way.

■
TWENTY-EIGHT
■

Buchanan's eyes flickered open in the Los Angeles hotel room. The telephone was ringing like a fire alarm. It was 4:45 A.M. Buchanan groped sleepily, picked up the receiver, and struggled to come awake. A long distance operator announced a person-to-person call from Washington. Frank Lerrick, the Bureau's assistant director, was on the line.

It was not a social call. "The Director," Lerrick intoned ominously, "is on the warpath."

"What time is it in Washington?" Buchanan asked.

"Almost eight A.M., Tom," Lerrick said. "And let me tell you—"

"It's quarter to five here, Frank. Most people sleep at four forty-five A.M., particularly on Saturdays."

"Most people don't have a director who was at his desk at seven A.M. on a weekend morning, Tom. Some sort of hell is breaking loose. J. Edgar wants a complete report on Garrett and Commonwealth Penn by Tuesday at noon."

That simple declarative sentence was enough to jounce Buchanan from sleep.

"What?" he asked.

Lerrick repeated. The Director had galloped in to work that morning as if he had a burr under his saddle. He'd been fuming noisily about Communists in the State Department, Communists in the university system, Communists in the fledgling television industry, Communists in the woodpile, and, for that matter, Communists in the Soviet Union. From this he'd transposed onto the Commonwealth Penn investigation. When, he demanded, would he see some results? Before Frank Lerrick could address the question, Hoover offered an answer. He would see some results on the second business day of the following week, he announced. He wanted "young

Thomas Buchanan," as he called him, summoned back to Washington immediately to personally bring him up-to-date.

"'Young Thomas Buchanan,'" said Lerrick portentously across the continental telephone line, "is, unless I'm mistaken, you."

"There aren't any results yet," said Buchanan, his indignation rising. "The investigation is ongoing."

"Tom, if you value your job, you'll think of something better to say than that."

"What else is there?"

"Well, I suppose you'll have to put the best coating on it," Lerrick said. "And you'll have to do it in person."

"Frank," Buchanan said, "I'm just making headway here."

"Staying at a ritzy Hollywood hotel for millionaire movie stars?" he said with a touch of reproach. "Having drinks with actresses about the town? Next we'll hear that you're taking nude dips in kidney-shaped swimming pools."

"Frank . . . ?"

"There's nothing I can do, Tom," Lerrick said. "The Director is fired up about this case. He wants a report in person and he wants it yesterday. Do you think I call you at this hour because I begrudge my agents their sleep?"

"I don't know. Do you?"

"Be on a plane out of L.A. today, Tom. I don't care if you have to fly back again next week. You know how this Bureau works. Get here pronto and give J.E.H. what he wants."

"Yes, sir," Buchanan said. Lerrick hung up. Five minutes later, Buchanan was packing. By seven A.M. he had checked out of his hotel.

He called on Ann once before heading to the airport. *Hold the Phone!* was in its final day of photography. The day's shoot included one of the initial scenes in the film. It was shot on a back lot of the R.K.O. studio, a set that was dressed to look like a suburban town somewhere in the comfortable middle class regions in the United States. In one scene Damon Forbes was to make a fool of himself—a recurring source of humor in the script, and a talent that Forbes seemed to have refined—by mistaking Ann for his own wife as she comes out of a grocery store. Ann, heavily laden with grocery bags, was to assume the man helping her into a car was her husband. The confusion was not to be solved until they got home, as the Forbes character played a vain man, who drove without his glasses, and Ann was to hold a bushy plant on her lap. Meanwhile, Forbes's actual film wife and Ann's husband were to be stranded together at the curbside, setting in motion the film's buoyant plot. The ensuing scenes, which would take place at Forbes's character's residence, had been shot the previous week.

Two scenes were shot in the morning. Buchanan watched from the side of the set. Joe Preston came nowhere near Buchanan, nor did Jesse Chadwick. During a break, however, Ann came to Buchanan and sat next to him. Impetuously she leaned over and kissed him on the cheek, which surprised him.

"Hey," he said. "That was nice. Any particular reason?"

"General principles," she said.

"How are things going?" he asked.

"All right," she said.

"How about Jesse?"

"Never came home again," she said. She sighed. "Maybe he's decided to leave me alone for a while. I don't know." After a moment, she continued. "After the wrap party tonight he and Joe Preston are on their way to Las Vegas with a pair of high school girls. The girls are here already."

Ann indicated a pair of teenagers sitting placidly on the opposite side of the set, awestruck by what they perceived as the glittery world of cinema.

"When are they going?" Buchanan asked.

"Tonight or tomorrow. Why?"

"Just wondering." He paused again. "I have to make a progress report directly to Hoover. I'm on my way back to Washington," he said.

"Today?" she asked, surprised.

"This morning."

She turned away. "Oh," she said.

"Something wrong?"

"I'm a little disappointed. I was hoping you'd come to the wrap party. Then maybe we could talk again tonight."

He was torn. "I won't be able to," he said. "I'm sorry."

"When will you be back?" she asked.

"I don't really know. Fact is, I don't know if the case will bring me back here or not. It probably won't."

"So you just drop into my life and out again? Just like that?"

"Ann," he said. "I'm concerned about you. Over ten years I never stopped thinking about you. But you're a married woman.

What's permissible in your film society out west here doesn't wash very well back east."

"What are you saying?"

"What I'm saying is, there are limits to what I can do for you. I can do anything you want on a professional level, if federal laws have been violated. But personally . . ."

"I'm another man's woman. Is that it?"

"With all my heart I wish you weren't," he said. "But you are."

He allowed a long pause. "Ann, you shouldn't squander your life with that man. No one should hold you in a bad marriage."

She looked nervously onto the set. "I suppose," she said, "I'll work up the courage to divorce him. Someday. But I don't have it yet."

"What more motivation do you need?" he asked. "He abuses you. He overtly sleeps with other women. You're still scared of Jesse, aren't you?"

"I have reason to be."

"No, you don't. If this 'goon squad' factor could be eliminated, would you feel safer filing for divorce?"

She thought about it. "Maybe," she said.

"You let me know," he said. He pulled a card from his wallet bearing his telephone lines in Philadelphia and Washington. He pushed the card into her hand.

"Now, there's one other thing," he said. "I had a visitor last night after I left you."

"Who?"

"Your father."

She turned to him again, her eyes wide. "My father?"

"Does that surprise you?"

"Yes. It surprises me very much. What did he want?"

"He wanted to know why I was investigating him."

"And what did you tell him?"

"I told him exactly why," Buchanan said. "What I still don't know is why he was on the West Coast."

Ann wore a blank expression.

"I assume, Ann," Thomas said, "that you didn't know he was in Los Angeles."

"No, I didn't."

"And you had no contact with him?"

"None."

"You'd tell me if you did?"

She paused slightly. "Tom, you saved my life two nights ago. I'd return a favor." Her eyes narrowed in thought. "What else did he say?" she asked.

"Only a few things," Buchanan said. "He told me where to reach him in Pennsylvania."

"Where?"

"At your home in Devon. And at the bank. He said he'd be there for the next few weeks." Buchanan took out the slip of paper. "Is this his handwriting?" he asked.

She looked at it and recognized it instantly. Ann Garrett nodded.

"You're absolutely sure?" he asked.

"Yes," she said.

"Thank you," he said courteously, folding the paper away.

"You recognized him, didn't you?" Ann asked.

"Of course. I just wanted to make sure we're talking about the same man," Buchanan said.

"How could we not be?"

He shrugged. "Your father told me that he'd personally talked you into breaking our engagement during the war," Buchanan said. "And he told me that he was completely innocent of any current illegality or wrongdoing."

First her face went red, then she thought about it.

"How's that sound?" he asked. "As legitimate as the handwriting?"

Ann seemed to disappear into a deep concentration for a moment, only to emerge a few seconds later, as if wondering exactly how to respond.

Jesse Chadwick's assistant director appeared before her. The next scene was prepped and the cameras were ready to roll, he said. Ann said she'd be there in a moment, but did not answer Buchanan's question. Instead, she sat facing away from him.

"Ann?" he finally asked.

"Tom . . ."

"Oh, come on, Ann. I'm not going to collapse into tears at this point over something that happened seven years ago."

"The first part's true," Ann said. "He never liked you at all. Said you were a typical unimaginative and boring son of the American middle class. Mediocre brains, average looks, not really equipped to excel in any important profession. Those were his words. He said I could do better, should do better and certainly shouldn't sit by for an entire world war when you'd probably get killed anyway."

"I see," said Buchanan with utmost civility. "And you believed him?"

There was a long, uneasy silence. "He could be very persuasive," Ann said.

"I'm sure," Buchanan answered. "But wasn't he away for much of the war himself?"

"Yes. We never knew when he'd be home or away."

"And he was in Europe, I believe," Buchanan pressed. "Did he ever talk much about it?"

"Why do you want to know that?"

"Because it bears on current-day business."

"He rarely said much of anything about the war itself," she said. "I know he was in intelligence work. That's about all."

"But on those rare occasions when he did say something, Ann," Buchanan pressed again. "What would he have said? Do you remember?"

"No," she said flatly.

"Maybe if you think a little harder . . . ?"

"Tom, what are you angling for?"

"An answer to my question."

"I told you. He didn't like you."

"And in that he's consistent," Buchanan said. "Because he likes me even less today. But I'm curious about his current occupation. He maintains that he's done nothing illegal."

"Tom," Ann Garrett said. "My father and I haven't spoken for five years."

"Think hard, Ann," he said.

"I would have no way of knowing," she said again.

"Ann, I think you're holding something back on me."

Ann's mouth opened to respond, but then Buchanan saw a growing resentment written clearly across her face, coupled with an incipient anger. He knew immediately he'd pushed too hard.

"Tom, two days ago you walked back into my life after ten years. Now you're walking out of it again, back to Washington, back to your job. I'm not about to bare my family's soul to you. Not today."

Buchanan nodded. "Fair enough," he said at length. "May I ask you one last question, then?"

She said he could.

"What about politics?" he inquired.

"What about them?"

"I was just wondering where John Taylor Garrett stood politically," Buchanan tried. "Did you ever have any discussions during the war?"

"Tom, what *are* you getting at?"

"Well, John Taylor Garrett worked with the other intelligence services, did he not? Did he ever make any statements on how he felt about our partners in the Allied effort? An opinion on De Gaulle, for example. Your father was in France. Or Churchill? Or Stalin? You were his daughter, Ann, and you weren't a little girl either. You were a young adult. Did he express opinions?"

"He spoke well of Roosevelt and Churchill, of course," she said. "Stalin too. I can recall some conversations. But then, back then we all were supposed to speak well of the Allied leaders, weren't we?"

"Yes, we were."

"So I don't really know what you're getting at."

"No?"

The assistant director turned up again. "Miss Pennington . . . ?" he asked. The message was clear.

"No," she said to Thomas.

Buchanan stood. "Thank you for your time," he said. "If I get back this way, we'll have lunch sometime. Meanwhile, if you have any problems . . ."

She nodded. He offered his hand. She accepted it. He was turning to go when she stopped him.

"Tom?" she said. She reached to him and held him. Impulsively she pulled him to her and kissed him again.

"Be careful," she said.

"You too."

He released her. She turned to walk back to the set. He was still watching her when she stopped a second time.

"Tom?" she asked. He waited. "Remember the story I told you about Dillinger's father? Dad always hated bankers and everything they stood for. I know that sounds preposterous, being what he is and what he does. But that's the case. He took us to see Dillinger, Senior, so that we'd know why he felt as he did. Does that seem inconsistent?"

"Not if viewed from a certain angle," Buchanan said.

"Then look at it that way," she said. "You're heading in the right direction."

"Thanks."

"Dad was wrong about a lot of things," she said. "Judgments on politics as well as on people. Know what I mean?" She was looking him directly in the eye.

"Yes, I do, Ann. Thank you." He gave her a gentle wave of the hand, wished her well, and left her to complete her film.

He drove directly to the airport and caught the next flight. There would be a change of planes at O'Hare in Chicago, a delay on takeoff from O'Hare to National Airport in Washington, and a turbulent flight in a DC-3 as the aircraft rode out the fringes of a snowstorm above Ohio. It would be evening when Buchanan looked out of the left side of his airplane and saw Washington Monument and the Capitol from the air. By that time he was exhausted.

But he was alive and in good health, much thanks to Frank Lerrick and his predawn phone call. From eight A.M. in Los Angeles outside the Commodore, Alexandr Filiatov had sat in ambush in his own car, a pistol under a folded newspaper across his lap, waiting for Buchanan to emerge from the hotel.

At noon Filiatov guessed that he'd missed his prey and had gone into the hotel to inquire. It was only then that the hotel informed the Soviet assassin that Mr. Buchanan had departed. The hotel graciously provided a forwarding address in Washington. Filiatov thanked the desk clerk and proceeded to the airport. He cursed violently to himself, but remained resolutely on the trail of his target.

■
TWENTY-NINE
■

From National Airport in Washington, Thomas Buchanan took a taxi to his address on 7th Street, S.E. On arrival, Buchanan paid the driver, turned, and walked up the wooden steps of the Raffertys' house. He turned the key in the door and entered. From the living room adjoining the entrance hall he heard familiar voices in casual conversation.

Mrs. Rafferty was talking about Bess Truman. Buchanan caught only a snippet of the conversation, but then Rafferty himself changed the topic back to Harry Truman. It was Rafferty's opinion, being a son of the Old Confederacy, that Harry Truman was "doing too much for the colored man." This was one of Rafferty's favorite topics, that and the Eleanor Roosevelt Clubs—to Rafferty, obvious hotbeds of sedition—that numerous exploited cleaning ladies in the South had formed. Buchanan had long since learned to keep Rafferty, if he wanted to rant, on the subject of the Washington Senators, where his fury was more constructively focused. On politics the man lived in the previous century.

But then Buchanan heard a third voice, a man's. He stopped and listened. For a moment he couldn't place it. Then he did.

"I think I hear Mr. Buchanan now," said the visitor. All conversation ceased.

Buchanan took one more step and stood at the doorway to the Raffertys' sitting area. He looked at the Raffertys plus their guest. "Hello, Mr. and Mrs. Rafferty," he said. "Hello, Jack," he said.

Jack Malone of the United States Secret Service grinned apologetically and stood. "I took the liberty of telling your landlords that you'd be back this evening. At least for a short time," Malone said.

"But how did *you* know I'd be back?" Buchanan asked, innately suspicious.

"I tried to phone your hotel in California," Malone said. "They gave me your forwarding number. And address."

"Something must be important," Buchanan said, "that you'd be here waiting in person."

"I think that's a reasonable supposition," said Malone.

"Mr. Malone has a job with the Treasury Department," said Mrs. Rafferty, impressed.

"Tom, you might want to repack your suitcase with a change of clothes, but I'd keep that coat on if I were you," Malone said. "We've got a drive in front of us."

Buchanan glanced at his watch. It was nine-thirty on a Saturday night. He was dead on his feet from the ten-hour journey from California. Even worse, there was a written brief to prepare for Hoover. "Now?" he asked with displeasure.

"If you care about getting your job done right," Malone said. "Yes. Now."

When Malone walked Buchanan back to the street, a car was waiting, complete with the same helpers as before. Special Agent Fred Clark of the Secret Service hopped out and opened the door. The engine idled noisily. Buchanan recognized it as the same vehicle that had transported him last time.

Malone went to the driver's side. Buchanan stood across the car from him. "Where to this time?" Buchanan asked.

"Just for a drive," Malone said. That was Buchanan's cue to get in and shut up.

Buchanan took his cue, tossing his suitcase in the backseat. There it landed on a case presumably belonging to Malone.

The doors slammed. Buchanan noticed that Clark was going to the car behind them. Special Agent Kirby was at the wheel of a backup vehicle.

"I hate secrets," said Buchanan.

"It's not time to talk yet," Malone said. "Believe it or not, our agency has a set of rules as to when I can reveal to a passenger where we're going. I can't do it yet. Not till we're completely sure we're clean."

Clean meant no one uninvited was following.

"Ready?" Malone asked.

Buchanan said he was. The car started to move.

As they had several days earlier, they drove through nighttime Washington. The city was again strangely quiet, even for a Saturday. It was cold enough for snow. To Buchanan, who had been in California a few hours earlier, the temperature was all the more chilling.

Buchanan sat quietly. The car radio was on, but Malone had the volume low. The broadcast sounded like a Blue Network pickup of a fake ballroom in New York or Boston. From the corner of his left eye Buchanan looked at the lines on Malone's face and wondered what percentage were job-related.

At the same time, Buchanan was growing to resent Malone. He was angry at being hauled out into a cold night when he would just as soon have collapsed in bed. He was angry at Malone's methods, his manners, and his missions. He was angry, also, he realized, that he'd just left a woman in California who was married to a man who abused her and with whom he could easily fall back in love. Malone, however, had excellent antennae.

"You don't seem in the best of spirits," Malone asked.

"I'm not."

"Anything I can do to help?"

"Sure. Solve my case for me, drop a brief on Hoover's desk, and ship me back to California for nine months of R and R."

"Anything more realistic?"

"Probably not," Buchanan groused.

After a small pause Malone spoke again. "Tom," he said, "I have a son eight years old, a girl five, and a boy three. They never see their father because the old man works at the White House. It's Saturday night, my wife's sister is baby-sitting, and I told my wife I'd take her to a movie. But here I am, same as you, because I have an important job to do. My wife is on my back every day to quit. But I can't. I promised the President I'd stay on for as long as he holds office."

"There must be dozens of men," Buchanan suggested.

"Maybe," Malone said. "But the fact is, I made a promise to the President of the United States. That means something. And I'll tell you something, Buchanan. I got three kids growing up and I have to fight for every second that I can spend with them. But they're going to be adults in the 1960s. It sounds far off, doesn't it? Well, it's not. It'll come and go like that." He snapped his fingers sharply. "The thing is, someday they'll ask me, 'Daddy what were you doing when the bad guys were trying to take over the country?' And I'll be able to say, 'Kids, I worked in the White House. And I fought against that with every ounce of strength my body could muster.'"

"Okay, Malone. Good pep talk. Don't worry. I'm with you."

"Thanks. You don't have kids, do you?"

"I'm not married."

"Well, someday you will be. You'll have little ones. And maybe you'll understand me a little better. After all, what do we do on this

earth that's important except keep it safe for our families and prepare it for those who come after us?"

"Jack, you should have been a priest."

"Nearly was," he said, a mischievous Gaelic smile crossing his
face. "Could have been too! 'Cept for I liked getting laid too much."

Both men laughed. Then Malone, as he drove, eased into the
subject at hand.

"Tom, I know you're trying to do your job as best you can. But
domestic politics keeps intruding, doesn't it? Let me bring you into
the picture as best I can."

"Please do," Buchanan answered.

"Senator McCarthy is about to go public on the Garrett case,"
said Malone. "He has a press conference scheduled for Friday,
March seventeenth. That's the end of next week. He seems to have a
pretty direct line on what you're doing." There was a long pause. "I
have to ask you this, Tom, so forgive me: I assume you're not telling
him directly."

"I am not!" Buchanan snapped.

"No, of course you're not. But Joe McCarthy is getting it from
the F.B.I. Probably straight from Hoover, let's face it." Malone
shook his head. "How do you feel about that?"

"I think it stinks!" Buchanan said with a rare flash of anger.
"How the hell do you think I feel?"

"Yeah, I know." Malone shrugged. "But when it comes down
to it, Hoover's your boss, right?"

"That doesn't mean Hoover can't be wrong. It doesn't mean an
agent can't think on his feet by himself. What is this, dammit, Jack?
An inquisition?"

"Want to hear more?" Malone asked evenly.

"Sure."

"McCarthy's going to claim Mark O'Connell as a victim of
Communist assassins in the United States. That should go over well
with the American public, don't you think? An F.B.I. agent killed
by Red gunmen on U.S. soil."

Buchanan remained silent, wondering if Malone knew O'Connell was alive. "Jesus Christ," he muttered.

"And Hoover's going to second the pronouncement," Malone
said. "Hoover plans to name O'Connell as a fallen hero of the
agency."

"Hoover's people harassed Mark O'Connell out of his job,"
Buchanan said almost instinctively. "The bureau does it all the

time. After years of work you fall into disfavor. Then they harass
you till you quit."

"Sure. I know. But that stuff goes on in any outfit, Tom. Office
politics. Hoover plays hardball like everyone else in Washington."

"Yeah. But try selling it to John Q. Public," Buchanan grumbled. "Hoover never leaves his office except to have a free drink or
have his picture taken. Never made an arrest in his life. Yet if
J. Edgar had any better a public image, he'd have sunbeams breaking from behind his head."

Malone laughed. Buchanan was weary and talking too much.
He realized it and fell silent. The two men rode without speaking
for several minutes.

In a certain pale light, Buchanan noticed, Malone looked ab-
surdly young. With the fluid movements of his arm on the gearshift,
with the poise with which he glanced back and forth between the
rearview mirror and the road ahead, he might have been an under-
graduate at Georgetown sculling on the Potomac. Yet he easily had
to be forty-five-years-old.

"The President says he wants to do the proper thing," continued Malone, "but he doesn't feel like having a spy scandal thrown
back in his face either. Mr. Truman seems to think he can trust you.
Of course, we have no choice. You're running the only investigation
of Garrett. You had a head start."

"By a few weeks," said Buchanan.

"The way everyone else sees it," Malone reminded him, "by a
few years."

"Ah, yes," Buchanan said, remembering time spent in 1939
and 1940. "Of course."

"Are you holding on tight?" Malone asked.

"What?"

"*Hold on.* We're about to jump the divider."

They were on Pennsylvania Avenue when Malone cut the
steering wheel as hard as he could. The car went into a U-turn,
spun tightly, and fishtailed. Its tires screeched and smoked. The
vehicle spent a solid two seconds in a skid, and Buchanan felt that
his insides were about to fly out the car door with him still inside.
Then Malone had completed the U-turn and the car was facing the
opposite direction.

Malone scrutinized his rearview mirror to see if anyone else
had done the same thing. He hit his breaks and went down a side

street only to emerge a few blocks later, and hit the accelerator in the opposite direction.

"We're clean," he said. "Doesn't that make you feel good?"

"What about Clark and Kirby?" Buchanan said.

Their job had been to watch for anyone who tried the same thing, said Malone. If anyone had, the follow-up car was instructed to stop and arrest whoever had tried, even if they had to crash their vehicle to accomplish it. But no one had. Malone lit a cigarette and offered one to Buchanan. Buchanan declined. Malone moved the car from third gear to fourth. Malone's eyes alternated between the road before him and the rearview mirror.

"What about all those files I asked you for?" Buchanan asked. "Wong. DeStefano and Garrett. Did you find any C.I.A. entries for them?"

"Sure enough," said Malone.

"Just tell me this: Garrett claims that his Chinese gangster and his Italian-American gangster have both done work for the government? Any truth to it?"

"Enough truth to complicate matters for you," Malone said. "Look, I have the files with me now. Right there in the backseat." Buchanan glanced back and saw an attaché case. "You can look at them now if you like," Malone said. "If reading in the car gives you a headache, you can look at them later. I just have to return them."

"Tell me where we're going now," Buchanan said.

"To a safe house in Maryland. We've got a Russian who says he wants to defect. He seems to know a bit about the unpleasantness up in Oregon."

"And who is 'we'? Whose defector is he?"

"Secret Service," he said. He offered a grin, suggesting that he had snaked the other services.

"How did you get him instead of the F.B.I. or the C.I.A.?"

"Interesting question," said Malone as he drove. "Instead of turning himself in to the police or tossing himself on the mercy of Hoover or Central Intelligence, the man got himself a lawyer. The lawyer had a tie to the administration. The contact brought it to Truman's attention and the President gave it to me."

"What's this Russian trying to do? Cut a deal?"

"Protect himself, I suppose," Malone said. "Not rot in prison."

"Where do I come in?" Buchanan asked.

"You're going to question him. Decide for us whether he *is* legitimate. Then we determine what we want to do with him."

"And by keeping him away from Hoover or the C.I.A., you can control the political damage if there is any."

"I said before, Tom," Malone answered with mild irritation, "The President has political concerns, too. Can't blame him." As he drove, his eyes slid sideways, from the rearview mirror to the road, to the side mirror and back. Buchanan wondered if he had developed the same habit. "Look," Malone resumed easily as if reciting from a script, "there's an election coming up this fall. You get four-hundred-odd reactionaries in the House of Representatives, a comparable number in the Senate, and America of 1952 will look like Berlin of 1933 all over again. You'll have Joe McCarthy riding into the White House making Adolf Hitler look like a candidate for the Nobel Peace Prize. Want that?"

"Truman asked me the same question. You guys must think you know my answer."

Malone laughed. "Very quietly," he said, "there's a lot on the line."

Then Malone was on the highway outside Washington, cutting a swath through the horsey Maryland countryside. Malone's foot pressed harder to the floor. The car's engine roared and responded. For several minutes their vehicle barreled through the night and ate the dark highway.

The towns rolled by: Silver Spring. Wheaton, Layhill. Ashton. Malone said little. In the darkness, entire vistas of suspicion and deceit began seething upward in Buchanan's mind. One by one in a dark, wild flight of paranoia everyone had betrayed him—Ann, O'Connell, Hoover, Lerrick, and Malone, and even President Truman—until the only good Americans he could trust were John Garrett and Senator McCarthy. Then, finally, the car left the highway, made a pair of turns on a dark country road, and was eventually upon gravel. Lights appeared, as did a Queen Anne house. Buchanan saw the figure of a man at a front window who disappeared moments after the car lights pierced the blackness of the driveway. By God, he thought, if this was what these espionage games were all about, he wanted none of them in the future.

Then Malone cut the engine. "Come along," he said. From within the house someone illuminated an outdoor floodlamp. They walked up a flagstone path along a suburban garden. And suddenly, with the light, everything seemed very American, very familiar, and much less ominous.

Malone led Buchanan into the house through the kitchen. Ma-

lone took the time to wash his hands at the kitchen sink. He introduced Buchanan to a pair of Secret Service agents, one of whom
had been the lookout above the driveway.

Then Malone brought Buchanan along to the next room. At
his entry, two men sprung to their feet. One had been seated on a
sofa, the other on a lounge chair.

One of the men was fiftyish and balding. The other was half the
first man's age. Buchanan looked at the two of them and guessed
that the older man was the defector.

"This is Bill Jaffe," said Malone, indicating the older man.
Jaffe wasn't defecting from anything other than Manhattan for the
weekend. He was balding and stout, with a reddish face. He was a
partner, Malone continued, in a heavy-hitting New York legal concern named Exman, Grossman, and Zacharius, names to be revered
in several New York circles. Buchanan had guessed wrong. The
younger man was the defector as well as Jaffe's client.

"Now," said Malone next, "I want you to meet the guest of
honor. George?" he said.

The younger man rose. In the presence of his attorney, the
Russian extended his hand and shook with Buchanan.

"This is Viktor Milenkin," said Malone. "Also known as
George Mulligan. Let's everyone sit down. I think George has quite
a story to tell us."

Buchanan settled into a chair to listen, remarking initially how
American the young Russian looked and sounded.

■
THIRTY
■

"These days I prefer the name Mulligan," the younger man
said. "I'm trying to put as much of the Russian stuff
behind me as possible." Buchanan was surprised at the
Soviet's flawless English. For a moment he wondered if
he'd misunderstood the purposes for which he was there. Mulligan,
or Milenkin, looked and sounded more American than half the
people Buchanan knew.

But then things became clearer. Jaffe, the attorney, spoke.

"My client, Mr. Mulligan," Jaffe said, "wishes to do a great service to the United States. He's willing to drop a Soviet spy network right in your laps, gentlemen. But, of course, my first concern is my client's safety, both from the Soviets as well as from certain segments of American law enforcement."

"What's that mean?" Buchanan asked, settling in.

"It means Mulligan has a story to sell us," Malone said. "And we're here to listen."

Buchanan looked at his watch. It was almost eleven P.M. Absently he wondered what Ann Garrett was doing out west.

"I'm sure you're using the term 'sell' figuratively," Jaffe chimed in quickly. "Mr. Mulligan is not 'selling' a story for money. He simply wishes to stay in his adopted country as well as render a valuable service."

Malone was loading a Webcor tape recorder, a big, bulky instrument, with six-inch reels of tape. As he worked, he looked to Buchanan.

"He's got a job with New York Telephone and a girlfriend in Brooklyn," Malone said, as if that explained everything. "What bigger piece of the American pie could any man want?"

Buchanan was sympathetic. "A good job and a good woman," he mused. "Any reasonable man would place a high value on both commodities. I can't think of two better reasons to wish to stay in an adoptive country."

"Thank you," Mulligan said.

"We can't make any promises," said Buchanan. "But I have access to the F.B.I. director and Mr. Malone has access to President Truman. If you help us, we can help you."

"I've advised Mr. Mulligan of his rights," said Jaffe. "I also know that the President would be more inclined to help him than Mr. Hoover would."

"I'm certain you're right," Buchanan allowed. Malone set a reel of tape. He was ready to begin.

"Who's doing the talking first?" Buchanan asked.

Jaffe, the attorney, was never short for words. "If the tape is running," he said, "a few things should be stated at the outset." Jaffe ran through his own name as well as his client's. He then stressed that Mulligan was there on his own volition and was not subject to any imminent arrest or deportation. He was there because he wished to help the United States, Jaffe said.

"That's nice," Buchanan said. "But I'd like to hear it from

him." Buchanan turned to Mulligan. "Why don't you tell us in your own words," he suggested.

"I will," Mulligan said. "Thank you."

And he began. For starters Mulligan took his audience as far back as he could remember, recounting his boyhood in the Ukraine. He remembered neither parent, he said, but he remembered his aunt Liliya—who would later become his adoptive mother—taking him strolling through the long stretches of squarish brick houses in the little mining town in the Donbas, where he'd been born. The houses had been built by one John Hughes, he pointed out, a Marxist Welshman who'd emigrated to the Soviet Union after the October Revolution. From his earliest years he could also remember the many new granite sculptures of Lenin erected in the time after Lenin's death in 1924. When he dwelt too long on this, his lawyer nudged him along to sections of his story to which American ears would be more receptive.

He told about his trip by steamship to America in 1929. He and aunt Liliya had settled in New York first, then had worked their way westward during the Depression, settling in northern California by 1931. His aunt had caught on as a billing clerk for a wire company, and on this solid foundation she and her newly adopted son settled in Palo Alto. He recounted vividly an American boyhood of the 1930s, and Buchanan, sitting in rapt attention, felt a strange empathy for him. Mulligan spent about an hour on this, working his way toward late 1938 when the United States Department of Immigration forced his family's decision and back to the Soviet Union they went.

Buchanan glanced at his watch. By now it was midnight and Malone changed the tape. Mulligan paused for a glass of water, and when the tape spun again, he resumed, moving quickly through his repatriation to the Soviet Union in 1939. More his aunt's decision than his, he said. Fact was, he would have been just as happy staying in school in California. Then again, he was only fourteen years old, and hardly capable of making a legal decision.

Then came the part that pulled Buchanan and Malone up on the edges of their chairs. Mulligan started to talk about the G.R.U. and his training in Moscow in the oppressive big building at Dzerzhinski Square. Here Buchanan began to interject.

"Do you remember the floor on which you were trained?" he asked.

"Fourth."

"Can you describe it?"

Mulligan did.

"What path did you take from the front entrance to the G.R.U.'s section?" he asked. "Please describe it in detail. Tell me about the security system, how many doors you went through, what the rooms were like."

Mulligan complied. This took seventeen minutes. Buchanan threw another dozen questions at him, and Mulligan patiently answered every one. The tape, Buchanan knew, would have to be reviewed by someone more authoritative than he. But at least he'd know whether or not Mulligan had ever been in the headquarters building of Soviet state security.

Presupposing that Mulligan was the legitimate article, Buchanan pressed onward.

"It was in 1941," Mulligan said next, "when I first met Colonel Andrei Klisinski."

"Who?" Buchanan asked.

"Colonel Andrei Klisinski of the G.R.U.," Mulligan said again. "The G.R.U. is Soviet military intelligence."

Buchanan turned to Malone. "Is this Klisinski anyone we know about?" he asked.

Malone shook his head. "Only what Mr. Mulligan is telling us," Malone said. "I ran it past a contact at C.I.A. We didn't find anything."

"He was my aunt Liliya's lover," Mulligan said by way of endorsement. "Klisinski found a spot for me right away, translating documents from the British and the Americans during the war."

As always, Jaffe sought to put the proper spin on it. "It should be pointed out that the British and Americans were officially Soviet allies until 1947. Mr. Mulligan was thus helping our war effort as well as the Soviet."

Buchanan let Jaffe's remarks pass without comment. He fished a small pad and pencil in his pocket. "I realize the name would be transliterated," he said. "But could I have a spelling?"

"K-l-i-s-i-n-s-k-i," Mulligan said with quiet cooperation. "First name 'Andrei.' "

"Unusual name," Buchanan said. "More Slavic than Russian."

"I've thought about that myself," said Mulligan. "The rumor was that he was, I mean, is a Pole. He was a leader of the Polish Communist Party during the war of 1939-45. Became a leader of pro-Soviet forces and was rewarded with a position rank of colonel in the G.R.U."

"What was your source on that?" Buchanan asked.

"Nothing very good," said Mulligan. "Mostly hearsay. But sometimes hearsay is reliable on such matters."

"And sometimes it's not," Buchanan countered. "Sometimes widespread hearsay is an attempt to fabricate a credible cover story. Right?"

True enough, Mulligan conceded. But in Soviet intelligence circles, a man's reputation often preceded him. And damned little got written down.

"A good point," Buchanan said. "Yet"—here he turned to Malone again—"if Klisinski was a Polish Communist, shouldn't we have *something* on him? Shouldn't there be a C.I.A. file or an O.S.S. folio, or something?"

"We should have something but might not," Malone answered.

"Have you checked yet?" Buchanan pressed.

"Yes. We came up empty."

Buchanan made an exasperated expression. "How could that be possible with a prominent officer?" he asked.

Malone shrugged. "Look at the Klaus Fuchs situation," Malone said. "The man was an overt member of Communist parties in Germany and France before going to England and America. Yet the intelligence services of every Western democracy fanned on him when he went to work on the Manhattan Project."

Security work was often the kingdom of the blind, both conceded, without even a one-eyed man to take charge. Buchanan turned back to Mulligan. "I'm just curious," said Buchanan. "And I suppose it's a small point: What language do you speak with Klisinski?"

"I've seen him only once in the last three years," Mulligan answered.

"That wasn't what I asked. Please don't be evasive."

Jaffe opened his mouth to protect his client, but Buchanan silenced him with a raised palm.

"I didn't mean to evade. We've spoken English and Russian," said Mulligan. "It depends on the circumstances."

"How's his Russian?" Buchanan asked.

"Just about perfect."

" 'Just about'?"

"He has a very faint accent that I've always taken to be Polish."

"And what about his English?"

"Even better," Mulligan recalled.

"And have you ever heard him actually speak Polish?" Buchanan inquired.

"No," Mulligan answered with just a hint of defensiveness. "Why would I? I don't speak it myself."

"But in Moscow perhaps?"

"It's not the type of thing a Pole would do," Mulligan insisted. "In Moscow a Pole would try to be even more Russian than the Russians, if you catch my drift."

Buchanan caught it. "Then we don't know for certain even if he *is* Polish?" Buchanan said.

No, they didn't, the Russian admitted. But it was unusual enough that Klisinski had something of a regal bearing. That in itself could arbitrarily arrange a funeral for a man in any intelligence service run by Lavrentii Beria. Beria was so much a man of the people that he'd murdered thousands of them himself. Finally realizing this in the West, Mulligan had figured that Klisinski must have been some turncoat Polish count with invaluable contacts both inside and outside the Soviet Union. Otherwise how could he survive?

"How old a man would this Klisinski be?" Buchanan asked, still taking written notes.

"Fifty-something," Mulligan guessed.

"And you said you even knew him during the war?"

"That's right."

"Then how could we not have something on him?" Buchanan asked Malone with considerable irritation. "Ask your C.I.A. people to try again on this one." Buchanan turned back to Mulligan. "Is there any other name we might know him by?"

Mulligan opened his hands in a gesture of helplessness. He didn't know of one, in other words.

"And where did you say you saw him last?" Buchanan asked.

"I didn't say. But it was in Battery Park in New York City several months ago," Mulligan said.

"You're kidding me! He was right here on American soil?" Buchanan said.

Mulligan nodded. He described the occasion and, for good measure—in an act that might assure his future position before a

Soviet firing squad—physically described his colonel as well. Buchanan listened incredulously.

"Don't you wonder how he seems to pass unnoticed across our borders?" Buchanan asked Malone.

That was no mystery to Mulligan. A forged passport was the key to trouble-free travel. He displayed his own as evidence. Buchanan took it and carefully examined it, from binding to photograph to the finely forged imprint of the State Department.

"This is really an excellent piece of work," Buchanan said with a wry sense of amusement. "Almost better than some of our actual passports. And some people insist that our Russian friends are unsophisticated."

He handed it back to Mulligan. "You wouldn't know what name Klisinski travels under? Or what sort of passport? Or whether he's in the United States currently?" Buchanan asked.

Mulligan said that wasn't the type of thing to which he'd be privy.

Buchanan found that credible. "Fine. Please go on," he said.

"It was about 1945," Mulligan said, "that Colonel Klisinski started talking about sending me back to the West." Here, Malone and Buchanan let the Russian speak for several minutes without interruption.

An assignment in America was something he relished in principle, he said, because he'd always held a certain affection for his second country. Or so he insisted anyway. It never even occurred to him that he was coming back to work against America's interests. It was a job, an assignment, an adventure. And in retrospect he wondered if Klisinski's courtship of Liliya had all along been nothing more than a sly recruitment rush.

Mulligan talked for the next forty minutes about his trip back to America, illegal entry in New York via an Albanian freighter, the switch of identity at the Hotel Astor, and the almost instantaneous assimilation into American society. In the middle of all this, Malone reset the Webcor with a third tape. Meanwhile Buchanan listened in fascination, his flesh crawling as Mulligan portrayed the relative ease with which he wove himself into the fabric of America. His attention drifted for a few seconds and he wondered if there were another ten thousand Red sleepers out there set to sabotage the interests of Uncle Sam. For no good reason he decided there couldn't possibly be.

Mulligan described his assignment in America. He was to find a job and disappear into mainstream American life. Then he was to serve as a conduit for messages, the drop point being the rocky foundations of the Williamsburg Bridge. He described the Saturday morning procedure, and made it all sound very simple to his audience.

Mulligan seemed a bit uneasy with what followed, but forged into it anyway. The messages he passed along to others, he said, were coded. He had no idea what they said. But being a curious sort of man, he was in the habit of taking a peek at them. "Just for the hell of it," he said. "Since they were coded, I wasn't really snooping, right?" he asked. That's how he saw the picture of Mark O'Connell in one envelope, then recognized O'Connell's picture in a New York newspaper a few weeks later. It didn't take a genius to figure out cause and effect, and that—inadvertently both he and his lawyer insisted—he'd sent a hit team on its way to Peterton, Oregon.

"Can you remember when this was?" Buchanan asked.

Mulligan knew exactly. It had been December 13, 1949, less than two weeks before O'Connell had been shot.

"Thank you," Buchanan said calmly. He noted the date on the pad across his lap. But Mulligan's eyes never left him.

"I'm jumping ahead," Mulligan said to Buchanan, "but in the most recent correspondence there was a very clear photograph also. It was of you."

For a moment a heavy silence passed around the room. Buchanan replied with more calm than he might ever have thought possible, considering there was a bullet out there somewhere with his name inscribed on it. "I'm pleased to hear that," he said. "That means we're all on the right track. Go on."

It was a male and female hit team, Mulligan continued, and for a moment Buchanan played with the idea of having to watch out for any couple he saw on the street. But Mulligan refined the nightmare a bit, relating how he'd passed some time at St. Peter's Lutheran Church in the Village, waiting to catch a glimpse of the Russian hoods who'd come in to pick up a message. He was sure there were at least two of them, he said, and described both.

"You got a good look at them?" Buchanan asked.

"Close enough to hear them as well as see them," Mulligan answered.

"Then you could identify them as well as describe them?" Buchanan asked. "And for that matter, you could identify our elusive Polish colonel as well."

Mulligan said he could, then entered a detailed description onto the tape. His account matched the one Mark O'Connell had given for the blond woman, though O'Connell had never managed a clear view of the man's face. For O'Connell the actual gunman had existed only in shadow, silhouette, and gunfire.

"Well," Buchanan concluded amiably when Mulligan had finished. "At least I know who to look out for now, don't I?"

Malone offered a weak smile of support. It was almost two o'clock in the morning.

The rest of Mulligan's dialogue was nuts-and-bolts stuff, almost as if he were reverting into a tiny boredom after pouring out the best that he had to offer. He said again that he loved America and wanted to stay and that he sure as hell didn't want to end up like Klaus Fuchs. That's why he'd let his girlfriend's family, the Litvinovs of Brooklyn, send him to a lawyer they knew. He wanted to stay, marry, work, and go to New York Knickerbocker basketball games, he said. He even had a favorite visiting player, Max Zaslofsky of the Chicago Stags, he explained, going off on a tangent. How could an athlete miss with a good Russian name like Zaslofsky? All that, to the tired ears listening to him, sounded very rational.

Buchanan spent another forty minutes throwing questions to him about his G.R.U. training, his answers to be reviewed by whatever C.I.A. contact heard the tape. Buchanan also took from him his fall-back position, his one means of instigating an emergency meeting with either Klisinski or another of Klisinski's legmen. The procedure was to reverse the pipe-in-the-stones trick, leaving a coded note to travel in the other direction.

"The colonel said that was a one-time-only procedure," Mulligan warned. "Only in cases of extreme danger."

Buchanan thought of Mark O'Connell shot down on a peaceful Oregon highway and Blake Warren stuffed into a trunk. He thought next of the two assassins loose in America looking for him. "That," he responded to Mulligan, "is exactly what we have now."

The interrogation moved toward conclusion at a few minutes after three in the morning. On the promise of his counsel that Mulligan wouldn't disappear, Buchanan allowed the Russian to keep his passport. His instructions were to return to New York. If there was any activity in the stonework under the Williamsburg, he was to report that to Jaffe from a public phone at least two miles from where he worked and lived. Jaffe would report to Buchanan. But aside from that, Mulligan was to maintain his life as usual. Indeed, this nighttime meeting had taken place when it had for that simple reason: Mulligan could disappear on a Saturday night and raise no suspicions anywhere. On Monday he would be back at work.

Malone took charge of the tapes, saying he would pass them to a C.I.A. contact for immediate review, no names attached. A judgment would be made on their authenticity.

Thereupon, the extraordinary conference broke. Jaffe and Mulligan started back to New York by car, a Secret Service escort with them. Malone and Buchanan left ten minutes later.

For the first twenty minutes on the drive back to Washington, no word passed between the two men. Finally Malone said, "Come on, Tom. Earn your salary. Tell me what you thought."

Buchanan blew out a long, tired, pensive breath as the car moved toward the city limits of the District of Columbia. "Does instinct count for anything?" Buchanan asked.

"Eighty percent of the ball game," Malone answered.

"I think he's telling the truth," said Buchanan. "Consider his position: He's showed us his passport. He's told us where he lives. If he's a plant feeding us bad information, he's a dead duck if and when a lie hits the fan."

"My thoughts also," said Malone. "But what's the angle tying Colonel Klisinski to John Taylor Garrett?"

Even approaching four A.M., when the car radio was reduced to static because most stations were off the air, that remained the key question. "You tell me," said Buchanan. He'd been awake for almost twenty-four hours now. His eyes were so tired they were burning. "Any guesses?"

"This Russian or Polish colonel is running a spy network in the United States," offered Malone. "Garrett is part of it."

"But where's the proof?" Buchanan asked almost rhetorically. "Where is a witness who would testify against him? Where is one piece of physical evidence? Where is one bit of financial documentation? Where is one incriminating recorded conversation? See what I mean? We've been all over Robin Hood's barn on John Taylor Garrett and all we have is an overall impression. We have nothing that would stand in court for two minutes."

"Yet Senator McCarthy wants to go with the charge and Hoover wants to feed him the information. And you work for Hoover."

Here Buchanan—overwhelmed with fatigue—grew very angry.
"None of this should bother Senator McCarthy!" he snapped. "He
can go with his scattershot charges anyway. It should create a
unique circumstance: Instead of smearing someone innocent, he
may be smearing someone guilty. But without evidence, as usual."

Malone grinned. His eyes, too, were at half mast.

"Can I change the subject?" Malone asked.

"Please do."

"If I know anything about Hoover, you've got a good shot at
locking horns pretty seriously with the old goat within the next few
days. Might cost you your job."

"I know."

"If it does, let me know. President Truman admires character
as well as loyalty. We might be able to find a spot."

"I'll keep it in mind. But I like my present career."

"If I recall," said Malone, "so did your friend O'Connell."

The car turned down Buchanan's block.

"Know what happened the night of the 1948 election?" Malone asked, still flirting with the same subject. "The entire Secret
Service detail that guarded the President had a choice. They could
stay with Mr. Truman or they could go guard Thomas Dewey, who
everyone expected would be the President-elect by the end of the
night. There were twelve men assigned to the White House. The
other eleven men read the polls and went to guard Dewey. I stayed
at the White House. The morning after, I was the head of the Secret
Service detail in the White House and the other eleven guys were
reassigned to the Treasury Building."

Buchanan laughed.

"That's what I mean about Truman. He rewards loyalty."

"Loyalty," said Buchanan, "or a good gamble against the
odds."

The car stopped in front of the Raffertys' house. There was one
light on downstairs. A single man was walking slowly past the doorstep, appearing for all the world like a drunk staggering home.

"As I said," Buchanan concluded, opening the car door, "I'll
keep it in mind." He stepped out, taking with him from the backseat his own suitcase, plus Malone's folio containing the files Buchanan had requested.

"Oh," said Malone. "One other thing." He started fishing
through his pockets. Buchanan held the car door open, leaned in,
and waited.

"When I contacted C.I.A. this afternoon," Malone said, "they mentioned something which may or may not be of interest."

Buchanan waited.

"Since 1948 they've kept open files on unsolved crimes in the United States involving foreign nationals. You know, the type of mixed bag of stuff that never seems to amount to much."

"And?"

Malone found the sheet of paper he was looking for. He handed it to Buchanan.

"Some Chinaman was shot in Philadelphia on New Year's morning. Local police can't make head or tail out of it. No local angle, no motive, no ID, no nothing. But I thought, hell, Philly is Garrett's territory, isn't it? And he's been involved in various multinational stuff, so . . ."

Buchanan took the sheet of paper, his eyes suddenly wide in astonishment.

"A *Chinese*?" he asked.

"Yeah. Why?" he asked. "Tom, you look excited. Does that mean something?"

■
THIRTY-ONE
■

Jesse Chadwick and Joe Preston arrived in Las Vegas with their new, temporary girlfriends the evening after completion of the principal photography on *Hold the Phone!* All in all, they felt pretty good about things.

The film was on celluloid, so there would now be fewer irritating problems with actors, unions, writers, and agents. Now it was simply a matter of seeing the film through postproduction. Chadwick did his own editing and Joe Preston rarely interfered with a director's final cut. The producer was too busy screaming into long distance telephone lines, bullying distributors, coddling theater owners, and ingratiating himself to reviewers. So Chadwick expected no trouble there either. He was even pretty sure of himself as a film editor. For a coarse, grossly amoral man, Jesse Chadwick had an amazingly deft touch with light romantic comedy. Correctly, whatever else his faults, he thought of himself as a man who could dependably put the essential final flourishes on a film, the touches that would make *Hold the Phone!* a commercial success and Lisa a star.

Yes, it was important to him that Lisa become a star. That way she had more value to him. Cash value for future appearances on screen, and barter value, when he swapped her for a night or two to some other Hollywood bigshot in return for a significant favor. A wife of little bargaining value was a useless commodity to Jesse Chadwick. So when he and Joe Preston arrived in Las Vegas with two precocious high school girls, Jesse Chadwick was a man with little to worry about. Or so it seemed.

One of the girls—the one who would accompany Chadwick— was a slim, quiet brunette named Meg. The other was a busty sandy-haired and giggly girl named Lynn. Both were fifteen, so Joe Preston, in procuring the girls, had taken some precautions.

He had sent them, for example, to the studio gynecologist before departure. Both Meg and Lynn had received pelvic exams and both had passed, meaning neither was a virgin. Thereupon, both girls had been given prescriptions for diaphragms. Joe Preston had been in the business long enough to know that every scenario— onscreen or off—must be planned carefully, with nothing left to chance. For a weekend bacchanalia, there was nothing quite as sobering as the threat of future lawsuits or pregnancies.

Birth control had forestalled the possibility of pregnancy, but Preston had also obviated the possibility of future lawsuits. Some men in Hollywood procured girls at casting or modeling calls, then carefully worked them away from their parents. Preston was far too clever for this. He knew that the type of parent who brought young girls to such calls were hell-bent on getting their daughters into show business, no matter what. These parents knew that the girls' virginity, even if it hadn't already been used as a bargaining chip for a first important film role, wasn't going to last much longer anyway. So Preston, when he invited girls away for the weekend, covered all angles. He went to the girls' homes while they were in school, *told* the mother or whatever parent he found that the girls were invited away for a weekend. "This," he would tell them as he looked them straight in the eye, "is your daughter's first big break in Hollywood. Naturally you'll be paid."

In exchange for the girls' services as "ingenue models," Preston would pay each set of parents five hundred dollars. He even

drew up a short contract of which he would keep both copies. He
insisted that the papers be signed on the spot and not shown to any
attorney. Then he paid the five hundred dollars immediately and by
check, it being Preston's theory that if they were dumb enough to
take it, he now had incriminated the parents just as much as himself. No recently converted Puritan would come screaming about
what had happened to her wholesome daughter—not when he had
in writing permission to take the girl away for the weekend.

The check, of course, was drawn out of the account of whatever film he was working on and came out of the postproduction
budget, the same as the entire trip to Las Vegas. That way Joe
Preston and Jesse Chadwick didn't pay a cent. The financing of the
film underwrote their basic short-term pleasures. Hollywood was,
as many men before them had noticed, a great way of life.

Both Jesse and Joe Preston booked into Bugsy Siegel's old hotel and casino in Vegas. It was their type of place. Siegel's demise
notwithstanding, it was still run by organized crime characters from
back east, which gave it the exciting, immoral atmosphere that both
men liked. Chadwick even had a cousin who was a Newark, New
Jersey, loan shark who operated with the protection of the same
crime family that now ran the hotel. It was an incestuous type of
place like that, where people saw old friends from tough old immi-
grant neighborhoods back east.

The best part about it was that no matter what went on, there
was virtually nothing to fear from the law. The local police and
politicians were in the back pockets of the gangsters who ran the
place, and the F.B.I. rarely caused trouble anywhere in the area.
For that matter, Hoover, as everyone knew, was a gambling man
himself who liked to play the horses in Virginia, California, and
Florida. Even J. Edgar liked to spend a few happy hours in front of
slot machines when he passed through Nevada. A few of the more
creative casino operators even had some "special" one-armed bandits that would be hauled out for important guests such as Mr.
Hoover, machines that were rigged to pay out eleven dollars for
every ten pumped in. That way, special customers left happy and
owners got little heartache from the law. Then again, J. Edgar Hoover also maintained that there was no such thing as organized
crime. Nor, insisted the Director of America's greatest crime-fight-
ing force, was there any network of crime families either coast to
coast or in the major cities of America. So federal law enforcement
was not a problem over which anyone lost sleep.

The first thing Chadwick and Preston did on arrival was take Meg and Lynn to their respective rooms and lay them. This took only a couple of minutes. Then they cashed checks, also as miscellaneous expenses from the film's postproduction budget, and spent the afternoon at the blackjack tables and the roulette wheels. Meanwhile Meg and Lynn worked a couple of the nickel slot machines for a few minutes, then changed into bathing suits, ordered drinks from the bar, and sunned themselves by the pool. They were too young to gamble or drink, but who cared?

At the gaming tables Chadwick lost $700 in three hours. Joe Preston, born under a more favorable star, had actually won $150 in casino chips by late afternoon. Being a film producer, however, it made sense either to lose other people's money completely—since he could always get more—or win big for himself. So as a prelude to getting up from the roulette table, Preston pushed his $150 winnings plus his $100 bankroll onto the six numbers thirty to thirty-six, meaning Joe would have $1250 if he won and nothing if he lost. The croupier called all bets, rolled the ball, spun the wheel, and the ball rode home on seven. Joe was down 100 of someone else's bucks, but big deal. It had been a fun afternoon and he could cash another check for some heavier rolling after dinner. Meanwhile, he and Chadwick retrieved their girls from poolside, swapped them, and took them back upstairs to gain release from the joyful tensions of the gambling parlor.

In the evening Chadwick and Preston were invited to a private party given by a handsome young hood named Paolo. Paolo was from New York and was currently one of the hotel operators. Chadwick and Preston were guests of honor, being visiting filmmakers. Part of the deal here was that the host be allowed to sample one or preferably both of the two California girls that Chadwick and Preston had imported. The girls by this time were increasingly drunk, and one of them, Lynn, was initially scared of the frequency with which she was starting to get pawed and passed around. But as she grew drunker over the course of the weekend, however, her inhibitions eroded and she, like her friend Meg, succumbed easily and even enthusiastically when passed from room to room. Jesse Chadwick and Joe Preston, meanwhile, availed themselves to a selection of the house girls that had been provided for the evening festivities.

All this socializing ran till three A.M., at which time Chadwick reeled back to his room two floors away. He found Meg on the sofa, half dressed and dead drunk. But he locked himself into the room with a red-haired girl of twenty-five named Tracy who'd been around the block for a few years in Las Vegas. Tracy was older and understood the services that some insatiably heterosexual men appreciated. She delivered them without the embarrassment, fuss, or argument that some younger girls displayed. For this, and for no other reason, Tracy was a salaried full-time employee of the casino.

Though neither Jesse nor Joe appeared for breakfast until two P.M. Sunday afternoon, the next day strongly resembled the first. This was, in fact, so much fun that Chadwick and Preston choose to extend their stay until Monday, even though Joe's girl, Lynn, was starting to be a pain. She claimed she was sick to her stomach and wouldn't come out of the hotel room, even if it did jeopardize her career in films.

All in all, though, it was a pretty great weekend and just the sort of release both men felt they needed following the rigors of setting a fluffy domestic comedy before the cameras. By the time they took a casino limousine to the airport on Monday night, there were only two clouds on the horizon—one seen and one unseen.

First, the visible one. Some of the stories about Jesse Chadwick's behavior in Hollywood had followed him even to Vegas. It had gotten around that on occasion he would lend out his wife, the rising actress Lisa Pennington, to other men who had done him favors. This had struck the fancy of Paolo, the young organized-crime bull who had money in the casino. Paolo had seen Lisa's previous film, the bathing suit epic shot in France. In fact, Paolo had seen it twice and had decided that he was going to get into bed a few times with its female star. Thus it had been upon Paolo's orders that Jesse Chadwick had been shown such a good time on this visit.

Chadwick was seated in the hotel's coffee shop on Monday afternoon when Paolo swaggered over to his table. He quickly dismissed Joe Preston, who had the good sense to leave without an argument. Then Paolo told Chadwick that on the director's next visit, Lisa should come along, principally in repayment for the fine time Chadwick had just been accorded. Then he explained *why* he wished Lisa to be brought along.

Here Chadwick made one of his infrequent mistakes. "Nothing personal, Paolo," he said, "but I'm not lending my wife out to some guinea hood."

Paolo had flown into a rage, leaping up from the table and

threatening to break a leg off the wooden chair and use it right there on both of Chadwick's knees.

Chadwick, stunned, calmed Paolo and apologized in the most servile language possible. This appeased the gangster. But thereupon, Paolo recounted another story that had traveled the two hundred miles east from Los Angeles.

Apparently, the story went, some young guy who also had designs on Lisa had appeared on the set of *Hold the Phone!,* had dumped Chadwick in front of his entire crew, and Chadwick hadn't even had the balls—or the muscle—to stand up to the guy. Worse, the man had been seen squiring Lisa around L.A. the same evening, and she'd even kissed him good-bye on the set the next afternoon. "The word we use for that," Paolo taunted, "is 'pussy-whipped.' " Jesse Chadwick, in other words, couldn't even control his own wife. A man with no balls and no muscle didn't last long in society, Paolo crowed. Chadwick would be the laughingstock of the Southwest if he couldn't even put his own house in order.

This, in turn, drove Chadwick into a blind fury, though he was careful what he said to the Italian. Instead, he muttered something about showing who was boss.

"So I can count on seeing Lisa here next time?" Paolo asked.

"If you'll be here, she'll be here," Chadwick said.

"She'll wear one of those bathing suits from the movie out by the pool? Then you'll send her up to my room?"

"Yes," Chadwick promised. The mobster seemed appeased.

It was quite a conversation. It took place right in public, and both men were given to the idea that volume enforced any point of discussion. So everyone could overhear. That led to the second problem for Jesse Chadwick, the one he didn't know he had.

Despite the fact that J. Edgar Hoover wasn't in town, two other F.B.I. guys were. They were Larry Herter and Jim Meadley, Mark O'Connell's old friends from the San Francisco office. When Special Agent Thomas Buchanan had asked for agents to cover the arrival of Chadwick and Preston in Nevada, he'd further recommended Herter and Meadley, they being familiar at least with certain aspects of the lengthy John Garrett-Commonwealth Penn investigation.

Meadley and Herter had covered Chadwick and Preston for the entire weekend, creating a pair of files, taking names, noting times and room numbers, and otherwise observing everyone's behavior with ever-mounting awe. Meadley and Herter were even sit-

ting right at the next table in the coffee shop when Chadwick had
his discussion with Paolo. And similarly, when Chadwick picked up
the telephone in his hotel room to hire some thugs to come by Los
Angeles and beat some obedience into his wife, an F.B.I. wire was
also on his line. So by the time Jesse Chadwick, Joe Preston, and
their two fifteen-year-old guests headed to the airport for the late
plane to Los Angeles on Monday night, Meadley and Herter had a
couple of sensational documents. They would mail them back east,
and those files would make for some spectacular reading back in
Washington.

Despite all this, back in Los Angeles Ann Garrett felt pretty
good about things. The drugs were gone and, it seemed, so was her
husband. She had a strange sense of elation now that the film was
finished, a sense that she'd performed well despite living through
the most troubled time of her life. Oh, there would be postproduction work on *Hold the Phone!,* but most of that was done by technicians. There would be little for her to do other than watch the final
cut as the film was put together.

That was, if Jesse would let her.

For today at least, Jesse was gone. Same as the drugs. Ann
took the car to Malibu, found herself a quiet stretch of beach, and
treated herself to a long, leisurely walk.

She enjoyed the solitude of the Pacific shoreline in the off season, the sound of gulls and wind, and the cadences of waves crashing on the sand. It was only in a moment like this, unpressed by her
husband or any other professional or personal obligation, that she
could put her head in order.

Yes, she told herself. Now that the drugs were gone she could
put her mind in order very nicely, thank you. And as soon as that
was straightened out, she could lend some structure to her life.

She walked a mile, maybe more. It was noon and the sun was
warm, suggesting the spring that was to come. This was the type of
air and atmosphere that had drawn her to California in the first
place. That, and the notion of acting.

She knew what she had to do next. There was only one real
way to take control of her life. She had to be single again. She had
to unload her husband. She thought back of all the violent and
escapist fantasies she'd had about him and she realized how mis-
guided they'd been.

Another man? Flight to South America? Murder?
Nonsense!

Tom Buchanan, stepping out of her past as he had, had reintro-
duced her to logic. It was simply a matter of enforcing the law of
the land. She had some money in the bank. She would get her things
together from the apartment. In the next day or two she would rent
for herself a small place somewhere in Los Angeles or Hollywood,
or maybe even a small apartment near Malibu. While Jesse was off
whoring, she would move out.

She would hire a good lawyer and sue for divorce. She would
negotiate out of her agency deal with Jesse's brother. And she
would take control of her own future.

It all seemed so clear, so real, so very possible on a bright
Monday afternoon, March 12. There was no way it wouldn't all
work out. She was so pleased that she almost started to skip.

She stopped two miles from her car, took her shoes off, and
walked in the wet sand all the way back. She was exhilarated. She
was free of the old shackles and ready to start her life again. She felt
marvelously young with a glorious future spread before her. The
past was done. Dead. Over. She was free again!

She arrived back at her car. She had a mad impulse to go back
to the apartment and call Tom Buchanan back in Washington. *And
what would I tell him,* she wondered mischievously.

The words came to her and she was astonished by them.

I'd tell him I love him, she thought.

For several seconds she stood by her car, thinking, the warm
Malibu air of the early spring riffling through her hair.

Well, sure enough! That *was* why she felt as she did. She was in
love again.

Damn! she thought. *Never imagined it would happen to me
again! Better get that divorce as soon as possible! Maybe in Mexico.
Maybe in Las Vegas.*

Vegas? What an irony! She wondered what little tart Jesse was
screwing. And even more important, she realized that she no longer
cared.

Tuesday, March 14. Shortly after ten A.M. J. Edgar Hoover
was roaring with anger. His eyes were practically popping, his face
was red, and Special Agent Buchanan could actually see a vein

throbbing on the side of the Director's neck. The Director was less than euphoric about his Commonwealth Penn briefing.

"That's it?" he asked. "That's all?"

"That's all," said Buchanan.

"So, no arrest is imminent?"

Buchanan began to backtrack over the Garrett investigation, citing the links he sought to draw between Peterton, Oregon; San Francisco; Washington; New York; Philadelphia; and Commonwealth Penn's headquarters in Bucks County. But the fact was, he said, he needed more time.

"Well, the fact is," mimicked J. Edgar Hoover, "you can't have it!"

Frank Lerrick sat to one side in the Director's office at F.B.I. headquarters in the Justice Department building. He lifted his gaze from the floor and sought to settle the air.

"J. Edgar," he said, "I don't think a request for more time is at all unreasonable in a complex case like this. I think this agent has been working hard. At some risk to his personal safety too, I might add."

"Personal safety?" Hoover snorted. "*Personal safety?* Who gives a good goddamn about a single agent's personal safety when Reds are overrunning this country? I'll tell you whose personal safety is at risk! Mine! Every morning when I get out of the car on Pennsylvania Avenue and walk that final mile to work, the country's safety is at risk because *I* am at risk! Don't you ever forget it!"

"We couldn't possibly, J. Edgar," said Lerrick. His tone was heavy with sarcasm. Hoover glared at him.

The Director looked back to Buchanan. "How much extra time are you talking about?"

"Two to three weeks."

Hoover hooted angrily. "Two to three weeks!" he mocked. "You'll have a new job in two to three weeks, and it won't be part of the F.B.I., I can damned well assure you of that!"

Buchanan couldn't resist. "Then I should start looking now," he said. "I've done the best any man could under trying conditions. So get off my back!"

Hoover looked as if he were on the verge of a stroke. He stared wildly at Buchanan. It was just possible no adult had spoken to him this way in years.

"You're just about finished in this man's Bureau, son!" Hoover shot back. "I'll promise you that!"

"Oh, calm down and give him some more time, J. Edgar," Lerrick said, pretending that there was little argument at all. Clyde Tolson entered the room without knocking, sat down quietly to one side, and said nothing. His presence seemed to settle Hoover.

"For what purpose?" Hoover asked. "This agent has traveled to Europe, gone up and down the West Coast on our expense, and had himself a grand old time. And what do we have? Fragments of a circumstantial case."

"I'm sorry, sir," said Buchanan, emboldened as his anger continued to rise. "But I fail to see what time element we have on this case. My understanding was that thoroughness would outweigh speed."

"Don't you argue with me, young man!" ranted Hoover. He pointed his finger accusingly. "You learn when to shut up. And don't you ever mock my authority in this country! Do you hear me?"

"Special Agent Buchanan is not mocking you, J. Edgar," replied Lerrick, his own impatience starting to show. "He's made a very reasonable request."

"I disagree!" Hoover howled.

"Then what *is* the time element?" Lerrick asked. "Where is this information going? Who has to have it and by when? If Garrett can be arrested, what's wrong with next week? Why not another week if we need some more time to make charges stick?"

"I want a conclusion this week," Hoover said. "By tomorrow, in fact."

"Absolutely impossible," said Buchanan. "If that's the situation, I'd have to hand you all the files along with my shield. It can't be done."

"J. Edgar, I beg you," said Lerrick. "Don't push a good young agent off the job. Please. Give him a week."

There was a full half minute of silence. It felt like an entire afternoon.

"All right," Hoover finally conceded. "Seven calendar days."

"Think you can have your arrest by then, Tom?"

"That's more reasonable than tomorrow," Buchanan said. "That's all I can say."

"You're both excused," said Hoover. That meant they were to leave immediately. Only Tolson stayed behind.

Outside the Director's office, Lerrick and Buchanan celebrated their small victory. Seven more days was a crash situation. But at least Buchanan had that much.

" 'Get off my back,' " Lerrick chuckled. "That's good. I don't think anyone has ever said that to him."

But later on the radio, Buchanan confirmed what the rush had been. Senator McCarthy canceled Friday's press conference and had now rescheduled for the Friday thereafter, the twenty-fourth. Buchanan noted the seven day's difference. Now for sure he knew where all his work was going: to prop up one of the rising demagogues of the middle twentieth century.

Thoroughly disgusted, he went back to 7th Street, S.E., packed his things, and returned to Union Station, where he caught a train to Philadelphia. For whatever purpose, it would be in Philadelphia during the ensuing week that his entire case would either stand or fall.

■
THIRTY-TWO
■

There were three of them seated in a booth. A waitress named Rose with teased hair and a pink dress set plates of pastry and hot coffee before them. All three paused until she was gone.

"Okay, okay," said Sergeant Fred Castelli as Mike Proley looked on quietly. "So we made some mistakes. So some sloppy police work was done. I'll tell you. It's not like we bailed out on the case. No, sir. It was in the active file all the time."

"That means we're working on that case among others," Proley volunteered. "We go through a lot of cases a year."

"Jesus, you're not kidding," said Castelli. "Since the war it's been unbelievable. Know what we used to call South Philly?"

"What?" asked the third man at the table.

" 'Baseball-bat territory,' " said Castelli. "People used to come out of their houses and settle their differences with a baseball bat. Now they use guns. You can't believe all the hardware that came back from the war."

"I can believe it, Sergeant," Thomas Buchanan said calmly. "And I'm not interested in criticizing local procedure on a homicide. I just want to know what I can about the Chinaman. That's why I'm asking questions."

"And what's it to you, again?" Proley asked.

"An ongoing federal investigation," said Buchanan. His response, vague as it was, fell somewhere short of approval around the table. "Sorry," Buchanan said. "That's all I can tell you right now."

"We're talking about the guy we found on New Year's morning," Proley said. "Right?"

Buchanan nodded. "And I wish to keep the inquiry as quiet and unofficial as possible. No use creating any unnecessary disturbances within your department, right? That's why I thought we'd meet here."

"Here" meant a table at the Melrose Diner. Unsolved homicides always seemed a little more promising over cheese danish and fresh coffee.

"Bullet to the head," Castelli said. "If I remember, it looked like he'd been shot somewhere else. Then the body was set on fire." He paused and turned to his partner. "Jesus Christ," he said. "I can't believe the F.B.I. is going to snatch this case away from us." Castelli lit a Camel. He expelled some breath and a cloud of cigarette smoke.

"I just want to know about it," Buchanan said patiently. "No one's taking the case away."

"That's what you Feds often do," said Castelli. "We do the hard-assed gumshoe stuff, then you guys come in and—"

"I'll go through the official channels if you prefer," said Buchanan, irritation creeping into his voice. "In fact, we can proceed right at the top. I'll have Director Hoover telephone your commissioner. That would mean that you'd have to present your files to your commissioner within twenty-four hours. I'm sure the files are all tidy and up-to-date, showing a great deal of current activity . . . ?" Buchanan let the suggestion hang in the air.

"No, no. That's all right," Castelli said. "We'll handle things right here. Between us. Unofficial."

"Thank you," Buchanan said. "I think that's a good idea. After all, I'm sure you grasp the significance of my visit. I'm going to steer you to a murderer. And you're going to get the collar."

This, to Castelli and Proley, seemed like such a good idea that it made them more talkative within a few minutes.

"So it was a bullet to the head?" Buchanan resumed at length. "Was the slug retrieved?"

"Yeah, I think it was. It was in his stomach. Traveled downward."

Much like the way Blake Warren died, Buchanan recalled. "Where is the bullet now?" he asked.

"At Fourth District Homicide," said Castelli.

"Then it would be available for trial? If there is a trial?" Buchanan continued.

"Sure." Castelli shrugged. "Unless someone took it." In Philadelphia, he suggested, not everything held as evidence remained where it was last seen.

"Can you get me a report on the ballistics test?" Buchanan inquired.

Castelli said he would.

"And what happened to the body?" Buchanan asked next.

The two Philadelphia detectives glanced at each other, then recounted the tale of how Mr. Lee, the vanishing Chinaman, turned up on a Sunday morning to claim the corpse.

"And where's Lee?"

Castelli told about the forged passport and the fake identity.

"But where did the body *go?*" Buchanan asked. "Someone had to take it from the M.E.'s office. Someone had to bury it."

"You looking to dig it up?"

"Were the proper X rays done on the burned corpse?" Buchanan asked.

Castelli said he doubted it.

"Then, yes. I'm going to have to find the body and have it dug up," said Buchanan. He had some X-ray records of Wong, he said, though he didn't admit that they were straight out of the C.I.A. file provided by one Jack Malone. If X rays could be matched, even on a charred body, Buchanan might have something that he could use in court.

Both cops seemed repelled. Castelli mentioned Bernie Gedmon at the M.E.'s office as the person to talk to.

Buchanan looked at his watch. It was ten A.M. on Wednesday morning. "Would this Gedmon fellow be working now?" he asked.

Finishing their coffee, Castelli and Proley said that he would. "If there's a steel table with a gutter in use," Castelli said, "you can bet Bernie's there working at it."

Rose the waitress happened past just in time to catch the remark. She tossed Castelli a ferocious scowl and slapped their check down on their table.

They drove to the medical examiner's office in Castelli's DeSoto. And there Buchanan's case smacked up against a brick wall again.

The erstwhile Mr. Lee had arranged for burial, all right. But a quick check of city interment records came up as cold as the corpse itself. There was no listing at all for any Mr. Lee having been laid to eternal peace in the days following his dismissal from Bernie Gedmon's office. Figuratively at least, it was as if he'd bounced up and walked away. In crime and politics in Philadelphia—professions between which the distinctions were usually vague—Castelli and Proley had seen a lot of things, but not that. Not yet.

"Sergeant," said Buchanan, stumbling into an unfortunate choice of words, "I wonder if you and your partner would care to start digging."

They would dig, as it turned out, at city hall, not a bad place to look for buried bodies. What the two detectives wanted, at Buchanan's behest, was a burial that looked like it could have been the Chinaman. But none could be found. So Buchanan suggested another line of attack. From Gedmon's records he obtained the name of the mortician who'd picked up the body. Life, Buchanan had frequently observed, sometimes has a strange and perfect geometry. And never was this more the case than here. The elusive, deceased Mr. "Chin" had been picked up by the DeStefano Funeral Home on Snyder Avenue, a parlor of professional bereavement which was, by happy coincidence, one of the many dubious but legitimate enterprises of Jerry DeStefano. Be it an irony or coincidence, Buchanan did not fail to notice: DeStefano had been the third man at John T. Garrett's last public supper at the Mayflower Club.

"Get me a list of funerals that DeStefano's parlor did during the two weeks after the Chinaman left the M.E.'s office," Buchanan asked. "That shouldn't be difficult."

"Anything else?"

"Yes. Two things. First, where does one find DeStefano himself?"

The two detectives looked at each other. "It has to be arranged," Castelli said. "And I wouldn't advise—"

"Please arrange it. Unofficially of course."

"What's the second?" Proley asked apprehensively.

"The maître d' at the Mayflower Club in Philadelphia," Buchanan said. "His name is Paul Evans. Thursday at about noon, I wonder if you could pick him up for questioning."

"Unofficially?"

"No. Officially. Accessory to murder. Just pick him up and hold him. Also, see if you can have your friend Gedmon there at the same time. That will save us some legwork. I'll do the rest."

Again Castelli said it could be arranged.

Across the continent in Los Angeles, it was a time of new arrangements for Ann Garrett also.

On Tuesday morning she found a small house a few miles from the beach in Malibu, wrote out a check, and signed a lease. The house was owned by a Mrs. Calderon, a widow who was thrilled to be renting to an actress. Ann seemed like such a nice young woman, Mrs. Calderon thought. Clean and wholesome.

That same day Ann started packing her personal belongings from the apartment she shared with her husband. Jesse hadn't appeared yet, which was fine with Ann. She heard he was in town, so she navigated in and out of the apartment carefully. She didn't want to run into him. She had only two or three carloads of things to take. Very little that she had acquired during the marriage still meant anything to her. Even the ring. She'd taken it off and placed it on his dresser. Moving out completely, she reasoned, would take only a day.

Then there was something else on her mind too: Thomas Buchanan and the questions he had been asking. She'd thought about them. The questions about her father. His politics. The falling out within the family. Who was she being loyal to, she wondered. Her father, who had disowned her, or a man who could have been her husband and who had saved her life? Under the circumstances, she had now decided, she was foolish not to answer his questions as fully as she could. She would call Thomas later in the week, she decided, after she had completed her move. And she would talk. Oh, would she talk!

On Tuesday evening Ann returned to the apartment to pick up a final armful of clothes. The living room was quiet when she entered. She closed the door and took two steps forward. Then she heard a man speak her name.

"Ann?" he asked.

She froze. Jesse appeared in the doorway to the bedroom. He confronted her.

"A lot of your things are missing, Ann," he said with a steadfast, menacing calm. "What's going on?"

She stood defiantly before him. She looked him straight in the eye from a distance of a dozen feet.

"I'm leaving you, Jesse," she said. "I'm moving out. I'm filing for divorce."

Jesse Chadwick's glare had a deadly stillness to it. "No, you're not," he said softly.

"I've made my decision, Jesse," she said.

"Have you?" he mocked. "Well, I've made one too."

Ann jumped in surprise when another man appeared behind her husband. At the same time, a second man emerged from the kitchen behind her. Both were silent. Neither looked like a stranger to professional violence.

"Oh, God, Jesse," she said. "I beg you. No. Please don't do this."

Chadwick's voice was icily calm.

"Lisa, when I was in Las Vegas, there was a man named Paolo who was laughing at me. He was laughing because that buddy of yours appeared on the set. Then you had the bad taste to be seen in public with him that night as well as the next day." Her husband came nearer to her, though not directly. It was as if he were circling for a kill. "You probably fucked him too, didn't you, you little bitch!"

"No, I didn't, Jesse. Please . . ."

One of the men had cut off the path to the door. Both men were big, broad-shouldered, and strong.

"Didn't I *warn* you?" he shouted. "Didn't I tell you that I had some friends back east who knew how to teach bad little girls a lesson?"

Now she was trembling.

"Well," said her husband. "I put in a call. My friends sent these two gentlemen from out of town. They're going to take you somewhere for a few days, Ann. You will live through this, but not by much. And when you return, believe me, you will never consider crossing me again."

By this time Jesse Chadwick was right in front of her, his face contorted with rage, his eyes dancing with fury and indignation. He raised a fist and brought it toward her.

Ann cringed, then fell away. She felt two steel arms grab her from behind, and one of the hands rose to cover her mouth. No scream would be heard.

But her husband's fist never landed. When she looked up, confused, the hand from behind still covering her mouth, she saw that the man nearer her husband had caught Chadwick's arm and stopped the blow.

"Isn't that our job, Mr. Chadwick?" the man asked.

"I suppose it is." He was still enraged.

"Then let us do it," the stranger said. The man released Chadwick. "Tell us again," he said. "Your exact instructions. What are we hired for?"

"Keep her tied up for a couple of days. Don't feed her much. Beat the hell out of her. Break an arm, maybe. Something that could be attributed to a fall. But leave the face alone. The face has to be photographed. Same with the tits. Don't mess them up. They get photographed too." He paused and looked at the two men. "There's five hundred dollars in it for each of you. Are those enough instructions?"

The two men looked at each other. "That's just about perfect," said the man behind Ann. He looked to his partner. "Do you need to hear anything more?"

The partner shook his head.

"Okay," said the first man. "Let's get on with it."

Castelli, Proley, and Buchanan drove to a quiet block in South Philadelphia where, waiting in the back of the funeral parlor, was Jerry DeStefano, of the DeStefano Funeral Home and the South Philadelphia underworld. DeStefano and Castelli had for years played handball at the same Y.M.C.A. on Broad Street. They were nodding acquaintances. Castelli introduced Buchanan to DeStefano, a short, wiry, black-haired man in a light brown suit.

"What's this about?" DeStefano asked. "Normally if there's a fed, I got nothing to say except through my lawyer."

DeStefano's lawyer's name was Irv, but he was noticeably absent. His place was taken by a pair of DeStefano's lieutenants, who made themselves busy by staring out the windows and keeping their backs to the conversation that followed.

"The body of Sammy Wong," said Buchanan. "I want it."

"No got," said DeStefano. The men were seated around a dark mahogany table.

"Yes," said Buchanan. "I'm afraid you do."

"This is a whites only funeral house," DeStefano explained. "We don't stuff and mount no niggers and we don't do no Chinese either."

"I didn't come here to be lied to," Buchanan said.

DeStefano's face came alive with rage. From the corner of his eye Buchanan could also see the expressions falling on the two cops.

"I said I ain't got it!" DeStefano exploded quickly. "And when I say that, shitface, it means I ain't got nothing else to say to you." DeStefano looked at the two police detectives. "Get this fuck out of here!" he roared, knocking his chair over backward as he stood up.

Buchanan didn't budge. Instead, he steadied his gaze on the mobster. The two police were nervous and trapped in between.

"Whatsa matter?" DeStefano hollered next. "I said, get him out of here!" DeStefano's two thugs began to gather behind him.

"Can't do it, Jerry," said Castelli softly. "He's federal."

DeStefano glared at all of them.

"I really thought," said Buchanan with infinite courtesy, "that you were going to be reasonable, Mr. DeStefano. But on the chance that you weren't," he continued, "I did take the precaution of reading a few files on you. Both F.B.I. and C.I.A."

"I did work for O.S.S. during the war," DeStefano said quickly. "Palermo to Calabria. I—"

"I'll do the talking, thank you," said Buchanan to the stunned gangster. "I know all about your favors to the O.S.S. But I also know that you're currently a very prosperous man in this city. And I also know that your current affluence is not entirely unrelated to a number of wire rooms around this neighborhood as well as the many slot machines that can be found in certain bars and barber shops along Snyder Avenue."

"You think you can close me down? *You?*" DeStefano laughed.

"Close you down? No," Buchanan shot back sharply. "But I can make your life damned unpleasant. Suppose I went back to Washington and cited your lack of cooperation. Well, let's face it. The F.B.I. can always use a few easy targets. A good Italian whipping boy, let's say. Capone's dead. Luciano's deported. And imagine how the police captains and inspectors in this city will abandon you before a federal racket investigation. All the people you've been paying off for years will be angry with you for not surrendering the remains of a Chinaman and wrecking what they pick up on the pad each week. They'll be just as happy to have you in jail and have someone smarter running your former operations. Why don't you sit down?"

Buchanan motioned to a chair. Grudgingly DeStefano sat. Castelli and Proley were more silent than the dead.

"Now," Buchanan concluded, "I still think you're going to be reasonable about your position. I know you didn't kill Sammy Wong. You merely buried him. But you left no record of where. Which is why I'm here."

"You're out of luck, you Scotch-Irish bastard," said DeStefano. "He was cremated."

"I doubt it."

"Why's that?"

"As I explained, I spent part of yesterday evening reviewing your F.B.I. file," Buchanan said. "I know how you think. An urn of ashes would be of no use to you at all. But a body that could incriminate a wealthy local banker in a murder case?" he laughed. "Well, that's something, isn't it? That's a commodity that should be kept for possible use—and profit—at a later date."

DeStefano said something about wanting to call his legal man, Irv.

"No, don't do that," said Buchanan. "Because if you do that, I'll do three things in return. I'll make a note back in Washington to have the tax returns audited for every business you own. Then I'll have every casket that you buried in since January of this year opened and examined. Who knows *what* we'll find there? I'll make sure the event is covered in all the newspapers. And third, I'll personally see that a sledgehammer and ax team hits at least a hundred of your one-armed bandits here in Philadelphia. But if that doesn't bother you and you want to call your lawyer Irv, I wouldn't *think* of interfering with you."

DeStefano seethed. At first he attempted to deny that he owned any business. Buchanan laughed and listed five from memory, including two in DeStefano's daughter's name. "Now, come on. Man to man," Buchanan pressed. He glanced at his watch. "Time is wasting."

DeStefano thought about it for another few seconds. The bulls that he'd stationed near the windows barely moved. At length he glanced at Fred Castelli, who gave him a slight nod of the head.

"No publicity if I give you what you want?" DeStefano finally asked.

"None," said Buchanan.

Castelli gave him a second nod.

"Ah, fuck!" DeStefano cursed. Then he began to talk. Sammy Wong—and DeStefano confirmed that that's who the cooked corpse had been—had gone into the ground double-decker style. DeStefano's parlor kept a few caskets on hand with some extra depth for just such purposes. The skeletal remains of Wong thus went into the earth in the same rosewood box as a DeStefano family friend who'd been mangled in a car accident. The bodies were one on top of the other, with a false bottom to the closed casket.

"Fine," said Buchanan. "Thank you." He turned to Castelli and asked which local judge would be fastest in granting a writ of exhumation. "I want to get the body up as soon as possible," he said.

"Don't bother with the legal stuff," said DeStefano. "My people can have it up in a few hours."

Buchanan didn't object. By ten o'clock that night Gedmon had compared the X rays of Wong's remains to the records in the C.I.A. file. There was enough similarity between the two to confirm the identity of the body.

That sent Buchanan home for the night, too anxious to sleep, and close enough to resolving the Garrett case to actually become excited.

He called Frank Lerrick at Lerrick's home in Chevy Chase and requested a full time F.B.I. surveillance on John Garrett. Lerrick said the surveillance could be put into effect with the first morning shift.

Then Buchanan tried to call Ann Garrett in California several times. He worried about her and, in a strange way, missed seeing her once he'd found her again after a decade. But each time he dialed, his call went unanswered. His anxiety over her increased, but he stopped calling when the hour grew very late. He had to try for some sleep. The next morning, he knew, he would bait a trap for his prey. And in doing so, he would either resolve the case completely or blow it altogether. But either way, the investigation of Commonwealth Penn would approach its conclusion.

THIRTY-THREE

As was his habit, and unlike many other chief executive officers, John Taylor Garrett was never the first to work at his own bank. He often came in at a quarter past nine, walked through the lobby of the four-story brick building on Lancaster Avenue in Devon, and proceeded to the staircase at the rear. A fit man, he bounded up all four flights, even at his age. When he arrived on the floor of his office, however, on Thursday, March 16, he knew immediately something was amiss.

"Ah, Mr. Garrett," said Eleanor Eshelbach, his secretary. "Someone to see you."

Garrett saw no one in the waiting area.

"Where?" he said.

The ill-mannered guest, it seemed, had already gone into Garrett's office and sat down, much against Mrs. Eshelbach's protestations.

Garrett pushed open the door to his office. He glared angrily at the man sitting behind the desk in Garrett's own swivel chair. The visitor had his back to the door and his feet propped on a wastebasket.

"May I help you?" Garrett snapped furiously.

Slowly the chair turned. Thomas Buchanan, seated at Garrett's desk, reacted calmly. He smiled.

"Good morning," he said.

"What the hell do you want?"

"A few minutes to talk," said Buchanan, slowly getting to his feet. "I was under the impression that banks opened at nine o'clock. So I was here right at that hour. I figured, fewer customers at that time. I'd cause you less embarrassment."

As Buchanan moved away, Garrett slowly rounded the desk. He pulled off the jacket of his suit and hung it on a corner rack. He regarded the younger man with extreme vexation.

"No embarrassment at all," said Garrett, cooling down. "You're just a damned nuisance barking up the wrong tree like a dumb little puppy dog." Garrett straightened his shirt and tie in a mirror within a cabinet. "A minor irritation. Not for the first time, I might add."

"With all due respect, Mr. Garrett," Buchanan said. "But you've been more than a minor irritation to me. And you're more than a nuisance to this country. That's why I'm here. Believe me. It's nothing personal."

Garrett eased into the leather chair behind his desk. "Maybe I'll just call the police and have you thrown out," Garrett said patronizingly.

"Two reasons you won't," said Buchanan.

"And what are they?"

"First, the local police know I'm here. I stopped by and told them. There are some pockets of enlightenment in the country," Buchanan said with amusement, "where F.B.I. credentials are held in respect. Even awe."

"This room, sonny, is not one of them."

"I know. That's why I took a second liberty. I disconnected your phone. I also deadened the alarm beneath your desk so you can't ring it with your foot."

Garrett's face was growing red. "And," Buchanan said, moving toward an early conclusion, "I figured you might have a weapon in your desk. I saw fit to pry open the second drawer on the right side."

Garrett glanced down and saw the broken lock. "That's illegal," said Garrett.

"So is espionage."

"Go to hell!"

"Your gun is still in there," Buchanan said, sitting calmly but motioning to the broken drawer. "I have the ammunition." He dug the bullets out of his jacket pocket and showed them to Garrett. "I didn't want you to do something impetuous that might cause you harm," Buchanan said. "I'll give the bullets back to you when I leave."

"I'm surprised you don't want to seize the gun for some test," Garrett said sarcastically.

"I doubt if you'd leave something lying around that would be of interest to me. Besides, the weapon in your drawer is a thirty-eight. I'm looking for someone who uses a twenty-two of foreign manufacture. May I?" Buchanan motioned to a chair where he intended to sit down. Garrett didn't answer. Buchanan sat anyway.

"I'm going to make some calls to Washington after you leave

here today, Tom Buchanan. I'm going to find out how you ever got hired by the F.B.I. Then I'm going to have you fired."

"I don't think so."

"Well, we'll find out, won't we?" he snapped. In his assessment of his own power, he was supremely confident.

"There's one thing about my line of work that's always indicative," Buchanan said. "When men who are under investigation start threatening to have me fired, I know I'm doing my job well."

At this Garrett burned.

"Why don't we have our talk?" Buchanan asked. "We're both wasting time. You're not going to be arrested today no matter what happens. So presumably you'll have work to do. I'm sure you'll want to make sure that the bank's affairs are in order."

Garrett leaned back in his chair, his arms folded across his chest. He could barely control his rage. "What in God's name is it that you want?" he asked.

Buchanan settled into his chair across the room from Garrett. "Much of yesterday I spent going through a stack of government files," he said. "O.S.S. Department of the Army. F.B.I. C.I.A. A lot of stuff, some interesting, some tediously dull. You know the names, in addition to your own. Sammy Wong. Blake Warren. Jerry DeStefano. I was hoping we might find a file marked Klisinski, after a certain elusive but ubiquitous colonel in Soviet intelligence. We have nothing yet, but I think we will soon."

Garrett didn't flicker an eyelash.

"Accordingly, Mr. Garrett, I would like to put a theory before you," Buchanan resumed. "I have a notion about what's going on."

Garrett's desk, to Buchanan's eye, suddenly looked like a frontier fort surrounding the banker. "No harm in listening, is there?" Buchanan asked.

Still Garrett was quiet.

"Thank you," Buchanan said. "I'll begin, if I can manage to decide where." He paused for a moment.

"Let's consider a Chinaman named Sammy Wong," said Buchanan. "Backtrack a bit. The man was an officer in Chiang Kai-Shek's army. He was from a wealthy family in pre-Mao China. The man was captured by the Japanese, then turned over to the Russians in the late 1930s. Why? Out of the goodness of the Nipponese hearts? I think not. Similarly the man was from the segment of the Chinese military that was fighting the Communists, yet the Russians welcomed him with open arms. Again, why?"

"You tell me," Garrett said.

"I don't need to, because we both know. Wong was, after all, your business associate for many years. He dealt opium all his life. That's where his family money came from, that's where his personal fortune grew. He dealt in the Chinese Army and I'd guess he had enough money—or access to enough money—to buy his way out of that Japanese P.O.W. camp. Fine so far. But then he goes to the Russians. What do they want with a drug lord? Nothing. But what would they want with a man who had firm—albeit unorthodox—trading ties with the West? Quite a bit. A man like that would be of infinite use after World War Two for one simple purpose. He would be able to finance espionage networks in the West. The Russians let him loose, provided him with extra passports where necessary, and allowed him to continue his business. He keeps some of the profits, the rest go to further Marxism in the Western Hemisphere. The problem is, he remains useless without a supporting system. Where, for example, does he keep all his money? How does it get laundered? How can it be placed in a bank in the United States where there is no chance that its true purpose will be uncovered and the assets frozen? The answer is, it has to be placed in a bank administered by someone sympathetic to his cause. For this purpose we do not call upon the Rockefeller or Mellon family. We must have a man known to the Russians as trustworthy. In other words, you."

Garrett frowned a bit and pursed his lips. "May I say something?" he asked quite cheerfully.

"Only if you care to."

"I've never denied that Sammy Wong was a depositor in my bank. Where he got his money, what he did with it, was no concern of mine. We've had that tiresome discussion before."

"Of course. But consider, Wong's deposits started to flow into Commonwealth Penn immediately after World War Two. How remarkably fortuitous for your bank! Here you were on the brink of ruin and this money just happened to roll your way."

"Business contacts during the war," Garrett said again. "And what the hell do you know of them anyway? You've never seen my bank's books in depth."

"Business contacts, yes. From the war, of course. But you were in Europe, Mr. Garrett, weren't you? You were in Europe and Sammy Wong was in Asia. Yes or no?"

"I was in Europe. Where he was, I don't know."

"You were in Europe, but for many months, according to your

own government's records, you were in liaison with several Soviet intelligence officers, particularly toward the end of the war. At that time you must have revealed your true sympathies to your Soviet contacts and offered your services after the war. According to this theory of mine, you must have been brought to Moscow and introduced to Sammy Wong. It was probably toward the end of the fighting in 1945. Or maybe even in 1946 when you again disappeared. In any case, the contact was made with Wong, and the Soviets decided that you would be one of their top men in the West after the war. And Wong would use your bank as a conduit for money to finance espionage activities in the United States."

"Bullshit. First of all, I would have no interest in financing Marxism. I'm a banker, for God's sake. A capitalist."

"You hate bankers."

"Who says?"

"Your daughter."

"Who? Ann? She'd say anything. She's a drug addict, a whore, and a liar."

"There's a place in my orthodoxy for your relationship with Ann," Buchanan said. "My guess is you weren't able to recruit her to the Soviet cause, same as you were able to recruit your other daughter. Ann has kept your secret, but you've never forgiven her."

Garrett continued tersely, addressing the previous allegation. "And second," he said. "I've never been to Moscow."

"I know someone who saw you."

"Don't try to bluff me. This is preposterous." He glanced at his watch. "The only thing that you've been right about is that you're taking my time."

But Buchanan was undeterred. "Problems arose, however, a few years ago. An Illinois bank was under scrutiny for various irregularities. The investigation was handled by an F.B.I. agent named Mark O'Connell. When that investigation branched onto a few associated institutions such as Commonwealth Penn, you grew nervous. It was time, you decided, to cover your tracks. You weren't sure quite what to do. My theory would have it that you conferred with Sammy Wong many times in person. Once was in a strip joint in San Francisco. Another time was at the Mayflower Club in Philadelphia. In actuality, you didn't really have much to say to Wong, because all this time you were planning to kill him. You just had to get him some time when the coast was clear and his guard was down. Such as New Year's morning in Philadelphia. You shot him yourself and set him on fire."

"Sammy Wong is alive," said Garrett, sounding quite bored. "I saw him in Canada two weeks ago."

Buchanan continued right on. "And in San Francisco you shot Blake Warren because you sensed that he may have known the full involvement between you and Wong. That is, that the relationship concerned more than an opium dealer and his banker. Warren might have known that you were, if not Marxist yourself, working for the Soviet cause in the United States."

Garrett sat transfixed, as if fascinated. "Absolutely fantastic. And how would you know about a meeting in some strip joint if I shot the only witness?"

"Because Warren wasn't the only witness. Mark O'Connell, who was working on a totally different case, spotted Wong meeting with you. Warren told Wong that an F.B.I. agent had seen the two of you together. Then Wong told you."

"But this F.B.I. agent? You said he was shot."

"That's right."

"I suppose I did that too?"

"No. Different weapon. The same gun killed Warren as killed Sammy Wong. I have the slugs and I have the ballistics tests. But a Russian hit team shot Mark O'Connell. Same as they're planning to shoot me."

Garrett laughed. "I wish they would," he said, trying to make a joke of it.

"I'll tell you something intriguing though," Buchanan resumed. "Do you remember the witness I said I had? Mark O'Connell survived. He's being protected under an assumed name. I talked to him most recently a few days ago."

The mention of O'Connell, and the first indication that he might be alive and talking, elicited a twitch in the left eye from Garrett, the banker's first discernible response.

"As I said, preposterous." Garrett rubbed his chin. "Oh, wait a minute. I'm beginning to see all of this. It's witch-hunt time, is it?" he snorted. His anger was evident. "And I'm to be designated a sorcerer by Hoover, Joe McCarthy, and all those people? I'm to be the next Alger Hiss, am I? Well, you can forget it. All you're doing here is spinning nasty fantasies. I'd fight every one in a court of law and I'd win every time."

"No, I don't think so."

"Why's that?"

"Because I'm going to link you to Colonel Klisinski also."

"Colonel who?" Garrett's tone was sharp and indignant.

"The Russian colonel, as if you don't know. Or was he a Polish colonel in his latest cover story? In any case, Mr. Garrett, Klisinski's blown. His whole network in the United States is about to be rolled up."

Garrett drew a long breath, exhaled slowly, and as usual evaded the issue. "Buchanan," he said. "I don't know what sort of stories Ann has been filling your head with, but let me tell you something. I hear things, okay. I have my ear to the ground. I know, for example, that you'll still be pursuing my daughter. And I'll tell you the real reason I don't speak to Ann."

Buchanan waited.

"Ann's a little whore," he said again. "Married to a little Hebrew film producer who buys her drugs, gets her high as a kite, then passes her around the Hollywood casting couches. Is this a girl a father could be proud of? Ann disgusts me. Her lack of morals. Her life-style. Her lousy choice of career and her lousy choice in men, present company included."

Buchanan fell silent. He felt like striking Garrett, but didn't. Instead, he fixed his gaze on Garrett and threw his final card.

"There's only one major aspect of this I don't understand," Buchanan said. "And that's where Zolling, the East German political officer, fits into this."

Garrett looked up. "*What?*" he asked.

"The East Germans must have known that there was going to be an important defection. And they knew it was going to come through London. Your daughter Laura compromised the operation, of course, and precipitated Zolling's death. But why was it *so* important to stop Zolling from defecting? As it is, you and Laura ran terrible risks to penetrate the American political corps in London. Risks, I might add, that contributed to your own exposure. What is it that Zolling knew? What was he going to reveal?"

Buchanan knew he had scored points. Garrett's cheeks were hot with rage. His hard eyes were fixed upon him. Somehow, however, Garrett found it within himself to remain outwardly calm, his arms folded across his chest.

"I expected that you'd come by with some silly story," the banker resumed. "Want me to show you how wrong you are?"

"Sure."

Garrett rose. Buchanan watched his hands carefully. Garrett crossed his office to a bookshelf and pulled from it a newspaper. "When was Wong supposedly murdered?" he asked.

"January 1, 1950."

Garrett flicked through the newspaper. "Here's an example of the shoddy sort of case you're building," Garrett said. He crossed the room again and presented Buchanan a Philadelphia *Inquirer* from January 9 of the same year. There on the society page was the journal's photograph of Wong, Garrett, and DeStefano dining at the Mayflower Club, a photo taken the previous Saturday.

"I apparently took my guest to dinner a week after I killed him!" Garrett intoned angrily. "Sure, you talked to my friend Paul Evans and Paul played you for the fool that you are! He never told you the correct date of our dinner. Said it was around the first of the year, but didn't say when. Then you got it in your mind that some barbecued corpse is Sammy Wong. But you didn't even bother to compare the dates. Some outstanding piece of detective work, Buchanan. Some case."

Buchanan stared at the newspaper as if his theory were collapsing beneath its own complexity. Meanwhile, Garrett's anger was approaching volcanic proportions as the banker sensed the kill.

"And a further question," Garrett ranted. "If I'm so alarmed at having been seen with Wong in San Francisco, why, oh, why do I go out to dinner with him in Philadelphia?"

Buchanan, almost trembling, shrugged helplessly. "It's, uh, the one angle I haven't worked out yet," he confessed.

Garrett chortled fiendishly. "You absolute moron!" said Garrett. "You don't have a case. You don't even have a theory that works."

Buchanan was without a response.

"I told you that you were going to get your ass burned if you hung around," said Garrett, "and now you have. You and your F.B.I. Director are nosing around something so sensitive that only President Truman and I know the full scenario. And you know what your role is? Low-level security. Just running some checks to make sure that our operation is leakproof. Which it is. What a fool you've been! Conjured up a whole theory around Sammy Wong's death, and you don't even have the date right." Garrett laughed contemptuously. "Here you go!" he concluded.

Garrett reached to the newspaper and ripped at the page that bore his picture. He tore out the photograph of himself and his two dinner companions. He crumpled it and shoved it into the breast pocket of Buchanan's jacket.

"Take this," said Garrett, "and stick it up your ass. Or maybe shove it up J. Edgar Hoover's! I understand he might like that. But in any case, get out of my office and get out of my life!"

"But, uh—"

"Just, *leave,* dammit! *Go!*"

Visibly shaken, Buchanan stared Garrett eye to eye for several seconds. The entire confrontation had reversed itself within a matter of seconds. Then, his face burning in apparent humiliation, Buchanan turned and walked from Garrett's office.

"I hope to God," Garrett said as Buchanan stormed out, "that you're finished here once and for all!"

Buchanan felt Garrett's eyes boring upon him like a pair of daggers as he strode from the room. To any observer, Buchanan bore the resemblance of a man whose career had just crashed. And Garrett, watching him go, stood in his own office basking in his self-proclaimed triumph.

For Buchanan, it would prove to be a full day. One hour later he walked into the office of Detective Fred Castelli of Philadelphia's Fourth District, Homicide. In a chair beside Castelli's desk was a frightened Paul Evans.

Castelli and Proley stopped talking when Buchanan walked in. Present also was Bernie Gedmon from the medical examiner's office. Gedmon was sitting on the edge of a table, munching a sandwich.

Evans's eyes went wide when Buchanan appeared. "I might have known," Evans said. "This has something to do with you."

"It wouldn't if you had told me the whole truth the first time," Buchanan said.

"What are you talking about?"

"Perhaps you're unaware of it, Paul," Buchanan said courteously, "but you've helped obstruct a murder investigation. That subjects you to arrest. I have every intention of letting these police officers arrest you and book you. Then I'll drive over to the club where you work and inform them that you're trying to make bail."

Evans had been sweating when Buchanan entered the room. The perspiration was rolling off his forehead now. Buchanan waited until Evans spoke again. "What do you want?" Evans finally asked.

"One minute of your cooperation. I'm going to ask you a series of questions. Your answers better be honest, because you're going to jail if they aren't."

More sweat rolled.

"If you chose to cooperate, you'll be taken back to the Mayflower Club, where you may resume your work. A plainclothes Philadelphia police officer will be with you all day. You will not leave his sight. You may not talk on the telephone with anyone. Nor can you endeavor to give any message or signal to John Taylor Garrett. If you do anything wrong, you will be arrested immediately. Do you understand me?"

He understood clearly, Evans said.

Buchanan reached into his pocket. He withdrew the photograph that Garrett had ripped from the newspaper. He placed it on the desk before Paul Evans.

"There seems to be some question about the whereabouts of a man named Sammy Wong," said Buchanan. "I say he's dead. I say John Garrett murdered him on New Year's morning." He nodded to the photograph and spoke directly to Evans.

"When was that photo taken?"

"Saturday, January eighth," Evans said.

"That's right. Now, who's in the picture."

Evans paused and stared at it.

"Well, come on, Paul," Buchanan pressed. "It's not something you should have to think about, is it? You know Mr. DeStefano, Mr. Garrett, and Mr. Wong very well from frequent visits to your club. Don't you?"

"Yes."

"Then, who's in the picture? It can't be Wong, can it? Despite what you told me once before."

Evans sighed. "Garrett. DeStefano . . ." Here he hesitated for several seconds until Buchanan cut in.

"You get one more chance to answer, Paul. Just one," Buchanan said. "Last time we discussed the incident, you intentionally misled me. I didn't know what you were doing until I came back to Philadelphia and learned that Sammy Wong had been murdered on New Year's morning. Then I realized the importance of the dinner at the Mayflower Club on January 8, the *reason* why Garrett wanted people to remember that he and his guests had been there."

Castelli, fascinated, opened a pack of cigarettes.

"Tell us who's in the picture, Paul," Buchanan said again.
"And tell us honestly this time. Garrett. DeStefano and who?"

Evans blew out a long, frightened breath. ". . . I don't know
the third man. Some Chinese guy. He looks like Sammy Wong. But
it's not him."

Castelli and Proley had difficulty following.

"Correct me if I'm wrong, Paul," said Buchanan. "But the
point was to establish that Wong was alive on January 8 and in the
company of John Garrett. So Garrett used a stand-in, an Oriental
from a Soviet spy network in the United States. That way Garrett
could never be accused of pulling the trigger on him one week
earlier."

"A Soviet what?" Evans asked.

It also accounted, Buchanan went on to explain, for Garrett's
making a display of the evening, particularly after avoiding public
contact with Wong for several years.

Buchanan turned to Gedmon and pushed the same paper before him. "Ever seen this picture before?" he asked.

Gedmon shook his head.

"How about the Chinaman?" Buchanan asked. "Ever seen
him?"

Gedmon looked at it hard. "Ooh, shit," said Gedmon.

"How about you, Sergeant?" Buchanan asked Castelli. "Same
question."

Castelli looked over Gedmon's shoulder. They both arrived at
the same conclusion. The man who had stood in for Wong had later
turned up again as "Mr. Lee" to claim the body.

"I think that makes a strong case for what I'm saying," said
Buchanan. "And it certainly establishes 'Mr. Lee' as Garrett's confederate."

In response, Paul Evans said he was scared to death and didn't
want to go to jail. In that case, Buchanan was quick to advise, he
might consider cooperating from this point forward.

Buchanan drove back to his Philadelphia office. It was nearing
evening now in the eastern United States, but was still afternoon on
the West Coast. He attempted to phone Ann, but—somewhat mys-
teriously—there was no answer at her number. He worried about
her safety, and the many threats her husband had made against her.
But he moved on to the concerns immediately before him.

He called Jack Malone at the White House. "Are you ready to move quickly?" Buchanan asked.

"As always," said Malone.

"Garrett used the alibi I expected," said Buchanan. "He thinks he's got a little time. Contact Mulligan in New York. Tell him to give the emergency signal. Bring Klisinski in for a conversation. If the colonel takes the bait, then we can roll Garrett's whole network."

"Does Mulligan need a bodyguard?"

"Definitely," said Buchanan. "Is that my department or yours?"

Malone said it was Buchanan's. Thomas said he'd arrange it through Washington. Better that than sharing with another agency at this point.

Then, with the end of his long investigation in sight, Buchanan also placed a pair of long distance calls to Shannon, Washington.

In his office in the Veterans Hospital, Dr. Alan Hamburger picked up the telephone. Moments later the operator put him through to the caller from Philadelphia. On the other end of the line, Thomas Buchanan inquired of the condition of the patient known as "Braverman."

"He's doing fine," Hamburger answered. As he spoke, he eyed a brunette member of the nursing staff as she passed his open door. " 'Braverman' will be up and around just as soon as he wants to."

"Still not walking?" Buchanan asked.

"Sitting in a wheelchair. Medically we've stopped the infection and stitched the flesh wounds. The bones that were damaged are knitting. Sure, there's scar tissue and some pain. But the man's biggest problems are in his head."

"Could he travel?"

"If he wants to," said Hamburger. "Hell, I'd just as soon discharge him."

"I'll see what I can do," said Buchanan.

Buchanan hung up. Minutes later he rang the hospital room of the patient. Helen answered, then gave the line to her husband.

"What I'd like," said Buchanan, "is for you to come east. Any way you could do that? Could you get to New York?"

"Depends on the purpose," Mark O'Connell said.

"Identification of a suspect," said Buchanan. "An arrest is imminent."

There was a pause on the line. "I'm not on my feet yet, pal,"

O'Connell said. "Helen will have to help me. I'm still rolling around in a chair."

If that was how O'Connell wanted to do it, said Buchanan, that's the way it would have to be. O'Connell said he could be in New York by Friday. Buchanan countered that a local F.B.I. agent would meet the plane.

Thereupon, Buchanan set down the telephone. He was content in the knowledge that he'd set his trap as well as possible. Now he could only wait and hope. He picked up the telephone a final time and called Frank Lerrick in Washington, requesting that a cable be sent to London. There MI5 and Scotland Yard would be jointly asked to take Laura Garrett into custody without any further delay or question.

■
THIRTY-FOUR
■

By nine o'clock the next morning, Buchanan sensed disaster. He walked past the Perry Street residence of Viktor Milenkin and saw no F.B.I. surveillance team. What had happened? Hadn't Frank Lerrick put the command through proper channels? Was the New York field office playing games with Washington's operation? Further, where was Jack Malone, who had said he'd fly up to New York from Washington?

Buchanan sat in the window of a coffee shop down the block. No one came or went from Milenkin's building. Finally Buchanan went to a public telephone. He called Washington. Frank Lerrick said a young agent had been assigned to guard Milenkin immediately at five A.M. with a full team to follow during the morning. Buchanan cursed under his breath. This was the way operations fell apart at key moments.

Next Buchanan called New York Telephone. No, Mulligan's coworkers said, he had never shown for work that day. Most unusual. "Oh, Jesus," Buchanan muttered to himself. Either Milenkin had set them up with a fabricated tale for some purpose, or . . .

Instinctively Buchanan's hand went to his weapon. He could feel the revolver riding on his hip, but he sought to reassure himself.

Once again this instinct was building within him, this feeling born out of years of experience.

He walked back to Mulligan's address on Perry Street, carefully keeping his wits about him. Again there was no movement around the building. He opened an outer door and stood in a vestibule where the mailboxes were located. The mail had been delivered for the day, and Mulligan's hadn't been picked up. He wondered if that meant anything. He decided that it didn't.

The inner door was flimsy. Buchanan put his hand on the knob. There was some give to it. He checked the street again, assured himself that no one was near, then turned back to the door. He brought his leg up and kicked in the latch with the heel of his right foot.

And ten dollars for breakage, he thought absently, imagining himself a student in high school. Funny the thoughts that pass through a man's head when there's cold fear in the air.

He pushed the door shut. Mulligan lived on the third floor. Buchanan began to walk up the stairs. Then he heard footsteps above him. From the cadence and the weight of the footfall, he guessed it was a woman. He was right.

He looked above him and saw a flurry of skirt and a flash of leg. He kept his gun under his coat, just in case. He glanced up. He saw her coming around the turn of the steps on the second floor.

"Hello," she said. She was dark-haired and wore a scarf. And she showed him a beguiling smile. She carried a small folio and looked like any other woman in her twenties on her way to work.

"Hi," he answered.

"Nice day, yes?" she said in passing.

She passed him and went down the stairs. At least she wasn't blond. He continued upward until he reached the third level. He heard her footsteps reach the ground floor.

The hall was painted yellow. There was a light bulb on the ceiling which was covered by a plastic shade. The light was on, but gave less light than the window at the rear of the hall. Buchanan had to turn a corner to find Mulligan's apartment. He did so carefully, with gun hand drawn beneath his coat.

He stood perfectly still and listened. A radio played softly within Mulligan's apartment. But he couldn't hear anyone moving.

He remained at Mulligan's door and realized that he was sweating furiously. Then another thought was upon him. It occurred to him that the sound of kicking the door in from below would have been enough to have alerted someone standing sentry.

Why hadn't the F.B.I. surveillance been assigned properly? Why wasn't the one agent assigned somewhere within view? He'd seen no one except the dark-haired woman coming down the steps. Who was she? Whose lover? Whose wife? Where was she going to work at eleven A.M.?

Then another impression was upon him, one which was the sum of its parts and more. It occurred to him that *Nice day, yes?* wasn't really the type of thing a New Yorker would say. It was distinctly foreign. Additionally she'd had her hair covered, so he could have been looking at a wig. Similarly her shoes weren't quite American. And for that matter neither were the rest of her clothes.

He leaned to the doorknob and damned if he couldn't sense the presence of a hand on the other side of it. He held the knob and moved his eye to the peephole. Sometimes one could get a blurred image of the apartment within by looking through the wrong way. But the hole was dark. Not black. Dark. There was a thumb or an eye or a hand on the other side of the door.

Then he knew that if one hand was on the knob and the other on the hole, this might be the best moment he had all day.

He stepped back from the door, spun around in front of it to pick up momentum, and hit the hinge as hard as he could. Just as he did that, the door started to open from within. Buchanan blasted it forward.

Alexandr Filiatov, on the other side, was caught in midstride. The door flew back and whacked him in the chest and chin, staggering him. But Filiatov's own pistol was out also, aimed, equipped with a silencer, ready, and coming up to fire.

Buchanan hit it with his arm and knocked it to the side as the gun discharged. Filiatov was off balance and staggering. He reeled two steps backward and fell over a magazine rack. But he brought the gun up a second time. Buchanan hit the floor but felt the whip-crack from a bullet as it sailed close to his ear.

It all seemed like it was happening in slow motion. *He's going to shoot me! He's going to kill me!* Buchanan thought. For what seemed like an eternity he was frozen with fear, and, in a vision that he would see for the rest of his life, he saw Filiatov's hand come up toward him a third time from a range at which the Russian couldn't possibly miss.

Buchanan's own revolver was extended outward. Instinct took

over. Buchanan felt two powerful blasts emanate from the palm of his hand, and he saw an explosion of red first in the center of Filiatov's neck, then in his forehead. The Russian, half standing while he was trying to shoot, was propelled backward and his arm flew wildly upward. The split second in which Buchanan's bullet arrived before Filiatov had been able to fire had saved Buchanan's life. The Russian's final shot hit the wall three feet above Buchanan's head as the assassin tumbled backward over the rack.

For a moment all was still. Then there was a spasm to Filiatov's body, followed by a vile, repulsive smell.

Very slowly Buchanan went to his feet. He stepped to the Russian and nudged the body with his foot. He rolled him over but didn't bother to feel for a pulse. There was a wound the size of a baseball in the man's throat, and the front of his head was blown away. Buchanan could see the man's brains. The desire to vomit was upon Buchanan, but he turned away and suppressed it.

Somehow he knew what he'd find in the next room. He stepped to Mulligan's bedroom, looked in, and for the first time in many years felt the overwhelming desire to cry.

There on the bed was Milenkin, his head tilted at an impossible angle, like a large bird with a broken neck. The man who had wanted so badly to live in America had died in America instead. Somehow Filiatov had gained entry to the building. Somehow he'd gotten the drop on the Russian émigré. Somehow, without much resistance, Milenkin had been shot in the head.

Buchanan took one step closer and saw how. Milenkin still wore what appeared to be his sleeping clothes. He'd been murdered in his bed, probably while he'd slept. Then the Soviet assassin had stayed to search the apartment.

As for the young F.B.I. guard, Filiatov had dropped him too. The young man, who appeared to be in his twenties, had somehow made a foolish mistake and had come into the apartment with his guard down, probably shortly after he'd received his assignment. He was dead on the floor on the other side of the bed. He had a single bullet wound in the center of his chest, and another in the head. The young agent had been shot from ambush, Buchanan deduced, then finished with a coup de grâce.

Buchanan looked at one victim, then the other. "Goddamned bloody murderers!" he cursed violently to himself. He fought back his own tears, tears for the young agent, tears for Milenkin and tears for Barbara Litvinov, who had lost her future husband. He swore to himself as he felt his hand sweating on the palm of his own holstered pistol. Someone, he vowed, would pay for this! Whoever had ordered this carnage would not live to brag about it!

Then he turned suddenly and jumped when he saw a human figure behind him at the apartment's front door.

It was the woman he'd passed on the steps. And this time it was Buchanan's turn to be on the short end of the situation. Marina Sejna had her own pistol raised. It was trained upon the center of his chest from a distance of twenty feet. In a space of time that has no measurement, Buchanan knew he was a dead man—he had allowed an enemy to get the drop on him, same as the young agent on the floor.

There really wasn't any escaping. She had him. Buchanan felt himself go white with fear. If he grasped for his weapon, he would be dead in an instant. If he bolted forward, he was dead just as easily. If he . . .

He thought of his childhood, his parents, his first love. For split seconds he savored each before dying.

He stared at the beautiful Russian woman whom fate had destined to be his executioner. "Whoever you are, you'll never get out of this country," he tried feebly. "Your only hope is to give up your weapon and—"

"Tom? Where the hell are you?"

Jack Malone's booming voice echoed distantly from midway up the stairs. Marina Sejna moved her head slightly in surprise, and Buchanan was all over his only opportunity. He ducked down low and moved behind the bedroom door frame. Bullets crashed into the woodwork around him and splinters flew toward his face. But his own hand was in motion. He thrust it around the door and fired twice in the direction where Marina had last been. The shooting stopped.

He withdrew his hand and felt his heart kicking like a boot in his chest.

"Jack! Look out!" he screamed to Malone's benefit. His words echoed through the still building. Then he heard a groan from the woman who had tried to kill him. Gingerly he peered around the door. He peered just at the moment when Marina, with a final gasp of life, raised her pistol and squeezed off a final shot.

Buchanan spun backward and felt the bullet part the air near his head an instant before it slammed into the wall. Then he heard her gun drop against the floor. He heard her body convulse with death and could hear a gurgle of blood in her throat.

A moment later he knew it was safe to step out. One of his shots had hit her in the lower abdomen. She was braced against the door. She was slumped over in death, the gun gone from her hand. Then, as he watched, she fell after it.

"Jack!" Buchanan howled.

He heard Malone respond from downstairs.

"It's over! Come up!"

Seconds later Malone appeared at the door, horror written all over his face, as he, too, surveyed the massacre.

Buchanan walked to the woman he'd shot. Her eyes were open and unfocused. He pulled a jacket from Milenkin's closet, stared at her for a moment, then covered her.

"Dead," Buchanan said. "All of them."

Malone hesitated for a moment, then spoke. "What in God's name happened?" he asked.

"Surveillance didn't get here in time," Buchanan responded bitterly. "Just this one poor bastard." He motioned to the murdered agent. "Why the hell weren't our teams in place?" he demanded. "How the hell long does it take to set a unit to protect a man's life?"

Malone let the question hang in the air. Then: "Garrett's slipped his leash in Pennsylvania," Malone said. "And the Soviet U.N. Mission in New York guided a diplomat out of the country last night," he said. "Took him to Montreal and put him on a plane to London. That's the normal route back to Moscow, from what I understand."

"Christ almighty!" said Buchanan.

"The passport was in the name of Klisinski," said Malone. "Our Colonel Klisinski apparently has full Soviet citizenship and complete diplomatic cover. Nothing we could do."

"What do you mean 'we'?" Buchanan asked, looking up.

"I talked to one of your superiors by phone an hour ago," said Malone. "A man named Frank Lerrick. 'We' means your Bureau as well as Secret Service at the White House. Assistant Director Lerrick said he couldn't get an arrest warrant for Klisinski overnight. So Klisinski's out of the country."

"What about Garrett?"

"There's an arrest warrant out for him. But he ducked his guard in Pennsylvania. Of course, he'll have half the East Coast looking for him. He won't get far."

"Don't count on it."

"Why do you say that?" Malone seemed surprised.

"Has anyone traveled on Garrett's passport?"

"Not as of an hour ago. And every U.S. airport is looking for him."

Buchanan pondered it. "I'm going after Klisinski," he said.

Malone shook his head. "I don't think so."

"Why?" Buchanan looked at him furiously.

"Your instructions from Frank Lerrick," Malone said. "I said I'd relay them. You're to cease involvement in this case immediately and report back to Washington. Have a report ready by the time you arrive."

"That's what he told you?" asked Buchanan.

"That's what he said."

"Then I'm off the case?" Buchanan asked with shock.

"Apparently," Malone sighed. "I'm sorry, Tom."

"If you talk to Frank Lerrick later," said Buchanan, "tell him to screw himself."

"Tom . . ." Malone tried to sound reasonable.

"And while you're at it, Malone," he said in conclusion, "screw yourself too."

Minutes later Buchanan was down the stairs and out onto Perry Street. He found a cabbie who was more than delighted to drive him madly to Idlewild. There, in a bizarre meeting at New York's international airport, he crossed paths with one Mark O'Connell in his wheelchair, freshly arrived from Washington State. It was only while waiting for his own flight—the next one to London—to depart, that Buchanan brought O'Connell current in the events that had put him in that chair. In return from O'Connell, he received the moral encouragement he needed to see the case to conclusion on his own.

THIRTY-FIVE

■

obert Sayre, the chief administration officer at the United
States Embassy, London, met Buchanan's flight at Heathrow.
It was past midnight G.M.T. and Sayre, with an embassy car,
provided transportation into the city. The roads were quiet
and wet on early Saturday morning, March 18.

For much of the first part of the drive, Buchanan was alone
with his thoughts, listening only to the squeak of the windshield
wipers in front of him. But by the time Buchanan arrived in England, much had already happened. And gradually Sayre brought
Buchanan up-to-date as he drove him from the airport into central
London.

Several hours earlier Colonel Klisinski had gone, Sayre explained, directly to the Soviet Embassy. There Klisinski was not
alone, as the past few hours had turned into a diplomatic Walpur-
gisnacht. That is, in addition to a fleeing spy, the Soviet Embassy
had a full-fledged defector on their hands as well, a woman who had
somehow received word from the United States that the time had
come to vanish to the worker's paradise.

"She's in the process of leaving the country right now," Sayre
announced. "There's an Aeroflot flight to Moscow at six o'clock
this morning. I know for a fact that the G.R.U. colonel is departing
on it. I assume the Russians are planning to put the woman on it as
well. They don't waste time getting their people out after an operation crashes."

"Laura Garrett, right?" Buchanan asked, although he knew
without waiting for an answer.

Sayre nodded. "She was in Soviet hands before we received
instructions to detain her."

"Naturally," said Buchanan.

"She knew ahead of time."

"They always seem to," Buchanan grumbled. About a mile
later, he asked, "I suppose you know about her father."

"We received a full transcript by wire just a few hours ago. It was sent and received while your flight was in the air," the foreign service officer said.

Buchanan was about to ask if anyone had managed to station some Scotland Yard or MI5 people at the airport. But then he soured on even asking that. Klisinski was safe in Soviet custody. So what did it matter?

"On the other hand," Sayre began, "if *John Garrett* arrives in London, since he's a U.S. citizen—"

Buchanan interrupted rudely. "Dammit! Can't Scotland Yard detain Klisinski?" he asked. "Can't someone stop him? There's a gallon of blood on his hands back in the U.S."

Sayre sighed. "The Brits don't see it that way, I'm afraid. Whatever Klisinski did, he didn't do it on their soil. And if he did, they don't know about it. Further, if he goes from the Soviet Embassy to a Soviet auto to a Soviet aircraft . . ."

"Then they don't have jurisdiction?" said Buchanan angrily. "Right?"

Sayre nodded. "I'm taking you to my office right now," Sayre explained a minute later. "I have a C.I.A. report. It might interest you."

"On what?"

"Zolling. The East German defector."

"The *late* East German defector," Buchanan said with no attempt to conceal his bitterness.

"Have it your way," Sayre said. "It's still Zolling. I suppose it's also your consolation prize if you can't stop Klisinski or Garrett."

Buchanan said nothing, but watched the quiet, dark neighborhoods of the outer regions of west London glide by the car.

They reached the American Embassy by one-ten in the morning. Sayre and Buchanan entered past the marine guards. Buchanan then stopped at the security room and checked his pistol, carefully following protocol. Sayre led Buchanan to a reading room for classified documents. Buchanan spent the next three quarters of an hour reading a background dossier on Hans Zolling.

Zolling was, as Buchanan already knew, a member of the East German Politburo and one of the satellite republic's experts on Soviet planning. He had been sending signals to the West for almost twelve months, and now the C.I.A. had promised to reunite him with Lili, the Danish cutie who'd caught the aging satyr's eye the previous summer. Lili had been the bait and the trap all by herself, if the report could be believed, and all the Americans were hoping to gain was an insider's view of the East German defense ministry. That, however, had been up until November 1949. Then Zolling had come across something else—something bigger and better, and figured that while he was on a roll, he might as well go for a house and a car in Florida in addition to the lithesome blonde.

The "something else" was a file freshly lifted from the office of Walter Ulbricht, the pewtery old Stalinist who was currently entrenched as premier of the Democratic Republic of East Germany. It pertained to Soviet military expansion in 1950. Zolling promised something earthshaking: He knew precisely when and where Russian-backed military operations would and wouldn't occur that year. Zolling promised all the blueprints, maps, numbers of troops, dates, and the degree of cooperation from Red puppet governments —as the report termed them—in Europe, Africa, and Asia. Zolling had everything, in short, for the British and the Americans to plan a swift countermove and blow whatever Red Armies were involved right back into the sea.

This was stuff of the most exalted quality, Zolling had sworn, and when the Americans gained possession of it, he joked, they would give him *two* blondes, *two* houses, and *two* cars. His C.I.A. contacts had been more restrained, but Zolling's offer was considered irresistible. So an American team out of London had been sent to bring Zolling and his file to the West. With credit to Laura Garrett, the team was captured, Zolling eviscerated and shot, and the file returned to Ulbricht before the earth could move for Western intelligence.

"God almighty," Buchanan thought to himself as he closed the files. It was an oath taken in amazement more than anger. Visions of John Garrett and Sammy Wong flashed before him, as well as the image of Colonel Klisinski, the globe-trotting G.R.U. officer depicted in the testimony of the late Viktor Milenkin.

Then that image faded into a more recent one of Milenkin, dead on his bed in Greenwich Village, a few feet from the slain young F.B.I. agent.

Buchanan drew a long breath and stood. How long had this case been going on, he asked himself. Just since 1949? Or could it be described as going back years? To the prewar era, or even into the time of John Dillinger in the 1930s.

He was exhausted. Many thoughts spiraled together, some of them not clear. Not yet.

He found Sayre waiting for him in his office. The diplomat looked at him solemnly.

"Seems like we missed out on something big with Zolling," Sayre said.

"Maybe. Maybe we can salvage things. Can you drive me to the Russian Embassy?"

Sayre shrugged. "Why not?"

Buchanan returned to the reception area and the security room. The security officer was reading a newspaper and seemed surprised to see him. The guard seemed ill at ease with what followed.

"Another man picked up your weapon, sir," the guard said to Buchanan.

"What!" Buchanan practically exploded.

"The man had F.B.I. credentials himself, sir," the guard said. "Explained that you were absent without leave from the United States and were not empowered to carry an F.B.I. weapon in a foreign country."

"You're telling me my gun was confiscated?" Buchanan asked.

"Yes, sir. My apologies, sir."

"What the hell office was he from?" Buchanan snapped. "London? Washington?"

"Chicago, sir. Said he was on special assignment."

"What?"

The long, long all-powerful grasping arm of J. Edgar Hoover, Buchanan wondered, or an ambulatory phantom? *Chicago?* But with an aircraft waiting for Colonel Klisinski, there was little time to wonder. All civility and courtesy had departed Buchanan now. He cursed violently to Sayre and asked to continue to the Soviet Embassy.

The Embassy of the Union of Soviet Socialist Republics was a grim place in any weather, but grimmest of all on a cold March night in a wet mist. By the time Buchanan arrived, an N.K.V.D. officer informed him that "the woman," as he called her, Laura Garrett, had already departed with an escort to the airport, where a Soviet jet awaited her.

"What about the colonel?" Buchanan asked.

The colonel was still inside, the guard said.

The colonel had also struck a pretty good deal. His diplomatic passport assured him of direct passage to the airport. Still a cautious man, he had sent Laura Garrett to the airport first. A messenger would call the embassy when Laura was safely aboard the Russian jet. Then Klisinski, having talked the English into clearing the area of police, would follow.

"When will the colonel be leaving?" Buchanan asked next.

In so many words, the answer was sometime soon.

Buchanan pulled a card out of his pocket and presented it to the Soviet guard. "Tell the colonel that we have some unfinished business," Buchanan said. "I'd like to meet him."

The guard refused to take the card. "Not possible," the Russian said.

"Why don't you let the colonel make the decision?" Buchanan pressed. "Unless you want to risk demotion for making it for him."

Buchanan was certain that the guard hadn't understood English well enough to comprehend the pros and cons of the suggestion. But he did summon a superior. Buchanan's card was taken within the embassy. Buchanan waited. Then ten minutes later an angry, bleary-eyed Soviet diplomat appeared and motioned at Buchanan.

"Please!" the Russian said. He summoned the American within the next series of doors.

Two uniformed Soviet soldiers then led Buchanan into a reception area. Buchanan looked at the soldiers carefully. He guessed that one was about thirty and the other slightly younger. And although he had no experience at such things, he guessed that both were officers, perhaps ranking around captain or major. He could tell by the way they swaggered and the way they expected to be obeyed.

In the room a pair of Soviet flags bracketed a color portrait of a beatific Lenin with sculpted beard. The room was shadowy with one dim light and only two chairs. From there the soldiers directed Buchanan down a gray corridor. Beneath an oil painting depicting the glorious seizure of the Kronstadt naval base in 1917, one soldier motioned to Buchanan to stop and raise his arms. The other man frisked him, complete with a firm grasp at the groin. Buchanan winced and the guards laughed. He wondered again who had taken his weapon, but knew that if someone hadn't, the Russians surely would have seized it there. Then the two soldiers spoke to him in Russian and led him onward. For the first time in his life he felt he was some sort of prisoner. A sickening sense of vulnerability was also creeping upon him.

They led him to a small room where there was a table and two straight-back chairs, one of which was badly chipped and scarred. In Russian they indicated that he was to sit in that one. The older soldier said something else to him in Russian. Buchanan guessed that he was to wait.

"Klisinski?" Buchanan asked.

The soldiers said something unintelligible to him. Then one said something to the other. They laughed and left.

Buchanan noted the time. It was almost two-thirty A.M. He waited, wondering if he was being placed there so that Klisinski could escape cleanly to the airport without their paths crossing. He decided that he'd give it another quarter of an hour.

Then another mortifying thought was upon him. He bolted up, went to the door, and tried it. The knob was stationary from within. In point of fact, he was their prisoner until someone in this embassy decided otherwise.

A few minutes later the door opened. Buchanan's gaze rose from the floor and settled upon a handsome man in his fifties in the brown and red military uniform of the Glavnoye Razvedyvatelnoye Upravleniye. The uniform was much bedecked with medals and gold braid and was clearly that of a ranking officer. And if the uniform was for shock or effect, clearly it had both, for Thomas Buchanan immediately felt himself on the defensive, particularly in this room.

The Soviet officer glared at the F.B.I. agent, then grinned slowly. Colonel Klisinski, as he was known here, was not above gloating.

In return, Buchanan stared at him, not in shock or a sense of surprise, but in anger as well as in recognition.

"My God, Thomas. You *are* persistent, if nothing else." Klisinski, as John Taylor Garrett now preferred to be called, straightened his uniform jacket. Over his arm was draped a heavy brown military greatcoat, strongly suggesting that the colonel was set to travel.

"I put you out of business at least," Buchanan said.

"Did you?"

"You're on your way to the Soviet Union, aren't you? Leaving the bank and one daughter behind."

Garrett nodded slightly. "Won't help you much at all, will it?"

Buchanan thought about it. "Who knows?"

There was an awkward pause.

"Can you imagine this?" Garrett mused. "The British are so eager to get me out of their decaying little kingdom that they've promised me a car and free passage. Of course I want no part of it," he said. "Who knows where they'd really take me. I'll use a Soviet driver."

"Oh, I suspect the British would play by the rules," he said. "Even if you haven't."

"*I* haven't?" He threw his head back and laughed. "That's a good one. Let me tell you something. To betray, you have to belong. I never belonged. You were right about a great many things. I hated the moneyed establishment in America as much as any man ever hated anything. I saw what banks did to people. I saw what capitalism did during the 1930s. An eighth of the country owns sixty percent of the property and ninety percent of the land. What kind of democracy is that? What kind of 'land of the people' is that?"

"So you went into banking to sabotage the system from within?"

"Not entirely," said Garrett. "Or, at least, not at first."

He had purchased Commonwealth Penn back in the 1930s, he said, out of his own American sense of adventure. He'd seen how the banks and financial institutions had failed ordinary people and he wanted to operate one differently. So he put his family name and money into the recovery of an institution that was itself on the verge of collapse.

"I wanted to be the local Robin Hood," he said with a trace of romanticism. "I wanted to provide a bank that was different, that could provide money to people when they needed it, not screw them when they were desperate. What I ran up against was the mentality of everyone else in banking. As soon as they knew what I wanted to do, they set about arranging for me to fail. Not once, mind you, but twice. It exasperated them that I'd kept Commonwealth Penn afloat in the thirties. But in the forties, when I came back from the war, they really had my number." He paused for a moment. "Let me assure you that when you learn to truly hate bankers, by extension you can learn to hate the entire capitalist system."

"But to stretch the point," Buchanan said, "by the late forties your enemies may have had your number, but you also had theirs. Am I correct?"

Garrett nodded. "Absolutely. I was in Moscow half a dozen times during the war. You had it figured out pretty well when we last met. By the late thirties I'd decided that the only thing that I really wanted for America was the complete destruction of the capitalist system. So during the war I made a point of befriending my Russian contacts. Gradually I earned their trust. I undertook special jobs for them. Sabotage the French and Brits here, undercut the Americans a little there. By 1944 I'd met with all the top Soviets. Stalin, Molotov, and Mikoyan themselves. They knew what I could do for them in terms of laundering money for Soviet activities in the West. So I had their blessing as well as their trust."

"So the whole reason you went into intelligence work during the war," Buchanan said, "was to—"

"To get as close to the great Soviet experiment as possible. And I'm damned glad I did." He paused as if far away in thought. "You know, Buchanan, I don't in any way envy you. How do you come to grips with the America you'll be living in for the next years? Men like Joseph McCarthy and J. Edgar Hoover are in the ascendancy. Already the shadow of the swastika is across the land. How do *you*, as a man who enforces the law, reconcile yourself to that? Or are you one of them?"

It was the first significant question that Garrett had asked Buchanan. The F.B.I. agent, groping for an answer for a second, stuck with his own line of questioning.

"And Ann knew how you felt? And Laura knew also?"

"Good Lord, of course!" said Garrett, actually shocked at the question and moving on from ideology. "I wanted them to work with me. Well, one daughter saw things my way, the other didn't. As it happens, I'm taking the better one with me. The other one I'm leaving behind." He looked at the younger man. "Of course, if you're still nursing that silly notion of romancing Ann, I suppose you'll have to stand in line."

"And Milenkin? And the young F.B.I. agent?" asked Buchanan.

"Did Comrade Filiatov kill them?" Garrett asked. He appeared to not know.

"If Filiatov was your Russian assassin, yes, he did."

Garrett settled back. "Well, good. A few small victories for us. Milenkin was a traitor. The young F.B.I. man was a perpetuator of the class oppression."

For the first time in his life Buchanan felt like drawing a gun and shooting a man for verbal provocation. Pity that someone had taken his weapon.

Garrett glanced at his watch. It was as if he had a plane to catch, Buchanan observed absently. Then Buchanan remembered that he did.

From his explanation of himself, Garrett launched into a protracted interpretation of the class system in America, a system which he at once said he hated yet which had nurtured him all his life. His thoughts were concise at first, then began to ramble:

"You have to remember that I have nothing against America or Americans," Garrett said. "My disappointment is that my country could never elevate its system of government. . . ."

And, "The struggle of the oppressors and the oppressed will continue through the better part of the century. It will eventually be won by the Soviet domination of air and space. . . ."

And eventually, with a taunting tone, "Mark my words on this. The next showdown between East and West will come in Asia. We'll see if America will have the courage to stop communism by force of arms."

"And that's what Hans Zolling was going to explain, was he not?" Buchanan asked, jumping all over Garrett's statement.

"What?" Garrett asked, faltering for a moment and realizing he might have overstepped even his own impertinence.

"Asia," said Buchanan, transposing from the C.I.A. report he'd digested just an hour earlier. "A military showdown. This year, is it?"

Garrett stared at him uncomfortably for a moment, then recovered and broke into a keen smile. "Think whatever you like," Garrett said. "I've been promised a dacha on the Black Sea. I'll be there comfortably by the time anything happens at all."

Buchanan had every impression that Garrett would be there, enjoying a newly privileged position in the classless Soviet society. He played with Garrett's final words and thoughts, wondering if the spy had uttered a few words too many or achieved a final crowning moment of disinformation. Buchanan had no way of knowing.

There was a knock on the door. One of the uniformed Soviet officers appeared and spoke to his colonel in Russian. Garrett translated some of it, announcing to Buchanan that he was free to go. Laura was at the airport and safely aboard her flight. That was Garrett's cue to leave. A Zil limousine waited across Archibald Park out front of the embassy at about a hundred feet from the entrance. The Zil would transport Klisinski to Heathrow, he explained.

"Come along," Garrett said. "See me to the door. You have to be leaving anyway. Just don't attempt any last-minute heroics. Our military people here are under orders to use the iron fist if necessary. Frankly I suspect they'd enjoy shooting you."

Garrett allowed Buchanan to leave the room first, then the two soldiers led them both back down the same gray corridor to the anteroom and the front doors of the embassy. Without speaking, Buchanan walked beside a man he considered a traitor and a murderer. And not only were last-minute heroics ill advised, Buchanan couldn't even think of any.

Outside, the night remained wet and pitch-black, perfectly matching Buchanan's mood.

The two men stepped outside the glass doors together. Garrett drew a deep breath and seemed to exult in his victory. At the same time, Buchanan scanned the misty darkness. From somewhere he felt something uneasy welling up inside him. Instinct again, just like he and Mark O'Connell used to say.

"So long, Buchanan," Garrett said, pulling on his coat. "I'm gone."

Garrett stepped off the curb, looked both ways, and crossed the street. There were no police in evidence and few nocturnal stragglers even in the park. Buchanan held his face to his hand for a moment as he watched Garrett step into Archibald Park and cross it to the Zil limousine that waited on the opposite side, its headlights slicing thin yellow cones into the darkness.

The Americans had no jurisdiction. The British recognized his Soviet citizenship. There John Taylor Garrett was, after all he'd done, a spy and a killer walking to freedom.

Garrett's pace quickened as he neared the center of the park. Buchanan was frozen to the spot, feeling much as he might if he were watching a film—or a bad dream—in which the conclusion was preordained. For a moment, and with great irony, he thought of Mark O'Connell some months earlier, himself alone out on an Oregon highway, anticipating disaster for days in advance, knowing that there was someone out there. . . .

And then Buchanan realized where his gun had gone. "Jesus Christ," he mumbled to himself. But he did nothing to stop the flow of events when he saw a very mobile man in a raincoat rise from the bench and turn toward John Taylor Garrett. Garrett saw him too, but somehow must have thought that, no, this couldn't possibly concern him. He'd played by rules, hadn't he? He expected civility under diplomatic laws. Who else was there to fear?

Garrett was shown instead a frontier standard of justice, as it might have been seen a century earlier in the wildness of the Pacific Northwest. The man in the shadows lumbered for a few steps and came very close to Garrett. In the final second or two Buchanan even saw Garrett accelerate and try to run. Buchanan heard him scream. But it was, of course, too late.

The gunman darted after him, pushed a pistol directly into Garrett's chest, said something, and pulled a trigger. It was a heavy handgun—sounding for all the world like the one Buchanan had just lost—and the eruption from it rocked the silence of the park. Only a single bullet was fired at first, and Garrett reeled backward. He staggered and somehow stayed on his feet. Then the killer, with utmost calm, extended his arms in a pose like an American policeman and fired a second round.

This shot sent Garrett sprawling backward against a bench and then to the ground. Buchanan started to run toward the fallen man, and he looked in the direction of the killer, a man who seemed familiar with fog and mist, and was able to slip in and out of them to great advantage. It would be recalled that there had been no police in the area at the request of the Soviets. And the gunman vanished in an instant.

Buchanan was the first one to the side of the fallen spy, but it made little difference. The assassin couldn't possibly have botched the job from that range and with that firepower. Garrett was dead. A crowd gathered slowly and a few minutes later—but long after the fact—there were constables. Curiously no one emerged from the Soviet Embassy. The two soldiers remained at the embassy's doors and watched without speaking.

"Who was he?" someone asked concerning the slain man.

Buchanan stared down. "A Soviet diplomat," he said.

"Who shot him?" asked someone else.

Buchanan never raised his eyes. "Could have been anyone," he said. "And whoever it was, he's gone now."

"Probably a political thing," someone else said at length. "You know. From all those East Europe countries the bloody Russian Army seized."

Buchanan nodded and offered that solution to the police. It sounded as convincing as anything.

THIRTY-SIX

S itting alone in a window seat on a Pan American jet bound for New York, Buchanan had the sense of never having known John Taylor Garrett at all. Rather, he had taken Garrett as an academic subject, having studied him in all his facets, then flunked much of the final exam.

Why *wouldn't* a few men of his social standing and generation have been attracted to communism? Why wouldn't many of them have taken the lessons of the Depression and applied them to social studies and come out with a formula for redistributing America's wealth? Why, when one thought of it, were banks held in such low esteem by so many Americans when John Dillinger was considered a hero? Why, when it came right down to it, did so many Americans hate banks?

How many men worked in banks in America? How many secretly sensed other ideals and aspirations. Of one sort or another, how many moles were there from within, he wondered.

Buchanan thought of Hoover's reception room in Washington, with mementos of the Dillinger era. Out of a hundred million Americans, he mused, how many considered the outlaws the heroes and the F.B.I. the villains? Idly he wondered if Garrett had a point. Was the shadow of the swastika already across the land? Time would tell.

He wondered how he would tell Ann her father was dead. He wondered how he might explain how he had died. Would she cry? Would she blame him? He wondered how she could spend a lifetime with the monster she was married to.

He gazed out the window. Go to Greenland, and turn left, he relayed mentally to the pilot. He was eager to go home.

Before him he had his written report on the Garrett case. He had the whole thing right there. He'd give it to Frank Lerrick and Lerrick would hand it to Hoover. Hoover would pass it along to Senator McCarthy and away they would go. A news conference. A major Red scare. Elections coming up. The 1950s already promised to be a fairly turbulent decade, an end to the carefree postwar era in

America when all the average man and woman worried about were the new car, the new house, and the new baby. This report would help darken the impending decade. So, Buchanan decided, when he got back to America, he would have to reword things accordingly.

He reread it and pushed it into a long manila envelope. He sealed it. He gazed out the window and closed his eyes.

He must have fallen asleep because when he opened his eyes again there was a pretty stewardess standing in the aisle, leaning to him and gently touching his shoulder to wake him. Outside, a bright sunlight engulfed the aircraft and flooded through the window. The flight was on its descent toward New York, the stewardess said, and the airplane would touch down on the runway within fifteen minutes.

THIRTY-SEVEN

"I had hoped," said Buchanan carefully, "to see President Truman himself."

Jack Malone sat behind his desk within the White House and shrugged. "I don't blame you a bit," said Malone. "But it can't be done."

Buchanan stared at him coldly and with increasing distrust.

"Look, Tom," Malone said, "if it were up to me, I'd march you in there right now and we could forcible evict the Canadian prime minister from the Oval Office. But things aren't done that way in this building. Appointments have a priority as well as a set schedule, and have to go through Mr. Truman's chief of staff. The President has a meeting with the Senate Democratic caucus at eleven A.M., lunch with ten midwestern governors, then afternoon appointments with the Israeli ambassador to the United States, the president of Mexico and—"

"What about tomorrow?"

Malone sighed. From memory he recounted, "Tomorrow's schedule starts at eight A.M. with a briefing by the National Security Council. At nine-thirty the Secretary of the Treasury has an hour scheduled with the President. That's already a problem because the

Secretary of Labor is booked in for ten-fifteen, and has been for a month. Later in the day—"

"I'm asking for only twenty minutes."

"I'm sorry, Tom, but it's hard enough for the Director of the F.B.I. to get onto the President's schedule, much less—"

"I saw the President once before," insisted Buchanan. "I want to see him again."

Malone opened his hands with a frustrated gesture. There was nothing he could do, he said. "You're missing the obvious, Tom," he advised.

"What's that?"

"Last time the President decided *he* wanted to see *you.* This time it's the other way around." Malone eyed the manila envelope across Buchanan's lap. "What is that? The final report on Commonwealth Penn?"

"Yes. But there's more," he said. All the names were in his mind, as well as in the report: Wong. Garrett. Zolling . . .

Malone held out his hand helpfully.

"Tom," Malone said. "I've worked for Mr. Truman for years. If you give me a document to be passed along to him, what in God's name do you think I'm going to do with it? Throw it in the goddamned Potomac? Do you think I'd still be in this job if I did things like that?"

Buchanan didn't answer. Malone's arm remained extended.

Buchanan stood. He passed a copy of his final report to Jack Malone. "See that he gets it this morning," said Buchanan, standing. "Eventually lives will be at stake."

"Word of honor," Malone promised.

"How much is that worth?" Buchanan asked.

Malone's voice was kindly, though a little fervent as he laid the envelope across his desk. "Tom, I know you've been under a lot of strain," he said. "But maybe you should go now. You're a good man, a loyal American. I like you. I respect you. And I'm going to pretend I didn't hear what you just said."

Toward noon the same day Buchanan stopped when he saw a familiar figure seated on a bench across the street from the Justice Department. Thomas crossed through traffic and approached the man. Buchanan had expected to see the familiar face, but not quite so soon, not quite so blatantly, and certainly not in that spot.

The man was reading a newspaper when Buchanan approached. Then he looked up and smiled.

"How are you feeling?" Buchanan asked.

"Not too bad," the former F.B.I. agent answered. He motioned to an empty spot on the bench beside him. "Sit down."

Buchanan did.

"On your way to see Hoover?" Mark O'Connell asked.

Buchanan nodded.

"It won't be fun," O'Connell warned.

"I'm prepared for it."

"Better be," said O'Connell. "Be prepared for the harassment that will follow it also."

Buchanan grinned. "I'm ready there too," he said.

O'Connell watched a Washington municipal bus for a few seconds as it discharged passengers. The cold weather had broken and there was a suggestion of spring in the air.

"I move around pretty good for a big guy, don't I?" O'Connell mused.

"How did you ever talk Helen into letting you follow me to London?" Buchanan asked.

Mark O'Connell laughed. "I made a bet with her," he said. "I said I wanted to go. She said not in a wheelchair. So I stood up and walked to the reservation window. Spent almost every dime on me to buy a ticket. Had to use my old F.B.I. credentials to get on the plane without a passport."

"And then you followed me?"

"You didn't make it very difficult," said O'Connell. "You told me right where you were going. And of course," he joked, "Helen's telling everyone I went fishing out in Oregon."

"What did you do with my gun?" Buchanan asked softly.

"Tossed it in the Thames, old boy," said O'Connell. "Threw it right off London Bridge. Sorry about that. I'll buy you a new one. But frankly, I always did want to throw a murder weapon in a river."

Buchanan grinned. "Well, it's something to tell your grandchildren."

"I'm sure," said O'Connell.

O'Connell looked at the Justice Department building across the street. "What happened with Ann Garrett?" he asked eventually.

Buchanan's expression changed as he answered. "You didn't hear? From mutual acquaintances?"

"No," said O'Connell.

"Her husband hired a pair of thugs to beat the hell out of her."

O'Connell waited for the worst. "And?" he asked.

"Our friends Herter and Meadley were covering Chadwick in Las Vegas for me at the time. Chadwick didn't know what his hired help would look like. So Herter and Meadley arrested them when they stepped off a plane in Los Angeles, posed as a pair of thugs, showed up at Chadwick's, and arrested him just as they were supposed to take Ann away."

O'Connell grinned from ear to ear. "Well done."

"It's only one of many charges now against Chadwick, from conspiracy to violation of the Mann Act."

"Must have been quite a weekend in Las Vegas," O'Connell said. Both men laughed again.

"As soon as all this is wrapped up," Buchanan said, "I'll be going back out to the West Coast to see Ann. See if I can revive the old relationship. I'll drop by Oregon when I can. I've always been partial to small-town cops."

O'Connell enjoyed the laugh. "Don't knock it," he said. "You may be one before you know it."

"I know," Buchanan said. He stood, shook hands with O'Connell a final time, and crossed the street.

A few minutes later Buchanan reported to his office in the F.B.I.'s suite within the Justice Department. Less than half an hour after arrival he was ushered past the main anteroom to Hoover's office, past all the old trophies, plaques, and artifacts, past the flags and the congressional citations and into the so-called Throne Room to see the Boss himself.

Hoover's cheeks were red and puffy on this occasion, his brown eyes smoldering. He wore a dove-gray suit with a white shirt, red boutonniere and dark regimental tie. He sat behind his desk and Frank Lerrick was stationed in a chair to the Director's side, his usual perch.

Buchanan felt Hoover's eyes burning into him from the moment he entered the chamber empty-handed. He sat down on a hard wooden chair that had been set for him in the middle of the room.

"Where's your report?" Hoover asked.

A slight hesitation, then Buchanan answered. "I don't care to write one," he said.

"Excuse me?" Hoover snorted.

"I said I don't care to—"

"*I goddamned well heard what you said, Special Agent Buchanan!*" the Director roared. "And just where in hell do you get off coming in here and saying something like that to me? Well? *Where?* Answer me that!"

"The case is closed and settled," Buchanan said. "I turned over the pertinent information to the White House. Anything else I give you is simply going to be passed along to Senator McCarthy for political purposes. I'm not going along with that."

"Who do you think you are?" Hoover roared. "You don't make decisions like that!"

"I just did," he said. "Sir," he tacked on irreverently.

Hoover leaned back in his chair. This was Lerrick's cue to speak.

"Tom," the assistant director said, "do us all—including yourself—a favor. Get your impudent ass out of here this minute, go to your office, and start writing. Have something to us by five o'clock today."

"No," Buchanan answered.

"Tom, it was bad enough that you went to London against orders. Don't make things any worse for yourself."

"I wouldn't think of it," Buchanan answered.

"What on earth is the problem?" Lerrick asked.

"Aside from what I just explained?"

"Yes."

"This Bureau is supposed to protect the innocent and serve justice. It does neither. You set me off on an investigation of John Garrett which you wanted to use solely to embarrass the White House. As it happened, I picked up on something much larger. Well, I'm not giving you the benefit of that. Similarly someone in this office made a decision to let Viktor Milenkin be killed. I find that unconscionable."

Lerrick stared at the floor. Buchanan glared at both of them, back and forth.

"You don't even deny it, do you?" Buchanan asked. "A protection team could have been in place with minutes. Instead, you stalled. You wanted Milenkin dead. Easier that way. Inadvertently, a young F.B.I. agent also died in all your bungling. Great for both

of you. Two more martyrs to your cause. Better statistics. Jesus
Christ! I can't convey to you how disgusted I am."

"Milenkin was a Russian," Hoover said.

"He *helped* us! So what if he was foreign born? So is Einstein.
Or for that matter," he added sarcastically, "same as Kosciusko or
Von Steuben."

"Einstein's a Jew," snapped Hoover. He turned to Lerrick.
"Who are the other two? Do we have files?"

From that point Buchanan could clearly sense his immediate
future. As far as the Bureau was concerned, there would be either
the "quick kill"—immediate firing—or the "slow" one—the letters
of censure, the petty professional harassments, the transfers to remote cold-weather F.B.I. outposts, and the reassignment to incon-
sequential or demeaning cases. All of it was more than he cared for.
There was still time to get out with relative youth, a feeling of
accomplishment, and a sense of personal honor.

Reaching within his jacket, he withdrew his letter of resignation and handed it to Frank Lerrick. As Lerrick opened it and
prepared to read it to the Director, Buchanan stood and walked
out.

EPILOGUE

The man who stood on a quiet beach in Malibu, California, on the evening of Sunday, June 25, 1950, hadn't shaved in two days. He walked by himself with bare feet through the wet sand. He wore a soft blue cotton shirt and khaki slacks which were wet at the cuffs from the surf. Every few minutes he looked toward a rise in a sandy hill. He was expecting someone.

He had been alone for several hours. The sun was setting, but the hour was already late. June 25 was one of the longest days of the year, sometimes in more ways than one. But this evening he was enjoying the solitude of the beach as well as the touch of the Pacific Ocean on his ankles and feet.

At a few minutes after eight he saw the woman he loved come across the top of the dune. Thomas waved to her. Ann waved back. Her pace quickened and she ran down the beach to join him. When they met, Thomas Buchanan held her and kissed her.

"How did it go?" he asked.

She shrugged. "This was my first callback on this script. I don't know. I may get the part, I may not. Should we worry?"

"No," he said. Between them they had enough money to last several months. But long before that, he was sure, Ann would have another role and he would find a job he wanted. In the meantime they could enjoy their leisure, the California sunshine and each other.

He took her hand and they walked together. "There is some bad news today," she said after a while.

He was thinking more in terms of her pending divorce, or the criminal charges against her husband. When he asked what the news was, Thomas was surprised when she handed him an evening newspaper from Los Angeles. It was an extra edition.

He stared at the headlines and stopped walking. Then he read the lead story. It concerned events from the other side of the same ocean that rolled gently at his feet.

Each year June marks the monsoon season in north Asia, so showers had fallen across most of Korea during the predawn darkness of that same day. The South Korean Army, after months of false alerts, had relaxed for a weekend of vacation. The frontier defense force between North and South Korea—four infantry divisions and a regiment—normally consisted of thirty-eight thousand men. But in actuality this weekend, due to attrition of personnel, personal leave, a traditional holiday in Seoul, and sickness, the force was closer to thirteen thousand.

The North Korean People's Army, meanwhile, had amassed an invasion force of ninety thousand well-trained soldiers. This juggernaut was supported by close to two hundred Soviet-made T-34 tanks, a low silhouette medium tank that had been the standard of the Soviet army at the end of World War II. Heavily armored and highly maneuverable, each T-34 carried an 85mm cannon and two 7.62mm machine guns. The T-34 had stopped the German drive on Moscow in 1944, had kept the Red Army entrenched in Eastern Europe since 1945, and had been a basic supply item for Red bloc armies ever since. This morning, rumbling across the thirty-eighth parallel and southward across the neck of the Korean peninsula, the T-34 and the tens of thousands of N.K.P.A. troops that followed would rise to new levels of achievement.

Thomas Buchanan felt a deep sickness in his gut as he read. No single soldier on the thirty-eighth parallel had heard the "first shot" of the war. Rather, at about five A.M. on a muggy morning in Korea, there had at first been rain and silence. Then a minute later there had been an eruption of artillery fire, the advancement of tanks, a hellish din, and explosions in every direction. The invasion of South Korea by Communist troops from the north had begun, as had what would be known in America as the Korean War. It had begun exactly as Hans Zolling had known it would many months in advance.

Buchanan folded the newspaper and looked at Ann. For weeks his final investigation as an agent of the F.B.I. had played upon his mind. For more than three months he had waited for the proverbial other shoe to drop. This finally was it.

"Want to take a trip back east?" he asked her.

"Where?"

"Washington," he said. "A final bit of business. Won't take long, won't change anything. But I want to do it."

"I'll go anywhere with you," said the actress known as Lisa Pennington.

"Fine. We leave tomorrow."

In the White House, Harry Truman had little to smile about. The Washington summer had already turned mercilessly hot and the air-conditioning was spotty at best. The national union of railroad workers was threatening a nationwide strike and the Democratic President had asked his Secretary of Labor to study the heretical move of nationalizing the rails, if necessary. But all of this was on the back pages of the newspapers.

On the front pages was the war in Asia. With astonishing swiftness America had been shaken from a five-year vacation from the cares of the world. By June 27 the President had ordered the United States Air Force and Navy to South Korea. Already both branches of the service were seeing combat and sustaining casualties. It might have been unofficial, but America was again at war. Soon meaningless, bloody patches of earth like Heartbreak Ridge and No-Name Hill would be before the national consciousness. And in another move that would be recalled with equally great importance many years later, President Truman that same day—June 27, 1950—also authorized thirty-five military advisers to be sent to the Republic of South Vietnam. For the first time in the twentieth century—in a precedent that would haunt the next five occupants of the White House—Communist military expansion would be met with American military force.

Downstairs at the White House, Thomas Buchanan sat where he had sat once before, in the office of Jack Malone, head of the President's Secret Service detail. Buchanan had fire in his eyes and mayhem in his heart.

"I can't believe what a low, conniving son of a bitch you are," Buchanan said.

"Why's that?" Malone asked calmly.

"You never warned the President. You never gave him my report. I had it all figured out. A Soviet-backed attack would come in Asia, probably Korea. That's what Zolling knew. That's why Laura Garrett took such a chance to prevent Zolling from defecting. I found out everything, cracked a Soviet network, made the correct suppositions, and you never told the President."

Malone shrugged. "Think whatever you want, Buchanan. You don't work here. I do. You're seeing only a small part of the picture."

"No," Buchanan said. "For that matter, I think I'm finally seeing the complete canvas."

"What do you mean by that?"

"Remember when I came back to Washington from California in March? You were at the Raffertys' house waiting for me. But the forwarding address I had left at the hotel was the address in Philadelphia. The only people who knew I was going directly back to Washington were Ann Garrett and the F.B.I. Right then I knew you were working with one of them. And my instinct was it wasn't Ann. J. Edgar Hoover's spies are everywhere, aren't they, Jack? You passed my report to the F.B.I. and they sat on it so that the President could be embarrassed. You people let a war start so the President could be humiliated."

"Bravo," said Malone, unimpressed. "Brilliant deduction. Three months too late."

"How long have you been on Hoover's payroll in addition to the Secret Service?" Buchanan asked.

"Six years. Since 1944. Summer of that year." Malone smiled amiably and continued. "The Director asked me to get a job with Mr. Truman as soon as Roosevelt started to consider him for vice president. And since I'm from Missouri . . ."

"I knew I shouldn't trust you. But I never thought you'd betray the President. Lives could have been saved if you'd handed him my report. But you didn't. You fucking bastard."

"That's all you have to say?"

"Pretty much."

"Good," said Malone calmly. "Because I figure I owe you one. And personally I have nothing against you. So I'll tell you something else. There was another reason that you were selected for the Garrett investigation. J. Edgar Hoover figured you were young, soft, stupid, and expendable. He didn't like you. It was always the Bureau's plan to fire you after the Garrett investigation, no matter what you accomplished. Fortunately you gave them good grounds by going to England against orders."

"And if I hadn't?"

"You were going to be fired for conflict of interest. You were investigating a man whom you knew. You should have pointed that out at the outset of the investigation."

"But I did."

"Sure you did," Malone said. "But who is the public going to believe? You, a fired agent, or J. Edgar Hoover, Mr. Crime Buster himself?"

"Jesus," said Buchanan. "You guys are worse than I ever thought."

Malone smiled. "You haven't seen anything yet. This country's going so far right over the next few years that you won't even recognize it by the time Joe McCarthy becomes president in 1952. So take a hike, Buchanan. That's all I have to say, unless you'd like to tell me who shot John Garrett in London."

"Go fuck yourself in hell, Malone."

Malone sighed and shook his head with disappointment. Then he took no chances over Buchanan's willingness to leave. He pressed a buzzer on his desk and two old acquaintances, Secret Service Agents Kirby and Clark, appeared from the hallway.

"Mr. Buchanan," said Malone by way of benediction, "just asked to leave. And, Tom? If I ever see you near the White House again, I'll have you arrested."

"I can take a hint," Buchanan said. He pulled away from Clark and Kirby, who stood behind him. "I'll leave by myself."

Buchanan emerged from the rear exit of the White House shortly after five o'clock that sweltering afternoon. He slung his jacket over his shoulder. Down the sidewalk a few paces past the marine sentry, he saw Ann Garrett waiting for him.

"How did it go?" she asked.

"About the way I expected."

"Anything you can tell me about? Or are these 'state secrets'?" Her tone was gently chiding.

"I'll tell you the whole story," he said, "from start to finish. There've been too many secrets already."

He wrapped his arm around her waist.

"There's a little Italian place called Cora's not far from my apartment," he said. "Good food, and better yet, a new air conditioner. We'll go there for dinner and I'll tell you everything."

"Sounds good to me," she said.

As they walked back to 7th Street, S.E., a flood of government employees poured out of the various office buildings of the capital. Traffic slowed in the heat, and the sidewalks became steamy and crowded. At a corner where Buchanan liked to buy his daily newspaper he stopped and gazed at the afternoon edition of the Washington *Star.*

The headline concerned the war in Asia. The President's picture appeared just below. On one side, Senator McCarthy's face accompanied an account of one of his sharp new attacks on leftists in the government. To the other side was a picture of J. Edgar Hoover, gloating indulgently as he received an award from a federation of local police chiefs.

Somehow Buchanan suspected that this image would stay with him for many years to come: the beleaguered President overwhelmed by events, surrounded by demagogues, but fighting valiantly. The 1950s, Buchanan concluded, had begun as one hell of a nasty decade. His arm left Ann's waist and he held her hand as they crossed Connecticut Avenue.

Then he drew a deep breath and took one consolation. At least, he reasoned, neither he nor Ann would again face the flood of events alone. And that was a victory in itself.